Looking Beyond the Ordinary

Janeé Thompson

First paperback edition April 2020
Second paperback edition March 2024

Book design by Benedicta Buatsie
Edited by Megan Joseph at Joseph Editorial Services

ISBN 978-1-7345264-1-7 (paperback)
ISBN 978-1-7345264-0-0 (ebook)

www.booksbyjanee.com

Author Note

This coming of age novel explores the unique difficulties of maintaining friendships, popularity, bullying, the pressures of sex, topics of abuse and mental illness, and how to cope with the many other issues that Black teenagers face in high school. **Due to mature content (language use and sexual activity among consenting teenagers who are of legal age), this novel is strongly recommended for readers ages sixteen and older.**

Prologue

Growing up, my mother taught me to never settle for less. In her world, complacency was weakness. Complacency was death.

It was the only household rule I had. Bring home Fs? Forget it. Dress like a bum? Disowned. Fragile? She ain't raise a weak ass bitch. And I, for sure, couldn't bring home a low life. I might as well write my own obituary. She lived this way herself and would be damned if she was dethroned by anyone.

Would be damned if I was dethroned either. *By anyone.*

Image was everything. If it meant shitting on everyone to maintain it, then so be it. Many people at school called me snob, siddity, uptight, and whatever other name they could call me except what I truly was – the flyest bitch in the school. But I didn't care. Sure, I was all those things they called me.

And? I earned my reputation. Periodt!

I was a freelance hip-hop dancer, making my way into music videos, shows, concerts, movies, and other gigs that would bring in some hefty pocket change for a seventeen-year-old like me. I wasn't living off mommy like most people at school who begged their parents for money because they couldn't get what they wanted off pitiful ass McDonald's checks. Do you know my momma would look upside my head like I was crazy if I even stepped a foot in McDonald's? You would never catch me in nobody's corporation uniform. As my momma would say, "You own; you don't get owned."

When it came to boys, I got who I wanted, when I wanted.

Listen. I wasn't even model material. I had a plain face and few curves. Not that wide-hipped, big-butt, no-waist, but big-boobs kinda chick you see on Instagram. I was about five-foot-seven and never wore make up. Didn't need to.

My hair was shoulder length, parted down the middle, and always worn straight. Never in a style. But what made me so attractive, especially to older guys, was that I was better than a lot of other seventeen-year-old girls. I was always competing with myself because there wasn't competition. Of course, there were some guys who couldn't handle someone like me. I didn't care. I didn't want them anyway.

Speaking of guys, no one would ever catch me dating someone who wasn't on my level. Like my momma said, "Without looks, style, intelligence, and money, he is worthless." There was nothing nor anyone who could prove me different or wrong. I got the best guy at school because I was the best choice.

Now see, I might have high standards and bougie ways of thinking, but one thing is for sure: I have a heart. A big one. That's something my momma didn't have.

It was the one and only thing I had but was unable to show. I didn't know how to show it. I had a lot of heart to give. It was just a matter of finding someone out of the ordinary, someone special who would accept me for me, and most definitely, *my momma.*

Chapter One

No other feeling beat getting out of English class first thing in the morning. Who did these teachers think they were, getting us to build what they called "critical thinking skills" at 7:30 in the morning in August? That type of brain power doesn't even kick in until about 10:30. *Whatever.*

I dashed out without looking back and headed to the highlight of my day: the upperclassmen kick it spot for the eight-minute passing time. The most hype hallway of any public school in the nation, hands down.

We called our exclusive crew of Juniors and Seniors the *D-Block*. Graffiti of our name decorated the halls in colorful fashion all over this raggedy ass school. No matter how many times we got suspended for vandalism while the janitors cleaned it up, D-Block was spray-painted or permanently marked by someone else shortly after. In the end, they just gave up, and they should've. We made our presence known and would put anybody in their place who tried to act like they didn't know what's up. Even the adults.

I moseyed towards the crew with my nose high and saw that everyone was already up to no good, bullying anyone unworthy of breathing the air of the block. Some random little white girl almost peed her pants being in a place she had no business.

"Hey! You! The fuck you doin' in our hallway?" one of our D-Block girls yelled to her.

She wasn't any older than a sophomore. Poor girl's eyes were goose eggs trying to find a route to safety. She tried to walk away but ended up running smack into another one of our girls who stood in front of her on purpose.

"You can't speak English, Cinderella?"

Then, one of them took the gum out of their mouth and pasted it into the girl's hair; the other poured a bottle of red juice on top of her head. It was all of two seconds before she ran in tears.

Shit like this was a daily ritual. Any person who wasn't well known dared not to come near us unless they wanted to be roasted or have something destroyed because that's literally all we did. Talked shit about people, joked around with one another, play fought, and threw Freshman in the garbage cans if they walked by. Nobody was safe, and that included staff. I mean if you could handle it, maybe you got informally invited into the crew, but that was rare. If you were joining us, it had to be through clout and personal connection.

I fully made my grand appearance to the block with laughter after that mini fiasco and saw Mike Harrison against the wall across the hall, ogling my silhouette. I bit my lip. It was the norm for any guy to look at me like I was a meal, but whenever Mike Harrison did it, my stomach flipped constantly.

"Why you lookin' at me like that?" I asked loud enough for him to hear.

"Get over here and find out."

I blushed when he winked his hazel green eyes and accepted his invitation to a hug, falling into his arms as if they were made just for me.

Mike was a heaven-sent physical specimen. There wasn't a single girl in this building who wasn't a groupie, begging to get in his bed because he was that fine. Six foot, with a clean-shaven face and honey brown skin; you couldn't beat getting devoured by his gaze! But no matter how tingly I felt about him inside, Mike was an old flame. Even though most people thought our fire was still burning. Every time I was near him, I wished we were together again.

"Let me get those," he said and plucked my schoolbooks out of my arms.

"Aww, isn't that sweet of you?"

"You already know I take care of you. What you doin' after school?" he asked in my ear. His voice rang in the pit of my stomach, a place forbidden for a girl my age to feel or to even recognize its existence.

"I don't know. I'll probably go to the dance studio. Why, what's up? You tryna come to the stu?"

"Nah, I was just asking. I got a hoop session lined up tonight with some of these goofs. Especially Martell's dirty mop water smelling ass."

Mike laughed and jerked his head over to the mutual friends he was talking about.

"Shut yo Daffy Duck lookin' ass up. You all hugged up with Jade, but you know that ain't going nowhere." Martell pushed Mike's arm the moment he returned the insult.

"At least I'm pullin' one. You too ugly to keep one entertained for five seconds."

"Bet I can pull your momma though."

Mike smirked and shook his head while everyone in the vicinity laughed.

"You lame as hell, boy. Wack ass your momma jokes. You can't even get a thirsty Freshman, let alone my momma."

Martell and Mike were best friends, but the way they talked and joked about each other, one would think they were enemies. I mean in a way, they kind of were since I was an insider to their friendship. They held an unspoken rivalry with one of them always trying to one up the other. Martell was just as popular as Mike, but he didn't have the groupies Mike had. Because of it, Martell kinda walked in Mike's shadow throughout high school. Sometimes I laughed at their jokes, but other times, I didn't because I really didn't know if it was serious. Plus, I didn't want to laugh at the wrong thing and offend Mike. I didn't care at all about Martell to be honest. For many reasons.

Just as Martell was about to answer Mike's dig, Martell fell forward as if he was pushed from behind. He fell forward so hard that he nearly landed on Mike's chest face first.

"What the..." Mike and I said in unison as we lifted from the wall.

Everybody froze, and all eyes fell on Martell, preparing for a fight. There were whispers, giggles, and our usual circle opened to give him space. Seemed like everyone knew what was going on, but I still searched for what happened. I followed everyone's gaze to put the pieces together when I laid eyes on a guy in an oversized hoodie. His face was barely visible since it was tucked inside of his hood like a sleeping turtle. All anyone could see were his ugly ass glasses and maybe his mouth. *Who was this creep?*

"Oh, look what we got here. LA's next jailbird." Martell chuckled and sized him up. "Who you think you pushing?"

Martell shoved the guy back. He didn't stumble much, but he put his hands up in surrender.

"It was an accident."

His mouth hardly even moved when he talked. I could see why Martell called him a jailbird because he had the whole hallway shook. Not only did he look withdrawn, but his eyes held this weird, open gaze. I couldn't explain, but his eyes weren't normal at all. Plus, anybody else in his situation, you'd have seen their skin go white in trepidation. Not him. He just looked so lifeless. Emotionless. Rigid.

Like he was a ghost.

Everything I felt inside about Ghost was written all over Martell's face. He was unsure if he should hit him, cuss him out, or let him go because Ghost's expression was as obscure as night.

"You accidentally ran into me. You can't see me standing here? What you on D-Block for anyway? Yo' filthy ass don't belong here."

No response. Just a blank stare.

"Hello? Earth to jailbird!" Martell yelled and knocked on top of his head. I giggled.

"Looks like your punk ass wanna learn the hard way. Let's get on his ass, y'all."

Everyone slowly closed the circle in on the guy and ripped him apart. Instantly.

"Boy look at those shoes! What the fuck are those? Some Reeboks? You look like you ain't been shopping for shoes since sixth grade!"

"That dingy ass hoodie!"

"Boy you look like a demon child. Get your spooky ass outta here."

"Damn, them pants look like they been through the ringer!"

"Damn boy, the bottom of them jeans look like you get chased by a dog every morning and you lose each time!"

I laughed, relieved for the return to normalcy. This ribbing session would probably never end. Everybody had something to say.

Why wouldn't I join? He was literally everything I physically despised in a man.

"Man, look. Just take this money with your low budget ass and buy yourself an outfit. Buy some soap too while you at it," I said and threw some chump change at his chest. Well, forty dollars wasn't chump change to him. The way he looked; it was probably worth millions.

Ghost hadn't said anything the entire time, nor did he appreciate my blessing. He just – took it. The heat, that is. Simply held his head down, stood there, and took it. Anybody else brave enough to stay would have done one of three things: try to rib everybody back only to get beat up, try to fight only to get beat up, or run for their lives. I had never seen anyone just stand there.

Eventually, it just got to the point where I stopped laughing and felt bored because there was only so much people could say without running out of jokes. The only thing left for him to say was, "Are you done?"

"Alright, y'all. Let him go," I said with a sigh. "This is over, we all know he's a bum."

Ghost tried walking around Martell, the ringleader of today's shenanigans, to head to class. But the determination to make him cry, make him run, or break him down like we did to anyone else was strong. So just like D-Block would do, many of them blocked his path to an exit. Whenever he tried to go around, he stupidly ran into someone and got pushed back. Whenever he thought he was safe, someone else stood in his way. I rolled my eyes with a smile. They just didn't know when to let it go.

"Martell, really?" I said.

"Nah, we gotta corner this nigga. He ain't no jailbird, he's

America's next school shooter. I gotta make sure he ain't gonna collect bombs or no AR-15 in his locker. Man, bro if you do got it, just give it to me. I'll have no problem spilling your guts. You worthless anyway."

Everyone laughed harder, and for the first time, Ghost reacted.

An eerie mix between anguish and sorrow flashed through his eyes. It was gone before anyone else noticed, but I did. It packed a serious punch. Enough to strike my chest and make me stop laughing completely.

Damn, who was this guy?

"Martell! That's enough. Let his ass go!" I yelled. Before I even realized it, I stepped away from Mike and moved towards the action.

"Mike you better get your girl! She sticking up for lame ass niggas now. What you gonna do about that, cuz?"

Mike just smiled and shook his head with a shrug.

"I ain't worried."

"It's not even about that. It's about you doing too much! You said what you had to say, now let it go," I said.

"Whatever, shorty. Aye Mike, get your girl," Martell said, and by the time he turned his head back around to give attention to his victim, Ghost disappeared. "Damn, that sucka is fast!"

The majority of D-Block was still hunched over in uncontrollable giggles.

"Bet that punk will think twice about pushing Martell again!"

I wasn't frowning solely because of what Martell had said. I never saw this dude before, didn't know who he was, and most certainly had never seen him down D-Block. If he could get someone like me to stop laughing amongst a hysterical crowd, then something was up.

"Who is he?" I asked Martell.

"I don't know his lame ass but I bet that mark will think twice about running into me without apology again though. Why you all on his dick? See look, Mike! You better keep Jade in check."

I turned my lip in disgust. Martell got on my nerves.

"Whatever. Don't worry about me, stupid ass."

I walked away in a huff. I had to check myself though. This is what we did on a daily basis. There was nothing new about what just happened.

So what had my panties in a bunch?

The fact that he had flown all this time completely under my radar, as weird as he looked, had me curious. If someone looked so out of place, out of the ordinary, I'd have noticed a long time ago.

So... who was he?

Chapter Two

TAKING INTEREST IN someone before they took interest in me was foreign. Any guy I've ever given the time of day had always publicly expressed their desire for me before I even knew who they were; including Mike Harrison. I had no romantic interest in Ghost at all, and probably never will, but he really had me thinking. Why was I curious about him when one, our contact with one another was literally less than two minutes, and two, he was the creepiest bummy looking guy I had ever seen in my life?

I tried to let it go, but my interest piqued again when I sat in my third period Physics class and peered out of the window to see Ghost standing at a locker – what appeared to be his locker.

Wait. His locker was in the Senior wing?

I was tripping. He and I were in the same grade level, his locker was so close to one of my classes, and I never even knew. Every day he was visible yet as invisible as the air we breathed.

I had to check him out. Carefully. Giving my friends, associates, and enemies any inkling that I was looking at someone like him wasn't ideal. Either way, it wasn't like I was looking at him because I wanted him. That was a hell all the way to the no.

A profile of his back was all he gave, but it was enough for me to see if that roasting session was warranted. And, well? It was. Too plain. Too hoodlum-ish. A dirty hoodie, terribly old black jeans, and some random, busted, non-brand shoes whose soles were seeing their last days. The hole in the bottom of his jeans was super apparent from the back, and I shook my head in disgust. *What a wreck.* He needed a personal stylist for sure. And a bath.

As I scrutinized deeper, hoping to see something new that I didn't see on D-Block, he turned around and gave me access to his full face. I ducked from the window so our eyes wouldn't slam together. So that he wouldn't think I was some stalker. Especially coming from someone like me.

I took a deep breath. *That was close.*

When I felt safe, I slowly peeked my head forward to finish snooping. His glasses were thick as hell. Couldn't he just get contacts? I wished I could've been closer, but even from afar, something was off about him. The kind of off-ness that had everyone on edge earlier. I really tried to pinpoint it, and I couldn't quite figure it out, but... those eyes... A school shooter was a perfect way to describe him.

Before I got a chance to process anything else about him, he tightened his hood and withdrew from the entire world as he made his way to class. I sighed, poking out my lip.

Just when I turned around in my seat to try and rid any thoughts of Ghost out of my head, someone was standing dead in my face with wide eyes. I jumped out of my skin, a part of me scared that I had been watched watching Ghost the entire time, and the other part? My personal bubble was obliterated! The minute I recognized who it was, I'd call her an annoying ass bitch before anything.

"Erica, what the hell?"

She was always the fly on the wall type that would flutter right into your grill at the most inopportune times. Such as this.

"He's cute, isn't he?" She smirked.

"What are you talking about?"

"Weren't you just checking out someone across the way? Jarell, right?"

"Who?"

"Come on, Jade. You were literally staring at Jarell."

"Girl, I don't even know who a Jarell is! You need to mind your business and get up out my face," I said with my lip turned and shooed her away.

"Alright. My bad, I thought I saw you looking at him. You were taking up for him in the halls. But you wouldn't do that to Mike, though. I'm sure he wouldn't like that."

Her fake ass really tried to sound apologetic, but I saw right through her.

"And you sure would know, since you like to stalk your way through my thoughts, huh? Hell, you know me better than me, let you tell it."

"I don't have to stalk anyone. I just figured somebody as fine and as smart as Mike shouldn't be messing around with someone who's got a sneaky little eye out for the lamest nigga in school, that's all. Maybe he should reconsider who he's dealing with."

"Coming from somebody who just said he was cute? That's interesting."

That sure wiped the ugly smile off her face. I laughed and rose to move to a different seat. She didn't budge, so when I stood up, we were practically nose to nose. Who did she think she was? I wasn't backing down from any challenge. She'd better ask somebody!

She opened her mouth to say something, but I put my hand up

to stop her.

"Ah. Shut up. Instead of worrying about what you think I'm doing, why don't you get outta my way and go 'reconsider' making a money move. Then you might know a thing or two about me since you should know I don't associate with broke bitches."

Since she was already way too close, I shoved her with my shoulder to head to a new seat. Many watched us, but when they realized there wasn't going to be a fight, those eyes redirected back to the teacher who began his lesson about gravity.

Erica delivered a dirty glare. I just laughed and motioned a check mark as I sat in my new seat. She was the type that wanted to be in my inner circle so bad just so she could try to destroy me and what I had going on from within. Definitely the wannabe type. B-List ass bitch who only made it to D-Block because she was a part of the cheerleading squad I was the captain of. Otherwise, her non-dressing ass would be getting bullied.

Girls like her were why I acted the way I did. No one could be like Jade Williams, even if I was caught staring at the lamest kid in school. But now, I seriously had to watch my back from her. She was a sly little thing, and she was going to do everything in her power to sabotage me about staring at Ghost.

The first person she was going to target was Mike.

An hour and a half flew by until it was time for lunch, and I let the thoughts of Erica and Ghost go. The hallways were always packed at lunch time, especially all the freshman that contaminated them with their immaturity. It just made me that much happier I had the opportunity for open campus.

Once I arrived in the cafeteria, I scanned around for Mike so we could get the hell out of here. He was usually waiting for me by the bathrooms to head out together, so when he wasn't there, I was annoyed. I stood near the bathrooms to wait.

As everyone walked by, I felt like all eyes were on me. Or at least they took a long glance as they passed and went on to their business. A crushing anxiety settled in my chest as I began to feel angry at Mike the longer I waited. He really had me out here looking like I got stood up.

I waited for five minutes, trying to play it cool until I couldn't take it anymore. I was about to give up and walk out of the school to have lunch alone, but he turned the corner and jogged in my direction. I went in on him as soon as he was in striking distance.

"You know you had me standing here for almost ten minutes, right?" I crossed my arms.

"My fault. I had got caught up with a few people in the hall. You mad at me?"

He smiled and nudged my arm as he got close to my cheek, puckering his lips for a kiss. If I was light skinned, I would have blushed a full-on crimson.

"Don't touch me."

I ducked my head, trying my hardest not to smile at him, but ended up failing anyway as the corners of my mouth tilted upward in defeat. He threw his head back in laughter.

"It's like that now, ma?" he said with low eyes.

"You get on my nerves," I said, still smiling.

"You like me anyway."

I cut him a glare, and just decided to let it go. He was with me now; I had what I wanted. I could never, ever stay mad at Mike. Boyfriend or not.

See, we broke up last year when we were Juniors. The history of our relationship was so tit for tat. He used to like me Freshman year, but I didn't like him back. When he stopped liking me, I started to like him. We then realized we liked each other, started dating, then realized it wasn't going to work. We were both too busy, with me dancing and him being the top basketball prospect at our school, to have any real time with one another.

So now, because we couldn't let each other go, we had this weird "friends with benefits" deal without sex. Well, that's what it was for him. I didn't want things to be this way, and I was done wasting time. He was truly, truly the only guy that met my standards, so I was down to fight for it. It was just a matter of how I was going to communicate that to him. At the same time, he just seemed to be happy with our status, so I didn't want to jeopardize anything.

We both walked out of the school building and headed to our favorite spot, Post & Beam down the street from school. It was a scorching day out in late summer, and the both of us hated being indoors, so we soaked up the warm breeze on the patio to eat.

For a while, we locked into our own thoughts and daydreams in silence. He always looked so handsome when he was in a pensive mood.

"My mom has been asking about you," I said as I stirred my ice water and waited for my chicken and waffles, hoping I didn't interrupt what looked to be some serious thinking. His eyes finally met mine and refocused, although a daze lingered in them.

"Word? What she say?"

"You know how she gets about you. Mostly about how she's happy that you're still around, and how she wants us to stick together and date. Even through college."

His eyes left mine and focused on his lap. A pall hit the

conversation. One of those loud silent types. I leaned forward, hoping to make him feel some sense of urgency to answer.

"I mean, y-yeah. That sounds cool and all, but you know I don't know where I'm signing to play ball. I could be going literally across the country to Miami," he said.

"I know. I told her that, but because my career in dance is already taking off, she thinks I'm going to be traveling as much as you do."

"Let me ask you something."

"Yeah?"

"What do *you* think? This ain't about your moms. What do you feel?"

I knew at times, I let my mother influence my decisions way too much. But it was only because I had never seen her ways go wrong. My mother never took a misstep. She never steered, guided, or told me wrong. My mother walked her talk; she wanted better for me.

"I think she's right that we can make it work. I want us to work, Mike. To be honest, we're at the stage where we gotta stop playing games and start making real decisions about where we're going with this. We're seniors. It's been all fun and games, but after a while, it's like… okay. What are we doing? What does our future look like?"

"So if I'm across the country and you're still in Cali, what would it look like? How are we making us happen? I guess I like where we are right now because if we make a move, we don't have that string or label attached, you feel me?"

"Well, I'm not planning on going to college, Mike. You know that already. That shit is a scam and I make great money already without it. You know I always make money moves, so I'm saying, I could travel with you. Wherever you go, I could make it happen. My name is already making waves, so it wouldn't be hard to find gigs. We could seriously be a money couple. You just have to be down. I'm down with you, and it's not simply because of my mom. It's because nobody else is on par with me the way you are."

Hmph. Look at me. Practically begging. Mike met my high standards, but I wasn't supposed to beg for his attention. Had me looking like a fool.

He mulled it over, picking at his drink as if it had suddenly become a disgusting plaything. I nearly wanted to get up and leave him at the restaurant to walk back to school his damn self out of spite.

"Well, are you gonna say anything?"

He smacked his lips. "I just think it's all uncertain. I think we should just keep things the way they are right now. You know, not complicate things and wrap things up in labels."

"What are you talking about? What's so wrong with labels?"

"There's nothing wrong with it, but it comes with a package. It's a name, but it comes with a responsibility, you know? Like the word wife is just a word, but there's a whole lot of things that come with being a wife you wouldn't just pick up if you didn't have that label, you feel me?"

"So you're saying you don't want to be together?"

My shoulders sank, and the tears stung the back of my eyes. *Was I really being rejected?* Me!? I willed the tears away. I wouldn't dare be caught crying over no damn dude. But I had to admit, this was a rejection I didn't think I could ever get over.

"I'm saying I don't want us to be wrapped up into what it means to be a boyfriend or girlfriend. Something happens to us as we move onto the next thing, and then it all falls apart. At least with what we have right now, we don't have all that baggage, but we can still appreciate one another. You dig me? So let's just leave things the way they are. We good like this, and we're both happy, right?"

Everything he said made no sense. I was borderline famous, I had money, I wasn't going to be strapped down to a scamming college, and I had dope connections. What was so wrong about being with me that he had doubts of making it completely official? I was *that* bitch, so I didn't want to accept a bullshit reason like potentially moving across the country as to why we couldn't make things work.

But I really had no choice.

It was his decision, and it was final. If I was smart, I'd just go along with it. It wasn't like he was saying we couldn't be friends anymore, or we couldn't continue having a sort of relationship... or acting like we were in one.

I would just have to come up with a real cool and slick answer for someone if they asked me if him and I were back together. Especially the Erica types.

Chapter Three

UNDERESTIMATION. THE EXACT motivator I needed to get what I wanted and to prove the naysayers wrong. I was good at that. Underestimation is one of the reasons I am here, at the age of seventeen co-running a dance studio with the famous Alise Marie at Hip Hop Emporium at Playground LA, one of the top choreographers in the country.

I might be young, but best believe I got the juice! I'd been doing this dance thing since I was three years old, starting off with gymnastics and ballet. When I started studying famous dancers like Jennifer Lopez, Janet Jackson, and now, Teyana Taylor, my time was completely dedicated to hip hop choreography, and I haven't looked back since.

Of course, I had plugs to get here. Plenty of dope dancers on the streets didn't get the blessing I got. You already know it was my mom that planted those seeds. When I was a pre-teen, she was dating a retired basketball player from the LA Clippers, Corey Marshall, and he had connections. When I really started getting into hip hop and expanding my gymnast background, I danced under some of the best choreographers around, particularly who had been good friends with Corey. These choreographers recognized my talent and had gotten me into several music videos with people like Ciara, Usher, and Missy Elliott and now, I've been able to establish good relationships with them.

That was one thing about my momma. She always invested in me.

Now, my mom and Corey were done, but those connections still stuck around, and I was thankful to Corey for that. He was still like a father to me. And as I co-ran the studio, many of our dancers weren't particularly happy being bossed around by someone young like me, but it didn't matter. I had more credentials than they did, and they were trying to get where I was. So, they had no choice but to follow commands. The only thing they could really say was that Alise had the final say, but she and I were on the same page more times than not.

Alise was a wonderful person to work with, and I was grateful for her mentorship, especially as I worked to finish up high school and run my cheerleading and dance team for which I was captain again this year. This was the ultimate way to get away from the mess that was always school, and especially, after Mike and I had our talk last week.

Although that was a plus, it didn't help my dance crew was fucking up tonight, so it was kind of a win-lose situation. Especially considering the biggest shows of the fall season for a big name was coming up. I couldn't take watching another person mess up. I went over and shut the music off without warning.

"Stop, stop! Listen. Let's make sure we hit that move right after the second eight-oh-eight ladies. Y'all dragging behind the beat. Let's run it back. If you need me to show you how it looks, let me know instead of messing up!"

To be in music videos or performing live on stage, one must be perfect. And when I say perfect, I don't mean close to perfect because everybody says, "There's no such thing as human perfection." I don't believe that. There *is* a such thing as human perfection if people worked at it and did what they were supposed to do. And you for damn sho needed to be perfect if you were dancing for Chris Brown's show! If he walked in this door right now and saw this, he'd be through with all of us and start looking for someone else.

"Listen, I'll be right back. Please have this right by the time I get back, or else I'm cancelling the concert myself."

I huffed and strutted to Alise's office to let her know it wasn't looking so good, and to ask what backups we had in case the original choreography didn't work. She was sitting at her desk with her chair back and her legs kicked up on the table, eating a salad.

"Hey, sis. Um, those girls aren't looking so good right now," I said immediately.

She rolled her eyes.

"Tell me about it. They weren't looking so good before you came here from school."

"What's up with them? Should we come up with a plan B or should we try to work it out? The concert is coming up and they can't even do a basic flare on the third count! I know Chris sent us the choreo, and I'm sure he wants it to be specific, but what do we do if they can't?"

"They can do it; we just have to push them. Make them do some wall sits or something if they mess it up again or threaten to recruit a whole nother mass of dancers. Actually, just tell them I said they aren't leaving this dance studio until everything is perfect. I can be here all night. Just drill em. Otherwise, we'll have to tell Chris no by tomorrow night so that he has time to find other folks. And before you leave, come back in here. I have some dope news for you that I know you'd like to hear."

"Really? What's it about?"

"You'll know when you come back," she said.

"Okay. I'ma go get them in order."

She winked and then turned her swivel chair away from me. I smiled with all the butterflies in my stomach. It was rare for Alise to share great news, and for her to have this sneaky little grin, it had to be something big.

I entered the main studio again and from the looks of it, they still weren't getting it right. I went over to shut the music off. Huffs and puffs echoed throughout the room and their body language was even worse.

"Alright, y'all. Listen. Alise said y'all have been trash all day. So here's the deal. If y'all want a cut from this Chris Brown check, nobody's leaving this spot until y'all get it right. Y'all will be here all night and sleep here if y'all have to. If not, we're calling the gig off. Y'all got until tomorrow night. Got it?"

Without a word, they all nodded.

"My God. Looks like y'all don't have a care in the world that y'all about to perform with one of the biggest names in the industry! Y'all look sad as hell – get it together!" I yelled. "Stacy, I want you to be in charge. Here's your chance to step up. Before I leave, I wanna see the morale up, you got it?"

Stacy nodded in agreement. "Yes, Jade."

"Thank you."

I headed back to Alise's office eager to hear the news she has for me.

"I left Stacy in charge and told them they'd be here all night until they get it right." She nodded with approval. "So, what's the tea?"

She clapped her hands together with a huge smile, opposite from the smug grin she had two minutes ago. My eyes widened in anticipation.

"First, I just want to say how awesome of a mentee you are. You've really grown into a leader, you're a great dancer, you take no crap and you have high expectations from the dancers and yourself. At the same time, you still know how to be warm and appreciate of them for who they are. That's a commendable trait to have. Especially from someone your age. I'm not much older than you, but you remind me so much of myself."

I nodded, for her to keep going.

"Anyway, I've been working on some things to expand our studio. I've been keeping this a secret, but I've been applying for some grants. I've talked to some important folks, and I've been accepted for funds to expand our studio to have a youth dance crew, and I want you to be the lead coach for that and hold classes, after graduating high school. These kids will have the same opportunities to dance under big names the same way adults do, but artists have to want them, and you're going to have to build their clout. How does that sound?"

My mouth dropped. *Me?* Be a head choreographer for the youth dancers and potentially be the reason why they're in music videos at a young age? Hell yeah that was an opportunity I couldn't pass up!

I tried to contain my excitement, but really, what other seventeen-year-old could do it better than me? I was about to be making millions! I could even start my own TV show with this and be in competition with some of the other dance crews out there! You know how crazy that would be? The level of competition? I was all for competition.

I had to settle myself. I couldn't just take an offer because it sounded great. I had to put my rational hat on and think it through, but honestly, I just wanted to celebrate getting the offer.

"Yo, Lise... this is crazy news! Are you really serious? Me?"

"Yes, girl! I told you I've been planning some things, but now that it's coming to fruition, I want you to be involved in the success of the studio since you've been such a vital asset to me and growing this studio to greatness since you were fourteen." I jumped up and squealed.

"Oh my God, this is huge news. I can't believe it! I need more details!"

"Well, yes, I need to tease out the details and everything, such as starting day, how we are recruiting dancers, the pay, and everything. I just want you to know I want you to lead it all but talk it over with your mom. Think about your postsecondary plans. Then holla at me, okay? Take as much time as you need, but not too long," she said. "Now get on out of here, I want you to celebrate."

"Bet! Thank you so much for the opportunity." I wrapped my arms around her, squeezing her tight before heading out of the studio.

Man! I had to be the dopest, most talented teen dancer in the country! Now, it was time to tell everyone. My mom was going to be stoked!

But, what about Mike?

I mean, I knew he'd be happy for me, but what about our future? Because at this point, my future was now going to look a whole lot different than what I thought it was going to be less than twenty-four hours ago. All of this just became so overwhelming, despite my happiness. I mean, I didn't know why it was overwhelming – I was basically hired for career employment before graduating high school

– but I mean, it was a lot of pressure and huge shoes to fill. I could do it though. If I could do everything else, I could do this.

I got into my car and quickly drove home. Faster than I should've been going on this road, but who cares? I couldn't wait to let Mike and my mom know the news. Whipping my phone from my pocket, I texted Mike first.

Me: Mike, you will never believe the news I got tonight! Are you free to talk?

Message sent. Now, I had to let my mom know the same thing.

Me: Hey mom, I have some great news for you when I get home that we should talk over-

The moment I looked up to watch the road, I gasped. Oh no. A red light and I was too close to the intersection!

I threw my phone down, gripped the wheel, and slammed on the brakes. A colorless body suddenly appeared in front of me and my whole life flashed before my eyes.

"Shit!"

I swerved over to the left, swerved to the right, and swerved back to the left to avoid the walking body in all black as my car did a complete three-sixty and hit a curb. My body flew forward, but my seatbelt pushed me right back into my seat with a thump.

Holy. Shit.

Thank God my airbags didn't activate. Thank God this wasn't a busy road! I took a deep breath to calm the wheezing, to get the air stuck in my throat out. When the smoke from the burning rubber of the tires cleared away, I looked back and the person who was wearing all black walked down the sidewalk in the opposite direction.

"Oh my God. I'm so fucking stupid!"

I slapped my forehead with a palm as hard as my heart pounded out of my chest. I almost killed someone, and all the opportunities I just got offered would've been down the drain.

I pulled the key out of the ignition and pushed the car door open.

"Hey! I am so sorry. Are you okay? I'm so fucking stupid; I should have been paying attention. But hey, try to wear some color next time! You could get hurt."

I called after the mysterious person as my long legs paced to catch up with him. What was I was thinking getting out of a car in the middle of the night to talk to a stranger who didn't seem to care that his life was on the verge of ending? But I had to redeem myself. No way was I letting this go.

He seemed to walk at a horse and buggy pace, but for some reason, I had trouble keeping up. The closer and closer I got, the more my chest fluttered.

"Hey," I called out to him, this time in a tremble.

Now, I was directly in front of *Ghost*.

My stomach flipped as the memories rushed back from last week's D-Block shenanigans. Fuck. Now this right here was awkward. He still looked like an evil turtle who would be happy if he never saw daylight again, especially with that stupid hood up. But the breeze from the night occasionally fluttered it away.

And that made the difference. All the difference. The difference that made my heart skip several beats when the wind blessed it opened and feel an uncanny sense of disappointment when it closed.

I wasn't expecting this. God truly took his time with Ghost.

Something about his bone structure trapped my heart – the perfect combination of high cheekbones and beady eyes. His lashes were thick and long, complementing his blemish free, milky brown skin.

And his facial hair.

The way his goatee grew into a thin, fuzzy beard and connected to his sideburns left me nearly gasping. It was a stamp of early manhood – a type of rough around the edges not even Mike possessed. That really any guy at school had possessed.

I was desperate to keep looking, but each breeze was so fleeting! My hands itched to pull his hood down forever just so I could openly stare and take him all in. I swallowed any words and thoughts from last week and admitted that he was *beautiful*. So beautiful, it was breathtaking.

I gazed at him for a while, but he simply looked around without a single sign that he was at all bothered. *Weird.* If someone stood staring at me like this, I'd be ready to run. It was only when he raised his eyebrow in confusion that I felt mortified for nearly killing him.

"Listen. I wasn't watching where I was going, and I almost hit you."

"Be more careful," he said with a clipped tone.

"Yeah. I should've been watching."

Now what? There was nothing left to say, but we still stood in front of one another. The chirping crickets filled the air with the smell of a warm summer night. The only thing pleasant about this whole ordeal.

"So... I'm Jade. From school. I guess being in this situation isn't who I am. People see me as this perfect person, but I mess up sometimes too. Not often, but I do. You know, like this whole situation. You should already know I'm not this airheaded, right?"

I was rambling like an idiot. And he just simply stood there, looking at the ground, moving his feet like he was bored.

"Um, yeah." I threw a side eye. "You do know me, right? I mean, who doesn't?"

"I know who you are."

"Well, aren't you going to acknowledge me?"

"For what? You ain't important." He shrugged.

I blinked.

"Whoa. I know I almost hit you, but that ain't no excuse to be rude. Especially to someone like me."

His eyebrows flexed. "Rude?"

"I didn't stutter. Yeah, rude!"

He made an amused sound in his throat. "You ain't a saint, Ms. Popularity. Especially the way you threw your money at me last week like I was some dog."

I wasn't ready to even think about apologizing for that. In fact, I wasn't going to.

"You needed it, if I'm honest." His eyes squinted. "And Ms. Popularity, huh? I'd prefer Jade. What's your name?" I asked.

"None of your business."

"I would like to know if that's okay with you. I'd like to know who I'm talking to; you know?"

For a long moment he stood in silence, withdrawing himself deeper into his hoodie by tightening it, removing any of the beauty I had previously saw from my view. As he did so, he traced the sidewalk with his foot. Like he investigated the ground. *So strange!* I was mesmerized by what he was doing until I looked up and realized my car was still in the middle of the street and opened. I sighed. I didn't have time to continue engaging in one-sided conversations or stand in uncomfortable silence.

"Well? Hello? Do you not know your name?"

He shot a sinister glare my way that would have sent anyone else running.

"My name is America's Next School Shooter. Asshole."

Damn. Forget that he called me out my name. My stomach churned as everything came back to me, including the guilt I felt when all those emotions flashed in his eyes after Martell said he'd kill him. I opened my mouth to say I don't even know what. Maybe that Martell didn't mean what he said last week, but I couldn't figure it out, so I just closed it again.

What the hell? What was wrong with me?

When I was quiet for too long, he shook his head and slid past and away down the street like a ghost. Quiet and enigmatic as he disappeared into the night.

Chapter Four

GOING THROUGH THE motions was the best way to describe a Friday like this. My mind was so preoccupied with nearly killing Ghost last night and waiting to tell Mike the big news about the studio that my mind was foggy all morning. I was going to tell my mom about it, but she was out of town, so I was left to think about telling Mike on my own. I was glad to share, but at the same time, I felt like telling him was a bad idea.

I came alive and aware of my surroundings when I got to school. I walked past D-Block because I didn't feel like watching or dealing with the foolery today, so I headed to my locker first. On the way there was Mike's locker, but it was empty. I opted to wait for him as the anxiety pressed into my chest. Would this be more of a reason for us to be together or to push him away?

It didn't take long for him to show up with my body getting all warm at his mere presence. Just looking at him made all the jitters disappear. He could make such a simple outfit look so sexy and effortless, even when it was a simple fitted white t-shirt, Adidas soccer joggers, and athletic flip flops. The older he got, the more attractive he got. I didn't feel this way all the other years the way I got all tingly inside for him this year.

"Sup, Jade?"

"Hey."

He wrapped his arm around my shoulder and kissed my forehead as if it was no big deal. As if his heart wasn't tripping over itself the way mine was when I looked at him.

"I got your text last night. You got something to tell me?" he asked and opened his locker.

"Yup. I'm both nervous and excited to tell you."

"What's wrong?"

"I just got an offer from Alise at the studio to run a youth dance crew last night. So, I'll have career employment before high school graduation."

"Word! You serious? That's wassup! Why you nervous about telling me this?"

My bottom lip protruded. "You know why."

He sighed and moved from his locker to face me.

"Listen," he whispered, using a finger to lift my chin. "Don't worry about us. Why don't we just celebrate the offer that was given to you? This is a big deal, shorty!"

"I know, but you know how I feel about you."

"But we can figure us out later, okay baby girl? You thinking about the wrong thing right now. Everything will work itself out," he said softly, rubbing my chin with his thumb.

"Okay." I smiled, but not convinced or satisfied with the response.

"I need to come check you out at the studio! That's just so dope man, you know how much clout you'll get doing this? How much she say she paying?"

"I don't know. I find out soon, though."

"Word. Well keep me posted, baby girl. Come on. I'll walk you to class."

I nodded, still feeling uneasy about the whole "us" thing, but was glad for his genuine excitement, nonetheless. At least he was willing to figure us out.

 He brought me closer to him and escorted me to class. All the girls watched us in desire, and I just shook my head with a smirk. They'd better keep dreaming.

We strolled through the halls like love birds and without a care in the world when suddenly, Ghost passed by us with a teacher leading his way. His head, again, was deep in his hood with his eyes lowered to the ground as he followed way too close behind her.

I really wondered about him.

And to think about it, I was probably the only person who saw him. Everyone else just bumped into him along the way but never apologized or even acknowledged his presence. Like he was invisible.

No. I tore my eyes away from him before Mike caught me. I needed to stop thinking about him. He didn't fit my standards. I acknowledged my mistake with nearly hitting him, and that was it. I did my part. Erase him from memory.

We were finally at my class, and I turned to Mike to see him off. To my pleasant surprise, he pinned me against the wall, his abdomen pressed against mine in a way that made me finally break out in sweat. I hugged my books and stared into his eyes.

"I'll see you later, okay?" he said, then kissed me on the cheek.

He needed to stop teasing me, knowing damn well a kiss on the lips was what I really wanted.

"Okay, big head. I'll see you after school. I'm gonna have lunch with Laurie today."

"Sounds good. See you soon," he said, walking away and leaving me in a daze.

The first part of the day flew by. I met Laurie by her locker, and we decided to stay in for lunch today, neither of us feeling particularly up for driving anywhere.

Laurie was my long-time best friend, since elementary school. Her parents and my mom had become friends since we lived in the same neighborhood. She and I were two peas in a pod and acted so much alike, it was almost scary. She was just your regular girl next door with blonde hair and blue eyes but had everything.

Her parents had high ranking positions in Fortune 500 companies, so they got her what she wanted when she wanted it. If she failed a class and wanted an A, her parents were the type to fix it for her by taking advantage of whatever powers they could impose over the school. Sometimes I felt some kind of way about how her parents operated, but I could never really name what I felt. Either way, it never trumped our friendship, although I could see it happening in the foreseeable future. I didn't know how or why, but I just did.

We grabbed something healthy from the salad bar and headed for the senior section. Much to my dismay, some baby ass Freshmen sat in our spots where they didn't belong.

"Y'all know y'all don't even sit here for lunch. Get y'all bum asses up," I said.

"We can sit here if we want to," challenged one of the girls, giving me a nasty glare.

"If y'all don't get up, you'll have a bigger problem than you already have, and I'll make sure of it. You know this is D-Block section so rise the fuck up and move your ass along," I said, and that was enough to make her and her little friend move.

"That's what I thought," I mumbled.

"Can't believe that girl tried that," Laurie said. "We have some bold kids around here. That's actually kind of good."

"Yeah, good for when we leave, but right now, they should know what's up."

After that, I completely disconnected. A part of me regretted sharing my news with Mike because by telling him, nothing had changed. He just evaded any further conversation about our future, and I for that moment, was fine. But now? I felt like shit.

"Jade, what's wrong with you? You've been quiet all day, and that's not like you at all. Are you okay?"

Laurie's eyebrows wrinkled with concern as she leaned over her salad. Hmph. I knew what that look meant. I wasn't ready to talk with her about Mike because that was just way too sensitive for me. The decoy I needed was Ghost to mask my true feelings.

"I need you to help me out with something. Do you know this one guy that's in our grade? I don't know his name, so all I can really do is describe him. He's really quiet and mysterious, and he wears a hood every day?"

Laurie chuckled, taking another bite of her salad. "Um, you know how many guys at school are quiet and wear hoods every day, Jade?"

"Okay, um... I don't know much about him, but he wears super thick glasses, he's literally always hiding in this dirty black hoodie that's way too big for him, and he walks around as if he's scared of showing his face to the world. He has this weird and scary kind of

... I don't know... ambiance about him, for lack of a better word?"

"Oh! You're talking about Jarell?"

Oh. Right. Erica had mentioned his name was Jarell after catching me staring a hole into him. But Laurie's response held a cacophony that caught me off guard, and it made me not want to even continue asking about him. I shrugged and shifted my eyes away from her.

"I think so."

"Eww, why you wanna know about him?"

"I was just aski-"

"Jade, you don't want to know about him. If anybody caught you asking this, you and Mike are a done deal!"

"What are you talking about? Why?"

"Haven't you seen him? He walks around with this weird look on his face that scares everyone! It's all in his eyes." She shuddered. "The only person he talks to is his special ed teacher who follows him around all day and sits with him in class while he does these weird movements with his hands and feet. They're probably fucking each other, I mean seriously, Jade. I'm glad I heard that Martell tore him to pieces. He's strange!"

"Do you know why he's like that?"

"Well, from what I've heard, he's a crack baby. That's been the rumor since Freshman year, but no one really knows much about him. He has no friends, Jade. Not even one since Freshman year. That's a red flag and shows you that he's creepy!"

"I mean, have any of y'all actually had a conversation with him to the point where you can make a judgement like that?"

"Hell no, none of us would ever talk to that creep. What, you're sticking up for him or something?" She glared.

"No! I ain't say anything about sticking up for anyone. I'm just asking questions."

"Well, if Mike was around, he'd be pretty upset. The way you're sounding, it's like you're down for him or something. Why did you want to know about him anyway?"

Laurie was being unfair. I understood we were on the popular side, and I wasn't innocent either when it came to excluding people out of our circle based on superficial bullshit. Actually, I was one of the head seniors in charge to do it. But this here seemed to be way outlandish. Everyone had friends, and maybe he had some that we just didn't know about. It just wasn't us.

Either way, there was no way in hell I was going to tell Laurie about my interaction with him, nor was I going to mention me almost killing him while I expressed my deepest remorse. And for damn sure I wasn't going into detail about how attractive he was! She would have said something crazy, like "You should have hit him because it'd be one less weirdo on the planet."

"It's really not that serious. I was just wondering because I've never seen him before until Martell and the crew ambushed him on D-Block and it had me wondering. You know it bothers me when I don't know people, girl. Especially when it's someone that weird looking," I said.

I tried to laugh it off, and Laurie looked like she wanted to believe me, but the qualm in her eyes told it all. I plastered the best fake smile that I could muster in hopes that she would just believe me and let it go.

"Okay, girl. Don't get any stupid ideas. I don't want that pretty little reputation of yours to be destroyed by taking too much interest in someone like him. Well, not your reputation as much as your thing with Mike. By the way, how is that going?" she asked, thankfully dropping the subject.

"It's been going great! We could never be better."

After the way this conversation about Ghost went down, I could see she was more judgmental than I would have thought. It was best to leave the topic of Mike alone.

"That's great! I love the both of you guys so much. You are going to make pretty babies when you are older, and you are going to be a power couple. You two just need to stop playing games and get on one accord."

"We will. Just give it time."

Chapter Five

IT WAS THE Lady Cougars Varsity cheerleading practice. Well, pre-season basketball practice for the varsity boys' team too since we shared half the gym with one another. It was the first practice of the sports season since tryouts over the summer, and I was a second-year captain. A squad full of seniors, one of the strongest teams we'd ever had, had me thinking about how we could participate in competitions to win some money and build our school clout this year. Not only that, but it would also build my versatility as a dancer and my future within this field if we started winning some of those competitions.

I was deep in thought about this while my team stretched to prepare for the intensity of today, but quiet snickers behind me told me they weren't stretching at all. I turned my head to see them all gossiping about the boys on the basketball team. I threw a hand on my hip.

"This is the finest basketball team I've ever seen in my life. It's time to get chosen by one of them," Laurie said. Without further ado, she turned around and bent over in a stretch, purposely pointing her ass towards the guys, showing off her thong underneath her cheering skirt.

I turned my head in disgust. First, it wasn't like she had an ass, okay? And second, they were practicing. Nobody on the team was going to see it.

Well. That theory was dismantled because Martell stopped to glare while the rest of his team ignored and did their drills. Ugh, his stupid ass would be the one. His eyes were wide and held a sexual hunger that I hadn't seen from anyone our age in a public setting before. The moment Laurie noticed, she bent over even more, smirking at him as he fell right into her antics. A teammate slapped his chest and told him to focus on training when they realized he was looking way too hard.

The girls behind me chuckled like Kindergarteners.

"Laurie, he's so fine. Did you see how he was looking at you?" one girl said with dreamy eyes.

"How could I not?" Laurie smirked.

"Look at his skin. I could drink him for hot chocolate. And his dimples. My goodness," the girl replied.

"Girl, that skin on those abs? To die for. Would love to see what he's really working with in those pants," Laurie said and licked her lips.

They all hummed wistfully. As much as I hated it, I had to agree with them. At the same time, Martell didn't need to be looking over here, especially if he was trying to become the star on the team he always wanted to be. He had to get through Mike first if he wanted that starting point guard role. Looking at Laurie as if he'd have sex with her right now wasn't going to cut it.

"Alright, ladies. Let's get our priorities in line. Make sure y'all getting the stretches right because I don't want anyone pulling any muscles and be out for half the season," I said.

"Girl don't be trying to act like Martell ain't cute," said Arianna, one of the senior cheerleaders. "Loosen up, girl. You know this a fine ass team this year. Let us soak this all up while we can."

I smiled, pulling my arm back in a stretch.

"Well first, I ain't interested in nobody but Mike, so I ain't looking at nobody. And second, we got priorities, okay?" I said in a joking tone, raising an eyebrow at her. I mean, I knew how to joke around and have fun. But at the end of the day, we had practice, and I was running it. We didn't have time to look at boys all night.

"Oh really? Just interested in Mike, huh?" chimed in irrelevant Erica, who was all the way in the back where she belonged.

"Yes, really."

"That ain't what I saw the other day when you were staring down Jarell across the hall from physics class last week."

"Who?" all the girls asked at the same time, turning their heads towards Erica, pausing their stretches.

"Jarell," Erica emphasized once again with a satisfied nod, and every one of them expressed a sort of disgust.

"That can't be true." Arianna shivered. "He's gross and a whole outcast. Jade knows better than to be looking at someone like that over Mike. Come on, Erica."

"I'm not lying. I saw it for myself."

She smirked that dumb ass smile of hers, bending over in a leg stretch with a stupid "gotcha" glow in her eyes that just made me want to snatch them out of their sockets. I had to keep it cool. I was the cheerleading captain, but damn if I wasn't so woefully tempted to kick her ass! I could just visualize my knuckles hitting the most vulnerable part of her nose.

"Stop making shit up, Erica. You know you didn't see me staring at anyone, let alone someone like Jarell. I didn't even know who that was," I said, crossing my arms and fully facing her. "And even if I was, you wanna be like me so bad, you probably would try to snatch him up for yourself."

"Oh, you sure had me fooled then because those eyes were locked on somebody that wasn't Mike. That's what I know for sure."

Erica giggled, and everyone shifted awkwardly. Everyone on this team knew I had Mike on lock, and none of them would dare, even drop a hint or thought about being interested in him for fear of what I'd do to them.

Yes, I was staring at Jarell. But it wasn't because I wanted him! I wanted Mike, and he was all I wanted. Nobody messed with my man. Ever.

Laurie shot me a puzzled look, waiting for me to denounce this accusation as soon as possible.

"You know what, Erica? Keep spreading lies about me and it'll be the last cheerleading team you'll be on," I seethed. "I'll have your ass suspended by the athletic director for creating rifts on the team. How about that, silly bitch?"

"Oh shut up and keep an eye on that nigga Mike you call yours. Because once he finds out you ain't interested in him, you never know who could slide right in because he can get anybody he wants."

"Girl, don't sit here and act like I ain't the one out here with the money and the clout. Trust me, you ain't gonna be the one to convince Mike to leave me. He wouldn't even be caught talking to you with yo' ugly ass," I said with a laugh.

"Alright, alright, stop. We're a team, and Erica, you're causing unnecessary drama. If Jade said she wasn't staring at Jarell, then she wasn't. Right, Jade?" Laurie intervened, watching me with hawk eyes.

"I wasn't staring at him," I said through clenched teeth. Laurie stared at me for a moment longer, searching for a lie. But she settled for a nod for now. This conversation wasn't over between us.

"Good. So let's leave it alone, especially before you get yourself suspended, Erica. And we all know we need senior cheerleaders this year for this hot team, so we can't cause trouble. So, tonight, let's go out and have fun together. Martell is having a block party at his college friends' place because his parents are out of town. You ladies down to go? It'll be the basketball team and some college hotties there," Laurie offered.

Although Laurie changed the subject, the tension in the air was so thick, only a chainsaw could slice it. The team came to a silent agreement to move on and accept Laurie's offer to attend the party later tonight. I didn't say anything yet because I was too busy serving a death glare to Erica, ready to pounce on her.

"You okay?" Laurie whispered. I nodded.

"I'll meet you at the party. Let's get back to stretching ladies so we can get done with this practice," I said and turned away from Erica.

Everyone else followed suit, whispering amongst themselves about I don't know what, but I didn't have the energy to deal. I fumed to myself while I stared at someone way more pleasing like Mike as he trained with the boys. They were some good-looking men, but Mike was something different. It just made me feel completely guilty that Jarell was even a thought in my head all day. Even if it was about nearly killing him.

Arianna was right.

Why would I even be staring at someone like Jarell when I had someone like Mike right in front of me that I could hug and kiss on all day? That's how girls like me got in trouble – simply not being grateful for what they had right in front of them. He was someone everyone wanted, but I had him. And from the looks of it, Jarell's grass wasn't anywhere near green, so I wasn't jeopardizing shit. Mike was a light skinned beauty with a drop of honey to give him the perfect brown glaze. He had eyes that would mesmerize anyone he laid his gaze on, and a smile that could kill. He was the typical pretty boy, but he had everything else going for himself.

I had to get rid of any thoughts about Jarell. Out of sight, and out of mind. Even though Mike didn't want to make things official right now, he was MY man and nobody else would dare to get anywhere near him. I just confirmed it for myself the moment he looked my way and gave me the sexiest smile. I bit my lip just to let him know I couldn't wait to get in his arms later. A wink in response let me know that my message was received.

Yeah, I knew where I stood. And nothing Erica did would change that.

Chapter Six

JANET ROBINSON WAS my mother's name. If you didn't know her name, get it together before she got you together. If you knew her name and you stepped to her, you'd better have something good to say, or something that interested her or else it didn't matter. She was very particular about her time. And you'd better not waste it.

I walked in the door from cheerleading practice to get ready to tell her what I hoped was interesting – the offer from the dance studio. It'd be the first time I saw her in a week. There she was, sitting on the couch with her legs crossed, red bottom heels, a body fitting black dress, and a glass of wine in her hand in front of a lit fireplace. The whole ambiance was set for a full-on romantic date here with the man of her dreams. Her hair was impeccable – not a strand out of place, and the makeup was just as flawless. A part of me wanted to ask if she was going out tonight, but the answer probably would have been no.

To be honest, I didn't think I ever saw my mother without makeup, even within the confines of her own house. She went to bed with it on, and if she didn't, that door was closed and locked. I never saw her weak or vulnerable. Ever. Or even heard her utter a single word that wasn't standard English. It was like she wasn't Black. And sometimes, she forced me to be that way, too. Well... she tried.

So, just knowing how she was, I was real nervous about breaking this news about the dance studio to her that I had been keeping inside since she was out of town on business endeavors. I wanted to tell her in person so that I had time to incorporate Mike in the mix of it all. She didn't like piecemeal news. The mind, the money, and the man. In her eyes, it was nothing more. Nothing less.

"Hey Momma," I said as I put my gym bag down.

"Hello, Jade. Don't put your crap by the door. Put the bag in your room."

"Sorry."

"So, what's the news? I know you said you have some big news for me. So, what is it? Make sure you stand and tell me though because I don't want that sweat on my white couch," she said.

"I already know, Ma. Anyway," I said and started smiling. "Alise has been working behind the scenes for a while to expand the studio. She's been applying for grants, and she got an offer to create a youth dance team. And she offered me a full-time position as head coach right out of high school."

"Oh that's great!"

Glad to see she was just as excited as I was. That made me even more stoked.

"How much did she say the pay was? If it's some bullshit hourly wage, don't even accept it. Wait for something better to come along."

"She didn't say yet. I was just happy to have been offered. She said she'll have details for me later, but to start discussing my postsecondary plans with you first as she teases that out."

"Okay, just don't accept the offer then until she provides details. You know how I feel about that low hourly employment with no benefits shit. Have you told Mike yet?" she asked, and I sighed.

"Not yet," I lied.

"Well, what are you waiting for? Why wouldn't you tell your man something like that?"

"That's the thing Mom. He's technically not my man."

"Why not? You're perfect for one another. Stop playing these middle school games and figure it out."

"I did! Well I tried. He said he doesn't want labels right now. That being his girlfriend and being my boyfriend isn't a good idea because it would require us to settle when neither of us knows where we're going to end up. I told him that's not the case and I'd be mobile since I'm not going to college, but he doesn't seem to believe me."

"You need to try harder. Maybe taking this gig at the studio isn't a good idea because it'll plant you here. You don't know how much time you'll have off to move around with him."

I gasped.

"Momma, you know this means a lot to me! Why would I pass this opportunity up for someone who doesn't even know if he wants to be with me?"

"No, the question is, what are you doing that's causing him to not want to be with you? Trust me, he wants to be with you. You just need to convince him that it's worth it. Try a little harder. I know you're used to getting everything easy, but when it comes to a man, that's something you'll have to work for."

I rolled my eyes. For the first time, everything she said made absolutely no sense. How could she ever suggest giving up my dream of running a dance studio for a guy?

This was the kind of thing that confused me about my momma. She always appeared so independent and strong, yet she said stupid stuff like this. I always wanted to know why she acted the way she did and why she had all these expectations of me but was so close mouthed about her history with men and even her upbringing as a kid. And I never questioned her either. Only thing I really knew was that her and Corey didn't work out, but I never knew why. Regardless, giving up my dreams for Mike was never going to happen.

"Well, there's a block party Martell's friend is throwing tonight down the street and Mike will be there. I'll try and get him to talk about it there."

"You sure it's not in Crenshaw? You know I don't like that trashy, hoodlum, thuggery of a place, but if it's Baldwin Hills, I'm okay with it. Just think about what I've been saying, alright? Don't let him make a fool of you. I didn't raise a dummy," she said, looking at me squarely, but her lips upon the wine glass.

"Yes, Ma. I'm gonna go get ready now, okay?"

"Alright."

~ ~ ~

The ride to Martell's friend's place didn't take long. This wasn't a place I was familiar with since it actually was in Crenshaw. I assumed that Laurie snuck out of her house to come here because her parents were not allowing this "party hard before eighteen" shit either. Especially nowhere near Crenshaw. They were the type of parents who loved Black culture and wanted separation from its people but forced her to Crenshaw to get a "diverse experience" and to be with me. I mean, I attended Crenshaw on my school choice and open enrollment, otherwise I'd be going to Beverly Hills by my *mom's* choice. But Laurie's parents were different. If they found out that she was here, she'd be grounded until graduation.

The curbs were packed with cars parked alongside it. Girls sauntered up the street with clothes barely covering their ass and shirts daintily covering their breasts; guys walked with mini liquor bottles in their hands, many with their pants sagged below their draws. This party was going to smell interesting.

With luck, I swerved into a tight, open space, parked, then got out of the car.

"Hey, hey! That's Jade!" some girls behind me whispered in awe.

"Isn't she the one in the music videos?" one of them asked.

"Yeah! She was in Bruno Mars' last video. She's pretty dope. Can't believe we're at a party with famous people here!" the other squealed.

I smirked and followed the crowd to Martell's friend's house as an unspoken collective, getting a few hellos from folks I knew and from strangers alike. You know, the usual.

The noise of the people and the music got louder and louder until we all finally arrived. Party lights were decorated along the fence, and people were making out, nearly having sex on the porch as if they owned the spot. My nose wrinkled in disgust. I made my way around to the back, and therein lied the action.

Opening the gate to the backyard was like walking into a steam room. The smell of alcohol and weed was rancid, tickling my nose to the point of a sneeze. Bodies were so close together that it was impossible to move anywhere without harshly bumping into someone, but it seemed like no one cared. Everyone was dancing, high, drunk, and having such a good time that drama didn't seem to be brewing, or even a possibility tonight. Hmm. Maybe Mike would be receptive to what I had to say if he was in the kind of mood everyone else was in. Or, on the other hand, maybe this wasn't a good time to be talking about our relationship. But if I didn't go forward with it, I wouldn't find the courage to do it any other time.

As I slithered between bodies, getting a few warm greetings on the way, I searched for Mike but ended up finding Martell against the wooden fence instead with someone shaking their ass all over him. His eyes were so fixated on where his dick and her butt met that he didn't even see me at all. Once the girl's head popped up, it was Laurie! Her eyes were glazed over with a huge smile on her face, and she was wavering on her feet. Martell wrapped his arm around her waist to provide stability and moved his hips to the beat.

"Jade! You're finally here!" Laurie squealed.

"Yeah, and you already drunk," I said with a thick voice I knew she didn't sense as I wiped the sweat from my forehead.

"You want some beer?" she asked.

"Nah, I'm good. You got a minute, though? I need to talk to you about something."

"Damn, Jade, you see me and her got a thang going on, don't you? You stay blockin' when shit ain't about you," Martell chimed in.

He pulled Laurie close to him as he pecked her neck. She giggled like a chipmunk and turned around to kiss him, completely ignoring me.

"I see what y'all got going on, but this is important, Martell," I said. "Laurie are you hearing me?"

"Don't look like she thinks it's that important, does she?" he asked with a smirk as Laurie marked her territory with her teeth into his neck.

I smacked my lips and just walked away. Laurie wasn't in a place to listen to me, so finding and talking to Mike without advice was going to be a lonely feat. My anger with Laurie now was a little unwarranted, but hell, I needed to talk to her about something serious. The way she completely dismissed me for Martell was wrong! Besides, the fact that she got this drunk anyway wasn't a good look, and she was going to be calling on me to save her ass from her parents.

As I scanned the party and continued moving through the thick crowd to find my damn man, I heard a deep female voice call out to me.

"Ay yo Jade!"

I turned my head, and it was one of my homegirls on D-Block who called out to me. She was a serious stud. "Come here!"

I walked over to her as one of her girlfriends danced on her. "Sup, Ro'Shae?"

"Aye, you might wanna check inside the house if you lookin' for Mike. You ain't gone be so happy about what you see, either. All these bitches out here talking about it, too. Just wanted you to know."

"What? What's everybody saying?"

"Just go inside and check it out, man. I ain't getting into no drama, I'm faded tonight."

I looked up and gazed at the house. The patio door was opened on the other side of the party, so it was gonna be a good trek before I got inside. I must have stepped on at least six people's feet, bumped into every single person, and broke out into a full out sweat before I reached the other side of the party to get in there. My heart pounded on the way, wondering what the hell Ro'Shae was talking about and hoped it wasn't going to fuck up my image. And once I made it inside a lump developed in my throat at the first thing I saw.

Oh fuck no.

Mike sat on the couch with three unknown bitches all over him as if he was their playground. One girl rubbed his chest and crotch, another girl had her lips all over his neck, and the last had her head on his shoulder. Whole time? He checked none of them for it. At all. In fact, he had a stupid, sleazy smirk on his face as he bit his lip and gave ugly ass neck girl more access. His arm was around her waist in a subtle move to push her closer.

Everything in my body broke as the lump sank from my throat to somewhere deep in my stomach.

No wonder he hadn't texted me back. This asshole was happy right where he was and that was a level of hurt I couldn't even begin to describe. I no longer wanted to do this. No longer wanted to be here. It was one thing to be shooed off by Martell and Laurie, but this was entirely different. This was crazy embarrassing. But now? I was about to blast his ass in front of these tricks.

"So this is what we're doing now, Mike Harrison? This is how your stupid ass disrespects me in front of all these people like I'm just some bum ass bitch? Look at me, and then look at them. This is what you're doing?" I pointed at all three with my eyebrows hiked.

I stood in front of him calmly with my arms crossed, but it felt like an earthquake on the inside. Those who were actually inside stopped whatever they were doing to watch us. Of course, with their cameras up and out.

With low, red rimmed eyes that were also glazed over, it was fully apparent that he was some combination of drunk and high. Without a word, Mike looked up at me and smiled a cute little grin that made me just want to slap it off his face.

"Jade! Wassup, baby? You tryna join us?"

He lifted from one of the girls and scooted over, opening a spot for me underneath his arm while the other three bitches slid over, but continued to have their grimy little hands all over him. *Was he crazy?*

"I don't share my man, thank you. Answer my question. What

the hell do you think you're doing, Mike? What is all of this?"

"What you mean? It's a party, girl, calm down."

"Calm down. Calm down? You out here embarrassing the shit out of me, and you're talking about some calm down? Are you serious right now?"

"Jade, chill out, you makin' this bigger than what it is."

"Then what is it? You got three whole girls all over you as if we don't have anything going on with each other. You know I don't roll like that."

"It's a party! Damn," he said, looking off to the side as he wrapped one of his arms around the girl's shoulder. In retaliation, the girl snickered and sized me up.

That was it. That was the last straw. He was blatantly doing this on purpose, and it was like I never, ever mattered to him. No wonder why he didn't want to make it official. He wanted to mess around and do this shit.

Without even thinking, I grabbed a drink that was on the glass coffee table and threw its contents right at his face, giving him a nice cool splash. I didn't care if it had alcohol in it. I hoped it did so it would burn.

"Oooh!" said the small crowd of bystanders.

The three girls gasped and moved away, shouting profanities at me and trying not to get any on them, but also made sure to ask if he was okay.

"If this was me with a bunch of ugly ass niggas, you'd be ready to fight. This is bullshit Mike, and we're done. You will not treat me like I'm some random bitch that you can toy with!"

He chuckled, pulling one of the girls closer to him with one hand, and wiping his face with the other as if was completely unfazed.

"Done with what? Because it wasn't like we together anyway. Last time I checked, I'm single, shorty. Remember that the next time you decide to throw a drink."

That was the dagger. The stinger. The comeback that went straight for my throat and stepped on it. Enough to bring the tears to my eyes without enough will power to hold them back.

"Fuck you, Mike," I cried, and walked away to exit to the front of the party as I heard the girls laugh.

"Yeah, get your ass outta here."

I slammed the front door open. Everything was blurry from the tears that had yet to come down, so whoever saw me at this moment, I didn't see them. To be quite honest, I really didn't care who saw me. I just needed to get out of there.

My legs just moved. Moved in any direction they'd take me, and that happened to be down the street and completely opposite of the party. This neighborhood was not the best to be running off angry without a destination, but I didn't care. *How dare Mike do me like that?*

I kept moving and moving until I found an abandoned park with a short wall around it. I found a place on the wall, and the tears that had been hanging on had finally fallen in a downpour. The last time I remembered crying was years ago. Years of whatever feelings piled up in my chest came out at this moment. I didn't know how long I sat that way. It was going to be as long as I needed because there was no way I'd be going back to my car in this pitiful state.

After a while, the tears naturally stopped, and the post crying phase came in full attack – headache and all. I was so upset with myself. Why did I let Mike get me to the point where I was crying out in public like a sad puppy? Trust me, this wasn't over. He didn't know who he was messing with. And it could have been worse; Erica could've been in the vicinity. Man, if she was there, I probably wouldn't have been out here crying because all my anger would have been taken out on her face.

I sat in silence to calm down and looked across the park's lot. A small figure was hitting fluid-like movements all on their own with nobody around. Strange. I rubbed the remnants of tears away to see clearly. Whoever it was, was dancing. Without music.

Ahh. This was just what I needed to calm down. Dance. An urge in my tummy wanted to walk over to dance with this person, but I instead opted to watch.

If I nodded my head to a beat I thought they were dancing to, they'd hit every cadence. The movements were so coordinated, so graceful, so peaceful, so on point. It was a beautiful combination of pop, locking, floating, and some other form of dance I couldn't quite register. A rare mix that I had never, ever seen done so well because it was extremely difficult to do. I knew I couldn't even do it myself, and I considered myself a well-versed dancer. They were dressed in all black sweats with a hood up, so determining whether they were male or female was impossible. Whoever it was belonged in Alise's studio for sure. It'd be even better if that person was a kid.

My legs itched again to move and this time, it'd be in the direction of the dancer, but that idea was quickly halted by my phone ringing. Looking at the caller ID, it was Laurie. If I wasn't a good friend, I would have declined her call, but because of my stupid heart, I answered anyway.

"Hey, where are you? Mike said you ran off somewhere!" Laurie yelled. I had to pull the phone away from my ear because of it.

"I left. It was too packed."

With reluctance, I walked away from the wall and back towards my car. The fact that Mike even had my name in his mouth had me hot. I didn't want him to ever mention my name again.

"Are you serious? Aren't you supposed to be my ride home?"

"Yeah, but you didn't seem to be too interested in me and what I was doing since you all over Martell and shit."

"Well, yeah, I told you I would be! Jade, you wouldn't believe what happened."

"What now?"

"Martell asked me if I wanted to have sex with him. He's waiting. What should I do? Get back here so I can tell you all about it!"

My heart dropped. The last thing Laurie needed to be doing was having sex with someone while drunk. That was considered rape, and she was only seventeen! She would regret it, and the way this party was going down, I was sure she was well on her way to getting ran through by the entire basketball team. And trust, even though that was my best friend, I knew the typical outcome with dicey situations like this. A criminal rape case on a bunch of basketball players wasn't anything our school needed, and I was going to stop it at all costs.

"Laurie do not have sex with Martell. You're drunk! That's not a good idea!"

"Why not? I've only had like two beers."

"Laurie, no! I'm taking your ass home, seriously. Because you don't know how to act. And you've had way more than two beers, I can tell."

"I'm starting to think you're jealous or something," Laurie countered, and at that point, I was appalled.

"Are you kidding me, Laurie? Jealous of what? This is how I know you drank way too much!"

"You're jealous that I'm about to get some and your man is getting attention from all these other girls that aren't you. And you're telling me you're not jealous by trying to stop what's happening between Martell and me?"

I had to remind myself that Laurie was drunk and talking out the side of her neck. Because that one hurt. Deeply. It was like her words dug into an already fresh wound and made it bleed again.

"Laurie, it's not like that. Listen, I care about you. Forget Mike and all of that. I don't want you to get hurt. Seriously, I'm going to come back, and we can talk about it, okay? Where are you?"

"I'm upstairs in the bathroom. Hurry up, because he's waiting."

Without another word, my phone beeped. She hung up on me. It didn't matter because I was already pacing up the front lawn and charging through the front door. The party was still as live as I left it. It was too bad that I couldn't enjoy such a drama free party because I was the one with all the drama. But from the looks of it, it was about to get busted by the police soon. Give it fifteen minutes. And fifteen minutes was more than enough time to get an underaged drinking Laurie up out of this party.

Sprinting up the stairs, the hallway was pitch black with closed doors on each part. How the hell did Laurie get up here without falling down? Which way was the bathroom?

"Laurie?" My voice trembled, afraid to take even another step forward.

"In here!"

I followed her voice and opened the bathroom door. Laurie was sitting on the toilet rocking back and forth. My God. She was completely wasted.

"Laurie let's get out of here. The police are on their way, and

I don't want you getting caught up in this shit," I lied, but it was a surefire way to get her out of there.

"Who on the way? You a damn lie."

A deep voice rang out, and I cursed beneath my breath. It was none other than Martell himself.

"Yo Laurie, I was waiting on you to give you that D you been wanting. And what you doing here cock blockin' again?" asked Martell, frowning at me the entire time he spoke to her.

"She's not having sex with you, Martell. Actually, you're lucky I'm here. It's a done deal, and if you were smart, you'd let me save your ass," I said, giving him a long, knowing glare. He knew exactly what the fuck I was talking about. He stared at me a while longer, his gaze giving away nothing at all, and then sneered.

"Yo, whatever," he conceded, and walked away. I wasn't sure if the alcohol had done half the work for me, or if he understood my nonverbal message, but that was the quickest surrender I'd ever experienced with Martell.

"Yeah, whatever is right. You'd better be tryna get up out this party anyway to save your damn basketball season because you know if y'all get caught drinking, your season is done. Take my advice or leave it."

He didn't say another word. Good. My focus was on getting Laurie out of here. I was just going to have to process this shit about Mike another time.

Chapter Seven

MY EYES STRUGGLED to open. When they did, the room twirled like a top toy, like the ceiling would collapse on me. I didn't drink last night, but it felt like I did. Laurie would feel ten times worse, if she would even get up.

My palms dug into my eyes to adjust to a new day. Everything about yesterday was terrible. Most of my time after the party was spent holding Laurie's hair back so that she could throw up all the beer she drank into my bathroom toilet. Just that alone was the cherry on top of all my frustrations because a part of me really wanted to drop her off at home and let her parents deal with this. But being the good friend I was, though I often feel like I shouldn't be, I didn't want her getting into trouble. Well, it was deeper than that. The real fear was that with her being so drunk, she would've slipped up and said something about her and Martell having sex to her parents, and it would be a bigger issue. So I just opted to take her back to my crib for the night.

Looking down at the floor with my blankets spread out, Laurie was still breathing deeply. Her hair was everywhere, a sign that she was still out. I laid back down and stared at the ceiling that was no longer spinning.

This was the first moment I had time to process everything that happened with Mike last night with a clear head, and it gut punched me. *How dare he disrespect me so blatantly?* In front of everyone. College kids, my peers at school who thought that I had him locked... it was embarrassing to say the absolute least. What was he thinking? Didn't he realize that he was destroying me in the process as someone who was well known? People were going to talk behind my back, and I had to be able to defend the fact that he, indeed, was still my man when I knew good and damn well he wasn't. Not to mention that he confirmed it.

Tears rolled down my cheeks again. The angrier I became for even letting him get me to the point of tears again, the more they started to come. Eventually, I just gave up and let myself cry. I had never felt so betrayed and hurt by the fact that someone like him didn't want me, as bad as I wanted him. I was too damn good to be feeling like this. What did I do so wrong?

Minutes turned into hours. Eventually, the tears stopped flowing. Laurie groaned and shifted awake with an inevitable hangover. In my peripheral view, she was sitting on her knees on top of my blanket, staring and waiting for me to say something. Or maybe she tried to figure out what the hell happened last night. Who knew. My eyes just stayed glued to the ceiling to avoid talking at all.

"Jade?"

I said nothing. I should have been able to be vulnerable around someone like her, but I couldn't. No matter what, I couldn't trust anybody. Not even Laurie.

"What's wrong?" she asked.

"Nothing, Laurie."

"Are you okay?"

I rolled my eyes.

"Are you upset with me? If so, I'm sorry. I didn't think I'd get that drunk. What happened? I don't remember anything after the party."

"It doesn't matter. You're safe. Why don't you go get some water in the kitchen? You need it."

"Good idea," she said softly, rubbing her arm in guilt. "I'll be right back, okay? Do you want anything?"

When she realized that she wasn't going to get a response, Laurie walked out and to the kitchen in apparent pain. She was going to have to stay here for a little while longer before she could even think about going home. Either way, I was glad for her leaving to the kitchen because that gave myself some time to get it together and put a wall around my feelings again. At least I tried to. When you haven't cried in years the way that I hadn't, and then to cry twice in a twenty-four hour period, building that wall up wasn't going to happen as quickly as I would have wanted.

She was back in no time, and I was still staring at the ceiling. She put a cup of water on my nightstand. I appreciated the gesture, but I didn't acknowledge it. She simply stood next to my bed, water in one hand and her phone in the other.

"Holy shit, my parents called me fifteen times between last night and this morning. Fuck! I hope they didn't call the police," she said as she frantically dialed to call them back.

I was sure her parents called my phone too, but I turned it off long ago. I didn't want to have to tell them the truth about what was going on with her and why she wasn't coming home. My day had already been terrible, so I wasn't in the mood to lie or make up some story to protect her.

"Hey Dad.... I'm so sorry.... My phone was on silent...... yes...... yes,

Daddy......I'm safe.... I'm with Jade...... I think her phone is turned off .... I've been here the whole time..... We just went out to hang with some friends last night watching scary movies .... I wasn't drinking Dad............ We just got back late and I spent the night with Jade......... can we talk about it when I get home? I didn't mean to not call you back............ okay......... okay. I'll see you soon......... Bye."

She hung up. Sighing, she sat back down on the floor with her water on top of the blankets and faced me.

"My dad is upset with me," she said. "I so don't want to go home to deal with that."

"Better now than yesterday," I mumbled.

"You're right. Listen, Jade. I'm sorry. I didn't mean to put you in a shitty situation. I just didn't think I'd get that drunk."

"It's fine, Laurie. It's over and done with now."

"Okay. I just don't want you to be upset with me."

"It's fine."

"I know you're still mad. But I'll just let it go. Hey, what was up with Mike yesterday?" Laurie asked with a frown. "Like, five girls were all over him all night, and he was just soa-"

"I don't want to talk about it. And you said some fucked up shit to me about him that I won't even mention."

"Sorry for bringing it up," she said instantly, and then shut up. Laurie was the type to press an issue, but she knew where she stood with me right now. Shutting up was the best thing she could've done.

"Listen, you should get ready. I'm going to drop you off at home," I said, swinging my legs over the bed to stand up.

She huffed. Clearly, she wasn't ready for that battle at home yet, but she really didn't have a choice. I've done enough already for her. She needed to suffer the consequences, even if it was just a little. Plus,

I just wanted to be alone.

"Fine."

We both got ready to go without a word spoken to one another. I checked my clock, and it was already ten in the morning. No wonder her parents were worried.

It wasn't long before we were both in the car. The first part of the car ride was quiet until Laurie broke it.

"So... why did you really stop me from having sex with Martell?" Laurie asked. Just by the tone of her voice, she had been thinking this the entire time that she was awake and was scared to ask.

"Because you were drunk. That isn't a good look. You would have regretted it," I said, giving her a side eye.

"But Jade, I really wouldn't have. It would have been better. I want to get this whole virginity thing out of the way because I don't want to remember my first time."

I turned my head to look at her like she was fucking nuts. Who wouldn't want to remember their first time?

I mean, having sex for the first time was always a dream... a thought in my mind. How it would be, who it would be with, and how it would feel. I had all the details down from what I was wearing to the lighting in the room. That was something everyone was looking forward to experiencing, and I'd be lying if I said I didn't think of it often. Simply thinking of Mike and I having sex for the first time always got me excited in a way that I would never tell anyone. I wanted to share that intimate moment with him, but I didn't know how that was going to happen now that he was a douchebag. Either way, it was still an exciting daydream to have.

"Laurie, that's the stupidest thing you've ever said."

"But is it? We're Seniors. Everyone around us has had sex.

Everyone talks about it. Everyone has been sharing their experiences, and I feel so left out of that conversation. I just want to get it over with and then start having a good time, you know? I'm ready, and I want to do it with Martell," she said. "I'm like the only virgin in our friend group."

"No you're not."

"Who else is still a virgin? None of the kids on D-Block, that's for sure!"

"Me, Laurie. I'm still a virgin."

She visibly did a double take. "You're not serious, are you?"

"I'm very serious. I've never had sex. When have you ever seen me participating in these sex conversations that you're talking about?"

"Well never, now that you say it. But I thought that – but you and Mike – never?"

"No. Never."

"But everyone has been talking about how you and Mike have sex. You know? They always talk about how lucky you are," she pouted.

"I want to know some of that luck, too. Me and Mike never got that far, though. That might be why he's dissing me. I don't know. But girl, you know my name is always in someone's mouth. Why do you believe what people say about me?"

"I don't! I mean, sometimes I do. Stuff like that, I do. Because you're so perfect. And you get guys like Mike that everyone is dying to have sex with."

I didn't say anything. That was the image that I wanted portrayed, so that was what was received. A part of me was glad for that, but I began to feel a kind of pressure that I had never felt before at this moment, and I didn't know how to explain it or even begin to cope with it.

"I don't know what Mike is telling people, Laurie."

"Well, it's a good rumor to be going around. Just know that. I mean, why haven't you guys, you know, gone all the way?"

I shrugged, turning the corner towards her house. "I'm scared, I guess."

Laurie shot her head towards me, and this time, started laughing hysterically. You see? This was why I couldn't be vulnerable around her. I couldn't be real or authentic. I always had to play the part in the image that I was trying to create. I could never just be me: a person with fears, with tears, or any other feeling besides confident.

"Why is that so funny?"

"Scared to have sex, Jade? Really?"

"Yes, really! What's so wrong with that?"

"Jade, sex isn't scary. Everybody has it, and I wouldn't hesitate to have sex with someone like Mike. And I'm sure plenty of guys wouldn't be scared to hesitate to have sex with you. Don't you want to get that first time over with, too?"

"No. I want my first time to be special," I rebutted. "I want it to be what I dream it to be."

"It'll be special, for sure. With a hottie like Mike! I just know it's big."

"Girl. Really? It's not just about the looks or it 'being big,'" I said, getting hella annoyed.

"Then what's it about? Because it's highly likely that the person who you have sex with the first time won't be the person you end up with in the long run anyway. I mean, you and Mike have that possibility, but for the rest of us, that isn't a reality. So might as well get it over with and fuck someone you think is hot." She laughed.

"Whatever, Laurie," I said as I pulled up to the front of her house.

I had never been so happy to get rid of her in my life.

"I'm just saying, Jade. You and Mike better get to it and hop on that bandwagon that everyone else is a part of!"

"Yeah. I'll see you tomorrow, okay?" I said, scratching my head and looking away from her, out of the window.

"Alright. Well, besides all of that. Thank you for everything, Jade. I owe you big," she said, opening the car door.

I didn't respond again, and this time, she let it go, getting out of the car and walked towards her house. The moment she was inside, I drove to the studio. I had to go and let off some steam.

When I arrived, it was empty, just as I expected it to be on a Saturday morning, but Alise's car was the lone car out front. People usually started showing up within the next couple of hours, so she had to open the studio. I kind of didn't want to talk to her either, but it was better than anyone else, to be honest.

I walked inside and she was nowhere to be found, which I appreciated. I just wanted to start dancing. So that's exactly what I did. I turned on some music, and just got in my zone, stretching to begin with. I closed my eyes and let my body work. Like nothing else existed, and everything that was going on drifted out of mind and into the universe.

After a while, I rose up and begin to dance. Lyrical was what I was feeling. A dramatic kind of dance with intricate moves and leaps. I found myself trying some of those moves that the random parking lot dancer did, but I just couldn't. Too hard, but it didn't stop me from trying. I loved a challenge.

As I was practicing and repeatedly failing, Alise walked out with a smile and started to dance with me. I loved when she did this. Competing with her was the best way that I grew as a dancer, and it forced me to try new things. Every time I danced alone, and she saw me struggling, she would come out to work with me. She was always sensitive to my needs, and I loved it. She knew I worked best under pressure.

She and I went at it for a while until a couple of hours went by. She gave me tips and encouragement, but was also in my ass a little bit, trying to push me to the next level and out of my comfort zone. I appreciated that.

We both stopped when we realized that the crews were going to be coming in the next thirty minutes, so she and I just sat down and relaxed until that time had come.

"You don't work today, so I'm surprised you came," Alise said.

"Yeah, I came to blow off some steam," I confessed.

"I figured. When I was watching you dance before I joined something seemed off."

I brought my knees up to my chin and secured them with my arms. "It was because of Mike. At some party last night, he completely disrespected me and had a bunch of girls all over him without saying a word. Laurie was two minutes away from being raped. A lot happened last night."

"Shit. I'm sorry to hear about Laurie. Is she okay?"

"Yeah, nothing happened. I had to save her dumb ass."

"Good. I'm glad she's okay. I won't even ask about it. Did you confront Mike at all about what he did, though?"

"Yeah, I threw a drink at his face and everything. I kind of regret that, but he pissed me off, Lise! Does he know who I am? I'm like the best girl around that he could ever get, and he does that to me!"

"You already know I know. What made him do that?"

"I don't know. He was just flexin' to be honest. I don't want anything to do with him anymore. He embarrassed me in front of everyone. I won't forgive him for that."

"I feel you. Anyone who does that to somebody doesn't deserve that person. But honestly, why don't you sit down and talk with him first though? Maybe y'all can work it out."

"Eh. I'll think about it. But enough about him. I want to talk about some good news. Last night, I saw someone who was super, super dope. A dancer. I was in this random parking lot fuming about Mike, and they were just dancing. No beat, no nothing. Just vibing, and it was the dopest shit I've ever seen. It was like a mix of four styles of dances, and they made it work. I wish you could've seen it! That's what I was trying this whole time today, and I just can't seem to get it. That's how raw they are."

"Well, did you go up to them and say anything?"

"No, because Laurie was in her crisis, so I had to go save her. I hope to see them again. I want to bring them here so you can check them out!"

"Well, you know how I feel about that. I usually like to pick up people who already have accolades already. If they're under sixteen, maybe you can pick them up for the youth crew. You can recruit that way if you so choose, but I don't recruit that way," she said.

"Yeah, I feel you. I just wanted you to see, that's all," I said. "Speaking of the youth crew and recruiting, have you teased out details about the offer?"

"Actually yes! It's looking like the salary is seventy grand a year for starters. And of course, as you become more experienced, hold more classes, and do more of your own shows, you'll be making more from sponsors and winning shows."

My mouth dropped. Seventy grand straight out of high school?

Not even counting sponsors and side gigs? Who would pass up that offer? At this point, I didn't care about Mike. He didn't care about me, and I wasn't going to stop my plans for someone who would openly and willingly disrespect me the way that he did. I would never forgive him. My reputation was way too important for me to be an idiot. The only person I needed to explain that to and convince was Janet Henderson.

"Word? Lise that's a snag! I'm accepting it, no other way to put it!"

"I knew you would." She smiled. "We can do all the paperwork and everything next week as I get everything together. But right now, take care of yourself, okay? You got a lot going on with Mike right now, and social shit that you need to get figured out. I'm sorry that happened to you."

"Yeah, thanks Lise. I'll think about how I'm going to move forward. You're the best," I said, hugging her, and she pulled me in and kissed me on the forehead.

Man. Sometimes I wished that Lise was my mother. Although she was only twenty-four, she was damn near motherly to me. I'd call her a big sis, then.

"Alright, see you soon. Good luck."

Chapter Eight

MONDAY WAS JUST like I thought it would be. The party in Crenshaw was the talk of the school. From everyone. As the grapevine weaved its way around, I listened out for any comments made about Mike and me. At first, I didn't hear anything. The gossip was mostly about how drunk and high everyone was and how the party got busted in the end. A couple of kids got arrested for underage drinking, and the college kid's parents came home. A lot of people were still at the party at that time, and I was glad I was long gone to avoid all that. But, for the most part, it was normal talk about parties on the Monday of school.

It was all fine until I reached D-Block after first and second period. This one girl who was funny as all hell but had no filter whatsoever, had said, "Did you see Mike getting all that pussy thrown at him? He must got that magic dick."

I didn't hate this girl. This girl and I weren't friends, but we got along. I could tell that she didn't seek to hurt my feelings intentionally because I knew her, and she *always* just said whatever came to mind with no regard for anyone. But boy was I pissed with her for opening that can of worms. Because that was what set the bullshit off. Laurie wasn't at school today because she still felt sick from all that drinking, so I couldn't have my partner in crime to back me up.

To make matters worse, Erica was in the hall listening to it all, and Mike hadn't made his way down to the block yet.

"Hell yeah, I saw his sexy ass getting all that action!" another girl said.

"Word, me too. I wished that would've been me!" said someone else.

"Of course they were throwing it at him. He's fine as hell, what did you expect?" said another.

And that's when I lost my shit. It was like I was invisible while they talked about him. The same way Mike made me feel at that party. And that was what pissed me off. He opened so many doors for other girls to disrespect me because if Mike disrespected me, then it was okay for them to do it. Nope. I was here to nix all of it.

"Excuse me, but do you know who the fuck I am? Y'all talking about my man. Am I not standing right here?" I yelled, shutting down the whole block. "Y'all already know what it is, so I don't know why you trying to pull this shit with me standing right here."

"That didn't look like your man on Friday. He was everyone else's man except yours," said one of the girls with laughter, and Erica followed up with her giggles, making sure I saw her laughing too.

"Yeah, well it wasn't y'all who was on him so who cares? He will never be with y'all thirsty asses. You can try all you want, but in the end, you won't get him."

"And it wasn't you either, his famous, rich bitch girlfriend. So, what's your point?"

"The point is that whether he played me or not, it's still me who he's still messing around with, and it'll never be nor has it ever been you. How about that?" I said, and then walked away in disgust.

I could've flipped this whole school upside down if I wanted to. If I was that childish. I knew that this shit was going to happen, and it was all Mike's fault. He was just giving everyone a reason to laugh at me, particularly my arch nemesis.

I went through the entire day unfocused. I didn't want to talk to teachers, didn't want to talk to anyone. I didn't go back down to D-Block for the rest of the day. I avoided walking down certain hallways and paths that Mike would likely be in order to avoid slapping the dog shit out of him.

Apparently, he had heard somewhere during the day that I was upset because he sent me a text asking me where I was so that we could talk. I ignored it. I wasn't ready, and I didn't want anyone seeing me lose my cool in this school. Not to mention, I was still cheerleading captain and still had practice later. I couldn't avoid that. It was going to be the topic of discussion there too. Well, at least it would try to be, but I would shut that shit down as captain. Even if my reputation was a little tarnished because of this situation, I still had to save face.

Later at practice though, I was surprised. No one brought it up at all in the locker room. Something was up. Because everyone would love to have a chance to see me down. Somebody had to have said something. I checked my phone before walking out to the gym and indeed, I had a text from Mike.

Mike: Hey, shorty. Listen, I know that you're upset with me. I know you're avoiding me. I want to talk this out some time, though. I was drunk, high, and I wasn't thinking. I shouldn't have disrespected you. If it makes you feel any better, I checked all those girls on D-Block and your cheerleading squad. They shouldn't have your name in their mouth because it was my fault. But also, you gotta realize that we're both single. I think you owe me an apology too for throwing that drink in my face. Anyway. Can we talk later?

I ignored it. I just wasn't ready.

Chapter Nine

ALL I THOUGHT about on the way to my car after practice was how much a shower was in order when I got home. I always appreciated a good sweat after dancing but sweating trying to perfect moves for the upcoming varsity game and practicing it over and over and over was the gross kind of sweat I didn't appreciate. One thing I could say was that we were ready for tomorrow's opening football game.

Hopping into my little Bug, I checked my phone for any additional text messages from Mike, and he hadn't sent anything. Good. I was glad he set cheerleading team straight because that made practice easier, but I needed a clear mind to think about what I was going to do with him.

I drove out of the parking lot from school and rode slowly down to the traffic light. When I stopped, I noticed someone in the crosswalk in front of me. It was Jarell. I hadn't seen or even thought about him. Forgot he even existed, but at this moment, my interest in him resurfaced like it was new.

Did he always take this route or walk this way? Did I not notice? Why was it that he and I seemed to always meet at a traffic light? Why did I even care?

He had his usual hood up tightened tight with his dingy, holey jeans walking like a lonely penguin, dragging his feet across the pavement and fluttering his fingers at his side. It was hot as hell outside today, yet this boy still had his hood up as if we lived in Iceland or some shit. I didn't understand. Was he trying to purposely have a heat stroke? Everything that puzzled me about Jarell was why I was so fascinated with him, no matter how weird, no matter how much I tried to forget him.

Once the light turned green, I pulled over to his side, not knowing what to say, but knowing I wanted his attention. Just to see what he would do or say.

"Hey! Wanna ride?"

He paused with a frown and turned his head, oblivious to where the voice had come from. As if realizing that he had shown confusion, he snapped back into his stoic expression, ignored me, and kept walking.

Not one to be told no, I kept driving along the shoulder to keep up.

"Jarell, it's Jade. Let me give you a ride. I won't let it rest. At least not until I can make up for almost hitting you the other night. Please?"

He huffed. "No."

"Why?"

He kept walking. I pushed harder.

"So you're just going to take a longer walk when you could be home way sooner?" I called out.

"Would you leave me alone? I don't give a damn about your ride."

"Like I said. It's the least I can do."

"No, the most you can do is stop bothering me."

"Really? Dude, it's ninety-five degrees outside, and you're walking with an oversized hoodie on. Get in the car. Hell, I can give you a ride every day if you want for the rest of the school year if that's what it takes to redeem myself."

It was an offer that I knew I would regret because I really didn't care how he got home daily, but it was something to say in order to get what I wanted for the moment. I was nosey and itching to know him more than how everyone else knew this kid. Especially since he was actually cute.

Jarell paused and stared at the sky through his sunglasses. He toyed with the idea until he finally shook his head. To my gratitude, he walked to my car, albeit reluctantly. I watched him like a hawk as he carefully stepped down from the curb.

A whole new smell took over when he got inside. While it wasn't putrid, he held a slight musk that made my nose wrinkle. I forced myself to ignore it.

"I'm starting to feel like you stalkin' me," he mumbled, pulling the passenger door closed.

"I'm not stalking you. I'm just trying to redeem myself for what happened the last time we saw each other. That's all. The least I can do is a favor," I said, continuing to watch him keenly as he got settled.

Any normal person would have said something about me staring, but he didn't. He simply kept his head turned as he looked out of the window, bunching himself up against the door.

"So. Do you walk every day?" I asked, driving off and turning down a busy street. Just to make small talk.

"Why?"

"I'm just asking."

No response. Just kept his head averted and cancelled me out.

"Apparently you do. Are you okay with catching a ride from me every day? I think it would be a nice way to make up for what I did.

And to – you know – get to know each other a little bit more. To be honest, I didn't know who you were until that whole thing went down on D-Block."

This time, he tensed up. But not once did he look at me.

"Where is this coming from? The fuck kinda game is this? Let's see who can be a good Samaritan? Are you betting money with someone about this so you can throw it in my face again?"

I sighed and smiled a sad one. Some days, although very few and far between, I wished that I could just start over elsewhere. Where I didn't already have such a grounded reputation of being an asshole because if anyone truly knew me, they'd know that I was different on the inside. *Sometimes.*

"I'm not playing games. It isn't fair to judge someone you don't really know; wouldn't you say?" I asked, tilting my head.

"You're really one to be asking?"

"That's also why I'm trying to make it up to you. You don't *really* know me, Jarell," I said.

"I know what you show me. You're sorry I'm not kissing your ass. So after you drop me off, you can go on pretending that I don't exist."

"Fine. Suit yourself."

It wasn't until that moment that I realized I was driving aimlessly with no sense of direction or any idea of where Jarell lived. It was also weird that he hadn't said anything or let me know where to go. That was as confusing as it could've gotten, coming from someone who would rather be in Hell than to be in a car next to me.

"Where do you live?" I asked.

"On W Fifty-Sixth."

"Okay, I know where that is. Damn, you walk that every day? That's a long walk from the school."

"I'm aware."

I huffed. I was done trying with his ass today because he was just going to be a dick. Shoulda just let his ass keep walking in the heat.

The rest of the car ride was completely silent until I was forced to talk to him when I turned on W Fifty-Sixth.

"Are you going to tell me where to stop?" I asked as I kept rolling slowly down the street. "Is this your house?"

"I think so."

How didn't he know where he lived? Now I was beginning to think he was messing around. Either way, I pulled over to the side. I did my part, and if he lied, he was going to have to walk from here.

"Alright, well we're here then. You also never answered my question. Are you cool with me dropping you off every day? If so, why don't you meet me in the teacher's parking lot after school around six? I have cheerleading practice directly after school and we're done at five thirty."

"If I want it, I'll be in the parking lot," he said and stepped out of the car, closing my door shut. That bastard didn't even say thank you.

"Relly, Relly!"

Before I could even open my mouth to say something slick through my rolled down window, a small girl that couldn't have been any older than five burst through the front door of his home and ran towards Jarell like a freight train. Knowing what I've observed about Jarell, I just knew he was going to tense up and maybe even back away, but Jarell wasn't at all bothered.

In fact, the most beautiful thing happened.

Where a frown and lines of sadness usually etched his face, he completely transformed. His features relaxed, and a small, toothless smile inched across his face. It was nearly the same beauty that I had seen the night of our near accident.

When the girl reached his side, she patted his legs, and Jarell bent over to swoop her into his arms. The moment she was up, she hugged his neck tightly as if she hadn't seen him in a long time. He hugged her back just as passionately and kissed her cheek. A warm, tingly feeling began to brew in my stomach and pass down to the soles of my feet. It was like he changed into a whole new person in thirty seconds.

"Relly, you're finally home! It's so hot outside, take off your hood!"

"Don't touch it. How was school?"

"It was fun. We worked on counting by fives, we worked on writing our letters, and we read a story in the library!"

"Sounds like a fun day," Jarell said, putting her to the ground, but tightly held her hand instead.

"Yeah, it was. And we played house for recess. Guess who I played?" she asked as she led Jarell towards the house.

"The Mommy," Jarell replied.

She gasped. "How did you know?"

It was the first time I had heard Jarell laugh. A deep, unique chuckle that was strong enough to make his head peel back. Pure music to my soul. Goosebumps.

"Because you're bossy."

"No I'm not! Be careful, of my bike. We're going to walk around it. Okay, we're at the stairs, now Relly. Step up." The little girl directed while still holding his hand, and Jarell cautiously stepped up. "Okay, step up again... step... step... okay we're at the last step, Relly."

Wait a minute.

I blinked. The warm feeling I had suddenly turned cold the more I watched this interaction. The more I watched, the clearer it had become.

My heart sank. This explained *everything*. It explained his mannerisms. It explained his preference to be withdrawn. It explained those thick glasses I hated so much. It explained why a teacher followed him around on the daily basis.

Jarell was blind.

I had never, ever felt such a weird combination of pity and guilt. My God. It was so clear no one at school had a clue about this. No one. I figured no one knew either because of the way they picked on him, bumped into him in the halls, and just generally had terrible shit to say about him.

For the brief amount of time I knew of Jarell's existence, I realized that literally no one at school liked him. *Why?*

When Jarell and what I assumed to be his sister were clear in the house, I sat there, simply shook. I barely knew him, but there was something about the emotion in his eyes that concerned me, or at least had me curious, and tugged at my heart. It was a feeling I couldn't name. Was it because he rejected me, and I secretly liked a chase? Maybe. Whatever it was, I decided I needed to keep an eye on him. His demeanor was so odd. So I guessed that was what I was going to do. Just to make sure he was good.

Chapter Ten

THE FOLLOWING DAY was the football season opener. September tenth. The biggest day of the fall semester for football players and cheerleaders other than Homecoming week. We all came dressed in our uniforms to show Cougar pride and had a pep rally later in the day. I was so excited about the cheerleading squad this year and couldn't wait to show off what we've been working on.

It was the only thing that was keeping me happy despite my drama with Mike and figuring out that Jarell was blind. But I had to get it out of my head. Being happy today was important if I wanted to make the impression I wanted on the football field tonight.

I headed to D-Block to talk football and cheerleading with the crew in high spirits when suddenly, a firm grip on my arm yanked me away from the corridor. I whirled around to give whoever it was a good punch to the face, but it was Mike. I dropped my fist, but then I reconsidered punching him. He would've deserved it. What was *his* problem?

"Boy, you were about to get the wind knocked out of you! Why you grab me like that?"

This was the first time I've talked to him since the party on Saturday, and I had no intentions of speaking to him either since I still wasn't ready to.

"Because it's the only way to get your attention. You've been ignoring the hell out of me. For what? I've apologized," he said, pulling me over into a side hallway where it was quiet and out of public view. Anyone would have loved to see a showdown between Mike and me. But he was smart. Too many of them wanted to see us fail.

"Yeah, and I don't accept! You embarrassed the hell out of me, Mike!"

"Jade, I was drunk. I wasn't thinking, and I apologized. What else do you want me to do?"

"I want you to leave me alone. You should have never given these little girls ammo to talk about me like that. You know who the hell I am around here! And you just out here making me look like a fool." I crossed my arms and looked away.

"And I shut it down! I did everything you probably would've asked for anyway. So I'm not understanding why you givin' me the cold shoulder, shorty."

"Don't call me your shorty. It's not just about the girls. You saying what you said embarrassed me too. You know, the whole single thing."

"That's because we are! That's why you should apologize for throwing that drink in my face."

I whipped my head around and looked at him like he was nuts.

"Apologize? I'm not apologizing for shit! Being single is not what I want, Mike. I don't want to be single. Your reason for us not being together isn't something I agree with. It doesn't make sense. You want me to still be loyal to you, yet you can do whatever you want? That's bullshit!"

"I'm doing it to protect us, not because I don't want to be with you."

"What difference does it make?"

"All the difference!"

He sighed, dipping his head in shame for raising his voice at me. Looking away from him, I shook my head.

"Jade. I want to work this out. You know I care about you, girl," he said calmly, grabbing on to my shoulders.

I turned my head again, not really wanting to make up anything with him. All I could see was that girl's mouth all over his neck. But another part of me felt like I was being dramatic. He did seem sincerely apologetic, and I couldn't deny that it would crush my entire soul if our friendship ended over some random ass girls that he probably didn't care about. And me giving him the cold shoulder would just push him away to other girls in the school, and I didn't want that either.

"You down to work it out?" he asked with this sad ass puppy dog face.

I couldn't help but grin. He got on my nerves, being all cute and shit.

"Fine."

"Good. Can I have a kiss?" he puckered his lips.

I rolled my eyes and pushed him out of the way. He chuckled.

"Don't try me," I mumbled, and then walked away from him with a smirk I hoped he didn't see.

I continued down to D-Block hugging my books to my chest. Damn it, there was only three more minutes left of passing time, and I wanted to talk about cheerleading! *Damn, Mike.*

When I turned the corner, a teacher brushed past in a rush, nearly slamming into me in the process. I frowned to tell her to watch where the hell she was going, but she was walking so quickly that I couldn't.

I looked closer at the back of her swinging, long blonde ponytail to see that she was Jarell's teacher.

Uh oh.

If Jarell's teacher was walking from D-Block so briskly, then Jarell wasn't too far behind. A million different thoughts ran through my mind about what our circle could've done to send her the opposite way in a rush. They probably were throwing things at her or talking hella trash. Who knows? But now, there was one person left who I knew was in danger.

The tension in the air thickened the closer I got to where our crew usually stood. A deep foreboding grew in my chest.

When I finally reached the end of the hall, my inklings were right. Our crew circle was spread open, and Jarell was standing at the very center surrounded as Martell stood in front of him and sized him up. Jarell's hand gripped his backpack with a tight, trembling fist while the other hand was stuffed in his usual jean pocket. His hood was up again and tightened as he looked at the ground.

"Looks like our future school shooter hasn't learned his lesson from the last time, huh?"

Martell walked up to Jarell squarely. The closer he got, Jarell turned his head to look away from him. By that time, Martell had gotten so close that he exploded Jarell's personal bubble. My heart rose to my throat. *Please, don't let anything crazy happen.*

"I ain't forget our last meeting together, but you ran off like a little bitch."

"I don't want any beef," Jarell mumbled.

Martell chuckled. "What's with this pussy? He ain't even a man. Dude can't even look me in the eye. Man up, boy!"

Martell pushed him roughly in the chest, and Jarell stumbled back. With threatening steps, Martell's sidekicks closed the circle in on him. Suddenly, I couldn't breathe.

I couldn't save Jarell again. Not publicly.

If I did, Jarell and all of them would know that something was up with me. Everyone would think that I had a thing for him. It would spread like wildfire to Mike and my other friends and who knew what would happen from there? At the same time, doing nothing wasn't an option either, now knowing that Jarell had a visual impairment.

"Look at his ass, y'all. Piece of shit look like he about to pee on himself. Aww, you gonna cry?"

"Hell no! He a monster, that nigga don't cry. His ass probably thinking of a way to kill us all right now!" Another person chimed in with their unwanted opinion.

"Aye, speaking of killing. Didn't I tell you to kill yourself like last week? Why you still here? Why the fuck you even on D-Block anyway? You know what happened the last time."

Jarell's face grew grim.

"Yo, look at his damn jeans. That hole at the bottom is so big, he can fit his big ass head through 'em," Martell said.

Martell continued to laugh and taunt Jarell while the circle closed tighter and tighter. He sensed it. He tried to back away from everyone, but none of them budged. As a result, Jarell backed right into someone's chest.

"Eww!! I got fleas now! Don't touch me, nigga!" she screamed, wiping away her clothes in disgust and pushed him back towards the center.

Martell pulled Jarell closer by yanking his hood back, exposing his head and removing all security that he felt inside of that thing.

Jarell instantly went to pull his hood back up. Amid him doing that, another one of Martell's boys ripped Jarell's eyeglasses from his face and crushed them beneath his foot with multiple stomps, producing harsh, crackling sounds that made me cringe.

"Yo!" Martell cackled. "Damn son!"

Jarell's knees struck the ground as he scrambled to pick up the pieces of his glasses. Nearby, another girl had his backpack and dumped its contents, scattering his books all over the hallway. All I could do was shake my head. It was one thing to throw Freshmen in garbage cans and have ribbing sessions on others, but harassing someone who was as withdrawn and insecure as Jarell was ... I didn't even know. Because I mean, it wasn't like they knew about him the way I now knew. He was going to get treated like everyone else.

As he patted the ground to find the remnants of his glasses, the guy who crushed them had his foot peeled all the way back, revving up to kick the wind out of Jarell in the stomach.

That was it. The last straw.

With no hesitation, I dropped my books and broke into a full sprint with my cheerleading skirt flying towards the perpetrator and stood in front of him, stopping the action at once by pushing him and serving a wild gaze.

"Are you fucking nuts?"

"What the fuck? Jade?" He threw his hands up with a smile. "Here you go again."

"Don't what me, Tazz, you know what's up. He's already down! What the hell are you doing?"

"This yo' nigga?" he asked, backing away from me with a smirk. "Cause it seem like you sucking his dick or something."

"Sucking his dick? Get the fuck outta here. You damn near was about to kill him!" I said, staring him down to the point where he shook his head, and backed off, mumbling that I was so lucky that I was Mike's girl or something of the sort.

Jarell was still down, trying to find the last part of his glasses in silence, and everyone else was watching me with this perplexed look. It was a pain having to deal with this because I was now setting myself up for some shit I was going to have to later defend, but it was better than watching a sightless Jarell writhing on the ground after being kicked in the stomach with no one to help him. I guess today was the day where my promise was going to be kept.

I ignored their gazes for now and bent down to help him. I collected his lenses and frames he was searching for and placed the remains in his hand, curling my hand around his to let him know that he was safe.

"Get out of here, now. Okay?" I whispered.

Without another word, Jarell rose up and quickly wandered away. Deep down, I prayed that he knew the hallway well enough so that he could get to his destination safely.

Once he was clear out of sight, I rose, and everyone was still looking at me like I was crazy. My heart was finally out of my airways, but that didn't stop it from beating like its sole purpose was for abuse. I feared that I would grow to be so unpopular to the point of ex-communication from D-Block. I just hoped it wouldn't be today for simply trying to do the right thing. Either way, I had to think of a way out of this and frame it in a way that was about them and not about Jarell.

"So that's the second time you played captain save a bum with that nigga, Jade. What's up with that?" Martell asked, and everyone stood by his side, waiting for an answer. "Something fishy is going on between you and that dirty ass mouse and I don't like the way you playin' my boy Mike. Mike out here checking girls left and right for you, and this is what you do?"

"Please, Martell. Ain't nobody got anything going on with him. Did you see what Tazz was about to do? He was about to kick him straight in the heart, and Tazz would have gotten suspended or expelled, either one of the two. You say you care about your boys, but it don't seem like you too excited to have them here without trouble."

"Naw, I'm not tryna hear that." He waved his hand. "Tell the truth Jade. What you got going on with him?"

"I don't have anything going on! And you better hear what I'm saying. I'm tired of saving you dumb ass niggas. I saved your ass from catching a rape case this past weekend, and I'm saving your boy from an assault lawsuit. Which one of you niggas are going to thank me instead of assuming I'm sucking his dick? Or, would you claim I'm sucking on y'all dick instead, since I'm actually working overtime to make sure y'all good?"

Crickets.

A wind of relief came over me, but I wouldn't dare let that show. I really, really had to be careful with how I was looking out for Jarell since I inadvertently and publicly made the decision to do so. I couldn't stop, now. Somehow though, I had to communicate with him to never, ever walk down D-Block again. Seriously. I didn't need anyone being in my business or deal with the drama that would come with it.

The tardy bell rang, and everyone dispersed with inaudible mumbles about me. I didn't particularly care about being late to class, so I picked up Jarell's backpack and cleaned up his scattered books. Looking at each one broke my heart.

They were all written in Braille.

I clutched them close to my chest, shaking my head. When his backpack was all finished, I took a trek around the school, dodging hall monitors to find Jarell's location. For back up, an old hall pass lingered in my purse in case someone asked me about my whereabouts.

I circled a corner and found him sitting on the bench in front of the nurse's office with his hood back up and drawn so tight that I couldn't see any part of his face. He was fiddling with his glasses in hand analyzing how broken they were.

Broken was an understatement. They were destroyed. Both lenses were popped out and cracked in more than thirds. The frames were wrangled to the point of dysfunction. My God. His teacher sat next to him, rubbing his back. I rolled my eyes at her. She was partly to blame for letting all that shit happen to him with her scary ass. I didn't even know why she was even walking down that hallway with him. I slowly walked up to them as their voices had become more audible.

"How are you going to tell your mom? Do you think you can get another pair?" the teacher asked.

"Does it look like I can afford another pair of glasses, Ms. Jenson? That's a thousand dollars."

One thousand dollars?

With a tight fist, Jarell crushed the remains of his glasses in his hand so easily that I stumbled at his strength. Not only that, but his entire hand also began to bleed from the broken glass cutting into his skin, and he didn't seem at all to be fazed. The blood produced quickly, and it wasn't long before his entire hand was trickling.

"What prescription are they?" I squawked out in a raspy voice, inserting myself into a conversation I had no business being in. I didn't have any sort of plan on dishing out a thousand dollars that I already had in savings, but it was a possibility.

"It's Jade," his teacher whispered.

"It's none of your concern. What are you doing here?"

"I have your backpack." I said, trying to find a valid excuse he'd accept for being there, and that was all I could come up with. I set his bag down in front of him and stepped back, placing my hands in my skirt pockets.

"Thanks," he muttered.

"Listen, Jarell. I-"

"You can leave me alone now," he interrupted, the base of his voice thundering through the empty halls. I flinched.

"Jade, just please go. He's really upset right now. You might want to try again another time," his teacher warned, but I ignored her.

"Jarell, I'm just trying to he-"

"Go away!" he yelled louder. "Matter fact, don't ever fucking talk to me!"

Jarell stood and stormed away from us towards the nurse's office. He searched for the knob and once he found it, he entered and slammed the door so hard it sounded like a gunshot. It echoed down the hallway, and soon heads poked out of their classrooms to see what commotion was going on. I was stunned. The nurse's entire door window was stress cracked from the impact.

Huffing in apparent annoyance, Jarell's teacher brushed past and followed Jarell, ending any contact and conversation between us. *Wow. That escalated quickly.* Looking down, Jarell left his backpack where I set it. I picked it up and hauled it over my shoulder, heading to my class. Hmph. Maybe I really didn't like rejection. If he wanted his backpack returned, he was going to have to see me.

Chapter Eleven

So much for trying to be happy throughout the day. My mind was so preoccupied with Jarell that I went home in a sour mood after the pep rally, which should have been one of the happiest times of this year. There was just so much to think about. Should I just give up on trying to help someone who didn't want to be helped? Or should I really continue claiming friends who'd bully a blind person? I was so disappointed in D-Block for the first time in my life. Hell, they crushed a thousand-dollar pair of glasses. There was no way in hell that Jarell would ever get a pair again. It was clear that they didn't even know he was blind, but they should have known something was off about him. That he had some sort of disability to the point where Jarell would look none of them in the eye. But then again, it was D-Block. A disability was even more of a reason to bully someone.

A part of me just wanted to find Jarell. Find him to make sure that he was okay, even though I knew he would cuss me out. He may have been calm by now, but with that bloody hand after crushing the remains of his glasses, he was probably in the hospital somewhere getting stitches.

I got out of my car after reflecting upon the day and walked through the front door of my house. I kicked the door shut and tossed my cheerleading bag down. A part of me wanted to go upstairs, hide in my room, and skip today's first game all together. But I couldn't make myself do it. Instead, I decided to eat dinner, even though I wasn't hungry. But if I went out on the field tonight on an empty stomach, I'd pay the price.

"Jade, pick up that damn bag. I don't know why you insist on putting it right at the front door when you know it should be in your room."

That was Janet for you. She was so particular about everything. Smacking my lips, I turned around to pick it up, but this time, I just threw it into the front closet. Hell, at least it was out of the way.

I went in the kitchen, and Moms was already looking at me like I was crazy. There must've been a look on my face or something because I didn't even say anything.

"What the hell's wrong with you?"

"What?"

"You look like you're mad at the world or something. You should already know my rule about your bag. You aren't upset with anyone but yourself," she said calmly with a chuckle. This time, she was sipping on coffee instead of wine.

I rolled my eyes. "I'm not mad."

I hopped up on the breakfast counter and reached for an apple that was in the fruit basket.

"Something's up. You better get your attitude together because you know your last first game is up tonight. You better not mess it up."

"I won't."

"And you need to eat more than that apple. Here's a salad," she said.

She pushed a large salad bowl my way. It was a leafy green chicken

Caesar salad, one of my favorite homemade by her. A little of that salad would go far.

"Thanks."

I ate quietly as Mom scrolled through her phone for a little while.

"I heard about that party last weekend," she blurted out.

"What about it?"

"First, you lied and said it wasn't in Crenshaw, so that's already strike one. And second, it got busted. And you were there, right? I hope you were not drinking, Jade. I'll put my foot so far up your ass if-"

"I was there, but I wasn't drinking. Actually, I left early. Way before it got busted. The party was too much."

"Did you talk to Mike?" she asked, and I rolled my eyes again.

How the hell did she go from me lying, to underage drinking, to focusing all her attention on Mike? I'd rather get yelled at about the former! Talking and even thinking about Mike was the last thing I wanted to do. I was already upset with how the day went, with Mike partially to blame even though I finally saw how sincere he was.

"No, I didn't. I was too busy partying, and he was too," I half lied, scooping a bite of salad into my mouth.

Her eyes widened.

"I'm starting to think that you don't really care about being with Mike. It's no wonder that he doesn't want you. You're not showing that you care!"

"It's not even like that."

"Then what is it? What the hell are you waiting for? I already told you Jade. The mind, the money, and the man. I'm not going to be around forever to advise you, you know."

"What exactly do you want me to say? You act like he's just gonna bow down and do whatever the hell I say!" I yelled, and she gave me that look that said if I raised my voice at her one more time, I'd be dead.

"Girl, watch your tone," she said. "Since you're acting crazy, I'll talk to the boy my damn self."

"Mom, no. Don't ev-"

"Shut it. Shut up. I've been doing everything else for you in your life and look at where it's gotten you. You can't do anything without me if we're being honest."

"It's not just you. I work hard too!" I said and felt a pang in my chest. I hated when she said shit like that as if I didn't spend numerous hours working on my craft. As if I had no autonomy over my own life.

"Hell, for the most part, it is."

"Well, you're not the one that got offered this seventy-thousand-dollar gig at the studio upon graduating high school. What part did you play in that?"

"Oh, so she finally told you the salary? And it's only seventy thousand dollars? That's what you're flaunting about? Honey, that's barely going to get you a one-bedroom luxury apartment in downtown LA, and you know it." She laughed, and then took another sip of coffee. "Try again."

Now, she was insulting. I loved my mom. I truly did, and I looked up to her. But she always, always shot me down while somehow finding a way to make amends by doing something for me that would be life altering. For the better, too. She left me no room to hate her. But for some reason, today, I was fed up. I couldn't even listen to her offend me anymore and then abide by her expectation of not standing up for myself.

So for the first time ever, I stood up and walked away in the middle of her talking.

"You better think twice about disrespecting me, Jade. Because God don't like ugly. You better pray for a decent performance tonight!" she yelled after me, and I ignored her, as much willpower as it took. I just grabbed my cheerleading bag from the front closet and left, heading back to school to do some practicing, preparing, and stretching on my own.

~ ~ ~

The bright lights. The roaring cheers. The blaring horns and snaring drums, the hyped football team. It was my favorite time of the year, but it had become one of the worst days. I absolutely hated fighting with my mom before performances. My mind would be swarming with negativity and not what the hell I was supposed to be focused on.

Get it out of my head. This was one of the biggest nights of the sports season, and our cheering squad had something to prove, especially to the opposing team. But nothing made me smile. Even Laurie kept asking me if I was okay, and I lied repeatedly to say that I was.

The opening cheer went fine, and I was glad for that after Laurie had given me renewed energy. Mike sat in the stands watching me with a smirk as we were now on the track doing our cheers in front of the crowd while the boys knocked each other's heads off on the field. I dished him little flirty smiles in return when I could, and everything was beginning to get better until my mom entered the bleachers.

Great. Just before halftime's big show.

As soon as the halftime buzzer sounded, my cheerleading squad ran on the field in excitement, chanting our favorite Cougar pride chants. We took our positions. Then, on came the music. I took a deep breath. This is what I lived for. The audience, the attention, the action. Dance was everything to me.

"Let's go ladies! Five, six, seven, eight!"

Then we hit our choreography. The crowd on both sides, our home crowd, and even the opponents, were really rocking with us. We were definitely doing something right.

But then, something happened. In the stands.

My mother approached Mike.

Fuck.

A nightmare brewed right before my eyes. I eyeballed her the entire time to make sure she behaved herself. Didn't think she had the guts to go up and talk to him! I thought she was just bluffing!

The further we got into the performance, music and dancing were completely off my mind, and instead, tuned into what was going on in the bleachers. The moment my mother reached Mike, he looked at her with pure confusion. Her body language was tense; she was probably yelling at him because the more and more she spoke, Mike's face became more and more peeved until he couldn't take it anymore. He stood up and now, was face to face with her.

Oh no.

The pressure was mounting, and I was coming up on a difficult stunt in this part of the routine, preparing to catch air stunts. But damn it, I just couldn't tear my eyes away.

By this time, a shouting match ensued, and I completely disengaged from our routine. Security was moving in on the situation while others in the vicinity held both my mother and Mike back.

Just as that was happening, Arianna was in the air hitting a split and then boom. I completely missed catching the lower part of her body as she came crashing to the ground.

Instantly, she screamed out in pain, holding her leg that was clearly sprained or broken. The crowd gasped, but the band kept playing and marching, drowning out Arianna's screams.

"Oh no," I whined, grabbing my forehead with a palm.

I had no idea what to do, so I knelt to her, feeling the weight of all the guilt in the world on my shoulders and tried to console her. She ended up shooing everyone away, needing air.

"Yo, Jade, what the fuck? You dropped her!" screamed one of my teammates.

"Yeah, what's up with you today? You could have killed her!" yelled another.

"You clearly don't want to be here, captain. Miss perfect ass bitch, you ruined the entire show!"

"Yeah, if you don't want to be a real captain, then get off the team! Don't try to tell us what to do if you're making rookie mistakes!"

Their screams, their grievances, their shouts were all directed to me at once, and I couldn't help but run away like a five-year-old. It was all just too much... my whole life seemed to be crumbling beneath my feet. On many levels.

I ran as fast as my legs would allow me and made it off the field and into the parking lot. Storming to my car, a familiar voice yelled after me.

"Jade! Jade! Jade Anastasia Williams, don't you hear me talking to you?"

My mom's screeching voice never sounded more annoying. A part of me wanted to sprint faster, but the other part of me slowed down because maybe it would be better for her to air out whatever she had to say rather than hearing all of it at home when I just wanted to be left alone.

"What!?" I whirled around, giving her a wild gaze.

Now, she was right in front of me.

"What the hell do you want?"

Then, I felt it. The one thing I was trying to avoid. The sting that rocked my head to the side so quick, I couldn't even think or process anything. My mother slapped me. Publicly. I heard a couple of gasps and laughs in the distance, and I could have just turned to dust and floated away.

"Don't you ever in your life talk to me like that. I let you disrespect me earlier, and you won't get away with it again! What the hell did you just do out there? An embarrassment!"

"Mom, *you're* embarrassing me! Why would you go talk to him?" I shouted. I completely melted down, was in full blown tears, and anyone nearby would have most certainly been laughing at me. Sure enough, I took a quick gaze around and some folks had their phones out, recording us.

"Girl, shut up! You look like a fool!"

"I watched you cause a fight at my last first game! You know how that makes me feel? And you got all these people out here recording me and whatnot!"

"It doesn't matter, Jade. You know what? Go home. We're going to finish this later."

She brushed by me, nearly knocking me over, and it took everything in my soul not to punch her. My hands were trembling. My body was shaking. Intense rage roiled through my body, and the only person that I could see right now standing in front of me was Laurie.

I dipped my head and sobbed. I couldn't look Laurie in the eye. No way in hell. Especially after I had the soul slapped out of me. With an arm wrapped around my shoulder, Laurie walked me to my car, whispering that everything would be okay. I took her word for it, but damn did it feel like the world was ending.

As soon as we were in my car and away from everyone, I leaned my seat back and bawled.

"I am so sorry, Jade. I'm sorry about your mom slapping you. I'm sorry about Arianna. I know you didn't mean it."

"I didn't! You know I would never do anything to make our team look bad!"

"I know. Everything is going to be okay. I don't think you should be so worked up. I think that if you explain what happened in the next practice, I think they'd understand."

"They're not going to understand, Laurie. Everyone wants to see me fuck up because they know I usually don't!"

"You're the captain. They have to listen whether they like it or not. Listen, it's going to be okay."

"Laurie, I fucking dropped her! I just took the attention away from the football game, and the season opener was a disaster. How is everything going to be okay?"

With my head down and into the crevice of my hand, Laurie pulled me in for a consoling hug. It was the right call because I needed it. Bad. The last time I got a hug from anyone was Mike. I'd been picking on Laurie for allowing me to be there for her when it seemed to never be reciprocated, but I was wrong. She was here. On time, and when I needed her to be.

Hell. Tomorrow was going to be a shit show on D-Block with me at the very center of discussion. Again. The perfect, popular Jade who talked shit about everyone, but never fucked up herself had done this. The dope dancer where mistakes weren't a thing because she danced with and for celebrities.

All of that was out the window. I wasn't afraid of my teammate being injured more than my reputation. And maybe that was the thing I needed to reconsider. That maybe, my reputation and upholding my mother's expectations weren't as important as being a better human being than she was. Because I wouldn't wish this type of embarrassment on anybody.

Literally nobody.

Chapter Twelve

I DID NOT go to school the next day. Sleep wasn't a thing for me, so school wasn't either. Never in my life had I been so publicly embarrassed and in tears the way my momma had me on Tuesday. Any hint of vulnerability at school was a no go, so I played the sick card while I watched everything unfold on social media. The video of Arianna falling, and the video of my mother and Mike arguing was all for everyone to display with upward of a hundred comments on each video. So many people were talking shit; I couldn't stay on there for long. I felt sick to my stomach with the thought of having to deal with all of that upon arrival at school. That is, if I ever decided to go back.

But Moms wasn't going to let that last for long. This morning, she had kicked my bed so hard that I nearly fell out of it from the impact.

"Get your ass up and go to school," she had said. "You are not sick, and I did not raise a punk."

So, I had no choice. I couldn't wait until I turned eighteen in a couple of weeks. Then she couldn't tell me shit.

The entire car ride to school I thought about what I was going to do or say when confronted about any of Tuesday's bullshit. I drove around LA for hours, purposefully getting myself stuck in traffic, just so I could think. The result was arriving to school late. Lunch time late. I just settled for the "pretending like none of it ever happened" tactic. Just avoid and deflect. Say it doesn't matter and deflect. Because those bitches at school didn't matter and still wished that they could be me at the end of the day. I worked myself up to think that.

But the one person I couldn't do that with was Mike. He was the only person that I truly owed an explanation, especially since he hadn't contacted me since.

So as soon as I walked into the school building before lunch started, I ignored all the eyes that laid on me. Ignored all the snide remarks and whispers. Ignored even Laurie asking if I was okay, and I went straight for Mike.

I rounded the corner on D-Block, and my heart fluttered when I saw him at his locker. He was fiddling about with his outfit and grooming himself in his mirror as I approached. He didn't even see me coming, which I was grateful for. I didn't want to give him a chance to walk completely away from me in front of everyone.

I reached him and opened my mouth to talk first, but nothing came out. I didn't think through my first words to him at all. My fist came up to my mouth to clear my throat. He noticed the noise and then me, delivering a fleeting glance.

"Hey, can we talk?" I asked just loud enough for him to hear. His eyebrows raised. "I'm so sorry about my mom. I didn't think she would do something like that. What did she say? Can we talk about it?"

"Not really," he mumbled, using his locker to shut me out.

"Why?"

"Because it seems like your mom is way too involved, and I ain't got time to be dealing with no baby shit with moms threatening me because she ain't getting her fucking way with her daughter. You grown, and you out here letting your mom run your life."

"Listen, I didn't tell her to do that. Can we please talk? I just want to know what she said."

"No."

"You're not telling me why. You're always down to talk, and we didn't even talk about what happened with you and your crap at the party, yet. So why is it different when I want to talk to you?"

He chuckled one of those chuckles that scared you. "You full of shit."

"How?" I blinked in confusion.

"You wanna know what I heard, Jade?" he asked and faced me squarely, his eyes holding tightly wound anger in check. Like he was going to hit me or something.

"What?"

"After the game, I met up with some of my niggas for a kickback. While I was there, I been hearing some shit around here about you sneaking around on me, and you got some nerve to send your crazy ass momma up in my face?"

"What are you talking about? Sneaking around?"

"You and some nigga named Jarell. I been hearing some shit about you staring at that nigga like you want him, that you been sticking up for him, saving him in the halls regularly, talking to him ... what's up with that, huh? At first, I didn't believe it because he's a fucking nobody, but then I kept hearing it, and something must be up. So, what's up? What you got going on with that dirty ass bum?"

I closed my eyes and took a deep breath, trying to stop my heart from racing. It was only a matter of time before this whole thing about Jarell got to Mike. It was especially more likely to happen when I didn't come to school. Because people were that damn miserable and wanted to see me lose. Especially when it came to Mike.

"Listen, it's not even what you think," I started, but was cut off by the roar of his voice and arms flailing in the air.

"Then what is it? Don't give me no fucking run around either."

"See Mike? This is what I mean. You're just *hearing* this about me, and you're already about to kill me as if I did something. But when I caught you with a bunch of girls, it's no big deal, right?"

"Fuck that, don't try to turn this shit on me. Fess up."

"I haven't and didn't do anything, Mike!"

"Yeah, right. So what do you mean when you say, *'It's not what you think?'* Something's up. Something happened."

"No, the only thing that happened was me saving Tazz from kicking Jarell in the stomach when he was already down the other day!" I shouted. "He would have gotten suspended."

"That lame ass excuse. You know good and well Tazz woulda been happy as hell to get suspended anyway to run on the streets with them Crips. Why did that even matter to you? Niggas get bullied all the time on the block and you ain't never said anything, never cared so what's the difference? What's so different about this nigga that you had to play captain save a bum?"

"Listen, you won't understand."

"Like hell, I won't. That's how I know something's up and that's the shit I'm talking about, Jade. You tell me you want one thing, all upset with me about something I did and felt bad for, but then you out here bullshitting. I checked all your homegirls, and this is what you do?"

"Mike, I'm telling you it's not like that!"

I wanted to slap him upside his head with one of my books. I didn't know how I could get him to realize that I was doing this to save our friends without revealing anything about Jarell to him. Tazz could've had a serious lawsuit on his hands.

"Nah, it's like that, Jade. You ain't really fucking with me the way you say you do. I can see that now."

"Yes, I do! What else do I have to show you that I do? I went crazy when I saw you with those girls. Any girl that talks about you, I'm ready to fight. I'm here to apologize about my mom. What else do I need to do?"

"You need to tell me the truth," he said.

"I am!"

"Listen. If I catch dude talking to you, kickin' it with you, lookin' at you, or whatever. Me and him gon' have a problem. You feel me?"

"Mike, no. You don't need to do that," I said. "You don't need that kind of drama. You're on the basketball team. You're going someplace. Why would you even let him get to you like that?"

"So you defending him? In my face?"

"No! Look, you're not in a good space right now. You're not listening to anything I'm saying, so I'm just gonna go. You're too much for me right now."

As soon as the words left my mouth, I turned and walked away. *How could he even dare to accuse me like this?* Either way, no matter what he said, I already made a promise. A promise to myself that I'd keep an eye on Jarell. Neither of them had to know. Being there for Jarell had absolutely nothing to do with me having a dating situation with him. That's what Mike didn't and wouldn't understand.

"I better not catch you with that nigga. I know that much."

I didn't say anything back. I just rushed out of the front doors and the breeze instantly hit my face. Yes. I needed to get out of there.

It felt weird to be walking outside alone during lunch. Laurie or

Mike were always rockin' with me, and Laurie still could have, but the importance of this alone time was paramount. I didn't know how much more I could take. Didn't know how much more arguing and negativity that I could withstand.

As I headed to my car and passed the courtyard, my heart slammed into my chest when my wandering eyes landed on Jarell sitting alone on a short tree stub eating a small sandwich and a bag of chips on the side. My trek stopped short as my mind grappled with whether to say something or not, especially after the conversation that Mike and I just had, but it wasn't like I was doing anything terrible with him. The feeling I felt after realizing that Jarell was blind was one I would never, ever forget.

Instead of talking to him right away, I settled for examining him as I decided whether to speak.

He still wore his hood in this hot weather, but the bandages on his hand were the difference. My inklings were right; he had gone to the hospital for stitches. Nearby, his special education teacher sat on the school steps, eating lunch while reading a book as well.

My feet moved in his direction until I was close enough to call his name. He beat me to the punch though; he turned his head at the grass shuffling beneath my feet. Today, he had on sunglasses. He looked so damn good in those things that I wondered again whether Jarell or Mike was more attractive. But reality checked me quick. Those sunglasses served as a reminder that his other glasses were crushed.

I waved his special education teacher down when she saw that I was approaching. She dropped everything and headed quickly in our direction.

"Hey, Jarell," I greeted him the moment she was in the vicinity.

"Jarell, it's Jade," his teacher said.

"Oh. Hey." Short and clipped.

He turned away from me again and fiddled with his sandwich. Looked like he only took about two bites out of that thing.

I stood for a moment, trying to collect my thoughts. Jarell's teacher had walked away once she realized it was a safe situation, leaving me alone to figure this out.

"Um… so… how's your hand?" I stuttered.

"S'cool."

"That's good. How many stitches did you get?"

"Ten."

"You really cut yourself deep."

"Yeah."

I didn't know what else to say that would explain me being there. As I tried to figure it out, Jarell threw his sandwich to the swarming birds and played with a sunflower in front of him, feeling its soft petals with his fingers. A huge bumble bee swirled around his hand as he touched it. It was going to sting him if he didn't move; it was his only good hand. It eventually landed on him, but he didn't move a muscle. Just continued to caress the flower petal between his thumb and index.

"You know that a bee is on you, right?"

"Mhmm." He nodded. "Knew it was around the whole time."

"How'd you know?"

"Heard it buzzing. You don't move, it won't sting."

"You're so calm. I'd be freaking out right now." I chuckled.

"Yeah. When there's bigger stuff to freak out about, you don't freak out about a planet saving creature," he said, and backed away from the flower with a deep breath. The bee flew away.

His words left me in tranquil. He had way bigger things to freak out about, yet I had a tantrum about something every other day that was nowhere near as significant as his problems.

"So, um, I was heading out to lunch. Probably go to Jack in the Box since I'm feeling something greasy. Wanna come?" I asked, rubbing my arm. I looked around the campus to see if anyone was watching me, and there wasn't anyone. Thank goodness. Besides, no one really came near the courtyard anyway.

He turned away and lowered his head. "Not hungry."

"You must be. You took two bites out of that measly little sandwich," I said.

"And that should prove to you that I'm not hungry. You should go away now."

"Why are you always shooing me away like I'm some house fly? I'm trying to be nice."

"And I'm not obligated to return the favor, so what's your point?"

"The point is... I don't know the point. I'm just saying you should stop being rude. Listen, the whole thing that happened on Tuesday in the hall? You didn't deserve that. I've been thinking about it ever since," I said, and knelt down to his level.

His entire body tensed and then, he just exploded.

"I don't want your sympathy. I don't know what it is with you trying to come all up in my life. I don't care about you, don't care about your apology, and I don't care about your fucked up friends. I don't care!"

"Jarell, please just hear me out. I can help you ge-"

"I don't need your help!" he bellowed and then rose up from the tree stump with his chips to walk away. By that time, his teacher rushed over to calm Jarell down, but it was too late. As Jarell tried to move in haste and far away from me, he completely missed a dip in the grass and fell, scattering his bag of chips everywhere, his sunglasses tumbling off his face.

"Fuck!" he shouted and punched the grass with his bandaged hand.

My eyes watered.

Goodness. He was so *angry*.

It was the kind of angry that you didn't want to see in people. That kind that produced so much pity, you didn't know what to do. The kind that would have you praying for the person even if you didn't believe in God. Anybody who saw this would have laughed, but for me, it felt like I had fallen myself. No matter how much he pushed me away though, it was so clear that he needed help.

His teacher helped him up and whispered something soothing into his ear while I rushed to grab his bag of chips. As I reached down for his glasses next, Jarell snatched my wrist unexpectedly into his better hand with a grip so tight that I almost yelped out.

"Put it down," he threatened through clenched teeth, and shot a glare in my direction that made me go cold.

Holy shit.

Now, I understood what people meant about Jarell being a monster. I nearly peed my pants.

His eyes were something serious. Especially since they weren't covered by thick prescriptions or those sunglasses. They were damn near demon eyes.

What happened to him? What could have happened that his eyes were so washed, grayed, and shaded over in blindness like that?

Immediately, I obeyed and dropped the glasses. His teacher's eyes were buck wide, and it was obvious she had never seen this side of him before.

"Let go of me," I whispered, trembling. How in heaven's name could he have grabbed me so on point like that? I didn't know what to think or believe. I was just shocked, and my nerves were getting the best of me.

He listened and let me go, getting himself up with his teacher's help. Then, she bent down and grabbed his glasses for him, leaving the chips on the ground.

"Jade, I know you're trying to help, but Jarell is in a bad place. Please. I'm begging you for the last time to leave him be. He wants to be alone."

I ignored her. Again.

"Jarell, why are you acting like this?" I asked.

"Listen. If you want to help, tell me where my fucking backpack is, since you're the last one to have it. That way you can leave me alone forever."

"When you stop being a dick to me, I'll bring it back. But until then, consider your wish granted. I'll leave you alone. And if you really want it, I'll be in the teachers' parking lot at six," I seethed, and then walked away from him.

That should have done it. Jarell wasn't going to get a new backpack or any new Braille books. He was left with no choice but to succumb to me.

As I walked away from him and headed to my car, I realized that I only had ten minutes left of lunch. Damn it, Jarell! Fuck it. I was going to be late coming back, and at this point, I just didn't care anymore. I wasn't going to college, so hell, what did it matter that I didn't come back to school anyway?

Chapter Thirteen

DAYS AND DAYS passed by, and there was no sign of Jarell in the teachers' parking lot after cheerleading practice to retrieve his backpack. As a matter of fact, I simply hadn't seen him at all for weeks. Day after day, I got my hopes up, convinced that he couldn't keep coming to school without his backpack and his books, but he did. What did he do in his classes without all his materials?

He probably didn't care. His attitude and stubbornness to avoid me at all costs was strong. He really hated me, and it showed.

Weeks turned into over a month. By the sixth or seventh week of not seeing him around, I gave up. I wasn't going to keep looking for someone who wasn't checking for me. I wasn't that type of girl; the boys swooned over me. Not the other way around. Especially over a guy of his caliber. I still wasn't giving up his backpack since he was a prick. He might as well buy a new one with whatever money he could find. Maybe that forty dollars I threw at him some time back.

Today was a typical day at school, but it was oddly mundane. D-Block was the chillest that it's ever been since school started in August. Not that I was around the block as much anyway given that so many people still couldn't stop talking about my blunder on the football field. The other part of avoiding D-Block was due to guilt since Arianna was on crutches. Seeing her was a constant reminder.

Mike and I weren't on the best of terms either, so I also didn't want people seeing us so distant. We talked of course, but it just hadn't been the same since our last disagreement. But either way, everyone on the block seemed tired. Maybe because midterm exams were coming, or it was just late fall season blues. I felt it myself. I had a couple of late assignments to turn in, which rarely happened. If it was turned in before the exams, that's all that mattered.

I walked to my English class well after the tardy bell had rung to turn in my late assignments before heading to Math and some teachers, including Jarell's special ed teacher and social worker, were in there having a meeting. I poked my head in, not wanting to be rude, but just to get in and get out.

"Can I come in to turn in these two assignments?" I asked.

All conversation ceased, and all four of their heads turned towards me. Visibly annoyed, my English teacher Mr. George waved me in.

"Next time, do it during passing time. You're well beyond late for class at this point, Jade," he said as I placed my papers in the homework basket.

"Oh well," I said with all the insincerity. Teachers don't be talking about shit anyway, so it wasn't like I was busting up something super important.

He picked up on the sarcasm because he rolled his eyes. I smirked. Just by the vibe, they were for sure going to start talking about me when I walked out of that door. So, I left but decided to stick around for a second to eavesdrop and see if my inklings were right.

"She's such a spoiled brat. Anyway. What's the status on Jarell, Mackenzie?" Mr. George asked.

Ms. Jenson let out a deep breath. "Well. I don't know. I've called home several times, but no answer. I am assuming his mother has been at work. I don't want to call her there because I know how upset she gets about that," she said.

"He was doing so well at the start of the year. We thought that this might be his year to make a turn around and finish high school strong," said another teacher.

"You know, I was hopeful because that's true. He was engaged in the schoolwork, really started to master Braille, and seemed more upbeat this year. But lately, he's been a ticking time bomb. Last time he was at school, he kept talking about how much he didn't care about graduating," Ms. Jenson replied.

"Yeah! I heard him say that too. Whenever I'd try to get him to participate in science talks in class, he would just shrug me off. Then stare at the ground for the entire class period, no matter what Kenzie would do to help him out of his funk or whatever it is."

Everyone sighed.

"That's too bad. Really too bad because he's so intelligent. I'd hate for him to throw his life away," Mr. George said.

"Yeah. He's been showing signs of depression and withdrawal more than I've ever seen since working with him. I'm going to get in contact with Jessica. As a psychologist, she can possibly make a home visit with the social worker and maybe get him to seek mental health services," Ms. Jenson said.

"Well, with his Special Education teacher a couple of years back, he recommended mental health services, but Jarell never ended up going. His mother didn't make that move, which I don't understand why. I doubt that as an eighteen-year-old male that you'd get him to do that now. You can recommend it, but that's only going to go so far," said the social worker.

"I understand that, but we have to try something. We must avoid him dropping out at all costs. He's just too close to having the requirements needed for graduation." Mr. George replied.

"It won't matter. He hates this school, Jeff. This place is like hell to him," Ms. Jenson countered.

"Where are all of his friends? Does he have anyone supporting him?"

"He has no friends," said the social worker. "We've been trying for four years to establish a friend group for Jarell, but he isn't interested, and no one is particularly interested in communicating with him either. They don't understand him, and he doesn't want people to talk about his blindness or to understand him either. It's honestly the saddest situation I've seen, and I've been working here for over twenty years."

"And the bullying is a major problem right now. We have to get a handle on that you guys," Ms. Jenson said. "Jarell was so upset when he got his glasses broken. I feel like that was just the last straw for him. These bullies are the reason why he can't make friends because they influence so many other kids."

"That is true. Why won't he tell anyone, though? That might stop the bullies," Mr. George said.

"It won't," said Ms. Jenson.

"Why won't it? How did he go blind anyway? He can't tell anyone?" Mr. George asked.

The table fell silent. I frowned, and leaned in closer, trying to see if they had started whispering, or if they felt like someone was there listening. My heart raced, planning to make a run for it if I heard footsteps towards the door. But instead, I didn't hear a single thing.

Just silence. For a long while. And then, "Why's everyone so quiet? What, no one can answer my question?"

"If you want to know, get your tissue ready, Jeff."

"Oh. Oh no. Is it that serious?" he said, a sense of premonition now laced in his voice.

"You'll need a whole box. I'm serious."

"Well alright. Someone grab my tissue by the door."

I gasped and moved to my class as quickly as I could. Not only was I afraid to get caught eavesdropping, but I also didn't want to stay any longer. A little angel on my shoulder kept telling me that it just wasn't right to stand there and listen to them, although I was curious as hell to know something so personal and pertinent about him.

I stopped just shy of my Math classroom door and thought... maybe I should go back to listen. My head kept telling me to go, but my legs wouldn't move. It was like the feeling you get stealing from a store when you're not a kleptomaniac. That feeling in your gut when you want something so bad, and if you stole it, you know you're a fraud. It was like that. I was far from a fraud.

I finally decided to enter where I was supposed to be fifteen minutes late, which the teacher had no problem reminding me that I was, and I basically told the teacher that I didn't care about her class. And it was true. My mind was occupied with Jarell.

What was his story?

For the rest of the day, I regretted not staying around my English teacher's door, but at the same time, knew it was the right thing to do. It left me confused and in wonder, playing different scenarios in my mind of what could've possibly happened to Jarell.

It was a thought until eighth hour. The library was my study hall with very few people, and I had brought Jarell's backpack along with my own work. It was the only way to satisfy this burning feeling I had inside, yet a weird sense of dread and feeling completely wrong for invading his privacy.

I kept telling myself to get over it. Don't think about it. Just open his backpack and see what's in there. Nobody knew it was his bag but me. I was safe, right?

When I unzipped it, it felt like I was on some surveillance camera as I slowly snooped around to find something juicy. To my disappointment and relief, I didn't find much. Only textbooks and a bunch of paper. Lots of it.

The more relieved I felt, the more I rummaged through, nearly crumpling his papers to see if there was any gold. Anything that I could find that would reveal anything new about him. But there wasn't. Go figure. He's not the type to keep things personal in a backpack.

Making the decision to let my guilt go, I took everything out of the bag and examined all his papers. I couldn't make out a single thing. Dots were everywhere. All over the place. I ran my hand across his papers and the dots were raised, feeling like a bunch of small pimples. *How cool.* I wished I could read Braille.

I found this little ruler looking thing and a weird pen thing, and I assumed that it was something he needed to write with. I set that on the library table and all the other unimportant papers. I felt around the bottom of his bag, but there was nothing. The only thing left was a stack of papers folded in half. I took them out with no hope, knowing I wouldn't understand a word on them, but to my surprise, this one I did. Just the top, though.

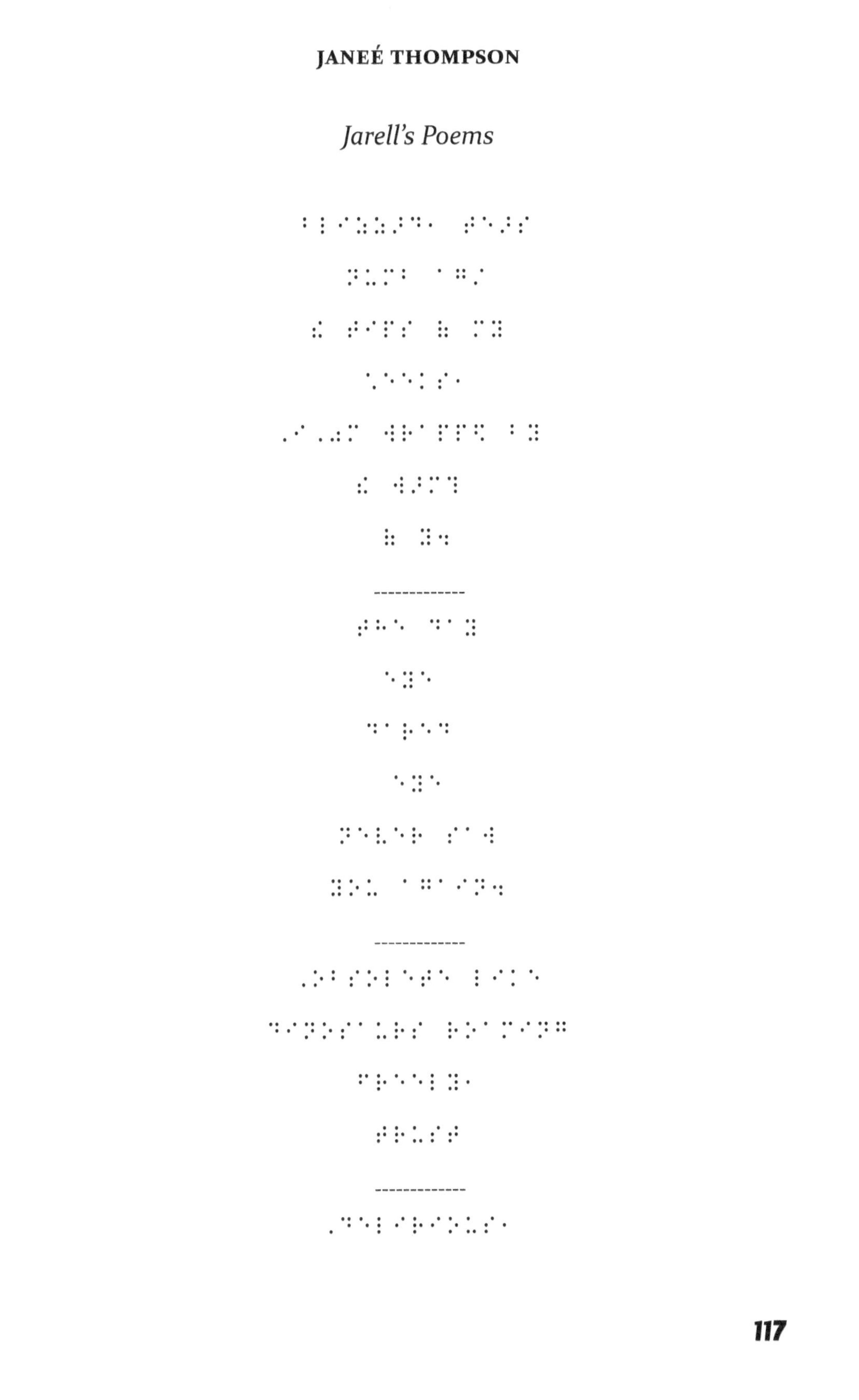

JANEÉ THOMPSON

Jarell's Poems

I couldn't make anything out. Dots everywhere. Did Jarell write these poems? What did they say? What did they mean? The lines at the end of the dots had to mean the ends of the poems, right? Hell, at least the heading of the papers was in plain English. Well, I guessed I found the gold I was looking for.

I took Jarell's poems, folded them as neat as I could and placed them into my back jeans pocket. Then, I placed his papers and everything else carefully back into his bag. Now that I had this information, I didn't want him having a single clue that I had seen it if he got his backpack back. Now, I just needed to find someone who could read them. I just knew it'd be the key to his heart that I now so desperately wanted to see.

Chapter Fourteen

IT APPROACHED HOMECOMING, my birthday, into November, and now over two months since I had last seen Jarell. Yet, he was on my mind every single day, and I still held access to one of his most prized and personal possessions in writing that I hadn't deciphered. Ms. Jenson knew Braille. She had to in order to work with him, but there was no damn way she would translate it for me if I asked, especially if she knew I possessed them. I even tried searching the internet to find someone who could, but to no avail. Something in those poems explained his story somehow.

I should've swallowed my pride and just asked the bitch, but I was too connected with D-Block for her trust. But what she didn't know was that D-Block, for me anyway, was deteriorating. I wasn't completely castigated because I still hung around each class passing time, although I didn't speak much. Like right now. Everyone around me laughed, talked crap about each other, and had a good time as usual as I pulled out Jarell's poems, probably looking like I had lost a loved one.

Laurie turned the corner with a smile on her face and headed straight to Martell instead of me, which was now the usual, too. They exchanged some inappropriate words quietly to each other; I could tell since Laurie did that stupid mousey giggle and Martell smirked, licking his lips. I shook my head, a little envious of their happiness since Mike and I were struggling. In the end, I couldn't help but to be happy for her. Even though Martell was the biggest of all dicks in the world, he still made Laurie smile, and I guessed I could give him credit for that.

"Hey, Jade," she greeted me all giddy and happy once their conversation was over and after I folded Jarell's poems away.

"Hey."

"Listen. Martell is so nasty. Talking about he'll lick the vanilla and eat me out in front of everybody. Who comes up with that?" She chuckled, and I laughed, shaking my head.

"Only Martell," I said.

"Damn right. I'll lick the chocolate off him." She grinned.

"TMI. Don't mean to change the subject, but I have a quick question for you that has been kind of eating at me. It's a weird question, but I just need you to answer, okay?"

"What is it?"

"It may sound strange, but do you know someone who reads Braille? Or do your parents know anybody who reads it?"

With a puzzled look, Laurie gazed around.

"No. I don't. Why?"

"Just wondering." I shrugged and waved her off. "Forget I asked."

Laurie gave a side glare.

"You've been acting real weird lately, Jade. I know I've upset you after the whole party in Crenshaw, and I know you've been upset about the whole cheerleading thing with dropping Arianna. You can trust me. Really."

I sighed and looked away from her.

"What's going on that you want to know something as random as needing someone to translate Braille for you?" she asked, and this time, I felt guilty for lying, but I still couldn't trust her.

"It's nothing major, Laurie. I just found a couple of poems that need to be translated. That's all."

"You're not lying to me, are you?" she asked, raising an eyebrow.

"Nope."

"Yes you are, Jade. Seriously. What is going on? You can talk to me. Really. Let's move away from D-Block," she said and grabbed my arm, pulling me away from D-Block's main artery and into a corner hall.

Now, my mind and heart raced. Even if I revealed that it was something for Jarell, Laurie didn't need to know Jarell was blind by connecting the dots. *Quick, think of something. Fast!*

"So spill, Jade. What's the problem?"

"Laurie..."

"Well?"

"It's honestly nothing. I found poems that need translation, but it's nothing serious. I promise," I said.

"I still don't believe you, but I'll let it go. So... you and Mike? Homecoming?" she asked.

"Yeah. About that. I haven't asked him yet. Or he hasn't asked me. I know he will though. I think we're going to end up working things out."

"Why do you say that? I see you both aren't on good terms lately. I heard he tore into you not so long ago, and it doesn't seem like you guys are repairing."

"Yeah, that's reason why I think he'll ask is because of how he reacted after people kept telling him about Jarell."

"So, was everything about you and Jarell true?" she asked, giving me another side eye.

"I mean, kind of. I was looking at him because I was wondering who he was. Then they damn near jumped him in the hallway and Tazz was about to kick him in the stomach when he was already down. So I came in and stopped it. They got all weird about it, and they went and told Mike."

"Jade, why do you even care about that dirt cake? Let him get jumped! He's not worth losing Mike," she said. "Seriously, he looks like the grim reaper."

"It wasn't about him. It was about Tazz, Laurie. He could've gotten in major trouble," I said, trying to defend Jarell without giving anything away. My scapegoat about Tazz wasn't going to hold up much longer.

"Yeah, okay. The way you're talking, it sounds like people aren't making this shit up about you and Jarell," she said.

"Laurie! Jarell and I don't have anything going on. What's up with y'all? Have y'all ever even seen me with this guy?"

"No, but you shouldn't get any ideas. Get rid of stinky boy Jarell."

I laughed and gave her a warm look as we both walked out of the corner hallway as we spoke Mike into existence. He leaned up against the wall close to the corridor to D-Block, and he literally blocked everyone out since his head was buried in his cell phone.

"Wonder who he's texting," I mumbled to myself, but Laurie overheard.

"Don't know. Why don't you go find out? He's your man," Laurie said with a shrug, and then left me alone to decide what I was going to do.

I sighed, rolled my eyes, and gave him a worried look he couldn't see. Laurie always spoke my language. Whether Mike liked the idea of labels or not, he was my man. Not only that, but his territorial ass also wasn't so hot about just the thought of me looking at Jarell, so I had that going for myself. And I needed to fix this.

With a deep breath, I approached him head on, giving him no ability to prepare for my presence.

"Hey," I greeted him shyly.

He looked down at me for a fleeting second before responding me with a very short, "Sup shorty."

"So...," I started, feeling discouraged, "you and I need to talk, don't you think?"

"About?" he asked.

"Us. And I don't mean *that* kind of us if that's what you're thinking. I mean that I miss our friendship."

"Aw, for real?"

"Mike, stop acting like you don't either. Seriously. Stop putting on this front because you feel salty about some rumors," I said.

"What you mean? That nigga ain't in no competition with me."

"So then why're you so distant? We really haven't spoken since that whole argument we had about him and my mom."

"All I'm saying is that I ain't got time for issues with nobody's mom, Jade. You too old for that," he said.

"I know, but I keep telling you that I didn't tell her to do this. Matter fact, I tried hard to get her not to do it. I just don't want her actions to be the reason why you won't talk to me."

"Why shouldn't it be? If we have any sort of future together, her actions show exactly how she's going to be. In our business. People like that don't change, Jade," he said.

"I wouldn't let her do that."

"Yeah, just like you didn't let her come up in my grill at the game?"

"Mike, I was cheering! If I was in the crowd, I would've stopped her. I don't think you're being fair, and at this point, you're just coming up with excuses and every reason not to be with me. If you don't want to deal with me at all, just fucking say so! Just know that it'll be a huge mistake because it ain't like no other girls out here doing what I'm doing."

With a sigh he lowered his head and then looked at me for a long while. Both of my eyebrows raised, looking for a response that, for once, wasn't bullshit.

"I'm sorry," he said. "You know I care about you."

"Then act like it!"

"Alright. I'm taking you to Homecoming. That's my official ask, and I ain't giving you a reason to tell me no. You're coming with me. Make sure you lookin' good, a'ight?"

I smirked.

"Don't I always look good? But thank you. And what else you got because taking me to Homecoming ain't enough."

"And we can talk more about us after Homecoming okay? This hallway shit ain't gon' work out."

"Hmph. Sounds like a plan that I'm holding you to."

"Alright, shorty. You got my word."

With that, Mike pulled me into him slowly for a long hug. Oh, how I missed that fresh cool water scent.

Chapter Fifteen

I HOPED MIKE wasn't full of shit. I felt good after our talk, but as usual, the more I reflected after our interactions, the more I felt like he was bluffing. Did he simply want to use me as a date to Homecoming?

Well.

I couldn't even lie. A part of my effort to reconcile was to use him for a date, too. What I look like coming up in Homecoming with myself or no date at all? That was a no go. Everyone else had dates, and they weren't even as poppin' as me. And I wasn't going to go with just *anybody*.

Either way, everything Mike said wasn't convincing enough to erase Jarell from my mind. He'd have to do better than simply asking me to Homecoming, and I was going to hold him to his word on talking afterwards. The other effort was truly to get us to where we used to be. I couldn't see myself with anyone else.

Speaking of Jarell, I ran out of options regarding how I was going to see him again. Getting someone to translate those poems for answers about him was harder than I thought, and I wouldn't dare to ask anyone at school about him. So, I figured I'd try to visit him at home after cheerleading practice. Last resort, and the thought of going there scared the shit out of me. I remembered he lived on

W Fifty-Sixth. I was going into this headfirst without even thinking about what I was going to do or say once I saw him, but I guessed that's how I'd been interacting with him from the jump anyway.

After an annoying and gossipy cheerleading practice, I headed to my car late since I had to discipline the team for being so off task. I checked the time to see if I could hurry up and take a shower before heading to Jarell's place, but it was already seven pm, and I didn't want to be rude and show up to a stranger's house so late in the day. Especially since our clocks were set back an hour to end daylight's savings. Guess I was going right away.

Hoisting my bag over my shoulder, I mentally prepared myself for the visit as I walked to my car when I saw a figure in the parking lot. An all-black figure moving fluidly to a sort of rhythm.

What the hell?

I approached cautiously, hoping it wasn't anyone dangerous. The closer I got to my car, the clearer it became. It was someone dancing. In fact, it was the same dancer I had seen in the park the day I ran out of Martell's friend's party at the beginning of the school year!

Holy shit! I was afraid I'd never see them again!

I walked closer, taking care not to interrupt. Pulling out my phone to record them was my first instinct, but the selfish part of me just wanted to see them totally for myself. If I had posted them on any of my social media, everybody would want to know who this person was and if they could dance for them.

Because goddamn was this person talented. Watching them this up close was even better. I couldn't even put a name to the style of dance. Mostly hip hop, but also other intricate styles mixed in between. Again, doing this all with no music, yet every step they took, every movement they made, created the music itself.

I watched for at least five minutes before the person completed a spin move, and by that time, my jaw was on the pavement. And so were my bags.

It was Jarell!

Wait, wait, wait! Hold the fuck up. Can't be.

I looked closer. Those sunglasses. Shoes whose soles were close to the end.

Indeed, it was him!

Wait. Jarell could dance? Like *that*!? But... *how*?? How in God's name could he do that? Without seeing? Without music!?

I was in awe. I could watch him all day and at that moment, I felt something new for him that I couldn't explain. Certain parts of his body stiffened while others moved like a river. A calm river. And the way his feet glided over pavement in torn shoes, anyone would've thought he was dancing over silk on bare feet.

He danced so passionately, like it was the last time he'd ever get to dance. His facial expressions evoked so many different emotions: happiness, sadness, anger, goofiness... this was the most expression I had seen from him.

At this point, I wanted to dance with him. I wanted to vibe with him just to see if we could. And that was the thing about his blindness that I appreciated. I wouldn't feel discouraged if I joined.

So, I stepped in without saying a word and danced with him, seeing if I could complement his style. This was honestly one of my favorite challenges of dancing at the studio. Freestyle dancing with someone you don't really know, yet making sure that you're in sync and connecting with the person at the same time. Elite level. But this was different. There was no music. This was the ultimate challenge – something completely new.

When I started to dance, he paused for a split second, startled. Nonetheless, it was short lived. He ignored and kept dancing.

And just like that, it was a vibe. He picked up on my moves quicker than I was able to get a hold of his, but when I did, it was magical. If I thought that Jarell was attractive then, he was a God now. As we danced together, his movements were racy – something I didn't observe as he danced alone. And totally unexpected. It ignited a part of me on the inside that usually ached and dreamed for Mike. The way my butt grinded on the front of his sweatpants in certain moves through the material of my thin skirt had me all types of hot. Did he feel it too? I couldn't tell because his pants were so baggy that gauging an arousal was impossible.

Either way, I had never seen anyone with such a sensual but disciplined disposition when they danced the way that Jarell did, and I've seen many, many, many dancers. He didn't even have to do racy moves to still be sexy. He just... *was.*

At the end of the dance, Jarell spun me out, leaving me in a couple of pirouettes and breathless. I watched him as he stopped dancing, and he simply stuffed his hands in his pocket, looking towards the ground.

Swallowing and recollecting myself, I had no idea what to say. Now, it was hella awkward. I didn't know whether to say something about the dance, ask him about school, ask where he's been, invite him to the studio, tell him I had his poetry, tell him that it was me... my mind ran as fast as my heartbeat at this point.

I settled on, "I still have your backpack," and squawked it out in a raspy voice.

A long, long pause ensued as he stood rigidly still without even giving me any semblance of recognition. He just turned his head and looked towards the street. And I just stared. Waiting.

"I... I know," he finally tore out of himself. He shifted his eyes from the street and looked at the ground again through his sunglasses, barring me from any surprise he might have felt about it being me.

"Do you want it back? It's in my trunk. Been in there for the past couple months."

"I know."

"Why are you out in the school parking lot so late? It's dark and almost eight."

"Fresh air. Didn't think anyone'd be around. Listen... I... I didn't know you danced."

"Yeah. I run a dance studio and dance in music videos for a living, but I don't freestyle much. Well, not as good as you do, now that I see."

Silence.

"Well... do you want a ride home?" I asked.

Another long pause. And then, a head nod so small that you could barely see it, even while I keenly watched. I found myself smiling at the gesture because this time, he didn't fight me. Didn't say anything snarky. Where head nods go, it wasn't enthusiastic, but it was something. A breakthrough.

"Come on," I said softly and headed towards my car. He walked closely behind, and even though it felt uncomfortable, I knew it was because he was blind, and it was his way of getting to his destination without asking for help. I sighed again. I honestly didn't even want him knowing that I knew.

We reached my car and we both got inside.

I watched him with intent again to make sure he was comfortable. Much to my disappointment, he tightened up his hood and scrunched up against the door as if wanting to take up the least space possible. I attempted to say something, even make small conversation, but he closed me off by looking out of the window and blocking any view to his face.

He wasn't ready.

I didn't press the issue this time. I felt so calmed by that dance that I just didn't want to fight him anymore about being unapproachable. So many other things were going on in my head anyway. How the hell did he learn to dance like that? What was his story behind dancing? Did he study anyone like I studied Janet, Teyana, and Laurie Ann? Could this be a way we could build our relationship? Through dance? Would he be willing to check out my studio? Did he see a future with dancing? We could have so many conversations about different dancers. We could dance together every day. We could vibe the way no one else our age truly could with our craft.

As I drove through the city at a slower pace than usual thinking of all this, it was a beautiful night. California always had dry, warm evenings but tonight was balmy as the palm trees sashayed with the wind. People were out on their porches with cigarettes and beer, laughing, joking, walking, and it felt so good to see. Especially in South Central.

What was Jarell thinking? Did he think about the dance, too? Did he feel the way I felt?

I would never find out. The entire car ride was quiet until the moment I pulled up to his house. The same little girl from last time was at the door waiting for him, calling out his name, and I heard someone yell at her not to come outside because it was too dark.

"We're here. Give me a sec and I'll grab your bag out of the trunk."

He didn't say anything. He just got out of the car and leaned against it comfortably and waited. I was so dumbfounded by his move that I caught myself gawking a little too long and then snapped out of it.

I said that I wasn't going to give his backpack up until he came to me, but today was more than I could've asked for. He wasn't rude, and he wasn't dismissive, even though sometimes his silence felt that way. But this time, it was different. This silence was a serene, comfortable kind where the both of us were just lost in thought. Even now, as he literally leaned on my car. Although I knew he wasn't going to talk about it, just by the tension in the air being released, it was super apparent the dance influenced his mood the same way it affected mine.

"Here," I said, standing directly in front of him and holding his bag out. He took it with ease and lifted it over his shoulder.

"Gonna head in," he said.

As he turned to walk away, I realized he wasn't going to say thank you for the ride, either. That was also too much for him, but you know what? I was actually okay with it.

"Uh, Jarell?" I called after him.

He stopped walking and turned his head slightly.

"Come back to school."

I meant every word and hoped he understood that I wanted him there. I really didn't know why because it wasn't like we talked or hung out, but it meant something for me for him to go back. I guess I just didn't want to let Martell and the crew win. Not this time.

He didn't say anything. Just slowly turned his head and walked towards the house, ruffling the hair of the little girl who greeted him at the door.

Chapter Sixteen

A Scorpio baby. A real queen's birthday. My birthday, November fifteenth, and there was no place I'd rather be than in the studio over attending school. I was eighteen, and more than happy to skip classes without repercussions to celebrate this day because Chris Brown was heading into the building to check out our crew for his LA performance. I was so excited for him to dance with us, vibe with us, and get shit done. The crew wasn't perfect by any means, but they were way better than they were a few months ago, that's for sure. Thank goodness Chris had to cancel and reschedule a couple of shows because had it been the original date, we would've been axed out, reputation tarnished. Because everyone knew that Chris was blunt and played no games.

The crew practiced all morning, perfecting their moves when Chris walked in. I smiled big. He was such an inspiration to me as a performer. It was rare when I got one of the people that I studied so close in the vicinity. I tried not to act like a fan girl because I should have been used to celebrities by now, but sometimes, you just can't help but to feel that on the inside. Did other legends feel that way about their own counterparts?

"What's up, what's up, what's up?" he greeted us lively and full of energy as he shook the hands of the ladies on the dance floor.

Alise and I stood next to each other, happy as hell. Because Alise owned the studio, was well known, and Chris always posted her on his social media accounts, Chris went straight to Lise, skipping over me as if I didn't exist and went for a hug. He hugged her so tight and lifted her up so high that she screamed in giggles. Being overlooked didn't feel so hot, but I wouldn't dare let it show. If he didn't know me now, he was about to know. That's what I did when big names did me like that.

Make sure they never forget you.

"Sup baby," he greeted Alise, and she hugged him back with a laugh when he finally put her down.

"You still flirting, huh?" she said as she pushed his shoulder.

"You already know what's good."

"Hey, this is Jade. She's under apprenticeship right now with me and she's pretty dope. And it's also her birthday today. She's been running the studio and handling business work for me for the past year or so. I moved her up to run the youth group as a part of the studio, and we're going to renovate an extension of the building really soon."

"Oh word? It's nice to meet you Jade. And happy birthday," he said politely, but it wasn't as vivacious as when he greeted Lise. I said thank you, and he continued to speak. "Yo, you got some big news since the last time I've been here. Congrats! You out here doing big things, Lise!"

"Thanks, man. It's just good to finally see you in town," Lise said.

"Yeah, I'm here and I'm ready to check y'all out. You ladies been working on that choreo I sent y'all?" he turned around and asked everyone.

They all responded affirmatively, and he nodded with approval.

"Alright bet. So let me check y'all out, and then we can make any tweaks or adjustments. Then, I'ma hop in like I'm performing with y'all. Make sure that we vibe. Sound good?"

Affirmative was the response again, and here we go. The nitty gritty. My hands were now sweating with nerves, knees trembled a little bit, and I had to remind myself to stop it. I had nothing to be worried about because Alise and I worked our asses off to get them to this point. We were confident that they'd pull through. If I was feeling this way, there was no way that Alise didn't feel worse. But damn her. She appeared so calm and stoic that I couldn't even read what she was thinking or feeling at all. Maybe I should just follow suit...

Chris' music came on, and the ladies danced the routine. Everything went really well, and then the hiccups came deeper and deeper into the performance. My eyes whipped over to Chris nervously, but he was simply watching with a pensive look that gave nothing away. I looked over at Alise, and she was doing the same.

Goddamnit, how was it that I was the only person worried right now?

"Alright, cut!" I yelled out and stopped the music. I may have overstepped my boundaries on this one, but I would just do it now and apologize later. It was for the crew's own good.

"Y'all were great at first, and then y'all got sloppy. Run it back. Tera, you're a step behind everyone. I need you to pick it up. Let's try it again, ladies," I said, and started the music from the top.

Neither Chris nor Alise said anything at my move, so I assumed everything was fine, and they appreciated my leadership. Either way, thinking too deep into it wasn't going to help because my focus needed to be on what the girls were doing.

Again, the beginning went fine... and then more hiccups... then even more hiccups... and then I just couldn't take it anymore. Here's the thing. They weren't about to embarrass Lise or me in front of Chris. If that's what they thought, then they had a whole nother thing coming. I stopped the music again.

"What the hell was that? You think you're going to go out in front of this man's audience and dance like that? What are y'all, nervous? Because you did just fine ten minutes ago!" I exclaimed, and the girls just stood quietly. "Tera, if I have to tell you again to pick it up, you're going to sit down. Let's go."

Irritated, I restarted the music, and I heard a frustrated huff from Alise behind me as soon as one of the girls screwed up again, and this time, she stopped the music. She didn't even let them get as deep as I let them.

"Against the wall, please," she said much calmer than I would have ever expressed, and they did as they were told. Chris sat quietly with a small smirk on his face. I didn't know what that meant, but it wasn't good. The rest of his body language didn't show that he thought this was funny.

"Individually. I want each of you to hit the choreography. Those who don't get it right will go home. Any little mess up, you're out of here, and you won't perform."

Whew! Now that was some pressure! Those ladies thought I was rough... when Alise got upset, she didn't play around! Maybe that was why Chris was smirking.

"Stacey. You're up first."

And one by one, the dancers hit the choreography. A couple dancers got sent home. Not very many, but a few. And now, Tera was up. And she was the biggest fuck up of them all. To the point where I had to push her off the dance floor.

"Get out, Tera. You're done. Let me show the rest of y'all how this choreography is supposed to be done. Some of y'all didn't get sent home, but you ain't selling shit. This is how it's done," I said, and I danced.

Danced from the beginning of the choreography to the end, hitting every move and pronouncing it as hard as I could to prove a point. To prove that none of them were on my level because they didn't act like they wanted to dance. They weren't enthusiastic like they thought they were, and it pissed me off. When I finished, I was nearly drenched in sweat, hair flying everywhere, and breathing like I just got into a fight.

"That's how it's done," I said glaring them down, and walked away. I didn't look at Alise or Chris because I was so mad. It didn't even matter how well I did... I cared more about the reputation of Alise and I to care.

"Damn girl," Chris said in approval with a surprised gaze. "You snapped. Yo. Do that again. Can we reformate with these numbers and stick Jade in there so that she can dance the part? Lise, you get in, too. I want to see how this will look with just you, Jade, and six other dancers."

Lise took on the job of the reformation, and then we danced, feeling relieved of all the cancers in the group. Everything went perfect. And although they could have been more enthusiastic, they still did what they needed to do. On the second dance go round, Chris came in to perform with us as well, and my breath was just taken away.

He was so talented. And the way it all came together was just amazing.

We vibed, practiced, laughed, were serious, and just generally had a good time with Chris. We danced for about four hours, perfecting the performance until he felt satisfied about it.

"Aight y'all, that's a wrap! We're going to continue working on this up until the show, okay?" Chris called out.

Everyone left the studio for the day until Lise, Chris and I were in the studio alone so that we could close up shop.

"Jade, I just want to tell you that I'm amazed by your talent. I should've known anyone working with Lise would be dope. I'd like you to join their performance next weekend but be my lead dancer on my other songs. I think they really vibe from your energy, and that's what I need on my stage. I ain't going without it. You interested? Show's already sold out," Chris said.

With wide eyes, I gazed at Lise as if I needed her approval or something. Shocked was an understatement. Lise looked at me crazy, like she would smack me upside my head if I didn't take an offer like this.

"Of course I'll take it! Sorry, I'm just shocked! Me?"

"Yeah, you! And you deserve it. You rocked that thang tonight. Let's catch up tomorrow morning here and we can practice and rock it out. Sounds cool? I'll also pay you hefty for your first on stage performance and for your birthday. My gift and pleasure. Sound cool?"

"Hell yeah, it's cool!"

And just like that, I had the best eighteenth birthday of my life. Didn't think anything could ever match it, past or future.

Chapter Seventeen

I WENT TO school for the second half of the day so that I was able to attend cheerleading practice after the studio. It was some stupid rule of the school for extracurricular activities that you had to attend school for at least half a day to participate. Since I was captain, I really had to abide by it. Otherwise, I would have gone home to bask in my birthday glory and everything else that had just transpired. I could hardly contain my excitement. I was really dancing for Chris Brown on stage in LA!

Thinking about some of Chris' moves today had me wondering if Jarell would give Chris a run for his money? I had only seen Jarell dance twice, so I really had no clue of his true capabilities. Chris showed what he can do on multiple occasions, and somehow, still managed to come out with something bigger and better than the last performance. Only way I'd find out is if I could somehow get Jarell into the studio. I hoped I'd see him soon to see what I could do to get him there. Since the last time I had seen him, he still hadn't been to school, which was about three days ago. So it was totally up in the air if I'd see him again without me making a visit to his house.

Cheer practice went quickly without me mentioning my birthday or the gig with Chris Brown, although of course, Laurie knew it was my birthday and wished me a happy one. In the back of my mind was everything going on was Mike. His birthday wish mattered most to me out of anybody. I hadn't received anything at all, which hurt my feelings. He had to know it was my birthday. Right? I worked myself up to believe he was doing this on purpose, making me wait in order to surprise me later or something. He had rest of the day to give me my due recognition.

I walked out of practice around the usual six p.m. and checked my phone for Mike, and indeed I had a message.

Mike: Hey. Happy birthday, I hope you enjoyed your day! See you soon ;)

That's it?! He needed to do more than that measly ass happy birthday. I texted back.

Me: Yeah, as soon as tonight, I hope. Thanks!

Mike: I wish I could, baby girl. But my little brother has an AAU basketball game up north in Fresno that I gotta be at tonight. Omw there now. Some scouts will be there to watch him, and I'd like to meet them as well. Don't worry. I will make up for it during Homecoming.

I rolled my eyes and threw my phone in my purse. That asshole... He wasn't going to get any negativity from me today. Not on such a great day like this!

As I walked out to the parking lot and to my car, Jarell was across the way sitting on a bench against the busy side of the street. This time, over his hoodie was an old Crenshaw jacket. The style from Freshman year. I grinned, instantly feeling my day become brighter. His random appearances no longer surprised me, so I hoped it continued. I was genuinely glad to see him and wanted to know how he was doing. Especially after that dance. He had to feel more connected to me the way I felt more connected to him. A connection that I didn't think I would have ever built with him if we hadn't danced. It broke new barriers – exciting barriers – and it was interesting to see where this was going to go.

"Hey Jarell," I said once I reached him.

"Jade," he said without any emotion. Forget that he always sounded like a monotone robot. I still couldn't get over how good he looked in those sunglasses as the sun lit up the cocoa brown features I otherwise wouldn't be able to see beneath his hood.

"What are you doing out here? Waiting for me to catch a ride? I knew you'd give in one day," I joked, and he didn't say anything. Just turned his head away. I kicked myself on the inside. *Too soon, Jade.* One day, I was going to talk to him without feeling like I was walking on eggshells.

"Sorry, I didn't mean," I started, but he interrupted me with a hand up.

"S'cool."

"Okay. Well, how are you? We haven't spoken since... you know... we danced."

"I'm good."

And then silence. Cars passed down the busy street, and I just didn't want to be caught talking to him by anyone driving by. Jarell was still my secret at the end of the day because I wasn't ready for any drama. Besides, I didn't know what else to say without making him feel uncomfortable.

"Okay, that's good. Well... I'm not going to keep you or bother you. I'll get going," I said and pulled my cheerleading bag over my shoulder.

As I turned to walk away, five steps were all I took before hearing his voice call out to me. A voice that made the hair of my neck stand because hearing him say my name was music to my ears. I turned around slowly and stopped in place.

To my pleasant surprise, he rose from the bench and walked towards me. Hood up, head down, hands stuffed in pocket, slow pace. I gazed like a hawk. Each step was calculated, careful, and small.

What if I reached out and touched him? What would he do? My hand itched to rub his back, maybe even give him a hug, but I willed the thought away. I just waited to hear him say something that he was clearly struggling to get out.

"I thought about what you said," he began.

"About?"

"About going back to school."

"And?"

"I got a home visit from Ms. Jenson earlier that same day. Were you two planning a tag team about me coming back to school?" he asked.

"No. I don't even like her."

"No teaming up about my backpack and giving it to me?"

"Um, no. I wanted you to stop being a jerk to me. And the night after we danced together," I started, not even sure if I wanted to go in this territory, "I really felt like some walls were broken. That we connected in some way that... I don't know... many people don't. So I gave you your bag back."

He stood silent, fiddling with his hands at his sides and dragging his feet periodically on the pavement. I smacked my lips and hit him with a side glare. I didn't have the patience to continue standing here with him. It was a waste of time, and it was getting dark.

"Jarell, I have to go."

"I'm coming back after Homecoming," he suddenly confessed.

"Why?"

He shrugged. "It's... I just need to finish what I start. Even if I don't think it'll help me much."

"Good. I'm happy for you," I said, trying not to let my excitement about that be heard. "Are you going to Homecoming this weekend?"

He scoffed. "No."

"Why?"

He shrugged again.

"Oh. Okay. Well, seriously, I need to go. I'm tired, and I want some rest. You want a ride?" I asked.

He nodded that small, little barely nod again, and I laughed. He was so cute. When he heard the chuckle, I could have sworn the corners of his mouth tilted upward, too. I couldn't tell for sure because his head was lowered, but it was, at minimum, remnants of smile playing about his lips.

"Alright, Ghost. Follow me."

"Ghost?" His eyebrows flexed.

"Yeah. I called you that before I found out who you really were. I found out your real name through the grapevine," I said, walking towards my car. He followed closely as he gave an amused sound in his throat.

"Better than America's Next School Shooter."

"I know, right? Sometimes, you maneuver and act like a ghost."

"Oh really?"

Smiling, I could get used to this. I truly could get used to us getting along like this.

"Yes, really."

"Y-you don't really think I'd do something like shoot up the school, do you?" he asked slowly, and I turned to look at him. I tried to read him, but those damn sunglasses! That's what made him so hard to truly get to know. Instead, I took what was available which was his voice and heard the insecurity.

"No. I don't think so," I answered at last.

We walked the rest of the way to my car in silence. I opened the car door for him, not realizing my actions were giving away my knowledge of his blindness. At this point, I still didn't want him to know I knew. It was still too soon, and just because he was acting different now didn't mean it would always be this way. I had to tread lightly.

I drove away and headed to his place. He still bunched up against the car door and looked out of the window. The way he always did when getting in my car.

"Jarell, guess what?"

"Hmm?"

"I'll be dancing with Chris Brown at the Staples Center for his Christmas concert coming up. I just got the news today," I said. I was happier to share this news than it being my birthday. For some reason, I felt like if I told him that it was my birthday, he wouldn't give a shit.

"That's cool," he said. See? Leave it to him to respond so dry with little emotion.

"Yeah, it is! I'd love for you to help and keep me sharp by dancing with me some time. I've never seen anyone dance like you. Honestly, you might give Chris Brown a good run for his money."

He didn't say anything. In fact, it seemed like he blushed because he lowered his head so that I couldn't see anything at all.

"So what do you say? You gonna help me out?"

"I'll think about it."

"Okay. Better than a no."

The rest of the car ride was a peace that neither of us felt the need to break. I pulled up to his house, and this time, the little girl from the last couple of times made it out of the house and into the dark to greet Jarell, yelling his name out as usual. Did she always sit at the window waiting for him? How was it that she always knew when he'd arrive?

"Kylah! Kylah, I know that you didn't just go out there in the dark!" I heard a woman's voice scream. I assumed it was his mother, and Jarell shook his head. I laughed. Next thing I knew, the little girl was at Jarell's car door, ignoring whatever her mother told her.

"Relly, you're finally home!" she said, jumping up and down in front of him once he was out. "I'm scared, Relly. All the lights are off."

I looked over at the front of his house, and it was pitch black. My heart broke. Damn, it was dark like this the last time I dropped him off. *Their electricity is really cut off… and has been for a while…*

"Shh. Don't talk about that. It took me a while to come home this time, huh?" he asked, and she put her little hand into his.

He didn't say thank you for the ride again as Kylah walked him towards the house just yapping away at him about her day and what new doll she wanted for Christmas. I was amazed at Jarell's patience and genuine love for her. A side of him I wished I could see more often.

His mother was on the porch now looking at Kylah like she was ready to pop her for not listening but rolled her eyes and opted not to once she passed her into the house. Instead, his mother pulled Jarell in for a hug and kissed his forehead. He accepted it with no hesitation and seemed to exchange words with her. Then, she looked up at me with squinted eyes. I waved to acknowledge her.

She must've told Jarell to go into the house because he disappeared inside when she ran towards my car. My heart started beating fast. I wasn't at all prepared to meet family. *Too soon, too soon!*

She clearly had no bra on as her breasts bounced up and down from jogging in the thin, oversized gown and slippers that she had on, and her hair was slicked back into a messy bun. I thought about my own mother. She wouldn't have dared done anything like this in public. *Over her fucking dead body.* I didn't even think I ever saw my mom without a bra. So seeing who I assumed to be Jarell's mom do something like this was actually refreshing. Liberating, and you could tell she didn't care. Could tell she was a free spirit.

Once she was at the window of my car, it was confirmed that she was Jarell's mom. Jarell looked so much like her that it was scary. But the other little girl didn't look as much like the two of them, so, who was she?

"Hey," she said, catching her breath. "Here's ten dollars. Thanks for bringing my son home."

I just looked at her. I didn't accept. I wouldn't accept.

"Ma'am, you don't have to do this. It's really my pleasure," I said, but she dropped it into my car anyway.

"No really. Take it. You don't know how much this means to me. This has never happened before where my son lets someone take him home. I don't have a car and haven't had one for a while. I can't pick him up myself, so he will walk miles instead of getting a ride or taking the bus. Thank you. I appreciate it."

"No problem. Just... don't give me money again," I laughed in a warm way. She did too.

"Don't wish something you'll regret." She smiled, and then ran back into the house, closing me off from their world.

I sighed. I would love to get to know her more. She seemed sweet and way more open than Jarell. Even given their current situation. It just made me even more curious. I wondered how I could be of help.

Without taking another moment to sit outside Jarell's home, I drove off in exhaustion, now thinking about if I was going to tell my mother the great news about the Chris Brown concert. In the end, I decided not to tell her at all. She needed to understand that throwing all the things she did for me in my life, which was what she was supposed to do as a mother, in my face wasn't going to fly. And it didn't mean that I couldn't do shit on my own. And I think by not telling her, she will have learned her lesson.

Chapter Eighteen

After a long and stressful day of shopping, I had found the one. The ultimate Homecoming dress and shoes for my last Homecoming dance that would shut the party down. Not too much skin, but it wasn't modest either. The back was opened, and the front was skintight, stopping just short of my knees. It was the perfect sequined dress to woo a guy like Mike.

At home, now to get ready for the night, I stood in the mirror fixing my hair into a nice pin up bun and slicking down my edges when my mother stopped at my bedroom doorway. She looked me up and down without expression. I tried not to tense up or feel like she judged my dress. Besides, she and I hadn't been in the best of places either since the football fiasco.

"Why you looking at me like that?" I asked.

"Just observing. You look like you're about to find you a whole new man at Homecoming. Or a sugar daddy," she said, turning her head away from me.

"I'm going with Mike."

"Oh? That's interesting."

"Yeah, it is. I'd still like to know what you said to him on the day of that football game since you keep telling me that it really doesn't matter. He won't tell me anything when I ask him about it. That'd be even more interesting."

"I just told him to stop being a baby and make it right with you. Someone had to say it, and it was clear that it wasn't going to be you. Like I said, I almost have to do everything for you to make anything happen."

For some reason, she saw that as an invitation to come into my room and sit on the bed.

"I don't know why you're mad at me for telling the truth. Mike is a great guy for you, but the both of you need to quit the mess. Money, mind, and the man. You two are perfect for one another and I don't understand why the both of you have struggled for this long."

"Maybe it's not for you to understand, Ma," I said, finally perfecting my hair. I stuffed my small formal purse with cash and my school ID.

"As long as you're living under my roof, it is."

"Whatever you say," I said, walking away from her and into the living room. I was already through with her. I was glad Mike had texted me to let me know that he was right around the corner.

Unfortunately, my mother followed, but I already had her canceled the moment I scrolled through SnapChat on my phone. I just didn't want to be bothered with her shit.

"Well... you have fun tonight, Jade. That's all I want to say."

My eyes slowly moved from my phone to her face. For the first time ever, she seemed sincere.

"Thank you." I blinked.

The doorbell rang. I still looked at her in shock, but that look changed to "please get lost." She wished for me to have fun, so there wasn't much else for her to say or much reason for her to stick around. I didn't need any confrontation between her and Mike on an important night like this. Well, it was an important night for me. She didn't get the hint, no matter how long I stared at her, so I just let it go and opened the door for him.

And *damn*. I could have nearly peed.

Mike always looked edible, but tonight, it was on ten. He had a fresh new taper hair cut with his curls tamed to perfection. His teeth were extra white, lips looked extra soft, and his fitted suit wrapped around his thin frame perfectly.

I must've swooned hard because he blushed and then looked up at me with knowing eyes, flirting back with a subtleness that made something inside of me purr. Panties might have come off if my momma hadn't been stupid enough to stand there.

"Hey," I said. Sheepish.

"Sup shorty. You ready to go?"

"Yeah. Come in for a second? I need to get my shoes on, and then I'll be ready."

"Sure thing."

He cautiously stepped inside moving no further than the foyer and leaned against the door after I closed it. I didn't want to make the situation more awkward by telling him to come in and sit down on the couch, so I hurried to my closet for my shoes.

Much to my demise, it took literally five seconds for my mom to say something to him, and that was about the time it took for me to come back and monitor it.

"It's been a while, Mike," my mother said, coolly. She was sitting on the couch in front of her ever-burning fireplace with her legs crossed and glared at him.

"Hasn't been that long," he responded.

"Hmm. Did my daughter have to ask you out tonight?" she asked.

I sat down to quickly strap up my shoes before this got any worse.

"No, she didn't."

"Mmm. Surprising. How'd you ask her?"

Come on, stupid shoe, I thought to myself, struggling to put the latch in the small hole.

"Didn't have to. We know what it is."

"Well, if you knew what it was, you would've come to wish my daughter a happy birthday on Wednesday, ain't that right?"

"Alright! Let's go," I said, finally getting the buckle right and stood up, almost falling over. I damn near sprinted to Mike while grabbing my formal jacket off the hook and led him to the door. That gave absolutely no time for my mother to respond.

"Yeah, let's go," Mike said with snark. I pinched him in the arm on our way out. He knew better than to fuel those flames. Especially knowing that Janet always had the last word.

Goodness. This wasn't good. If Mike and I were going to have a future together, their relationship needed some serious repairing.

Once we were clear outside and away from her, I looked him upside the head.

"What?" he asked with a bewildered look.

"Why would you even do that?"

"Man, I ain't finna let your mom run over me like that. She be wildin'," he said.

"I know but let me handle her. You don't have to make the relationship between y'all worse," I said, and we started walking towards what looked like someone else's car that he'd been driving. It was a sharp, black Jeep Wrangler. We were definitely about to turn some heads rollin' up in this. Just how we liked it.

"Whatever you say, shorty. Aye, you like this whip though?" he asked, opening the front door for me like the gentleman I always knew he could be.

"Yeah, whose is it?"

"It's my Uncle's. He let me borrow it tonight."

"Oh word? That's wassup. It's nice. It's the latest one?"

"You already know." He licked his lips and rubbed his hands together.

"Cool! So where we meeting up with Laurie and Martell?" I asked.

"Man, that nigga said that he want some alone time with her, so we just gonna head to the joint. You cool with that?" he asked, leaning on the car.

I huffed. I already knew what was going down, so I anticipated that I'd be hearing a story Monday morning about how she had lost her virginity and how good or bad it was. Knowing her, she'll be talking the entire lunch period.

"Yeah, I'm okay with it. You think they're... you know..."

He laughed.

"Knowing that nigga, he wouldn't waste any time."

"I agree."

With that, we drove off and headed to the school. The car ride was quiet with us in our own thoughts, which I was glad for because it gave me some time to think about how I wanted to deal with Mike for the rest of the night. Especially since he promised that we'd talk.

I checked the car clock, and it was already nine thirty; the dance started at eight. The parking lot was packed, so it was a nice way to be fashionably late and to also walk in with Mike to let bitches know that I was still the one who ran this show. Besides, now I was about to execute my plan. We weren't going to be in this dance very long. My plan was to stay in there for maybe about twenty to thirty minutes, and then let him know to head back out to the car so that we could talk like he promised. I just hoped that he didn't get too preoccupied. We had a pretty good DJ, so it wasn't far-fetched for anybody to get caught up with dancing.

"Ready to head in?" he asked the moment he was parked.

"Of course."

With my arm wrapped around his, we walked inside the school. The ladies wore super cute dresses this year, which surprised me, and the fellas looked way more handsome in their suits. Everyone was having a good time from the looks of it.

Still locked arms, Mike and I made our way deeper into the crowd of the party, and that's when everyone started giving us stares. Especially the girls. I just wiggled my fingers, waving at them all as we walked down the gym line. *Pure envy*. I loved it.

"Where're we going?" I asked.

"To my niggas," Mike said, and I assumed that was either his basketball team or our friends on D-Block. It was both. Everyone was in a small little crowd huddled up, dancing and laughing. Once he appeared, they acknowledged us with a warm welcome. Laurie was in the crowd as well, but she didn't look drunk or wasted. *Thank God.*

"Hey, Laurie," I said, still holding on to Mike. He didn't seem to mind. Matter of fact, it appeared like he enjoyed me being the trophy on his arm.

"Hey! Oh my God, you two are so cute! I'm so happy you came together!" she squealed.

Mike and I both looked at each other awkwardly, and I laughed. I let go of his arm, and we separated to do our own thing. I needed to know the tea about her and Martell. If anything had happened.

"Hey, so I thought we were meeting up to walk into the dance together?" I asked Laurie once we were away from everybody and semi one on one.

"Yeah, well Martell wanted some alone time."

She had a sneaky little smirk; a story to tell was written all over her face.

"What happened?" I gave her a side glance.

"Nothing major. You know… just a little boob action that's all. We hadn't gone all the way. I plan to tonight, though."

"Do your parents know you're with him?"

"God, hell no. They think I'm with Samantha. We haven't been friends since Sophomore year, but they think we still are."

"What if they find out?"

"I'll deal with that when the time comes. I see you and Mike got your shit together, huh?"

"Not quite. I'm actually going to pull him outside to talk in a minute. Girl. He showed up on my doorstep looking so fine, I thought I was about to strip at the front door."

"Hey, you might wanna get a little action tonight as well."

"I doubt it," I said, staring him up and down. I couldn't lie. With the way he was looking tonight, I wasn't in any position to be ruling out that possibility.

"Yeah right. We'll see about that."

Laurie and I gossiped some more and mingled with our friend group as the night progressed. A few girls tried to shoot their shot with Mike, but he turned them down without even mentioning my name. See. He was always so smooth and intentional and just… *ugh*. There was no way that I could leave this night without making it right. Making us right. The more I stared at him throughout the night, swooning over him, the more impatient I became. The plan was at minimum, twenty minutes. It really was. I only made it to fifteen.

"Hey." I walked up and whispered in his ear. A part of me wondered if that triggered something inside of him because it wasn't just some normal "hey."

"Sup?" He turned towards me with a low gaze.

"Can we talk outside for a bit? It's kind of getting hot and crowded in here, and I want some fresh air. And also, to talk alone with you."

Tilting his head to the side, he seemed to toy with the idea since he was having fun with his boys. In the end, he did agree, and the both of us walked outside together. I gave Laurie a sneaky wink on our way out, and she giggled.

The moment we were outside the dance, Mike unexpectedly grabbed me by the waist and pulled me closer to him, kissing on my neck. I screamed out in laughter.

"Boy don't be doing that! You scared me!"

"Aye. I just wanna let you know how good you look tonight," he whispered in my ear.

And Lord. When I tell you that I felt tingly all over... I felt like I wasn't in my own body.

"Well, I did it just for you," I confessed.

"Oh word?" he said with a raised eyebrow.

"Word. Let's head to your car."

"Aight, bet. So you looking all good just for me, tonight? You must want something," he said.

"Yeah. I want to talk just like you promised."

A twisted grin crept across my face, nullifying his suggestion that I was after something else other than trying to make it right with him. I didn't want to send the wrong impression. Besides, my dress was a way to lure him to talk. Not to actually have sex. I didn't even think we were in the right position to have sex, as much as I desired it. We were so hot and cold that it wouldn't have been a wise decision anyway.

We made it to his truck, and the both of us sat in the back seat. Now, I was nervous. My plan had worked to perfection so far, and now that I had him, what was I supposed to do? What was I going to say?

"So. What's up?" he asked.

I swallowed. I had no idea how to begin this conversation without pushing him away or creating another argument.

"You're the one who promised that we'd talk," I said.

"Yeah, because that's what you wanted."

"So you're only doing it for me and not also yourself?"

"No, I mean, it'll be good for the both of us."

"Okay, so then let's talk about us."

"What about us?"

"Well, first. I asked my mom about the incident on the football field. She finally told me what she said. I am so sorry about her. I just don't want you to think that I put her up to it as I've been telling you for the past month," I said.

"To be honest, I didn't know what to think. All I knew was that she came out of left field on some bullshit."

"I know. Forget her, I don't want to talk about her. I just want us to go back to the old us. Where we are true friends, care about each other, don't argue as much, and you know... like we were dating. Right now, I feel like everything is forced."

He sat and reflected before responding with a sigh.

"Yeah. I miss the way we were too, shorty."

"Do you? I just feel like things have been so awkward. And you've been just a serious asshole with me sometimes, and ... I don't know. I just want to move forward."

"I mean, I really ain't start being like that until I heard about you and that Jarell nigga."

"See, that's the thing. What you're hearing isn't really what it is."

"There's gotta be some truth to that. Why you got people walking around talking about you taking up for a bum ass nigga like that? Come on, Jade. You know that me and that nigga don't even compare. How would you like it if I was rumored with some bum ass girl?"

"That's the thing, Mike. You weren't rumored. You were caught at a party with bum ass girls. By me! And when I wanted to address it, you flipped it on me, talking about how I was messing around on you with Jarell!"

"But the difference between that and this situation was that I owned up to it and apologized. I made it right by checking them girls. I said sorry. I was drunk. You didn't apologize at all. You started pointing the finger and shit."

I dropped my head. He did apologize. But that didn't make what he did okay. And that's what I needed him to realize. What I had done with Jarell was essentially nothing.

"Yeah, because you actually did it in my face, Mike. I hadn't done anything with Jarell."

"Who is this nigga anyway, and what does he have to do with you?" he asked.

I took a beat. I didn't want to give away a thing about Jarell's business to Mike. Hell, I didn't even want to talk about Jarell at all because he was honestly my little secret, and for good reason. I didn't want anyone knowing about our communication with each other.

"He has nothing to do with me. I just stuck up for him in the hallway. That's it. That's all. I think you're making this bigger than what it needs to be."

"Alright. I'll take your word for it. But the fact remains that if I catch you with that nigga, something ain't gon' be pretty."

I laughed and pushed his shoulder.

"I kinda like it when you're aggressive like that."

"Yeah. And I like it when you look at me the way you do," he said with a raspy voice, and pulled my chin towards him.

And just like that, our lips met. His lips were just as soft as I imagined them to be when I opened my front door. There was nothing in this world that I would rather have than for bitches to be jealous and never have this type of intimacy with him.

What started as a soft kiss turned into a full blown, heated make out session with my back flat across the backseat of his uncle's Jeep. An achy tension between my legs appeared, and I didn't know what to do or say to him about it, so I just kept kissing. The more I ignored and continued kissing, the more intense it got and the hotter my skin became.

I got even hotter when Mike's hands roamed up my dress, cuffed my breasts, and fondled them. I moaned in excitement.

"You want this, huh?" he whispered in my ear, and I moaned again helplessly.

Then, I heard it. And then I saw it. The condom.

He took it out of his pants pocket and ripped it open in one tear with his teeth. *Oh shit.* This was getting too real. We started kissing again, but this time, my mind was running sprints.

What if I wasn't good enough? I'm not ready! We're not ready. It was only one talk to make it right, and we're already about to do it? Having sex in a car? For my first time? Well, it's his first time too. What if the condom broke? If I get caught having sex in this car, I'm a hoe. I'll be called a hoe by everyone. What if he'd think that I'm a hoe too? What if I get pregnant?

"We should probably stop," I said, raising up from the seat and wiping my mouth of our mixed juices. I couldn't take any more of my thoughts interfering.

"What? Why? Girl, you trippin. You know you wanna give it up," he said as he exhaled, and then dove his face right into the crevice of my neck again, digging his teeth in for a hickey.

My stomach fluttered and my mind raced for the right words to say, but it was just too much. I dreamed of such moments with Mike. I didn't see myself having sex with anyone else. But it had to be different than this. I couldn't go out like this.

"Wait, Mike. Stop. Please," I whimpered, and gently moved his body away.

He pulled back, giving me an impatient look.

"I-I just... I don't want to be some cheap fuck in your car, Mike. If we are losing our virginities to one another, I want it to be a little more special than this."

He growled in frustration, rolled into the adjacent seat, and stared at the ceiling of the car.

"You've gotta be fucking kidding me," he finally said.

"I'm not! Why can't we take this somewhere else and make it real?"

"Why can't we just do it now? My dick is rock hard with a condom opened and you're talking about making shit special. You and I both know we got some needs. You know you want this," he said, biting his lip.

He rolled back on top of me, kissing my neck with his hands wandering up my thighs, then higher up towards my crotch, his hands grazing the outside of my vagina. I stopped him with full force and moved his hands off me. I couldn't allow this to happen. I was more than a fuck in the car.

"I said no! Why wouldn't you want to take this home, or to a hotel or something? What am I to you?"

"Because I don't care, Jade! Fucking in the car is no different than fucking in a hotel! That whole virginity thing is overrated!" he yelled, punching the seat next to him.

Wow. This man really didn't care. Didn't care about my feelings, didn't care about what I wanted, and frankly, didn't care enough to respect me if he thought that he could have sex with me in someone else's car, taking my virginity along with his bad decisions.

At this point, I hadn't felt any more done with Mike than I felt right now. For him to brush something off as special as this was to me wasn't okay. We were friends, yes. He cared about me sometimes, yes. But I could see now that I was nothing more than the rest of the girls when it came down to sex. He was letting this sexual tension get the best of him, and he was changing – he damn near raped me. This wasn't the Mike I always knew. Or maybe, this was the Mike I didn't allow myself to see.

"I have a question," I said.

"If it ain't 'can we do it now,' then I don't want to hear it."

"Are you even a virgin? Because the way you're acting right now got me questioning," I asked.

With his head resting against the seat, he turned and gave me a look that said nothing, but yet, told me everything.

"You aren't, are you?"

"Why does it even matter?"

"Who was it?"

"I never gave you an answer. So what the hell you mad for?"

"Your silence tells me everything I need to know, Mike!" I screamed, punching him in the arm.

"It doesn't matter! I'm not a virgin, and ain't nothing you can do to bring it back!"

"Wow. Fuck you. Take me home. Now."

"Are you serious, Jade? You just gonna leave me hanging like that because I lost my virginity to someone else when we ain't even together? I swear, you have your head so far up your ass about yourself that you think niggas owe you everything!"

"You lied to me!"

"No, I didn't. You just can't accept the truth."

"Take me home! Take me home, *now*!"

"Fine. I'll take your overdramatic ass home," he mumbled and pushed the car door open. Then, he got in the driver's seat slamming the door shut and left me in the back.

My eyes burned with tears ready to fall, but I kept them away. He wasn't going to see me like this. I wouldn't ever give him the satisfaction of getting me as upset as he got me on the day of the college party. But damnit, I felt so much worse than that day. This was icing on the cake, and in my mind, I was officially done with him. There was nothing he could really do to re-earn my respect and move forward after this kind of dishonesty. He'd need to do some major ass kissing if he wanted to even be acknowledged.

The entire ride home, I had to regulate my breathing before I took my heel off and whacked him in the head with it. I looked at my phone, and it was literally only eleven o'clock. I was eighteen. A senior. I should have been walking into the front door past midnight after partying with my friends, but here I was.

Once he pulled up, I hopped right on out without a word, and he drove right on off without a care in the world. He didn't even see if I'd make it into the house okay.

One thing was for sure. I didn't want to go through the front to face my mom. Matter fact, I didn't want to go inside at all. So I just stood on the porch thinking of my next move. In the end, I resolved to go to Jarell's. I didn't know the outcome of doing something like this, but it couldn't be any worse than what's already happened.

Chapter Nineteen

WEST FIFTY-SIXTH STREET. Here I parked. Boldly. Right in front of Jarell's small stucco home at nearly midnight. His home looked as reticent as one would expect. Jarell's neighborhood wasn't the best place to be at night since it was usually populated with drunks or weirdos walking around, but I was desperate. I wished to be anywhere else but home. Anywhere other than with Mike. And somewhere where I could release. At this point, that was with Jarell. As crazy at that sounded.

When I turned my car off and peered at the house, all of the lights were off. Pitch black. It then dawned on me that his little sister revealed that their electricity was off the last time I dropped him off. Must've still been their reality. I really hoped someone was awake.

I inhaled and got out the car. My hands were shaking, and my breathing picked up pace each step I took towards his home. I closed my eyes and tried to think of something quick to say if someone had opened the door.

How should I knock?

Should I knock softly? Should I knock with urgency? No... in this neighborhood, that's a sign of a threat.

Knock on the damn door, Jade!

I gave the door a light rap that was short, audible, and quick. I stepped back and held my breath in anticipation. I looked behind me to make sure no one was watching and whipped my head when I heard the doorknob turn.

My heart felt like it had stopped beating.

The door groaned its way opened a little bit, and Jarell's mom peeked through the crack in confusion. I leaned my head to the side to see more of her.

"Can I help you?" she asked with much attitude.

"Um... hi. Is Jarell home?"

"And you are?"

"Jade. The one who's been dropping him off here from school."

Her eyes widened with relief, and she pulled the door open fully so I could see her. She wore the same pajama gown that she had on the last time I saw her as her nipples poked proudly through it. Her hair stuck out like a porcupine on one side with the other side matted.

Yeah, she looked a little tattered, but she gave me the warmest smile I could've ever gotten from anyone. Jarell's mom was just an adorable, short little lady with a cute spirit. Jarell was so lucky.

"Oh, hey, honey. You left Homecoming? It's fifty degrees. You must be cold with that dress on, right?" she asked and attempted to fix her hair.

"Not really. My jacket is pretty warm."

"Well I mean... I guess you can come on in anyway. Don't want to leave you outside," she said with hesitance as she looked behind herself. "Let me light some candles real quick."

I reluctantly stepped inside as his mother made her way through the darkness and lit quite a few candles on their coffee and end tables. Wow. This totally confirmed their electricity being out.

Once the place was adequately lit, I gazed around and instantly felt out of place. Like I had overstepped a ton of boundaries, especially in such a rough time in their lives.

Little toys and barbies scattered the living room floor like landmines, and a thick blanket lay wrinkled on top of the couch. An old, antique, rickety box TV with an antenna sat across the couch.

"I'm so sorry. I had fallen asleep out here," Jarell's mom said as she scrambled to clear the blanket. "And Kylah will be cleaning this mess tomorrow morning."

I nodded as I continued to take in the environment. The walls were a little dirty and plain. And I could have probably touched the ceiling without even jumping. It was stuffy to the point where I could hardly breathe. The couch was outdated and looked as if it had been pre-used several times before finding its home here.

My goodness. This was nothing like home.

Now, I understood how Jarell felt whenever he'd get into my car.

"Make yourself at home. Take a seat before I call Jarell in."

I didn't want to be rude and say no, so I took a seat on the couch and sank in it to the point where I didn't think I'd be getting up when it was time to leave. I hoped to not be sitting here long. I felt like I was going to catch lice on this thing.

"Jarell! Jarell, baby can you come on out?"

After about ten seconds, Jarell strolled out of his room with his hoodie and sweatpants. His groggy eyes and head were uncovered, the first time that I'd ever seen him without wearing both. I was mesmerized. His beauty was really something serious.

"Hey, there's someone here to see you," she said softly, walking over to him and kicking away any toys from his potential path.

"Someone to see me?" He frowned.

"Jade is here to see you. She's sitting on the couch."

His frown deepened.

"What the hell are you doing here?" he blurted out, and a pang hit my chest. No one ever addressed me in such a disgusting way. I didn't know if he meant it, or if he was surprised, but I had to remember who Jarell was. That I was building trust, and one good moment with him wasn't going to guarantee peachiness moving forward.

"Jarell! Apologize to her. She came to see you at this time of the night, and you should be thanking her for taking you home all the time," his mom scolded him with her arms crossed. "Jade, has he been thanking you?"

"Um..." I started to lie, but Jarell interrupted me.

"Ma, it don't matter. Jade, what are you doing here?" he asked again, this time with less brute.

"Can we meet outside for a second? I really need to ask you something."

"For what? Isn't it Homecoming? Why aren't you there?"

"Jarell!" His mom yelled this time.

"What? I'm just asking!" he said, throwing his arms in the air in frustration.

"Cut it out!" she said through clenched teeth.

"Fine. Let me go put my shoes on," he mumbled, retreated into his room, and shut the door.

Shaking her head, his mother turned towards me and gave me an apologetic look. I gave her a half smile and shrugged.

"I am sorry about my son. I don't know why he's so rude."

"Don't worry about it. I'm used to it."

"That's not something you should get used to. Jarell knows better than to treat a lady like that. You see, I've been trying to get him to get out more and to talk to his peers. He's so lonely. I worry about him."

I didn't know what to say. My heart just hurt for him. Not only did he behave this way in school, but also at home, and the person who loved him the most even felt the ramifications of his behavior.

"He's mostly in his room making origami or sitting at his open window, thinking for hours. Sometimes, Kylah will get him to play with her, but for the most part, he's so secluded. Sometimes I drive him out to the countryside when I had my car and let him explore and hike because he likes that, but he only wants to do it alone. I'm so glad you came." She touched my thigh in a motherly way that surprisingly made me feel warm. Her touch alone made my body relax a little bit. I placed a hand over hers to let her know her words were appreciated. I still didn't know what to really say. I was learning more about Jarell than anything. I wanted her to talk more.

"Is Kylah your daughter?" I asked.

"Yeah, that's my baby." She smiled. "My cute and full of sass baby. She just turned five a two months ago."

"Aww, well Jarell's being a great big brother when he plays with her."

"Yeah, he takes a lot of pride in being her big brother. It's the only time I really see him come alive. Even when she wants to play barbies, he hates that of course, but I see my son come alive with her in ways that I used to see, but don't anymore."

"Yeah. I'd like to see him come alive more as well."

"Maybe you can be the one to bring it out of him," she said.

I opened my mouth to respond, but Jarell came out of his room with additional attire – sunglasses and his hood. His mom gave me a glare that not only suggested our conversation was over, but also one of hopelessness.

Man.

If I could feel anything intangible from this house, the invisible weight of despair literally pressed on my shoulders. No matter how warm, sweet, and friendly his mother was, there was something going on behind her smile that surfaced every now and then for the little snippets of time I spoke with her. It was a suffocating feeling I didn't know what to do with.

What was their story?

I desperately wanted to know, but I didn't want to feel entitled to their business either. I just wanted to be there for Jarell. And that's it.

"Hey, you ready to head outside?" I asked him, struggling to rise from the couch but eventually did.

He didn't say anything. He just walked past me and went straight out the door. I looked at his mom, and she just shook her head and turned away from me.

"Thanks for inviting me in, Ms...?"

"Ms. Hendricks," she said. I felt awful. Her body emanated such angst, and at that point, I just wanted to get out of there.

"Thanks Ms. Hendricks."

Without another word exchanged, I walked out of the door to Jarell who was sitting on his porch. I shut the front door and sat down next to him.

"So what are you doing here?" he asked. "At this time of the damn night? At my house? We don't let people inside our house. No one."

"Well first, your mom apparently does. And two, I had a rough night. I really need a release, and I'm... I'm asking you to dance with me. Please."

He pondered, and I was okay with that. It gave me time for me to reflect on what just happened over the last fifteen minutes.

I couldn't believe their living conditions. I now understood Jarell's clothing and their repetition. The only nice thing he owned, that I rarely saw him wear, was his old Crenshaw jacket. My mind ran ragged, trying to think of a way that I could help his family without being too forward. Without being offensive.

As we sat in thought for a while, suddenly, he stood from the porch and walked towards the gate.

"Where you going?" I asked.

"Follow me."

With hesitation, I followed by his side. I felt more of a need to protect him than anything as he traveled down the street. But when I saw his confidence, I let go of the fear.

In fact, watching Jarell maneuver up close and personal was mind boggling. He often fluttered his hands out to the side like I'd always seen before, and I didn't know what that did for him, but it was a clear necessity. The first time I was about to yell at him to watch his step from the curb, I didn't even have the chance because he was already down and on his way forward. He dragged his feet when he walked, and it bothered me at first, but I got used to it. I now understood why his shoes were on their last days.

Sometimes he would touch things to feel his way around such as streetlight poles or stop signs. At no point did he raise his head. He kept it down, and he never spoke a word. It was cool because I enjoyed observing. The whole thing was very interesting, especially without his use of a blind cane. I wondered what his mother truly thought about him navigating the streets by himself like this. There was no way in hell I would let my child just walk alone while blind. But that was neither here nor there. He probably told his mother that he needed some independence.

We walked for about ten or fifteen minutes, then he finally led me to an old park with a couple of swing sets, slides, and an open concrete space in the middle with a couple of streetlights surrounding it.

Without further ado, Jarell went to the concrete and began to dance like I had never been walking or standing with him. He had completely canceled me out, and I didn't know if I felt grateful for that or not. I mean, I guess it was great because I didn't have to feel any sense of awkwardness about how we were going to start dancing together.

Deciding not to make it a big deal, I started dancing, and it was just as magical as the last time, but we danced separate from each other for the most part. I found it much more difficult to dance alone in silence, so I didn't and couldn't understand how Jarell did it. When we finally were tired out and could no longer breathe, the both of us sat down on the pavement and caught our breath peacefully.

"Jarell, you've gotta tell me how you started dancing. How'd you get so good? Especially without music?" I asked. He shrugged in return.

"It's just something that I do and something that I'm always gonna do."

"Yeah, but... how'd you get *this* good? You study people?"

"I've studied Mike and Breezy in the past. I also just have a good ear too. It pays to listen, even if it's just to the wind around you," he said.

This is what I loved about dancing with him, too. It opened him up in ways that I wouldn't be able to do, like dance was the key to his communication. He didn't always give super comprehensive answers, but it was something. He talked. And that's all that mattered to me.

"That's fascinating. I really admire Janet, Teyana Taylor, and

Laurie Ann. They're some of my inspirations.

"I can tell. Never had someone keep up with me before, so it's cool."

"Yeah. Thanks," I said, wanting to ask him how he knew if he couldn't see, but I didn't want to go there. "So, I'm going to ask you again. Are you going to come to my studio? I would really love to have you and for the lead choreographer to check you out. Jarell, she's got to see your work."

"We'll see." He shrugged. "How was Homecoming?"

I see what he did there but decided not to fight it. With Jarell, you really had to be careful picking your battles.

"It was terrible," I said. The memories of Mike and his bullshit tonight flooded my head again. I just wanted to forget about it because at this point, I was forgetting about him.

"Why?"

"Because. Just the people there. It was all bad," I lied badly, and he could tell because he made a little sound in his throat.

"Them your people. Don't understand how it could've been so bad."

I puckered my lips and thought of something. Maybe if I was just honest and opened up to him, it would encourage him to do so as well. That was going to be a major challenge, considering I wasn't the vulnerable type, but he had to see beyond that part of me. I didn't want to be like my mother anymore, who was impossible to see. She was as non-transparent as it came, and after realizing how hurt I began to feel after every interaction with her, I wanted to be different. I wanted Jarell to be the first person to see me for me. And I wanted to be the first to see who he was.

"Alright, alright. Fine. You got me. The short version of the truth is because Mike tried to have sex with me, and I said no. Then he got all asshole about it and took me home. So I got really mad with how he treated me, and I needed to just blow off some steam with a good dance."

He tilted his head slightly with a confused frown.

"Why didn't you do it?"

I blinked.

"Because. Well... a few things. We aren't ready. I wasn't ready. And the way he was going about it was just... it was really messed up. You can tell he really doesn't care about me."

"What does it mean for you to be ready when it comes to someone like him?"

My eyes grew as wide as saucers. Didn't think I'd get a question like that from Jarell. At all. He was so calm, and it didn't seem to faze or embarrass him that he asked either. Wonder what made him so interested?

"Just feeling comfortable with the person and feeling like they would treat me special. Mike didn't do that tonight. I don't think he ever will."

"Why? That's your boyfriend, ain't it?"

"Hmph. No. To be completely honest, we haven't been together since Junior year. It's just... it's just a friend thing that we've had going on."

"So you been putting on a front for everybody..."

"Basically."

"Why?"

"Don't know at this point. It's a waste of time, and I'm just ready to move on. It's really because he was someone that could keep up with me and was on my level, but I feel like I'm chasing a nigga who ain't interested, I ain't down with that."

"So, you never did it with him?"

"No. It would've been my first time, and he just was looking for his. He only cared about himself. Let's just put it that way."

He nodded without much other expression. *Ha. Damn.* I would never be sitting in front of anyone else, not even Laurie, spilling out my truth about Mike like this. It honestly felt liberating but scary all at the same time. Honestly? I wouldn't rather have it any other way. Especially knowing my truth would be safe with Jarell.

"Have you ever had sex, Jarell?" I blurted out without thinking and instantly wanted to take it back. It was way too personal, and I just wanted to kick myself. Just because I was spilling about stuff like this didn't mean that he was going to. There was no way he was going to answer that question without some sort of snark. Maybe even snap on me for asking. *How could I be so stupid?*

But to my surprise, he laughed. Heartily. For the first time, I saw teeth.

He had the most perfect smile.

There was a little gap in between his teeth, and he may have needed braces, but it suited him so well that it didn't even matter. My goodness. He was more beautiful than I had first considered. I didn't know if he laughed because he was embarrassed at the question or if he actually thought it was funny, but who cares? He gave me a laugh, and it was the most treasured thing that I would keep in my heart and forever remember.

"What? It was just a question," I said, laughing away the anxiety.

"Why do you wanna know?" he asked.

"Because we were talking about it."

"But we were talking about you."

"So?"

He didn't say anything. He just had a lingering smile and looked at the ground.

"Oh, so you're not gonna answer that, huh?" I said, nudging him lightly.

"I didn't say anything."

"Exactly, that's the problem. Well, you don't have to answer. It was stupid of me to ask anyway. Why didn't you go to Homecoming? Aren't you coming back to school Monday?"

"Yeah. And I don't do dances."

"Why? You're a dancer."

"I hate people."

I smacked my lips and gave him a disbelieving glare.

"Really, Jarell? Dancing has nothing to do with people. Why do you walk around hating the world so much?"

"Because the world hates me."

I smacked my lips. He said that with so much conviction, and I could tell he truly believed it. From what I saw each day, I couldn't blame him for feeling that way.

"The world doesn't hate you, Jarell."

"Easy for you to say. What do you know?"

"I know because I don't. Your mom doesn't. For damn sure your sister doesn't. Listen. I know that I can be really annoying to you. I probably piss you off more than anything. But I want you to know that I'm here for you. I don't know if you've noticed yet, but no matter how bad you treat me, I keep coming back."

"Why?"

"I don't know. There's just something about you... I don't know. That makes me realize that I take a lot of shit for granted."

I didn't want to tell him what I had heard during my eavesdrop escapade the other day. Or that I actually did have a heart I've always wanted to show but didn't know how because I was trying to uphold this stupid image for myself that everyone had already bought into.

"Okay, and?"

"And so I want to make a promise. A promise to you," I said.

"A promise? To me? Shit. You're setting yourself up, ain't you?" he asked, raising an eyebrow.

"No, I'm actually dead ass serious, and I want you to hear me out."

"I'm listening."

"I want you to know that I'm here for you. I know I haven't given many reasons for you to believe me. Nor have we known each other long. But I serious. I'm here."

No response. I didn't expect one. I just wanted him to take it in. Now, I had to keep my word for real because who knows what Jarell was like at the core? Did he take things like this to heart? Did he care about anything I just said? Did he wear his heart on his sleeve and show if he'd be disappointed or elated if I followed through on this promise or not?

What I knew for sure was that he was going to test me in multiple ways. To see if I was real. And trust me. I didn't want to be some fake ass phony to someone like him. Because for Jarell, I knew deep down, the stakes were too high to be playing around with his emotions.

Now, was he going to continue being my secret? I didn't know. But all he needed to know was that I was here. And that I wasn't going anywhere. Not even on a love thing, but as a person. As a friend.

"I'll believe it when I see it," he finally spoke.

"You got my word."

Chapter Twenty

THE DAYS AFTER Thanksgiving leading into December were a blur with routine. I went to school, to cheerleading practice, and then left to find Jarell waiting for me in the parking lot. I dropped him off at home, went to the studio to practice, and woke up the next morning to repeat. I didn't talk to anyone much during transition times, nor was I interested. Laurie kept trying to get me alone so she could tell me her stories about Martell and everything that happened after Homecoming, but I wasn't even bothered with that.

The only thing I cared about was seeing Jarell at school again. He was back to his old ways of walking through the halls with his head down, following behind his special ed teacher during passing times. He was just as invisible as he was before he dropped out; no one noticed his absence, and no one noticed his return. It amazed me how he could move through the world so forgotten. Like the physical space he occupied had never been acknowledged and never will be.

So, any time I saw him in passing, I always stopped to say hi and ask how his day was going. No matter who was watching. At first, he didn't like it. Probably because it surprised him, or maybe because he was ashamed. But the more I did it, the more he warmed up. He'd give me a small, toothless smile and nod his head. Lately, he'd been saying hey in return. His hellos sounded more like gratitude than a greeting, and it broke my heart. It was hard keeping him a secret.

The more I interacted with Jarell, the more I felt done with Mike. I didn't realize how serious I was when I felt absolutely nothing any time I saw him at school or at cheerleading practices. To top it off, whenever we passed by each other in the halls, not a word was spoken. Not even a glance at one another. Soon enough, all the girls noticed that we weren't speaking, trading glances, or that we weren't anywhere near one another on D-Block.

And then the talk started to happen.

About how he dumped me, about how he cheated on me, about how I cheated on him, about how I wasn't giving up the pussy, and all this other nonsense that I just didn't even feed into. Laurie kept asking about what really happened, and I just shrugged every time she asked. Even my cheerleading team tried to get me to talk about it, but I wasn't interested, and my feelings weren't hurt. I was about to gain so much clout from being in Chris Brown's concert that this little school drama didn't matter anymore. All these other little girls could have him and whatever he was slanging.

Speaking of Chris Brown, today was the big day. I woke up bright and early on this Saturday morning to prepare for Chris' concert. The plan was to stop at the studio for a quick run through and then head down to the Staples Center. I hadn't even told my mother about this gig like I told myself I wouldn't, but now, it was time to.

Who I did intentionally invite, which would add an extra layer of salt to my mother's feelings, was her ex-fiancé' and my father figure, Corey. She was going to find out sooner or later, but I didn't care.

And most of all, I invited Jarell. Surprisingly, he accepted with a simple yes. Nothing more, nothing less. Although Jarell couldn't see, simply being backstage with the ability to meet a dancer he admired probably meant the world to him.

Packing my bag for the big day, I was all set and ready to go when I went into the kitchen and saw my mother making coffee. I hoisted my bag over my shoulder and swallowed. Even though I wanted to spite my mother, I was still nervous doing it.

"Hey," I called out.

She turned her head towards me.

"You're up early," she said.

"Yeah. Getting ready to head out."

"Where you going?"

"I'm performing as a lead dancer at Chris Brown's concert tonight so I'm gonna do a few run throughs to prepare."

That made her nearly spill her hot coffee onto her business pencil skirt.

"You're performing for who? Come again?" she asked with wide eyes.

"Chris Brown. His concert is tonight at the Staples Center. I'm performing as his lead dancer."

She set her cup down and gave me a long glare.

"Jade Anastasia. You weren't going to tell me something like that? You waited until the day of? Are you kidding me?" she said, now walking towards me, and I stood my ground. I wasn't going to let her intimidate me anymore.

"No games being played here," I responded with conviction, and at this point, she was right in front of me. Face to face. Nearly nose to nose. I knew what she was thinking, but she wouldn't dare.

With pursed lips, her eyes squinted, and she took one step back.

"Why didn't you tell me?"

"Because you walk around here thinking that you run my life. You take the credit for every little thing I do. I'm not letting you take this one, Janet," I said.

"Oh. So it's Janet, now?" She blinked.

"Yeah. That's how you've been acting lately. You haven't been acting like a mom."

Shaking her head, she pressed her lips thin. I was so nervous. I had never, ever stood up to my mother this boldly before.

"That's how you feel?" she asked.

"That's what I know."

She nodded slowly. I didn't know what was going on in her head, but she was too calm.

"Fine, little smart ass. I'll be a 'mom' and come support you. I was going to head to Las Vegas for the weekend to do some fashion stuff, but I'll cancel and come to your show. When is it?"

"Seven."

"Alright. I'll be there."

Nah. She was defeated too quickly. She had something up her sleeve, and if she had any kind of thought to ruin my performance, she had a whole nother thing coming. I wasn't playing around with something like this.

"What you trying to do?" I asked, giving her a side eye.

"What do you mean?"

"You backed down way too easy. I feel like something is up with you."

She laughed. Not a genuine one, but definitely something sneaky.

"I'm pissed right now. But I'm not trying to do anything. I'm going to come and support. I put too much work into you not to. This is the payoff for me too."

I rolled my eyes.

"Here's your ticket," I said, pulling out a front rower out of my bag and set it on the counter. "Later."

~~~

My makeup was flawless. My outfit sexy. And the thunderous crowd during the opening acts screamed relentlessly, so I almost couldn't even imagine what the crowd would be like when the main act came on, which was Chris. We had another hour before we were set to hit the stage, and Jarell sat in my dressing room with me since Chris allowed it. Jarell didn't get a chance to meet Chris yet, and I was super excited for him.

Although he didn't say it, Jarell's restrained excitement about meeting Chris was obvious since he talked with me more than usual in a happy mood. In addition, he wore clothes I had never seen him rock before. The hoodie and sunglasses were the same, but this time he sported some black fitted joggers and white low top shoes, which was much more presentable than his holey jeans and sole-ripped shoes. I wish he would ditch his hoodie, but that was going to be a challenge.

It was a waiting game for him to meet Chris, but eventually he was going to come inside to check on me as I was freshening up my makeup. Just as I was doing so, there was a knock at the door.

"Ooh, Jarell! It's Chris!" I whispered.

With a smile, he laid back on the sofa all cool and shit without speaking another word. It was such a front, but that was Jarell. At least he gave a smile.

"Come in!" I yelled out.
~~~

The door to my dressing room opened, and in walked someone who wasn't Chris.

It was my mother.

She had on the same pencil skirt business suit with that nasty, strict air that screamed arrogance. Nothing – not her hair, her outfit, her makeup – was out of place, and her prissy attitude was a perfect match. My heart started beating fast because I didn't expect her to come back here, especially since Jarell was in the room. I stood up, trying to figure out what the hell to do or say. *Who let her back here?*

"What are you doing here?"

"I wanted to say good luck before you head on stage. Is there a problem?" she asked.

I closed my eyes, rubbing my arm. "No. Thank you."

Then, she pointed at Jarell and scanned him up and down with obvious contempt. "Who's this?"

"This is Jarell. Jarell, this is my mother, Janet."

A part of me so badly wanted to tell her that it was none of her business and to get the hell out, but I didn't want to show Jarell just how damaged our relationship was becoming, especially since he had a great relationship with his mother.

Jarell rose up and walked towards us, and that was the biggest mistake he could've ever made. I just knew she was about to verbally insult him.

"Nice to meet you, Ms. Janet," he said politely and put his hand out for her to shake.

She stepped back in repulsion, glaring at his hand as if he had reached into a toilet and had feces to give her.

"Um, no. Disregard the handshake. It's okay. You aren't Jade's boyfriend, are you?"

"No. He's a friend," I spoke for him.

"Oh. Whew. Didn't think you'd be that stupid to date a bum. Well, I'm going to head out, now. Corey's out there surprisingly. You invited him and not me?"

"Listen, I'm not doing this with you right now," I said, waving her off, feeling disgusted.

"Hmm. Okay. I will go out and sit next to him and find out myself."

"Great."

"Well good luck to you," she said with her nose in the air without even acknowledging Jarell anymore. I tried to wrap my brain around everything that just happened and looked at him. His shoulders now sunk, and he looked towards the ground with his sunglasses. My God. How awful. Of course, she'd be the one to throw a wrench in a great day like this for Jarell.

"I'll see you after," I said, rushing her out and then closed the door in her face. I took a deep breath, and Jarell was already sitting back down on the sofa with an expression I failed to read.

"Jarell, don't worry about her. She's a little off."

"I see why you've been an asshole to people. Look who raised you."

"Yeah. Thankfully I think about the things I do and say, and I'm not so much like that anymore," I said, even though his words did hurt. But I had to continue to understand that I was once his enemy. That I had broken his trust long ago that he was trying to repair. I couldn't let words like that get to me because they were the truth.

The energy in the room fell from a high to a low with neither one of us saying much until another knock came at the door.

"Come in!"

The door slowly creaked open, and this time, it was who we

wanted to see in the first place.

"Hey, Chris," I said with a smile as he walked inside.

"What up girl, you looking good. Good to see you. You ready?" he said after licking his lips and pulled me in for a long hug that was almost sensual. It was interesting how the tables had turned. Just a month ago, he had skipped right over me like I didn't exist and now, he was nearly greeting me with as much passion as he greeted Alise. I call that the *Jade Effect!*

"Good to see you as well!"

"Who this?" Chris asked with a closed expression, but his tone suggested genuine curiosity. Jarell stuffed his hands into his pockets and looked away.

"Chris this is Jarell, one of my friends. He's here to attend the concert with me and hang out backstage. Jarell this is Chris Brown. I mean, you know Chris, Jarell," I said.

"Sup. Good to meet you, bruh," Chris said, offering his hand out for Jarell to shake up with him. When Jarell didn't accept it, I signaled to Chris that he was blind. Chris gave a big "aha" head nod in understanding.

"Thanks. It's nice to meet you too," Jarell said and put his own hand out. I smiled. Jarell was smart to do that. Chris acknowledged it and pulled him into a man hug.

"Chris, Jarell is a really, really dope dancer. Like no lie. It's crazy. You'd enjoy vibing with him, and he might give you a run for it. But I know he won't dance to show you because he's really shy."

Jarell smacked his lips, clearly pissed that I mentioned it, but I didn't care. I just nudged him with a smile, and eventually, a small smile lingered at the corners of his mouth.

"Oh word? Well let me know when you ain't so shy and I'll check you out. You're in for some good music tonight, though. I'm glad you came out. And your good friend here 'bout to kill this shit."

"Ha! You already know." I nodded with a smug grin.

"Let's do a quick run through. Nice and light. We're on in ten," Chris said.

"Let's do it."

"Good to meet you, Jarell, bruh."

Jarell nodded in respect and gave him the peace sign. And with that, we danced a light run through with the team, and Jarell stood quietly on the side and vibed out. He looked so cute over there in his own little world. An element of him that I rarely got to see.

After the quick run through, our crew and Chris all got together and prayed for a good performance, and then got hyped up, jumping up and down to get our energy flowing. This was it. This was the biggest performance of my life. This was about to put me on the map more than any cheerleading event I've ever done, any music video I'd been a part of, anything. I had to kill it. The future of my career lied in this performance.

"Hey Jade," Jarell called out to me just as I was about to run out on the stage.

"Yeah?" I turned my head.

"Good luck. You're gonna do great," he said, and that just made my entire day. He sounded so sincere, and for the first time, I felt Jarell's true heart. It was the best feeling.

"Thanks, Jarell. I really appreciate it."

And now!

I hit the stage with the brightest lights and the largest crowd I had ever faced. The jitters were there, but I cursed them and got rid of them. And we performed. Danced our asses off. I pretended to be

Jarell. I pretended to see nothing. No one else existed except for Chris and me. And energy. That was all that was there. That was all I allowed myself to see and feel. And that got me through the performance.

Before I knew it, it was over faster than it came, and the reception that I had gotten from everyone was completely overwhelming once the concert was over. Hugs from everywhere. Stares in awe from everyone. It was insane. It appeared that I was just as much of a star as Chris was, being his lead dancer. It was amazing, and I was on cloud nine. I wished that Jarell could've seen it, but he knew that I did a good job the moment he heard the reception. He just sat in the background and smiled, seeming genuinely happy for me. He hadn't said anything yet because everyone kept bombarding me, but I knew he would later on our way home.

The last people to get to me were my parents. I couldn't have been happier to fall into the open arms of my father figure.

"Oh baby girl! You did an amazing job!" Corey said, hugging me tight and lifting me from the ground. I screamed out in laughter. "Damn! I had no idea you could dance like that. I mean, I know that I've been investing in your dance since you were little, but you've grown up so much and really have perfected your craft. I'm so damn proud of you!"

"Yes, baby. That was awesome. Congrats," my mother said, holding her hands together and placing them in front of her.

"Thanks, y'all. I really appreciate your support."

"It was good to see you, Corey," Mom said.

"Likewise."

"And also good to see you're still in my daughter's life."

"I mean, just because we're done doesn't mean that our relationship has to end," he said.

"I mean, I would have expected that it would, so I'm glad to see you're still around. Considering that she invited you before she invited me to this show. How long have you known about this performance?" she asked, and it just sucked all of the positive energy out of the air once again. *Ugh.* I could see why Corey left her.

"Maybe about two or three weeks ago?"

"Hmph. That's interesting. She didn't tell me until today."

He shrugged awkwardly. "I don't know what you want me to say."

"You know the reason why I didn't tell you, Ma. Stop acting like you don't know," I interrupted.

"Well, as someone who has had an influence on your life just as much as Corey has had, you'd think that I would know as soon as he did."

"The difference between you and Corey is that he doesn't go around belittling me because he thinks that he deserves every ounce of credit for everything that goes right in my life."

"Excuse me?" She squinted her eyes. "How dare you insult me in front of-"

"Janet. Janet, let's not do this here, alright? Jade had an amazing performance, and you should be celebrating that and not making it about yourself."

"Thank you!" I exclaimed.

"Corey, don't tell me what to do with my daughter!"

"I'm not telling you how to parent. I'm telling you what makes sense in this space right now."

"You don't need to tell me that either. I'm a grown ass woman."

"Yeah, and that's why I left your ass, and that's why you single now."

And the arguing and bickering didn't stop there. It turned into a full-on shouting match. I wanted to slap the shit out of my mother. She ruined everything. She always did.

I huffed and was about to walk out, but I remembered Jarell. He was awkwardly standing by looking towards the ground but was clearly affected by what was happening. I didn't want him to be in this mess. He was supposed to have a good time and not have to worry about any of my family drama and dysfunction.

I walked to him and grabbed his arm to walk out of the building. I'd thank Corey later because he knew where my heart was, but now wasn't the time to stick around and let him know.

The first couple of steps that Jarell and I took towards the exit doors were halted by my mother yanking my arm back and slamming me into her chest, leaving Jarell hanging without me.

"What the-"

"Shut up!"

Then, she began to whisper so that only I could hear.

"If you think for one second that you are going to walk around with that nasty bum on your arm, you better think again. I will disown you; I swear to God I will. I raised you better than that. Who do you think I am!" she said, each sentence becoming incrementally louder than the last.

"Get off me," I snatched away from her. "You don't have any idea who he is, and the worst thing I've ever done in my life is listen to you about who I can and can't be with. Get out of my way."

Shoving her off me, I grasped Jarell's arm and quickly walked towards the exit, hoping that Jarell wouldn't trip over his feet at my abrupt move. The tears burned at my eyes, but I wouldn't give her the satisfaction of upsetting me on one of the best days of my life.

Once we were outside in the back of the Staples Center, I

screamed to let out my anger and frustration. It came right from the depths of my stomach, resulting in a raw throat. My body shivered, my fists balled up, and I had to wonder if it was a culmination of anger with my mother, Mike, and everything else within the past couple of months. Either way, even though the scream had hurt, it felt so good to release.

To the point where I had forgotten that Jarell was there throughout it all. As I stood seething, he came up to me with caution. I could read nothing he was feeling or thinking; part of that was because of his sunglasses.

"What?" I asked bitterly as he approached.

Without a semblance of emotion, Jarell reached out and rubbed my back. He didn't say a single word, and it was the best thing he could've ever done. The shaking stopped, and my breathing slowed. The more it did, the deeper of a massage he gave of my shoulders and neck. I closed my eyes and let the tension release that I felt in the upper half of my body. It wasn't a professional massage, but Jarell took time to work out some kinks and tensions that were spot on. I must've been truly stressed for him to feel that tightness.

"Thank you, Jarell."

Still, he said nothing. At that moment, I trusted that just as much as I said I'd have his back, he'd have my back too.

Chapter Twenty-One

DAYS PASSED BY after the fiasco at the concert. I still lived with my mother, but we no longer communicated. She wasn't around anyway due to her travels with her developing clothing line, so I was happy to have such a big house all to myself. I couldn't lie and say that I didn't feel lonely, but I took that time to be grateful for the peace because I was getting blown up by everyone about my performance at Chris' concert. Both at school and outside of school alike. So many different celebrities wanting me to perform in their music videos and concerts, so many compliments, videos going viral, and I didn't even know what to do about it.

At this point of my life, it was time for me to hire PR and an assistant to handle bookings, answer emails, and all of that. Because it was now spiraling out of control, and I was actually interested in many of these offers while wanting to handle things in a professional way. To dance with Ciara, Cardi B, and Omarion on live tours were dreams! If my momma had any sort of sanity, I would have hired her to be my manager, but that was completely out of the question. Never, ever would make that decision.

So this time was very stressful, but it was good stress. Either way, I was happy for Christmas break to unplug. The money was coming in fast from the concert, and it was hefty. And I meant, *hefty*. Like Chris promised, for my birthday and to start my business with Alise as a jump start, he decided that half of his proceeds from the show would go to me.

At this point, if I wanted to, I could probably move out of my mom's spot right now, get an upscale downtown spot on my own, and be okay for the next six months without any other forms of income. But better things needed to be done with that money. Some of that money was going to build up for an assistant/PR, some to my new position as a youth dance coach, and I had some things up my sleeve for the holidays for Jarell, so it was something to look forward to.

Not to mention the fact that I was just tired of school. Senioritis was making its whole presence known, and I was just ready to be done.

After breaking the boring and mundane cycle between Jarell and I at the concert, it had been pretty easy to get him to dance with me every now and then leading up to Christmas because talking about anything just wasn't who he was. Any time I'd try to get him to engage in meaningful conversation, he'd purposefully keep it short and sweet. I wasn't okay with that, but I had to compromise. If he wasn't going to talk, then I wanted him to dance with me. So just about every other night, he and I would go dance in the empty park he had taken me to on Homecoming night.

Oddly, the more and more it did approach Christmas, Jarell had been requesting for us to dance before I could, as if needing a release or like he was running away from something. I never asked him about it, but I did want to know. I indirectly got my answer when I one day asked him if he was excited about Christmas. He had said that he was never excited about Christmas – that it was one of the worst seasons of the year. I figured it was because his family either didn't celebrate it or couldn't celebrate it. The latter broke my heart. It didn't matter though because those issues were going to be resolved. It was already in the works.

One night after a dance a pretty passionate dance between us though, I had gotten a sort of breakthrough. I had asked Jarell if he could just check out the studio just once. Literally, just once. He knew that I wasn't letting the question go, and in annoyance, he had finally said yes just to get me off his back. He said it was going to literally be the first and last time that he would. I was so happy that he was going that I told Alise to be at the studio first thing in the morning today. She had already said that she'd be there doing some business, so it was all settled. She also asked me why I wanted her to be there, but I told her it was a surprise. So she was in for a treat. He said that he'd do it once, but if Alise was going to offer him some cash to work with her, he might think differently.

On a Sunday morning, Jarell and I walked into a quiet studio, usually how it is during the early afternoon hours of the day. It was just how I liked it, especially when I wanted to freestyle before the dance crews came in and the place got hectic. Alise was the only person that was here all day also sharpening up her skills and handling the business of the studio.

"Lise?"

My voice echoed throughout, letting her know I was here with my special guest. The lights were off, so she was probably in buried in her office somewhere.

"Hang on, Jarell, okay? I'm going to grab Alise really quick. Stay here."

Leaving Jarell standing there without giving him a chance to rebut or respond about being here, I jogged to the back to Alise's office to find her nose deep into some paperwork that looked like some serious business. She was pensive, and eyes frantically scanning; she hadn't even heard me call out to her, much less heard me even walk into her office.

"Alise," I called out louder this time, and she snapped from her intense focus, shooting her eyes at me.

"Oh, I'm sorry, Jade. I was just reading some information about building renovations. What's up? You about to freestyle?"

"No, but I got someone here to show you who will freestyle."

She gave me an annoyed glare, which caused me to speak faster before she could nullify my request to see him.

"It's that same guy I told you about who was dancing in this random empty parking lot who I thought was dope as hell."

"Oh, so this is your surprise? Who is this person?"

"His name is Jarell. You should check him out, and maybe he can join us! I mean, really work with us."

"I trust your judgement, but you know I usually don't watch people freestyle without knowing how they dance with a crew first. Especially during my office hours."

"I know, I know. You tell me this all the time that you hate when people tell you to check other dancers out, but this is my first time ever doing this. And you know if I'm coming here to tell you to check this dude out, that means he's extremely good."

She stared at me a while before her body clearly gave in.

"You lucky I love you. I guess if I should listen to anyone, it should be you." She smiled and rose up from her desk. When she stood up, some papers fell onto the floor because it was so filled with them.

"And if you don't like him, I promise to organize your desk.

But I probably won't have to do that because you'll like him. I know dopeness when I see it."

"Whatever, sis. I'll take you up on that desk organization offer, while your desk over there looking all clean and shit."

"You know I will do it for you anyway, whether this was a bet or not."

"You're right."

She chuckled, and we both walked out into the dance studio to find Jarell withdrawn into his hoodie and walking slowly around the studio as if examining the place. The moment Alise saw him, she had a weird look on her face, as if he was repulsive. She gave me a look and a raised eyebrow as if I was sure he was going to be any good. I sighed with a smile, vowing to explain to her later.

"We're back, Jarell," I called out to him.

His head tilted upwards to acknowledge the fact that he heard me and traced his steps towards the direction of my voice. He stopped just short of us, keeping his head down, his eyes averted, and his hands snuffed in his pants pockets. Whew, this introduction was going to be awkward. They were both skeptical for very different reasons.

"Jarell, this is Alise, my partner in crime here at the studio. She's the CEO and I'll be running the younger dance crews when we graduate! I've been under her mentorship for some years now. She's danced under many, many people," I said as giddy as I could, and Jarell was completely emotionless as I gave him this information.

"Nice to meet you, Jarell. I'm Alise," she said with a polite tone, but you could tell that she was a little clipped and short on patience. She stuck her hand out to shake his, and of course Jarell didn't see it. I just looked at her with wide eyes and shook my head, pulling her hand down. She frowned, giving me a confused look. I mouthed to her that I would explain later.

"Good to meet you," he said, never once looking up, but skirted the floor with his foot.

"Lise, Jarell and I are friends from school now after having been strangers, even enemies, and he's an extremely talented dancer, and I'd like you to check him out."

"Okay. I'm out of my dungeon so you gotta be good. Show me what you got, kid."

"What do you want me to do?" he asked.

"Well, your homegirl said that you freestyle, so I wanna see what you got."

"Jarell, I've seen you do many things, but can you do something that you've never done or shown me before? What about some African inspired type of dance? They got some pretty cold new dances out in Nigeria."

"If there are any new dances in Nigeria, I clearly wouldn't know them," he said bluntly.

"Really, Jarell?"

Jarell shrugged like he didn't have a care in the world. His entire body language screamed that he didn't want to be here, and now wasn't the time for him to be acting like this. I clenched my teeth. Now, he was getting under my skin. My credibility was on the line here, and here he was acting like a clown.

"Jarell, stop playing. I'm going to put on some music. Do what you will with it. If not, Alise and I will just dance if you're going to act like this."

"Alright." He shrugged again and walked away from us.

I wouldn't dare look at Alise. I wasn't ready. I knew she was pissed with me for wasting her time, but I would deal with that later. For now, I had to save face and start the music. In the meantime, I had to think about how I was going to tear Jarell a new one once we were alone.

Walking away from what I already felt was a steaming Alise, I turned on a song with an afro beat and hoped for the best. I still didn't look at Alise as I started vibing to the music myself and warming up my body in case Jarell wasn't going to dance. Matter fact, Jarell had walked away, but I could tell that he was beginning to vibe to the beat too because he started nodding his head. Then, after a while, the Jarell I knew came through. I knew he couldn't resist. A true dancer like him couldn't ever resist a good beat.

And he started dancing, killing it like I knew he would.

I put this song on purposely so that he wouldn't dance in his comfort zone, even though he was pretty versatile anyway, and damn did he accept the challenge. What I saw was Hip Hop, and something else that completely surprised me. He went on and infused a combination of Caribbean and African dance. My God. It was like he was straight from the Motherland. He hit every clap, every snare every beat with his body in some way, or he slowed it down, sped it up... I couldn't describe it.

As I studied him intently, it was clear. Jarell could probably out dance anyone he came in contact with, and that included famous dancers like Chris Brown. I had never, ever seen such talent, and most certainly had never seen him dance in this style before.

He was in a zone.

There was just something about the element of his vision loss that brought his sense of sound and movement to an elevated level that no one else had. He was so fluid, yet so crisp, and no matter how talented I knew I was; I wasn't on his level. Not by a fucking long shot. I always studied his moves, but I could never, ever do them on my own. I couldn't even consider replicating anything that he had just done.

I turned to look at Alise and by the look on her face, she was shook. She had the same look on her face that she had when she was looking at the millions of documents on her desk, but her eyes were way more engaged. I knew Alise, and I knew her well. When she looked at someone like that, she was in awe.

"Watch this," I nudged her, and walked over to Jarell to dance and vibe with him. There was something about the way that we danced together that felt so right. A rare connection I don't think anyone could ever have. I couldn't dance as well as him for sure, but I could keep up. I always found myself improving as a dancer whenever we got together and vibed.

He and I danced together for the rest of the song, and it flowed into another afro-beat song until it ended, and he and I both laughed in exhaustion when we were finished the way we always did.

"So, Lise what do you think?" I huffed, pulling my hair up into a ponytail. Jarell was standing by with his hands on his hips, catching his breath.

"Wow. I'm speechless to be honest." She blinked. "That was a level that I haven't seen in a long, long time. Like... wow. Jade, I know you're a great dancer, but this dude right here is an uncanny type of talent. You were right. Jarell, where'd you learn to dance like that? How long have you been dancing?"

"Since I was young. Just taking free time to practice," he said, stuffing his hands back into his pocket and looking away from her.

"That's a raw talent. Like, celebrity status talent. I could probably put you in a live concert right now without any choreography, and you'd kill it. You have an ear and an energy that I've never seen from anyone before."

He smiled shyly.

"Thanks."

"Have you ever considered dancing for a studio, lead a studio, or teaching dance?" she asked.

"Nah, not really."

"Well, you should join us! We would love to have you. Someone like you added to our crew would blow any other studios in LA out of the water," she said. "What do you think?"

My mouth dropped. Okay. Shit like this never happened. Alise *never* recruited someone on the spot like this. She'd always tell them that she'd think about it, that she needed to consult with me, or even just flat out say that she isn't accepting dancers or instructors at the moment. Because I knew this, this was a huge deal.

"Of course he will!" I shouted with glee.

"I'll think about it."

We said it simultaneously. I looked at him like he was crazy.

"What do you mean you'll think about it? Jarell, you have too much talent to keep that all to yourself."

"I said what I said. I'll think about it."

"Jarell, are you being serious? Alise is offering you a job doing something you love, and she never, ever does this. Stop playing around."

"I don't see why you think I'm playing. Nice to meet you, Alise. Thanks for inviting me," Jarell said, and proceeded to walk to the studio exit.

At this point, I had to take a deep breath in order to stop me from slapping the living shit out of him.

"Alise, I'll be right back," I said, not even able to look her in the eye, and ran out of the studio. I caught up to him pretty quickly because he didn't make it that far.

"Jarell what the hell is wrong with you!" I yelled. "Why would you just dismiss her like that? Do you understand that she's one of the biggest choreographers in the country?"

"I don't care if she was Jesus. I said I'll think about it. It's not like I said no."

"Saying you'll think about it is just like saying no. What the hell is your problem? You know my own reputation is on the line too, right?" I asked, pointing an index to my chest.

"Oh, I see. It's all about you, isn't it?"

"No, it isn't about me, but yes your choices do have an effect on my life. I'm trying to make it about you, but you're so damn shut off that it's impossible."

"Jade, I don't have to be what you want me to be!" Jarell turned around and faced me, throwing his arms in the air with a plethora of emotions in his eyes that he tried to keep in check. I was so up close to him that I could see right through his sunglasses.

"It's not that I want you to be what I want you to be! I just want you to live up to your full potential!"

"But this is my full potential. You leaving me the hell alone and letting me decide what to showcase or keep to myself is my full potential. If you haven't noticed, I'm blind, Jade. That already takes a significant part of what I can and want to do out of my life. I dance to contain all the anger in me. Sometimes, I want to keep certain things to myself. I want to enjoy them because I like them, not because I want to be someone's showcase or help others. I don't care to be known!"

"Oh my God! Why do you hate the world so much? What is wrong with letting others see who you are and your capabilities?"

"I hate the world because the world hates me. How do you not see this? Look at the way your mom treated me, Jade. She wouldn't even shake my hand! No one cares to see who I am."

"I do! I fucking do, Jarell. Because I care about you. I'm not doing this for shits and giggles. I'm doing this because you have something so raw, you are so gifted, and you can seriously take advantage of it."

"No, you don't care. You think you do."

"I do, Jarell!" Before I knew it, I was sobbing. I didn't think I'd get this emotional about him. But there was something about Jarell that I just couldn't let go, and I was determined for him to see it. I wasn't giving up.

"I do. Am I the nicest person in the world? No! Do I deserve any of your fucking friendship? No! But damn it, I treasure it. I treasure every moment you give to me because after every stupid thing I've done or said, I didn't deserve any part of you. And you've changed me so much that you don't even realize..."

"How? I haven't done anything. It's been four months, and this is what you're saying? I don't believe any of that shit." He turned his head away.

"Seriously? I barely even hang out with my old crew anymore. People are shutting me out because they see how I interact with you now. And you wanna know what? I don't care. I thought I would, and it sucks sometimes, but I don't care. You put life in an entirely different perspective for me. I can't really name why I care or whatever. Maybe because I'm so tired of trying to maintain my popularity. I just feel like I can be myself around you... the person that I believe I really am."

"What was wrong with being yourself regardless? Before you even decided you wanted to talk to me? Why do you have to put up this fake shit?"

"You don't understand."

"Well, maybe some time you can help me understand. And until then, I'll take a raincheck on working for this studio. Because that's not who I am, and I won't pretend that it is."

At that, I completely exploded.

"Jarell are you serious? I've been working overtime, kissing your ass to show you who I truly am, and that's the type of shit you say to me!? At least I'm working on not putting up this front. You can't even bear to come out of your fucking sweatshirt!"

The minute those words came out of my mouth, I instantly regretted it. I didn't mean it like that. I didn't. But I was so upset. He just froze and looked my way. I couldn't even read what he was thinking. His body language, his face, everything was inscrutable.

"That's how you feel?" he asked.

"No. It's not." I sighed, running a guilty hand down my face.

"Then that's my point. You're saying that you didn't mean it because you're scared that you'll lose whatever ground you feel like you've gained with me. That's how I know you ain't real. Tell the fuckin' truth!"

"Jarell, I don't feel like that! You want to know why? Because you actually do come out. You've opened up to me so much that I often wonder how I even deserve it because of all the shit I've done. But I'm thankful for it. Damn it," I said, and then broke into more sobs.

He stood silent for a while, fiddling with his hands and feet while I cried and tried to get myself together. I was so upset with him, but mostly, with myself because of my own actions, and how I had to work twice as hard to build the trust I was seeking.

The entire time, he said nothing. Usually, I would've been upset that someone got me to the point of tears again. But now, I didn't care. I wanted Jarell to see me. I wanted to challenge his thoughts about how he expected me to be. What I was displaying wasn't some front. This was who I was. These tears were for him, and they were real. And I was dead ass serious.

As time passed, I felt an energy of regret emanating from him. It was all in his stance. Finally, his weight shifted, showing some sign of life.

"I'm sorry," he confessed.

"For what? For me standing in front of you crying and laying my bare ass to you? I don't know what more you want me to do, Jarell."

He sighed and ducked his head.

"Yeah. I know. It's just... hard."

"It's hard for the both of us, Jarell. But I'm trying. I really am."

He said nothing. He just nodded.

"Listen. I know you're trying. I do see that. I just don't want things to fall apart, or for you to decide that you don't want to ... I don't know... be friends with me anymore. That shit'll piss me off."

"I made a promise to you, Jarell. I just didn't say that because I felt like it."

"Yeah. I know."

I took a deep breath. This was the first time that Jarell had ever apologized to me. I didn't want to make a big deal, but this was a big deal. Of all the times that he's been a jerk and should have apologized, this was the one time that actually mattered. And hell yeah, I accepted his apology. I knew how hard it was for him. But he just needed to understand that I was doing my part. And that I was working hard to show it.

"Listen, forget about the studio. I'm just glad you came and danced. Okay? That's all that matters to me. That you came in to do something that you loved. And if you don't feel comfortable, that's something I'm going to have to accept."

He nodded. "Yeah."

I laughed. He was so damn dry. That's all he could say to that? I shook my head. He humored me.

"Can we hug it out, now?" I asked with a smile.

"Too soon," he uttered, and then walked away towards my car.

I laughed and followed behind him.

Touché, Jarell. Touché.

Chapter Twenty-Two

IT WAS TRADITION for my mother and I to wake up early at five o'clock in the morning to open Christmas gifts. Today was no different. Although I was eighteen and becoming way too old for Christmas gifts, there still was a spirit about the holidays that always made me feel loved and at home. Plus, it was the only time that I woke up in the morning without an alarm. It was a day I resolved to put the recent bullshit between my mother and I to the side and really enjoy our time together, although it took a lot outta me to get to this point.

In addition to me just wanting a positive day with my mom, I woke up excited for so many other reasons. With my hefty checks for my performance at the Chris Brown concert, I bought hella Christmas gifts with it, particularly for Jarell's family. I just hoped they'd be excited about them and not feel weirded out by it. I had taken a lot of time thinking about what I was going to get them, so I hoped it wasn't for naught.

I rolled out of my bed and rubbed my eyes, heading towards my mom's room so she could get up to open presents. I didn't want to, but I got her a few things as well. At the end of the day, she was still my mother, and it could be worse. I could not have a mother at all.

The fact that I was even going to her room to call her out was weird because she was always up before me and waking me up. I hoped everything was okay.

"Ma?"

No answer. I knocked lightly on her door and put my ear up to it. I didn't hear anything, so I turned the knob. It was surprisingly opened, and I peeked inside. Her bed was empty but made to perfection. Where the hell was she?

"Ma!" I called out louder and walked from the bedroom hallway towards the kitchen. Maybe she was making her morning coffee, but I didn't smell anything. I peeked into the kitchen, and no one was there.

"Where is this woman?"

As I gazed around in panic, on the breakfast counter there was a piece of paper with handwriting that looked like hers. I took a good look at it.

Jade,

I flew out to New York City this morning. There is a Christmas fashion show here, and I will be having a few models trying on and modeling my new pieces. Please take care of yourself on this Christmas. I will see you when I get back after New Year's.

Mom

I couldn't believe her. Really? She couldn't tell me that she was leaving on Christmas? Why would she even do that? She couldn't catch a later flight after we spent some time for the holiday together?

She was wrong. So wrong. Okay, I didn't tell her about my concert because it was for good reason. I wanted to prove a point to her that I could succeed without her taking credit for everything. But simply leaving your only child to celebrate Christmas alone? No matter how old I was, this was meant to be family time. The two of us. It wasn't like I had any other extended family around. My grandparents were on the other side of the country. I didn't know my father's side of the family. Corey was reporting for Christmas Day NBA games. So if I wasn't going to Jarell's today, what would I have done?

I couldn't continue looking up to her anymore. She was petty, vindictive, manipulative, and she just didn't have the character of someone I wanted to be anymore. I used to admire her so much because of what she had done for me, but really, I now understood she was also doing it for herself. So she could gain recognition as well.

Deep in my soul, I wanted to take those gifts I bought her to the homeless shelter. They would be so much more grateful than she. But again, I had a heart. She would just see them when she got back into town. But I hoped she didn't think there wasn't going to be some conversation about this.

Ripping the letter into shreds and throwing it away, I gathered the gifts I bought for Jarell and his family into one spot before I showered and got ready. Today, looking good was important because I had some big things planned. I put on a cute Christmas dress and a Santa hat and felt like I was ready to go.

I walked my Christmas gifts to my little car, nearly tripping a few times because I had so many gifts in my hand and couldn't see. I made it though and took the fifteen-minute drive to Jarell's.

When I arrived, my heart palpitated. *I have never done anything like this before, and what would Jarell and his mom think about all of these gifts? Would they be upset? Would they ask me to leave? Would they be suspicious or embarrassed?*

I walked up to the door of Jarell's home, and again, it looked abandoned. His neighbors at least had some Christmas decorations up; people were outside walking around with Christmas bags and kids were outside with their new toys. But Jarell's home was bereft of any holiday spirit, and it almost made me wonder if anyone was even home. I'd give it a try. Even though I was nearly trembling, I hoped they were here.

I stepped on the porch, shifting the gifts and packages in my hand. I struggled to ring the doorbell, but I managed. I made sure the gifts weren't covering my face when someone opened the door because I didn't want either of them to be freaked out.

Jarell's mother was the one to open it, and her face registered a puzzled look, staring at all the gifts I was about to topple over.

"Hey Jade. Um...who are all these gifts for?" she asked, looking me up and down.

"Merry Christmas! How are you? They're for your family. I would love your help," I said giddy as hell.

"What? Gifts from who?"

"Me!"

Her mouth dropped.

"What? Now Jade. Why did you do this?"

"I can explain as soon as you help me in."

She sighed, running her hands through her long hair, looking guilty and stressed out. "Fine. Don't want you in the cold. Come on in. Let me take some of these off your hands."

I walked inside and let her help me take the heaviest of load to put on the floor. Then, she closed the front door.

"You didn't have to do this. You're still in high school, sweetie. I can't accept this. I'm not even sure what possessed you to do it," she said, shaking her head.

I swallowed the lump of embarrassment in my throat when suddenly, from the back of the house, I heard quick little pounding footsteps make their way closer until Kylah's cute face appeared with a huge smile. Small beads of sweat lined her forehead as if she'd been active all morning. The moment she saw all the presents, she froze as her gray eyes had become as big as stars.

"Oooh, Santa finally came, Mommy! Can we open?" she squealed.

Ms. Hendricks' head tilted back, knowing she now had no choice but to appease her child.

"I suppose he did, baby. You were a good girl this year," Jarell's mom said, unsure, hugging Kylah close and wiping her sweat away. She gave me a closed look and shrugged. "Guess I'll call your brother out. Jarell! Come on out! Santa came!"

"What are you talking about?" Jarell called out from deep into his room.

"You heard me. I said Santa came. Come on out and see all the gifts."

There was silence from the back, and Kylah swirled around the presents, trying to figure out which ones were hers. Her mother grabbed one of her little active hands, stopping her from ripping open one of the boxes too soon. With a shaky smile to keep from crying, I kneeled to her.

"Hey sweetie. What's your name?" I asked, even though I already knew.

"My name is Kylah. What's yours? Are you Santa?" she asked.

I chuckled.

"My name is Jade. I'm Santa's helper for the day," I said. "Santa had to go back up north to get more gifts for the other little kids, so he told me to deliver your gifts for you."

"Really!?" she said, full of innocence and beauty. Her mother watched her lovingly.

"Really. So you want to wait until your brother gets out here? You don't want to open Santa's gifts without him."

"Okay."

I rose up, and Jarell was standing in the middle of the hallway with his hoodie and old, ragged pajama pants on. I took a deep breath and took him in. His head and eyes were uncovered again, and the more and more I saw him this way, the more attractive he became. I just wished he'd take off that hoodie.

"Mom, I thought I told you not to worry about gett -"

"Jade's here with Santa's gifts." Ms. Hendricks said, interrupting him.

"Oh really?" He raises a brow.

"Yeah. It appears that he has gotten us a whole lot this year," she responded, gazing at Kylah.

"You didn't put Jade up to this, did you?"

"Now why would I go and do that? You know I'm not like that, Jarell," she retorted, giving him an indignant look, and sat down.

"Relly, she's Santa's helper. Can we open the presents now?" Kylah whined, moving in closer to me and giving me a hug. I just adored her personality, her outgoingness, and willingness to love. I was a complete stranger, and she was all over me like she'd known me for years.

"No, she's not." Jarell huffed with crossed arms.

I shifted, staring at him, ready to respond when his mother, again, interrupted.

"Yes, we can open the presents if your brother stops being such a worrier," Ms. Hendricks mumbled.

"Yeah, Jarell you shouldn't worry. And I *am* Santa's helper," I said, supporting his mom, taking the opportunity to stop him from ruining this moment. I really wanted this to be special.

"Relly, can we open the presents? Please?"

"I guess," he said, leaning against the doorway in the living room. "I'm not going to open mine, yet. I want to know why you did this, Jade."

I knew this wasn't going to be easy, but I cleared my throat to try and find the right words to explain.

"Jarell. Seriously? Sit down," his mother said.

Rolling his eyes and deciding not to argue, Jarell walked towards the couch and sank in it the same way that I did when I first sat on it. I was so grateful for his mom. She helped me play this along quite nicely.

"Okay, Kylah. The first gift is for you."

I handed her a huge box, and her eyes lit up.

"Ooh, I get the biggest one!"

I laughed and stood back to watch her reaction. I took out my phone to snap some pictures for memories. Kylah wasted no time in tearing the wrapper open and looking at what she had in front of her. She screamed in excitement when she realized that she had gotten a doll house.

"Mommy, mommy look!"

Jarell's mother smiled genuinely at her daughter and laughed. Even though she didn't want to accept the gifts, I could tell that she was so glad that her daughter was able to have a Christmas.

"There's more, Kylah," I said, and gave her two more wrapped up boxes.

"Ooh mommy, Relly, there's more!"

"Open it and see what it is," I said.

Without another word, her cute little hands tore into the wrapper, and she screamed again when she saw that she got two new barbie dolls. Hugging them close to her, she closed her eyes and cheesed all twenty-eight of her primaries.

"What do you say to Jade, honey?"

"Thank you, Jade!" she said, and ran to hug my legs. I looked down at her and ruffled her sandy brown, loosely curled hair. She giggled and then ran away to play with her new toys. She didn't even stick around for her brother or her mother's gifts. A part of me was glad though because this was about to get personal.

"Alright, Jarell. It's your turn," I said, and my heart started beating fast when I reached out to place the box in his lap. I didn't know how he was going to react to this, so I held my breath.

He touched it reluctantly and explored the shape of the box. Though he had tried so hard not to care about this moment and to be angry that I had brought gifts, he failed miserably.

He shook it to see if he could hear anything. Then, he tried to smell it. I laughed at the wonder on his face. The little kid in him was surfacing and it was so adorable.

"Open it, Jarell," his mother said, impatient because she wanted to see what he got herself.

With a wistful breath and an air of anticipation, he tore the wrapper off. I got my camera ready and snapped a few pictures. When he felt the leather in his hands, he realized it was something that could be opened. He frowned in confusion and felt around for its opening. When he opened the box, his mother screamed.

"Ahh! Oh my God!"

Suddenly, I was tackled, and my phone tumbled out of my hands. Knocked over with a huge hug by Jarell's mom. I couldn't even see Jarell's reaction, but I laughed at her, a little physically hurt from the abruptness of it all, but I would deal with that back pain later. On top of that, his mother burst into tears.

"Thank you," she said through her sobs and melted down on the couch, crying into her hands. I blinked. I had no idea getting him this gift was this special to her. It warmed and broke my heart at the same time.

"Jarell, you asked me why I did this, why I brought all of these gifts. Well, after your glasses got broken, and after spending time with you, I felt like what happened in the hallway that day was unfair. I saw how angry you were, and at that time, I had no idea how important your glasses were."

His mom was still sobbing. "I had paid a thousand dollars for those. All with my overtime money. I was working almost twenty-hour shifts to get those things."

Damn.

I looked at Jarell. He was smiling in disbelief at his brand-new glasses. Not only did they replace his broken ones, but the frames were designer with the latest technology. On the left side of his glasses, his name was inscribed. On the right side was a mini camera, OrCam, that could tell him his surroundings and help him navigate the world even better than he already knew how. His hands were all over them as he felt its inscription and the smoothness of the frames. Then, he stood up. With slow and careful footsteps, he stopped right in front of me.

"What?" I said, shaking in my boots.

To my pleasant surprise, Jarell reached his hands out and pulled me in for a tight and long embrace.

That's when I lost it. Not only did Jarell show appreciation in such an intimate way, to watch Christmas gifts transform a family within minutes like this was priceless. To produce this kind of reaction from someone as withdrawn as Jarell, words couldn't explain the overwhelming sense of love blooming in my chest.

"You don't know how much this means," Jarell whispered in my ear.

"Jarell, you deserve them. You're welcome." I wiped my tears away.

Smiling with gratitude, he backed away and sat back on the couch to feel his glasses, taking them on and off, listening to the OrCam feature in disbelief.

"My goodness, I'm such a mess, I shouldn't be crying like this," Ms. Hendricks said with laughter, wiping at her eyes too.

"He deserves it. Really. And I hope you're not offended, but I have something for you, too," I said, walking over to my Christmas bag. I placed the package in her hands and stepped back to watch. This time, I made sure to step back so I wouldn't get tackled again. Because if she reacted like that to Jarell's gift, I knew she was going to really go nuts with what I was about to give her.

Taking a deep breath, she tore the wrapper open from the box, opened it, and immediately started crying again.

"What the... how much money is this!?" Ms. Hendricks exclaimed.

"Three thousand dollars."

Jarell's mouth dropped opened, and his mother looked at me with wide eyes.

"Jade? Where did someone your age get this money? This isn't illegal, is it?"

"Ms. Hendricks, I'm a professional dancer. I have been dancing for four years."

"Ma, remember I told you that she danced for a sold-out Chris Brown concert? That she invited me to?"

"Oh yeah! But wait...why? What did we do to deserve it? You haven't known any of us for long at all. Are there any conditions with this money? I feel so weird taking it."

"Well... can I be honest?"

"Please. I need to understand why you're offering me so much of your money."

"The second time I dropped Jarell off, I overheard Kylah say your lights were off. I noticed it was dark for weeks whenever I'd drop him off, but I didn't want to say anything. I just thought this might help."

"Wow. Well, thank you. And to know that I was about to lose this house at the end of this week. Now I can get the lights back on too!"

"Ma don't be sharing stuff like that," Jarell scolded with a frown.

"Hush, Jarell. But Jade, you could have saved this!"

"I could have, but don't worry. It's my gift to you."

She fell to her knees, bawling. I kneeled down and rubbed her back. I cried with her. Seeing the impact of poverty was heartbreaking. I had never seen the effects of it so up close, thanks to my privileged life. Yeah, I'd seen homeless people, but to me, they weren't *people*. In this situation, I knew them personally, and now I knew that they were about to lose their home to live on the streets within days. I was so glad I had made this decision. Even if it seemed odd. Something inside told me to just do it.

"Let me stop crying," I said, wiping at my eyes as I stood up. "I'm taking you all out to lunch for the holidays. I promise that's my last gift." Ms. Hendricks rushed and hugged me again. Tight. That was the moment I wished that I had a mother like Jarell's. A mother humble enough to show gratitude.

Because I arrived so early in the day, I got to spend quality time with Jarell and his family before our plans for lunch. I got to play with and know Kylah more, and her love for Barbies. She was the smartest little girl, had an expansive vocabulary, and her imagination was out of this world. I got to know his mother a little more and what she did for a living, which is clean hotels on multiple shifts. After a couple of hours, Ms. Hendricks excused herself to get Kylah bathed and herself dressed, and that left me alone with Jarell.

I had never been alone with him in such an intimate and personal space like his home, so I felt kind of weary of how he was going to handle it. While we were alone, he didn't talk much, but he was the most relaxed I'd ever seen him. His arm was spread over the back of the couch, his feet up on a rickety coffee table, daydreaming about I don't know what. The silence was unnerving.

"What are you thinking about?" I called out to him, rubbing my arm in guilt.

"About all this," he whispered. "About what just happened."

"I hope you're okay with what I did for you and your family."

"You really know how to make a first impression, don't you?" he asked with a raised eyebrow. The rest of his face was completely unreadable. "That money will definitely get the lights back on."

I didn't know what to say. Or what that even meant. Or if he was serious or not. I was lost for words.

"I'ma head to my room to get ready. You wanna come?" he asked softly.

I did a double take. *He was actually going to invite me into his room?*

"Are you sure?" I hesitated. I didn't know why I felt so uneasy about going into the room of someone of the opposite sex. Maybe because I had never done it before. Not even with Mike. And no guy has ever made it into my room.

"Yeah. What's wrong?" he asked.

"N-nothing. I just… never thought you'd ask me something like that."

"I usually wouldn't. But you're here. And I… I'm glad you're here."

My stomach fluttered. So *that's* what Jarell was actually thinking. I could sense how much he struggled to admit it. Seemed like he wanted to say more about how he felt, but just didn't know how. For the first time since we began this… relationship… friendship… whatever to call it, I felt the barriers he erected were truly crumbling away.

"Thank you, Jarell. I'm glad I came too. My mother flew out to New York this morning and left me. You know how she is, so this is a breath of fresh air."

With a small smile, he gave me a look of appreciation. Then, he put his hand out towards me. I looked at his hand.

"What?"

"Your hand," he said as if stating the obvious.

"What about it?"

"Give me your hand, Jade," he said plainly, and I blinked. In shock, I put my hand in his, and it was surprisingly soft and gentle. I stared at the way our bodies had come together in such a small, but close way that I didn't even realize he was trying to help me off the couch.

"Follow me."

I did as instructed, and he led me to his room. The minute I stepped inside; my jaw dropped.

It was a wonderland. Jarell had what looked like origami hung up everywhere, and they were some of the grandest masterpieces I had ever seen. There were birds. There were flowers. There were animals. There was everything. I blinked several times just to make sure that what I was seeing was real.

It was official.

Jarell was the most talented person that I had ever met. No wonder why his little sister was full of imagination... look at how her brother spent his time!

"Jarell! This is amazing!" I whispered in awe.

"Oh. The origami? This is nothing," he shrugged as he placed his glasses case on his dresser.

"Jarell are you kidding me? This is awesome! Don't try to downplay this!"

"I guess."

"How often do you do fold?"

"Everyday."

"Really?"

"Yeah. I have nothing else better to do. My mom doesn't have a car to take me on nature hikes anymore, so I just brought nature into my room, really."

I walked around his room looking at some of all his different kinds of creations. I touched them gently. They were so well done. How could he do things like this without vision?

"This is crazy."

"Yeah," he said, and then sat on his bed with a sigh. I walked over and stood in front of him, touching an origami piece that hung over his head.

"You know, Jarell? You make me appreciate life so much. Just the little things that I would have never valued before, I think it's a big deal now. I mean, I'm even thinking about just the simple ability to create origami with having my vision to do it. None of this would have mattered to me four months ago."

"Yeah. It's why I always thought you were crazy whenever I'd hear you freak out about little shit at school. I was like, this girl is siddity as hell. Don't understand a thing about life, for real," he said bluntly, and I nudged him with an embarrassed smile.

"Whatever. I'm working on it, you know."

He chuckled, his head hanging low.

"Jarell?"

"Hmm?"

"Thank you for allowing me to get to know you and your family better. And celebrating Christmas with me. You really didn't have to."

"You're saying thank you? I need to be thanking *you* a million times over," he said, giving a weird look in my direction.

"Like I said before, you deserve it, and you've changed me in some ways."

"Yeah. And believe it or not, I've learned from you, too," Jarell admitted, his head tilted to the side in reflection.

"Really?" I said with excitement.

"Really. I mean, you annoy me, get on my nerves, and test me, kind of like my little sister, so I learned more patience."

With a gasp, I punched Jarell in the shoulder in jest, and he laughed out loud.

"That's not funny, jerk," I pouted.

"Nah, but for real. You did."

"Well, I'm glad that I was able to be something for you," I whispered, and then looked at him head on. His eyes were one thing I always thought about, but I never noticed how edible his lips looked. Hell, his entire face. I just imagined how beautiful he was going to be when his growing beard filled in.

"I got a feeling you're staring at me," he said in a low voice. Immediately, the heat in my cheeks rose.

"What if I am?" I asked.

"Then you're in trouble."

"What kind of trouble?"

"I don't know. You would know though."

"I would?"

"Yeah," he said, kind of breathy, his voice becoming as low as his eyes.

"You mean, this kind of trouble?"

With that, I leaned in close and pressed my lips lightly against his. His lips felt just like they looked. I was so tempted to kiss him fervently and get my tongue into some action, but I had to hold myself back. Much to my pleasant surprise though, Jarell felt the same way. He pulled my body closer, and suddenly, his hands went to my cheeks to deepen the kiss.

"Oooh!!! Mommy! Jarell's kissing Santa's helper!"

We heard the voice, and Jarell and I both jumped. I gave Kylah a mortified look, and Jarell shook his head in embarrassment.

"Kylah, get out," Jarell said.

"Mommy! Jarell is kissing Santa's helper!" Kylah skipped out of Jarell's room. "Mommy! Mommy, guess what?"

"What, Kylah?" his mother said with exhaustion.

"Relly is kissing Jade!"

"Mind your business, Kylah."

When we heard that, Jarell and I busted into laughter, and Jarell pumped his fist like he had won, hissing a "Yes." That made me laugh harder and I wrapped my arms around his shoulders, giving him a final hug before lunch.

Chapter Twenty-Three

THE TIME AFTER that wondrous Christmas Day had been a blur. I was on cloud nine thinking about the kiss between Jarell and I, the impact I had made on their family, and our lunch together. Surprisingly, Jarell's mother didn't ask anything about the kiss that her daughter was so excited to tell. We mostly talked about other things like our childhood memories, movies, our favorite Disney characters, and other lighthearted things to make us laugh. I was happy for that because they deserved to talk about happiness to get a break from their hard life.

It was weeks past New Year's Day and into February. Jarell and I talked frequently, mostly outside of school and away from prying eyes on our rides home as we settled into our mundane routine again. We never mentioned anything about the kiss, but just the way we interacted since then, even if it was about very surface level things, I felt just how comfortable we had gotten with each other as my heart began to grow even more for him. He opened up a little more, but not as much as I would've hoped. And every time I dropped him off, I couldn't wait to see him again. I often wanted to stop by his house after I left the studio to spend some time with him, especially after that kiss, but I forced myself not to. I didn't want to seem too thirsty.

Much to my surprise, late into February on a Sunday morning, I had gotten a phone call from Jarell about taking him out for a hike on the nature paths in the outskirts of LA. He reminded me he's been wanting to go, but since his mom didn't have a car, he hasn't been able to and was hoping I would go with him.

I, of course, took the opportunity. I missed him and I was so bored here by myself in this big house without my mother. She had literally come home twice since Christmas. Both times? I wasn't even home to see her. And both times, she had left a letter saying that she'd be doing business for a while in both Miami and Atlanta. And to let her know if I truly needed anything.

The whole while?

The Christmas tree was still up. With her presents underneath.

I didn't want to admit how heartbroken I was about all of this, mostly because I kept myself occupied at the studio, but I was. So, this hike was actually timely. I could do some thinking myself and spend time with someone who was becoming a favorite person in my life.

So I obliged, put on some leggings and boots, and picked Jarell up to head to the hiking paths. When we arrived, Jarell requested to take me on the less hard route because he liked the nature better there. It wouldn't have mattered to me anyway because I wasn't familiar with any of the paths; I was just along for the adventure.

Within the first five minutes of the hike, I got tired out fast. I wasn't used to this kind of exercise, but it didn't seem to bother Jarell at all. In fact, he chuckled at me when I stopped to take a break when I was out of breath. Then, he found a large stick on the ground to assist me in walking up the inclines. That helped me out a lot, so now I was more willing to engage in conversation with him. The way this path looked, it looked like we were going to be spending the day here.

"Alright listen, Jade. Now that you're getting used to the paths, I want to give you a heads up. Usually, I camp this place alone to just have fresh air and to think, so I'm limiting your questions of me to three. You're probably thinking all types of ways to see what you can get out of me today," he said, but I could hear the humor underneath.

I laughed out loud. Damn. It was six months that we've known each other, and he already knew me this well. I definitely had some tricks up my sleeve to get him to talk about topics that I wanted to talk about.

"Three!? Really, Jarell? I can't be limited to three. How about five?" I said, looking at him sideways.

He gave me his second and rare full-on laugh, showing his beautiful smile again.

"No, Jade. Three it is. And that's final."

"Really? Fine. Well, I'm making a deal. If my maximum is three, then your minimum is three," I said, crossing my arms.

He laughed louder.

"What? No."

"Jarell, you have to play fair. You can't lay rules on me when I can't lay rules on you."

"Nah, it's my alone time!"

"Yep, and you wouldn't be getting it if I didn't bring you here."

Yeah. There was no way he was winning after that comeback. He smacked his lips and ran a hand over his face with a twisted smile.

"Yeah. Take that L. Your minimum is three."

"Whatever. What's your favorite candy?"

I punched him in the arm lightly. He winced in fake pain, and it took everything for me not to laugh.

"That's a wack ass question. The rule is that you have to ask deep questions."

"What? You can't be making up rules as we go!" he exclaimed with a frown.

"Jarell, just humor me. Oblige me. Please? I've played your quiet, safe, and simple game for too long. Can you just play my game once? Just once?" I pleaded, grabbing onto his arm.

He grumbled and rolled his eyes.

"God. You ain't coming with me next time."

"Okay. I can accept that. As long as you oblige me today."

"Fine."

"Alright. You're first."

"Why you so snooty?"

"Jarell!" I screamed, and he gave me another laugh. Jesus, was it music to my ears.

"I was serious that time!" Jarell said with a wicked glare and a twinkle in his eyes.

"I'm not snooty!"

"Alright, alright. Um... what made you start caring about me so much?"

Great question. Now this is what I was talking about.

"Much better. Honestly? You caught my eye after that showdown in the hallway at the very beginning of the year between you and Martell. You were so withdrawn and quiet. That's why I call you Ghost. Nobody knew who you were, and people had different things to say about you. So, I wanted to find out for myself. And then, I damn near killed you on my way home from the studio one night, and I felt really bad about it, but that became my excuse to get to know you better. And then, I really started to like you. Even though you got on my nerves being an asshole to me, you honestly have the best personality. You're so authentic and dry, but it's funny, and I enjoy it. And I just grew to care about you ever since."

Jarell nodded without any expression except his eyes. Again, gratitude. I've come to know that all his feelings lay in his eyes, ironically. He had to have felt good on the inside because it was rare for someone outside of his mother to tell him that they truly cared.

He really wasn't going to say much after that, so I interjected.

"Alright. Now I'm going to ask you a couple of questions."

"Go for it."

"How do you navigate the world without vision? I'm amazed at how you can just find your way without a blind cane or without anyone's help. How do you do it?"

This moment was a textbook example. Here he was, walking through tumultuous hiking paths with just a thick branch, yet he simply walked through them like it didn't faze him at all. At times, he stumbled a bit and I would pause in fear that he'd hurt himself, but he would just find his footing again with his branch and keep moving. It was amazing.

"Well, because I can't see, my other senses are very strong," he said. As he spoke, he reached out to touch some of the tree bark to find his way as we walked. Suddenly, he stopped.

"What are you doing?" I asked, my eyes tracking his every move.

No response. He just ventured off the path and headed for the trees, pointing his branch towards the ground.

"Jarell, I wouldn't do that," I warned, but he ignored me. He simply knelt to touch a bed of beautiful reddish flowers that had blossomed. Not only was I in awe that he knew where they were, but that they were blossomed in February.

"This is a Petunia flower," Jarell said. With a smile, he retraced his steps towards me. I watched in awe. He was completely in his element, completely himself amongst nature, and my heart melted. "Because we live in Southern California, some flowers still blossom in the winter."

"How'd you know what they're called? How'd you even know they were there without seeing them?"

"I can smell them," he said, and handed me the flowers.

"Awww. Thank you, Jarell," I said, blushing. They smelled so sweet. I would treasure these flowers as long as they lived. They were his first gift to me. And as simple as it was, it meant everything.

"But to answer your original question fully," he continued, "I just come to a place over and over again, really. And I memorize its paths and landmarks by touching. If I'm with someone, I listen to their footsteps closely so I can follow. I wear my hood up because in my head, I count my steps sometimes. If I have my hood on and have my head down, I can focus on counting better, and it'll appear like I don't want to be bothered. So I really hate when people bump into me in the halls at school or interrupt me anywhere because then I lose count."

Wow. Everything he said just made so much sense.

"So, the steps from your car to my porch is about thirty-three steps. I do this because I don't want to use a blind cane. I don't like the idea of people knowing I'm blind. Then they'll really take advantage of me."

"Wow, Jarell. That's fascinating. So I'm assuming that you pretend you need Kylah's help into the house when I drop you off…"

He chuckled.

"She's a little kid, Jade. Anything to make her feel important is what makes her happy. So, yes. I pretend that she's helping me."

"Such a good big brother. What about your hand and feet movement? Why do you use your hands and flutter them to the side like that all the time?"

He smiled.

"You know that's your second question, right?"

"What!? Jarell, that's a follow-up question to my first one!"

"Nope. Your questions about how I knew the flowers were there were follow-up questions." He smirked.

"Really? Whatever. Go ahead and answer."

"Yes. That's why I use my hands like that or drag my feet. I do that to feel my environment on the ground or the temperature. And also to tell the time. When I'm outside, I feel the direction of the sun with my hands too, and that tells me what time of day it is. So right now, the sun is beaming on my face in front of me. That not only tells me we're moving east, but it's about eight or nine in the morning."

Looking at my watch, it indeed was 9:17. Holy shit! Not only was he fascinating, but he was also smart as hell. There's no way I would have thought to do that if I was blind. I'd just be as helpless as a newborn, probably asking anyone I felt that was around to tell me the time. That's how spoiled I was.

"That's cool stuff, Jarell. You honestly amaze me."

"Yeah." He blushed. "Thanks."

"It's your turn."

"Let's see... what happened to your real father? That guy at the concert wasn't your real dad, right?" he asked.

Oh, well that was an easy question. It wasn't like I had a relationship with my real father. I didn't even remember him to be honest, and I never wondered about him anyway because Corey had done such a great job with me as my stepdad. Plus, my mom never mentioned him and wanted me to erase him from my mind. Not only for my sake, but also for her own. She didn't want to admit that she was a teen mom to some thug. It would ruin her entire self-image.

"Yeah, that's not my real dad. That's my stepdad. My real dad? He's in prison. According to my mom, he's sentenced to life for getting involved in some murder when they were younger. My mom was seventeen when she got pregnant with me and so was he. So he was just getting into some shit he shouldn't have been in and got caught up with some older guys, assisting in the murder."

"Oh. We've got something in common then," Jarell said, leaning smoothly against the bark of a tree.

"What?"

"My dad was killed before I was even born so I never got a chance to meet him. He was in some gang, my mom used to tell me."

"Damn. Two Black men's lives ruined over silly shit."

"Right. Alright. Your turn. You only get one last question, so make this good because I ain't answering shit else," he said with a small smile.

The pressure was on. There were so many things I still wanted to know about Jarell. He was so mysterious, and I could play this game for hours on end. Like, how come he never stood up for himself to bullies at school? How did bullying at school make him feel? How come his family was in such poverty? What did he plan to do with his life in the future? How did he see his future with him being blind? Was he ever scared to be blind? How long had he been blind? What could he actually see? Has he ever had a girlfriend, and for how long? *Which question did I choose!?*

"Do you write poetry?"

Jarell frowned.

"What?"

"Do you write poetry?"

"Why?"

"Well…" I started, but now, at this point, I didn't know how I was going to break it to him that I had found poems in his backpack and had kept them. Now that I had brought it up, I had no choice.

"Well what?"

"Well, when I had your backpack for those two months you weren't at school, I kind of went through it to help me figure out some things about you and where you might be. And I couldn't read anything because everything was in Braille. But then there was this…"

And with that, I pulled Jarell's poems out of my leggings pocket. They were still neatly folded and almost looked untouched. I reached out to hand the poems to him, touching his hand and he slowly accepted. He ran his hands over the writing slowly, biting his lip with this weird, closed expression.

"Is this your poetry?"

With a deep sigh, he nodded.

"Yes. It is. Why did you think it was okay to even go through my stuff like that? None of this is any of your business."

"I know, and I'm sorry. I never ended up getting it translated anyway so I don't know what anything says. I was wondering, could you tell me what at least one of them means? Only if you're comfortable, of course."

With this continued blank look, he shook his head.

"You've used all your questions." He shrugged.

My mouth dropped. That fucker! It was true; I did ask all my questions, but that first question was a leading question to my real question!

"Jarell, that's not fair!" I exclaimed.

"It's fair. I told you to make the last question a good one. You're the one who decided you wanted to ask if I wrote poetry or not."

"Are you serious?"

"Dead ass."

"So you're really not going to share?"

"No. And to be honest, you won't understand them."

"Of course I don't understand them; they're in Braille."

"Not even that. If I read them to you, it wouldn't even make sense."

"So if that's the case, can you read them? Not like I'd understand them anyway, right?"

"You've used all your questions. Sorry, Jade."

"Fine. Forget I asked," I said, folding my arms and continued to walk up the hill.

A half smile spread across his face.

"You'll be aight."

"Whatever dude. You have one question left."

"I'm honestly done with this game." He shrugged.

"Really, Jarell? Can you ever finish anything you start?" I asked. It was kind of a low blow, considering his situation with graduating and dropping out of school, but whatever.

"I didn't start it. You did."

"Don't be an asshole. Finish the game, Jarell. It's not hard to ask a question."

He rolled his eyes and continued up the hill in silence. I sighed. *Fine.* At least he engaged for most of the game. I couldn't even complain. I guessed that I should honor his alone and reflection time. Although, according to his mom, he had had more than enough reflecting in his room when he closed himself off from the world.

Not a word was exchanged until we reached the top of the path. It was a beautiful sight, overlooking the city of LA. Literally breathtaking. Something I wished the both of us could experience. I felt sad for Jarell, that somehow, he was stripped away from knowing such beauty. He didn't seem to care, though. With his head raised high and his eyes closed, Jarell soaked up the cool breeze of the day and completely canceled me out. I just let him.

After a while, probably after too long, I was ready to go. Now, Jarell was sitting near the edge of the cliff with his knees up and his forearms resting on them, not seeming to want to leave at all.

"Jarell, I'm ready to go," I said.

"Go ahead. No one's stopping you," he replied.

"I'm not leaving you up here alone."

"Then sit down and chill."

I huffed. "Fine."

Impatient, I leaned against a tree next to Jarell and looked at my phone. It was past noon. We'd been here for three hours. And it was going to take another hour to get back down.

"Do you still love Mike?" Jarell randomly blurted out, and I blinked.

Where the hell did that come from?

"What? Why?"

"Do you still love him? That's my final question."

I sighed. Well... Did I still love Mike? Did I even love him in the first place?

Did I even know what love was?

"No," I said. "No, I don't and never did love Mike. Cared about him, yes. A lot. But I don't think I ever loved him."

"Interesting," he nodded. "Interesting that you'd want to entertain him. Even have sex with him then."

"What's it to you?"

"Nothing. Just found it interesting that you'd fight for him, fight over him, and would want to have sex with someone for your first time if you never even loved them."

"You don't have to love someone to have sex with them."

"You don't, but it makes it pointless."

"Okay, know-it-all. I take it that you're having some hot, meaningful sex with the one you so dearly love. Good for you, perfect heaven-sent angel," I said.

"Thanks." He smirked. I turned up my lip. I didn't know why I felt so sick inside after he said that. An image of some faceless girl on top of Jarell, riding him like there was no tomorrow burned my psyche, and I suddenly felt hot and the need to throw up.

"Whatever. Can we go now?" I asked.

"Yeah."

"You should come over my house. I'm bored there with my mom being gone."

"Hell no. What if she comes back?"

"She won't, Jarell. She's gone for another few days. Maybe even more."

"I don't know." He shook his head.

"Please Jarell."

"I'm not going to that bougie ass side of town. Forget about it."

"I understand Jarell, but it's just this once. It's been an entire month since she's left. None of this money shit matters when you have no family."

Oddly, a huge lump developed in my throat. I tried to swallow it away, but that actually made it worse.

"Fuck," I hissed in frustration at my eyes burning. And right then, I just started bawling. Out of nowhere. Didn't even know where it came from. *Nothing.*

"Sometimes I just feel so alone. My father is in prison. I don't know any of his family. My mom's family is on the east coast. Corey is reporting for the NBA. My mother only wants anything to do with me if I'm producing some sort of money or perfection. She's never even told me that she loves me. Ever. I have no one, Jarell. Even when to the world, it seems like I do. Even when there are so many people around me, I feel alone. Every fucking day," I sobbed. Then, completely broke down in my hands.

Jarell was quiet the entire time. I didn't expect any words or care to even look at him. I just basked in my own misery for what was a hurtful revelation.

I truly felt alone, no matter who surrounded me.

Didn't think I'd be the type to say that. Hell, was it even valid? I had no right to feel this way, standing with someone who had absolutely no friends at all. But hey... I couldn't help the way I felt. Now, it was my truth.

I cried to myself for some time until I felt Jarell's presence. He was a man of no words until I turned to face him squarely.

"Come here," he said and opened his arms for a hug.

I obeyed and sobbed into his embrace. And he just held me. Strong. And I appreciated it.

"Fine. I'll go with you," he finally said.

"Thank you."

Chapter Twenty-Four

"**WELCOME TO MY** home."

Placing my small, red bug in park in the driveway, I turned off the car and gazed over to Jarell. His hood was up, and his face was emotionless as he stared straight ahead out of the windshield without responding. I sighed, rolled my eyes, and watched him again, waiting for a response.

Still. Not a word.

I squinted to get a closer look at him. What did he see? Could he imagine the possibilities of what a richer neighborhood looked like? Did he envision the cul-de-sac we lived on that was lined with two and three-story homes and Mercedes Benz and Maserati's parked in their fronts? What was he even thinking about?

The entire car ride here had been silent, and although he didn't scrunch up against the car door the way he used to, which was a win, his silence still bothered me. Particularly since we had broken so many communication barriers, and he just took us four steps back. And his silence barred me from any measure on how he felt about coming over here. It didn't help that it was dark outside as the sun had gone completely beneath the horizon. That gave him an extra layer of security and ability to hide from me beneath his hood. Either way, no matter how he felt about coming here, I was glad he did. I was glad he swallowed his discomfort for me. For my sake. That right there told me a lot.

"Ready to head in?" I asked.

"Guess so."

He sighed and pushed the car door open to get out with his backpack that lay between his legs. That prompted me to do the same, except mine was in the back seat. I walked over to his side of the car and linked his arm with mine to lead him inside the huge, empty home that echoed with our every step. My heart thrashed while thinking of what I should do now that he was here. Should I give him a tour? Should we stay in the living room area instead of going up to my room? How were we going to spend our time?

School was tomorrow, yet it was still early in the evening. It was more than enough time to get into something before bed. I barely knew what he liked to do other than dance, origami, and walking in nature.

"Let's go upstairs to my room," I decided as he fluttered his hands at his sides and dragged his feet across the linoleum tile. If I wasn't crazy, I'd have thought he was nervous or something.

"You sure?" he slowly asked.

"Yeah. It's fine. I got to see your room. Why can't you go to mine?"

"I never said that I couldn't. I just wanted to make sure that you were... never mind."

"What? Say it," I prodded as he, for a split second, looked concerned, but it disappeared.

"Never mind, Jade. I'm following you."

He hauled his falling backpack over his shoulder again and followed me up the stairs to my room. I wondered what was in his bag other than overnight clothes.

"Here we are! You can give your bag to me. I'll set it somewhere safe," I offered, but he shook his head.

"I'll keep it."

I shrugged. "Okay. Well, make yourself at home. Take your shoes off. Take a seat on the bed. Do whatever you need to feel comfortable."

Jarell nodded and sat on the edge of my king-sized bed and kicked his shoes off. I walked by and picked them up to move them out of the way, taking note to buy him a new pair of shoes soon. With crossed legs, Jarell acclimated himself to my room without much other movement. He looked as uncomfortable as he does when he gets into my car. I tried to lighten the mood.

"So! What do you want to do? Wanna have a movie night? Dance? Do homework? Want to go down to the game room and play? What else do you like to do?"

"It's whatever you want. I'm here for you, really. You wanted my company, so I'm here for that," he said.

"Okay. Well why don't we just stay in my room? I have a bathroom and everything you'll need up here anyway. How about I put on a movie and order pizza?"

"If that's what you want to do." He shrugged.

"Jarell, don't be a pill. I want to make sure that we both do what we want. Actually? How about this? How about we do some origami as I play the movie? You can teach me a thing or two about how to create such masterpieces."

At that suggestion, a smile creeped slowly across his lips and stopped just as the corners of his mouth slightly tilted up. I laughed.

"Sounds like a yes," I said.

"What do you want to make?"

"A bird, maybe?"

"Alright. That's a good place to start."

"What movie do you want to watch? Or should I say listen to?" I rose from the bed and walked over to my tall movie collection on the built-in shelves on the wall.

"I'd rather listen to music."

"Okay. Well music it is. I'll just put on my Spotify playlist."

"Bet."

Jarell bent over and opened his bag, rummaging through his overnight clothes for paper he had neatly tucked inside. Once he pulled them out, I noticed the papers were all different kinds of beautiful, bright colors that made me smile. The fact that he even had those papers in there told me he was planning on doing origami here regardless of what I wanted to do. Or at least while I was asleep.

Moving from my bed to the floor, he spread the papers out and sat down with his legs spread wide.

"Come here," he invited with a soft voice.

Giving him a fond look, I turned on my playlist and crawled to the floor, sitting next to him.

"Pick a color," he said.

"Lavender." I pointed.

"I meant grab the color you want, Jade. You know I can't see where it is." He chuckled with a joking glow in his eyes that caused me to giggle. I was glad he didn't get offended or trip out on me. I could tell he was getting comfortable. Just a little bit.

"My bad, sometimes I forget. What color do you want? So I can give it to you."

"Turquoise."

I handed him the paper, and in the meanwhile, he collected all the other unchosen papers together and set them to the side.

"Alright. I'ma make something real quick, and you're going to make the same thing I make. Okay?" he said.

"Sounds good to me. Let me order pizza while you do that. You good with pepperoni?"

"I'm good with anything."

"Alright."

Jarell went on and created his origami while I ordered the food. He was still creating the masterpiece when the pizza got here. By the time he was finished and we both had eaten, it was time for us to create the bird together. He had just finished his plate while I was looking at his completed origami piece.

"Jarell, this bird is amazing. It's so intricate. How do you do this with so much detail?" I asked, staring at it in the palm of my hands.

"Just a matter of touch. That's all. You don't really need to see," he said, wiping his mouth with a napkin.

"Show me your ways."

"Alright." He sat back down on the floor and spread his legs out. "Bring your paper and come sit in between my legs."

With a shy grin, I cleaned up our food, grabbed my lavender paper, and sat in between his legs as my back met his chest. The warmth of his body made me feel so cozy and protected that my heart raced. Never in a million years did I think I'd ever feel the way I did for Mike, but for Jarell. It was to the point where I was nearly shaking. I wondered if he felt the same. If his heart was skipping beats because he was so close to me.

"Alright. First start by folding the paper into a triangle."

"Easy enough," I said and folded my paper into a triangle. He watched calmly over my shoulder as the heat of his breath on my neck warmed my skin. I shuddered slightly, praying he didn't feel it.

"Done."

"Alright. Now fold the longest part of the triangle down so that only the tip is showing."

"Done."

"Here's where it gets hard. I'm gonna use my hands to help you fold the way I want you to, okay? So fold the paper like this."

He reached around my body and held my hands in his, showing me how he wanted me to fold the paper. My eyes fixated on the point where our hands joined. Any direction he had given me about how to fold the paper floated through one ear and out the other. Our brown complexions were almost an exact match, but his skin sported something else that my unblemished tone didn't.

His hands and knuckles were covered in healed scratches, scabs, and bruises, indicative of possible rustling, tussling, and fighting. Which was interesting because for the four years I went to Crenshaw, I had never seen him fight. It made me wonder if his hand had healed from those stitches when he crushed his glasses on the palm side.

"Jade, are you listening?" he whispered in my ear. That made the hair on the back of my neck shoot right out of their cuticles. I blinked, coming back to reality.

"Um... maybe?" I bit my lip.

"What's wrong?"

"N-nothing."

He looked at me with suspicion.

"I'm serious. It's nothing."

"Alright. Well pay attention then and move your hands with me," he said. "I'm trying to show you how to fold this."

"What if I can't?"

I turned around to face him squarely, and he looked towards me with low eyes.

"Why can't you?" he asked with a raspy voice.

I didn't answer. All I could find myself doing was stare at his lips, wondering if they felt as plush as they looked tonight. If they tasted as moist and soft as I remembered. But I was scared. I had leaned in to kiss him the last time on Christmas, but to do it in my space and in my room felt so different. We were now alone, and the possibilities were endless.

He just stared at me too, letting the piece of origami we practiced with fall into my lap. Unfortunately, I could read nothing. Not a single sign of what he felt.

I just went with my gut.

I shifted towards him and laid my head on his shoulder. Just to show my gratitude. Just to show how happy I was that he was here with me. He stiffened, but I didn't care. I just took a deep breath, taking in his scent, which was surprisingly a refreshing combination of a cool fragrance mixed with his natural aroma.

I wondered what his skin tasted like, too.

I've kissed a man's neck before and left hickies. It was Mike Harrison during our Sophomore year in the hallway when we were both wide-eyed, innocent, and scared. It had been racy and fun, but this here was different. This moment brought a level of genuine closeness that I had never felt before.

I pulled back and watched him to take in his reaction. Now, Jarell's eyes held so much emotion that there was absolutely no way for me to decipher and tease apart what was in them. I didn't know if that was good or bad.

"You smell good," I whispered.

I buried my face into the crevice of his neck this time, fully taking in every inch of his flesh. My lips brushed against his soft, mocha skin that I craved to explore.

And I went for it.

I kissed him lightly on the neck a couple of times while at the same time, feeling extremely fearful. My heart fluttered as his entire body became even more tense. My lips softly met his skin, placing my stamp upon him. I instantly felt discouraged, yet it made me feel emboldened. That maybe he'd just give in and follow my lead.

So my tongue left my mouth and grazed him as I left kisses in between.

He let out a long sigh and reluctantly tilted his head a bit to give me more access, which made me feel a little better, but there was something about this whole thing that just didn't feel right. No matter how my body felt. It just seemed that we both wanted this to happen, but at the same time, we largely did not.

Jarell let me kiss him for a while until I eventually felt his full resistance.

"Hey. Jade. Listen," Jarell called out gently. My tongue left his neck. "We shouldn't."

He put his hands on my shoulders and pulled my lips away from him. He bit his lip with guilt as I gave him a similar look.

Yeah. He felt the same way I felt.

It just didn't feel like it was the right time. He was here to stymie the loneliness I felt, not to take advantage of my mother's absence for something that would potentially lead to sex. As I sat on his lap and thought about it, I came to a painful realization.

I was doing this because I was vulnerable. Vulnerable about feeling so alone, and I was projecting that onto him.

He probably knew that. And now I felt awful. I shouldn't have put that kind of pressure on him. We hadn't even talked about or acknowledged the first kiss that we had together, let alone trying to navigate this.

"You're right," I said.

"Maybe we should just get ready for tomorrow," he said.

I nodded, separated myself from Jarell's body, and rose from the floor. I checked the time. It was approaching ten o'clock. My fingers ran through my flat ironed hair as I tried to collect myself and think about what to do next. Jarell took a deep breath. He turned his head away from me and looked towards the ground, clearly feeling some type of way.

Damn.

All of that was intense.

Very intense.

I blinked several times, feeling a bit embarrassed and moved towards my dresser to get out clothes to sleep. As I did, Jarell got up, leaving the origami on the ground and sat on my bed with his back towards me. I took that moment to strip and put on a tank and boy shorts, which were my pajamas. Jarell didn't even notice or say anything. Instead, he had simply sat on the edge of my bed fully clothed in his jeans and hoodie, thinking to himself, looking at the ceiling. I would've paid to know what was going through is head right now.

"Jarell, are you going to undress and come to sleep with me?" I had asked.

"Nah. I'm good."

"You're not getting in my bed with those dirty clothes, Jarell. That's an absolute no."

"Then I'll sleep on the floor." He shrugged.

"Really?"

"I'm not going to sleep in the bed with you, Jade."

"Fine. If that's what you want to do. Is there anything you'd like me to wash tonight?"

"Nah."

"Jarell." I gave him a look. "Let me at least wash your hoodie."

"No," he said firmly. "Absolutely not."

My eyes had widened, and then I rolled them. Sheesh. Why was he so connected to that piece of filthy, oversized cotton anyway?

"At least your underwear and socks, Jarell. Can you do that?"

He sighed, finally figuring out that he wasn't going to win.

He had given me his socks, and in privacy, as I turned my back, he had given me his boxers to put in the laundry.

"Thanks," he had mumbled.

Nothing much was said after that. I put Jarell's clothes in the larger laundry to be washed later and when I came back, Jarell was cuddled up on the floor next to my bed on my plush rug. I gave him a sad look but decided not to fight it.

"Do you want a blanket at least?" I asked, but he shook his head.

I felt shitty for ultimately allowing him to sleep that way, but I was also too exhausted to even fight him. Especially after everything that had just happened.

I sighed and got into the bed, just letting it go. I shut the music off and turned the lamp off.

"Good night, Jarell. I'll see you in the morning."

Chapter Twenty-Five

The sun shone brightly the next day through my huge windows and its curtains. I woke up confused, since the sun usually struggled to peak over the horizon by the time it was ready for me to get up for school. I grabbed my phone on my nightstand in a panic to check the time since I didn't hear my alarm, and it was indeed nine o'clock. Shit. School started two hours ago.

I sat up, and my head throbbed.

"Shit," I hissed.

I couldn't keep missing school, especially if I was the cheerleading captain.

I squinted my eyes opened, hearing slight movements and breathing down below on the floor. I had forgotten Jarell spent the night, unfortunately, without getting in the bed.

Finally waking up and fully adjusted to a new day, I peeked over my bed and down at Jarell. He had his arm over his head shielding himself from being seen, but his chest rose and fell even and peacefully. A huge part of me didn't want to wake him because I just didn't feel like facing him after what happened last night. I had no idea how he was going to perceive me or how we were going to move forward. But I had to get him up because for one, he wasn't very familiar with my home for me to leave him here. And second, my mom may come back tonight. I didn't want to get caught up with that. Especially since I had my own bone to pick with her.

"Jarell," I called out. He didn't wake.

"Jarell," I said louder this time, and he groaned.

Shifting again, it appeared he just turned to a different side and went back to sleep.

"Jarell, seriously. Get up. It's nine and we need to be in school in the next hour. We're already hella late."

I shook him this time, and he groaned again in frustration. He snatched away from me in anger, lifted up, and just sat there, trying to wake himself up. I sadly watched him, knowing that he just wanted to be left alone, but I had to do it.

"I'm gonna shower," I said. He still sat with his head down. "You can shower in the guest bathroom. I can walk you there with your bag if you want."

"Yeah."

I smiled small. He was so grumpy.

Grabbing his backpack, I also grabbed Jarell's hand and led him to the guest bathroom. His steps were groggy and slow, and he looked awful. His eyes were red, and he looked like he didn't sleep well. I wanted to ask him about it, but I already knew he wouldn't answer anyway. Seeing him like this made me feel even more terrible that I was forcing him to go to school.

"Jarell after you shower, I'm going to take you home."

"Thought we were going to school?"

"No. You need rest. Sleeping on the floor isn't good sleep at all."

"Nah. I'm going to school."

Once we made it to the bathroom, I gave Jarell some towels and turned on the shower water so that it would be one less thing for him to have to figure out.

"When you're done, let me know when you're dressed too so that I can walk you to where you need to go."

It took us about thirty minutes to get ready. I wasn't particularly cute for school today, but whatever. It just wasn't the time for it. Jarell was in the living room sitting on the couch waiting for me when I gathered all of my cheerleading stuff and made sure the house was cleaned before leaving. I stepped in front of him when I was set and gazed at him one more time. I sighed as he stood up, sensing I was standing there ready to go.

"Jarell? About last night," I started, but he put his hand up.

"S'cool, Jade. Don't beat yourself up about it," he said awkwardly.

"Wait. Just let me finish. Please."

He exhaled, throwing a genuinely patient look my way.

"I know I was wrong for doing that, Jarell. I hope you don't think I'm some... I don't know... some thirst bucket who was looking to get you alone so we could ... you know ... do things."

He laughed.

"I don't think that at all about you, Jade. I know where it came from."

"Yeah, and it wasn't a good idea."

"Yeah, that's why I stopped you. I wasn't gonna take advantage of that moment, Jade," he said softly. "I would never take advantage of you like that. Okay?"

My heart melted. It was literally the first time I had ever seen him be completely vulnerable and show himself to me. His soft side. The true colors beneath his nonchalant demeanor.

"Aww, Jarell. I really appreciate that."

"It's the truth. I'm sorry that you feel alone."

"Yeah. Well, since you came, I feel better. I just want to say thank you. You didn't have to stay with me. I treasure every moment we have together, and I'm glad you trust me enough to come to an intimate space like my bedroom."

He nodded.

"It ain't a big deal. You ready?" he asked, picking up his backpack from the floor.

"Yeah." I nodded.

We headed to school, and by the time we made it, it was fourth period. As the both of us walked towards the building, something dawned on me.

"Oh shit, Jarell. It's the first day of fourth quarter! Damn it, this is like the worst day to be late. It's graduation season, now!"

"Oh, yeah. I forgot about that, too."

"You got your schedule in your bag?" He nodded. "Let me see it."

Jarell shuffled around in his backpack for his schedule, and he finally found it because it was folded a certain way so that he could remember the difference. Smart guy. I took my own schedule out and looked at it, comparing the two.

"We have gym together this quarter. Seventh period!" I smiled. I was so glad to have a class with him as high school was winding down.

"I hate gym," he said.

"I know. We have swimming this quarter too. I'ma have to get braids or something."

"That's even worse."

"Well, Ms. Jenson will be with you, right? She's going to get in the pool. She's not going to let anything happen to you."

"Yeah, I know. I just don't like being around people, especially like that. I'll probably be in the special ed pool anyway, so I'm cool with that."

"Yeah. Everything will be okay," I said.

Finally, we had reached the point in the school where we had to go separate ways.

"I'll see you seventh period, okay? Have a good day, Jarell. I mean it."

"Yeah. You too. Jade?" He called out to me when I started to walk away.

"Yeah?"

"Give me another hug."

I smiled. I loved how open he was becoming. And the more he did, the more I cared nothing about displaying our friendship openly.

With my arms stretched out, Jarell met me halfway and we embraced one another as we buried our faces into one another's neck. I took in his raw scent, and it was a breath of fresh air. I pulled back and smiled. He returned it, of course not even knowing I was smiling at him.

"Have a good day, Jarell."

"Thanks."

We both went our separate ways with Ms. Jenson meeting up with him halfway down the hall, and me heading to D-Block. The bell had just rung for third period to be let out, and the halls quickly filled up. Once I reached the kick it spot on the block, my friends were already congregated. I headed straight for Laurie because she was the only person I wanted to talk to anyway.

As I approached the group and they noticed me, every one of them dished me a weird look. The only person that didn't have that look was Erica. She had a silly smirk on her face she always had when she felt like she had one-upped somebody. *What the hell was going on?*

"Why y'all looking at me like that?" I asked with a frown. "I literally just got here."

"Oh, she just got here, y'all. Wonder where she could've been," Erica said, looking up at the ceiling of the school as if saying 'I told you so.' *This bitch...*

"Yo, Jade. What the fuck is wrong with you? You on some bullshit. Talking about you ain't fucking with that dirty weird boy," Tazz said. "Lying ass bitch."

"What are you talking about, Tazz? And watch your mouth talking to me like that."

"Nah, stop fucking fronting because as soon as Mike come in the hall, I'm showing him this shit," Martell chimed in, and then displayed his phone.

My heart dropped. His phone showed pictures of Jarell and I walking in the parking lot after school, riding in my car together, and today, hugging in the hallway. I took a deep breath and shrugged my shoulders, backing away from the phone. Who was that damn thirsty to be having tabs on me like this? It had to be Erica. I just knew it. She was looking for literally any way to destroy me.

"So? That's what y'all mad about?"

"Nah, we mad because you on some lying bullshit and you fucking around on a nigga everybody wants," one of the girls in the circle said.

"Yeah, and you playing my nigga Mike, and I ain't with the shits on that," Martell said.

"I don't know why y'all care so much," I said, and looked at Laurie. She was frowning at me, shaking her head.

"Why Jade?" she asked. "What is so special about him that you're messing around with him like that over Mike? He's fucking creepy, dirty, a crackhead, and he has no friends. Why would you want to get yourself in that situation with him?"

"See, what y'all problem is, is that you don't know shit about him. There's nothing wrong with him and there's more wrong with y'all than anything he got going on," I said, crossing my arms.

"Oh hell nah. Fuck that," many of them groaned simultaneously.

"I'm just telling you the truth. Get to know him some time. You might think differently."

"Hell nah. Fuck around and catch Ebola," some guy said, and everyone laughed.

How ignorant. I scoffed in disgust and turned my lip at them. I was about to walk away when Mike appeared in the hallway, walking down with Martell who was showing him the pictures. Mike had a frown the entire time, but it deepened the more pictures of Jarell and me that he saw. When Martell was done showing him, he had whispered something, and Mike's eyes snapped towards me. I huffed and looked away, not wanting to hear one goddamn thing he had to say.

"Jade, so you lied to me.'"

"Nigga, I didn't lie to you."

"Get the fuck outta here. Every time I asked you about that nigga, you was saying how much you ain't had shit going on with him, you barely know him, and now this is what the fuck I find out? The proof is right there shorty. In the pictures. You can't hide or deny that shit."

"Last time I checked Mike, you don't care about me. You got a new bitch all up on you every single day, and you worried about me? Please, ain't nobody thinking about you," I said, waving him off and tried to walk away.

With a tight grip, he grabbed my arm and yanked me back towards him.

"Don't you dare disrespect me like that," he seethed, and I snatched away from him.

"Who you think you touching? Don't you ever put your hands on me like that again! Who the hell do you think you are?"

"I'm the nigga that has sustained your popularity all this time. That's who I am."

"Boy bye. Are you serious? I got whole ass bands from dancing with Chris Brown. What money you got? What clout you got? If anything, I've sustained you. So get up off me. I've moved on, Mike. And you should too. Hell, it looks like you already have. I don't care about what you got going on anymore. Don't care about you. Bitches, you can have my sloppy seconds."

"Sloppy seconds?" His eyes bucked. "Oh, so you think you bad now and can talk all that shit, huh? I ain't none of these little niggas and bitches you be checking out here, Jade. I'll ruin your ass."

"Do it then. I ain't worried."

"Yeah, you should be. Then, you'll love how much I ruin that dirty ass nigga too that you lied to me about. We let his soft ass go twice, so he's due. I'll show that bitch what happens when you mess with a real nigga's girl."

"Go ahead. Touch him. Your whole ass basketball prospect will be ruined and you won't be going no damn where for college. How about that? Since that's your only claim to fame."

Licking his lips, he stepped back. He tried not to show it, but he knew he had been defeated.

"Okay," he nodded in a threatening way. I swallowed.

"What you need us to do, cuz?" Tazz asked Mike.

"Not a damn thing!" I shouted. "If y'all lay one finger on him, it'll be the last finger that touches something."

The guys in the circle laughed.

"What you gonna do, cupcake?" Martell said, and everyone laughed at me.

Shaking my head, I walked away. Now, I was truly going to have to stick by Jarell's side publicly. And I was okay with that because our relationship and friendship that we had was way bigger and more important than anything these low lives had going on here.

There was no way I was going to allow anyone to touch Jarell or put him in danger. I would protect him by any means necessary, even if that meant ruining college prospects, expulsion, or anything. I was going to let Ms. Jenson know now. I was going to let the counselors know as well. I was going use every tool in my toolbox. He needed someone to stand up for him more than ever from the world and the fucked-up problems that it came with.

Chapter Twenty-Six

I came home from school early before the basketball game tonight and moved past the foyer to see my mother sitting on the couch with her legs crossed. *Oh. She was home. Surprise.*

She was wearing a red bodycon dress that stopped just above her knees and nude heels. Her lips were also red, and her hair was pulled back into a tight bun as she sipped on a thin glass of wine. I just stared at her, feeling disgusted and she stared back with cool glare.

"Hey," I mumbled, and then attempted to walk by her to head up the stairs to my room with my cheerleading belongings. Looking at her pissed me off, and that told me right there that I wasn't ready to deal with the hurt she caused by leaving me alone for the holidays. Not only the holidays, but for damn near two months. With everything that happened today at school, I didn't have time to even build up enough walls erected around the vulnerability I had been feeling to deal with her.

"Uh uh. Get back here," she said, putting her leg up onto the coffee table so I couldn't walk by. I could have easily stepped over it or walked around if I wanted to, but I didn't. I looked down at her, and there was fire in her eyes and her lips were pressed thin.

When she realized I wasn't going anywhere, that I was actually going to listen, she kicked me back towards the living room door with her foot, causing me to stumble a little bit. It was enough to make me look at her like she was crazy. Especially since the heel of her shoe dug into my thigh, which caused for some pain.

"What did I do?" I asked.

"Girl, don't ask me a stupid question like that."

Then, she pulled some clothes from behind her back.

"Whose clothes are these? Who the hell was in my house while I was gone?" she asked, holding them up in the air.

I closed my eyes and sighed, cursing on the inside. I had totally forgotten that I told Jarell that I would wash his clothes that he left here. Now I whole heartedly regretted that decision because I didn't even think about my mother coming home today to even see the laundry.

"Answer me!" she screamed, and I cringed, turning my head away. "And don't you lie to me."

"They're Jarell's," I whispered.

Slamming his clothes down on the couch, she stood up. She was tensed, and her eyes were ravaging. She walked over to me, and again, I didn't back down. I was eighteen years old. She wasn't going to lay one hand on me without a fight. I didn't care anymore. I had enough of her controlling, power hungry bullshit.

She pointed her finger at my face. I looked at the finger, and then at her.

"This is my house. Mine! I will not let you have some dirty savage stinking up my house. That bozo better be glad I didn't catch him to kill him because he probably stole from here for his broke ass family. You have no say of who you can have in here. Do you understand me?"

I could feel every breath that she took when she said those words.

Every little spit that came out of her mouth. She was that close to me. And I simply stood there and took it. Because I couldn't believe that this was the woman I once called my role model. Now, she was a completely different person in my eyes. I squinted, trying to figure out if I knew her. At all.

"Listen to you, Momma. You are disgusting. A disgusting human being. You don't know anything about Jarell. Jarell is a better person than just a quarter of what you are."

Then, she slapped me. Again. I didn't feel an urge to hit her back like I thought I would. I just kept my face turned, and I let the anger continue to roil within my veins.

"You little girl, you will learn not to talk to me like that!"

"I'm not your fucking little girl anymore," I said through clenched teeth, and she slapped me again.

"Keep cussing in my face. Come on. Come on. I got more."

She baited me, and the anger kept roiling beneath my skin, and I felt myself start to get extremely hot.

"You disrespect my home, and you have the nerve to cuss at me? How dare you. I run this show. You don't! You don't have shit without me. I made you. I did! And I can take you out. Keep talking, Jade. Come on! Keep talking!"

Now, I was shaking. My boiling point was near, and the tears began to puddle in my eyes. My fists began to ball.

"What are you gonna do? Hit me?"

I took a deep breath, and then unclenched my fists. The tears started to fall down. The hurt that I felt for her leaving me for the holidays and what happened at school today, and Jarell... it all came to the surface. Hitting her wasn't worth it. I didn't want to hit her. What I wanted was a mother. A real mother. A mother who would show me who she was on the inside. A mother who would take off her makeup just once so that I could see who my real mother was. A mother who took off her clothes so I could see the woman who carried and loved me. A mother who showed me her mistakes and how she learned from them instead of hiding behind them. I needed a mom. A real mom.

"What the hell are you crying for? You did this shit. You did! You brought that bum here without my permission. What the hell are you thinking? It's like you listen to nothing I say! You will end up taking care of him. You will end up having to spend money on him. You will spend all your energy on him; you will lose yourself. And he will suck it all out of you and keep asking for more. Do you want to live that kind of life with a bum like that!? He's nothing but a piece of dirty scum from the streets with no future. That's what you want?"

"That's not who he is! He's blind, but you have no idea how he operates!" I screamed.

"That's even worse! Oh my God," she huffed, throwing her hands in the air. "Not only is he a bum, but he's also disabled? What has really gotten into you? I didn't raise you like this! Snap out of whatever kind of funk you're in. This isn't you. This isn't."

"No Momma! What I've been showing you so far in my life isn't me. This is the real me!" I shouted, pointing at myself.

"Well if this is the real you, I don't want her. I want what I raised. I raised you that way for a reason. So you don't make the same dumb mistakes that I did. Jade, when are you going to understand that!?" she screamed over me.

"I'm not making the same mistakes! Jarell is more than you're making him sound like. He's a person. A human being. And he is special."

"Yeah, special alright. Special Ed. You need to get rid of him. You *will* get rid of him."

"Really, Momma," I cried. "This is horrible. You can't treat him like that. I will not let you talk about him like this."

"I don't care. I don't want to ever see him in this house. I don't want any of his belongings in this house. I don't want you speaking about him. That's final. If you don't like it, there's the door. I don't want to ever see him again. And I don't want to see you with him either. If I do... consider yourself out of here."

"You know what? Fine. I'll leave. I can't take being here anymore anyway. You're a horrible mother. You left me on the holidays, and now you're kicking me out because you're judgmental? Because you already have an idea about a person that you haven't even taken a second to get to know? I don't want to be in a household with someone like that. I don't! Jarell has more heart than anyone I know, yet people treat him like he's a parasite. It's not right!"

I rushed past her and stormed over to the Christmas tree.

"Bye then! Silly spoiled girl! You'll come running back when he has wiped out all your money because you take care of him."

"Whatever. I'll be out of this house by the weekend. But I'm leaving tonight, and I'll be back to get all my stuff. Oh, and Merry Christmas," I said, throwing several boxes at her, hoping one struck her in the face. She put her hands up and moved, dodging them for the most part. "I hope the karma falls on you, Janet. Because you're the shittiest human being I've ever met."

"Shut up, you little bitch! I raised you and gave you all those opportunities!" she screamed at me, and for the first time ever, I saw the tears puddle in her eyes. "I didn't have to have you! I was seventeen! I could have aborted you. I could have had my whole life ahead of me without you. But I gave you that life, Jade. I gave you the best life I could possibly offer to you because I love you and this is what you're doing?"

"Really, Ma? That's what you say to me? Why are you like this? Why do you want me to be this way? Why is it that you're so damn controlling with these ridiculous standards? I can't live up to that anymore!"

"Because, Jade! All this little crap you're doing now, running around with that bum, is the same stupid shit I did at seventeen. And I got knocked up. I got knocked up by your punk ass daddy who decided to be an accomplice in a murder. My parents warned me about guys like him my entire life, and I never listened. I was just like you. Had so many opportunities to have a great life. And the minute I got pregnant, my parents put me out. I had to figure things all out on my own. I succeeded, but I never, ever wanted you to live a life like that. I wanted you to have the best that a man could offer. The best opportunities you could have to be successful. I did that for you. I did! All on my own with a little help from Corey. So do you see? Do you see why I push you to be with someone like Mike and not that scum of the earth? He's going to put you in a situation you can't get out of!"

"No, he won't! You don't know him!"

"Jade, listen to me. Yes he will! Why am I even arguing with you? You're going to do what the hell I say or you're out of here!"

"Fine and you want to know what? I don't care how you were raised. You acting this way towards someone you don't know is not okay. So I'll be just like you. I'll take credit for all of my success, and I'll do what I want to do with my fame. I'll act like everything I've done was on my own. I'll disown you like you have now disowned me. Now. How's that, from your little bitch?" I seethed in her face, and then went upstairs to pack a bag.

I had no more tears left to cry. I was just searing with anger. I couldn't even think straight.

Once I had my simple bag packed with underwear, bras, a cozy outfit and a toothbrush, I rushed down the stairs and headed to the front door. Janet was sitting on the couch, her knees shaking as she sipped her wine. I kicked her Christmas presents out of the way, slammed the front door shut and went to my car. I knew just the person to go to who would let me stay for a few days until I dug into my savings for some money to buy my own spot. I had given quite a bit of that money to Jarell's family, but I would be okay for a little while before I graduated and became a youth choreographer. In the meantime, I would probably have to take some deals from the offers I had gotten from others. But then, that means I couldn't save that money for PR and an assistant. I sighed deeply as I walked out of the house. It was an abrupt move to leave my mom's place and just the financial piece part was simply hard to think about. But I'd manage. I just wanted to be far away from her.

Chapter Twenty-Seven

IT HAD BEEN three weeks into March since I stayed with Alise. When I showed up to the studio and vented to her about everything that had transpired between my mother and I that night, she easily accepted my request to stay with her until I filled out my apartment applications and got accepted. Not only that, but Alise was considering hiring me early to run the youth studio before graduation after knowing my situation. She hadn't set anything in stone yet because she wanted me to focus on my studies, but she let me know that she was thinking about it. I was so thankful. If she hadn't said yes, I would have asked Corey, but living with him would have required me to attend a different school, and I didn't want that.

As all of this drama went down and thinking about the financial piece, a moment of regret came over me for giving Jarell's family that much of my money. I instantly swallowed that thought when it came. I had so much more saved, and Jarell's family had absolutely nothing. I felt horrible that the thought had even surfaced to my mind. I would be okay for a few months, but I definitely couldn't just sit on my ass and spend up my savings for living expenses; I would have to do some gigs here and there and start thinking of my freelance work outside of dancing.

Speaking of Jarell, he had no idea that I had been kicked out. He had much bigger problems and a new one had come along with him as far as graduation.

Since he and I had grown close, Ms. Jenson warmed up and began to communicate with me about him since I was the only person he seemed to listen to in the school.

And also, since I had told her about Mike and the crew's threats towards Jarell.

Thankfully, she said that she'd keep an eye out and let the principal know so that she could keep her eye out as well. But besides all of that, she had also revealed to me earlier this week that because he had dropped out for over a month earlier in the year, he had missed significant instructional time, which jeopardized his chances of graduating on time.

Now, he had to make up for lost time.

Ms. Jenson wanted to motivate him by giving him an opportunity to attend an additional study hall with me, being that he wasn't particularly fond of studying with her during the last period of the day. She said that he'd much rather do origami instead, which wasn't very productive. He didn't listen to her no matter how hard she tried to get him to study, so she used me.

I was all for it.

Any time I got to spend one on one time with Jarell, I cherished it, and I wasn't going to miss that opportunity. So she set it up, and now, we had eighth period study hall together in the library. Away from everyone. I understood we had work to do, and I needed to play my role in helping him get his work done so that he could graduate, but often times, it was so hard not talking to him about other things and flirting. That time together was just an excuse to grow even closer.

So now, here it was. Eighth period on a Friday, and I was already in the library waiting for Jarell. My books were out, and I was already getting to it because I had a test Monday that I needed to ace. I was interrupted by Ms. Jenson walking Jarell up to the table.

"See Jarell? Jade's already got her books out and studying," she said when she got closer. "Seems like you are going to have to do the same."

Jarell didn't say anything. He just kept walking, and I smiled. I could tell that he was annoyed being around Ms. Jenson. He probably felt that way since he's been at this school. She was literally around him every moment of the day; this was probably his one time of privacy away from her.

"I can take it from here, Ms. Jenson. Thanks," I said, trying to help him out. It was funny because the relief that he displayed on his face was so apparent. I laughed aloud.

"Alright. I'll see you after school, Jarell," she said and walked out of the library.

Jarell pulled up a chair and sat down with a huge sigh and rolled his eyes. I continued to laugh at him. Jarell was so funny at times. When I first met him and started noticing him, his expressions and emotions were often completely unreadable. Now he let his guard down and frequently couldn't even hide how he felt. It was so refreshing.

"Be nice, Jarell," I said, giving him a flirty look.

"I wasn't mean. I could've been."

"Well, you weren't nice."

"I don't think you'd be very nice either if you had someone following you around all day," he said.

"I understand. I was just joking."

"I know."

Jarell reached into his backpack and grabbed his big textbook, which looked like biology, and threw it onto the table. His paper and stylus came after. I had taken biology in like tenth grade, so I didn't remember much, but I could try to help him.

"I got a test on Monday," Jarell said in a deadpan voice.

"Same! Except I have a test in Physics."

"Glad I ain't taking that class."

"Biology ain't no better. Do you need help studying? You can help me study for mine, and I can help you study for yours."

"I really don't want to study to be honest," Jarell said, putting his head down.

"Jarell. Come on, you have to do this. You know I want to see you walk across that stage with me."

"Yeah, yeah, yeah. You know anything about sexual and asexual reproduction? That's what we're testing on."

I licked my bottom lip and smiled.

"Depends on what species you're talking," I said.

"Any species."

"Well, I suppose you'd know all about human sexual reproduction, right?" I asked.

"I'm asking you."

"And I'm wondering what you know."

He smiled small, and then laughed. He knew I had him backed in a corner.

"I mean, I guess experience is the best teacher when it comes to human sexual reproduction," he said, blushing and opening his book in order to hide what he was feeling. He was super cute when he did stuff like that. "I can't tell you what I know. Only what I've done."

"What've you done?" I asked and gave him a sinister look.

"I'd have to show you."

"When can you show me?"

I wanted to see how far I could push this exciting envelope as my stomach fluttered a million times over.

"Whenever you're ready to be shown."

"What if I'm not ready to reproduce?"

"You don't have to reproduce."

"But you're learning about reproduction. What if I'm not ready?"

"Then you're out of luck."

"And I guess you're out of luck on your test," I said, and he laughed aloud again, showing all thirty-two.

"Then I won't be walking across the stage."

"Oh, yes you will."

Jarell and I went back and forth, continued to flirt, and got absolutely nothing done. We had taken so much time goofing around that it was close to being dismissal time; it wasn't even worth studying anyway. I'd do mine at home, and I was sure Jarell would take his load home as well. Besides, it was better that way. I could come over there and truly help him study without trying to do it after a long day of other activities.

So that's what we did. Study hall ended, Jarell and I collected our books and belongings and walked out of the library together. Ms. Jenson saw I was with him, so she didn't bother to walk Jarell out. I didn't tell him, but I knew he'd be thankful for that.

"What are you doing after school today?" Jarell asked as he and I approached the front door of the school to leave.

My heart raced, and it wasn't because he asked that question. Everyone's eyes were glued to us. Literally everyone. Freshmen to Seniors alike. I was enjoying my time with him so much in the library that I forgot the news was spreading around the school that I had cheated on Mike with Jarell. That those pictures with him and I were spread around. That by me walking around with him, I was basically confirming it was true.

It was the first time that we'd ever walk in such a populated space together like the front doors after school.

Jarell honestly acted like it wasn't a thought to him at all, which surprised me. I didn't know if he was aware of the talk that was going around and just didn't care, but did I feel a little nervous and weird about it? Absolutely. At the end of the day, this was still a major step for me. Giving up school popularity for another person was foreign territory.

When I didn't answer his question after a while, he spoke out again.

"Did you hear me?" he lowly said. Like he had been abandoned and was talking to himself. My heart ached a little for him. This was a learning curve on his end too, just as much as it was for me.

"I'm right here. I heard you. Sorry. I um… I have a game later tonight to cheer at. Then I'm gonna go home. Well, to Alise's spot."

"Why her spot?" he asked.

"Um…y-yeah. We should probably talk about that. Let's head to the courtyard, okay?"

"Is everything okay? Did I do something wrong? Your whole mood just changed," he said.

"No. I promise. I was just… I was just thinking about something. Let's go."

I grabbed onto his arm and moved. We finally made it through the thick of the crowd and prying eyes into the courtyard where less people were. If I was going to be walking with Jarell and taking him home, I would rather wait until the parking lot cleared out. For his safety. I also needed to collect myself after getting so many weird stares. My anxiety was through the roof right now.

We made it to the courtyard and stood next to a small garden of flowers. I needed something like this if I wanted to return to equilibrium. A calm place was also needed if I was going to tell him why I had gotten kicked out of my mother's house.

"I have to tell you something," I said, facing him squarely and grabbing his hands into mine. One walking by would have for sure guessed that we were together if they saw.

"What's wrong?"

I sighed, and then sat on a stone bench. His expression changed from generally happy to worried and confused.

"My mom put me out," I confessed.

"Why?"

"Well, when I came home from school that day that you spent the night," I started, and he nodded, "she found your clothes in the laundry."

"Are you serious?"

"Yeah. I didn't think she'd look in the laundry basket coming home from a long trip. For me, the laundry would be the last place I'd check out if I'm traveling home. But maybe she was putting her dirty clothes from her trip into the basket and saw yours."

"What did she say?"

"She basically just said I was disrespecting her house, and that I should leave."

Of course, I wouldn't tell Jarell all the nasty things that she said about him. That would crush him.

"She kicked you out because of that? No parent kicks their kid out for having some guy in the house. You know how many people actually get caught doing that in high school?"

"Yeah, but she takes that really serious."

"No parent takes it that serious."

"She does, Jarell."

"Would it have been the same if it was Mike?" he asked reluctantly.

I didn't know what to say. I didn't want to lie to him, but I didn't want to be phony either. I had to remember that Jarell had intuition and senses out of this world. He would know if I was lying.

"To be honest, no. It wouldn't have. But Mike is different. She's been pushing me to be with him since we were Freshmen. Trust me."

"I believe it, but don't try and butter it up," he said, and turned his head away from me. "She kicked you out because it was me."

"Jarell," I said softly.

"S'cool," he nodded without any expression, but his lips were pressed tightly together, and his jawbone flared. I didn't want him feeling like this anymore. I was happy with the talkative Jarell from ten minutes ago. I needed that in my life, and I just didn't want him shutting down on me.

"Let's talk about something else. I don't want to ruin the mood with my shit. Listen, you asked what I was doing after school today. Like I said, I have a home basketball game to cheer at tonight. You want to come? It's a rival game, and it's the finals; a lot of people are going to be here. It's going to be pretty live."

"You're asking me? Knowing I hate people? I'm good. Good luck at your cheer thing," he said politely, and then sat down on his favorite little tree stump.

"Thanks. But Jarell?"

"Hmm?"

"We should get together after the game. Tomorrow. Maybe to study for our tests on Monday since we didn't get much done today."

"I'd like that," he said.

"What do you want to do besides study? Maybe you can teach me more origami," I said, and his face lit up. Probably unknowingly, but it was so cute to watch. He smiled faintly at the idea, and then ducked his head, just now realizing that he was showing too much. I laughed.

"I can make that happen."

"Perfect."

I was about to tell Jarell that the parking lot should be cleared out by now, that we should get ready to go but my worst nightmare, Mike, Martell, and a few other guys, were walking in our direction. Before I could even say anything or get Jarell out of there, they surrounded us with no room for an escape. If my heart was racing earlier, it was on a NASCAR track now because I had no idea what ideas those boys had up their sleeves to do.

"Who's here?" Jarell whispered, hearing the footsteps. "What's wrong?"

"You're what's wrong, nigga," Mike said, and that caused Jarell to turn to the direction of his voice.

"Mike, what do y'all want?" I asked, irritated as hell. What the hell did they want with us? Mike and I were over. Forever. He made that choice.

"I'm tryna figure out from this diseased ass nigga here why he thinks it's cool to steal somebody girl, and why his new girl snitched on us to the principal," Mike said, and Jarell frowned.

Much to my surprise and horror, Jarell swung his legs over the tree stump and slowly stood up to face Mike. *Holy shit, Jarell.* I stood up quickly and got in front of him. There was no way I was going to let this go down. No possible way. I understood that Jarell was starting to get fed up, but at the end of the day, he was still blind. I didn't want him getting hurt.

"Move out the way, Jade," Jarell mumbled. "I'm tired."

"Jarell no," I whispered in panic, my hands on his chest to stop him.

"I just wanna hear what he has to say," Jarell said.

"Look at this crack baby getting bold. You wasn't doing all that when we damn near jumped your pussy ass the last time. Dude was finna cry. What you think 'cause you got a new lil girlfriend that you all hard now?" Martell said with laughter.

"Shut up, Martell!" I yelled.

"What do you have to say to me because I'm not scared of you," Jarell said to Mike, and if I didn't know any better, all through Jarell's voice screamed threat and to get lost. I think Mike felt it too because he blinked, taken aback, but frowned again to hide his apparent fear.

"Nigga, nobody scared of you either," Martell jumped in. "Scared to catch your disease if anything."

"I'm not fucking talking to you," Jarell said and turned his head towards Martell. It was the first time I had heard him curse in a while.

"Ooooh!!!" Martell started laughing along with the rest of his weak friends that found this so amusing. "Careful there."

"What the hell was you doing with my girl? I know you a lame and all, but everybody in this school knew what was up, and your dusty ass thought it was cool to just slide up on through, huh?" Mike said, stepping closer to Jarell.

Jarell didn't budge. I just held my breath, wondering what the hell I would do if Mike laid a hand on him.

"If I'm a lame, I wouldn't know that y'all never were together, would I?" Jarell raised a brow.

"Oh, so you was telling all our business to this nigga too, huh Jade? Interesting," Mike said, cutting me a death glare. I swallowed and rolled my eyes.

"It ain't your business if you didn't make her your business," Jarell said.

"Shut up, you bitch ass nigga," Mike growled and then pushed Jarell. He stumbled but didn't fall.

Then, I went straight into protective mode. My right hand left my side, cocked back, and then it stung. My hand did. And Mike's head rocked back so hard that I nearly looked at my own hand to see if it had truly come from me. I had slapped him. As hard as I could, and now, his face was completely red with my handprint.

"Damn," Martell gasped, looking at Mike for what he was going to do about it.

His other friends looked at me with wide eyes, and then at Mike.

"Whatever you wanna do, bruh," whispered one of the guys, and any nervousness that I felt had shot through the roof. That means, as men, they'd be down to hurt me for hurting him. And I wouldn't truly have that much protection because of Jarell's condition.

"Mike, don't you ever, ever touch Jarell again. I don't know why you came out here, but we are done. You had a chance to be with me, and you messed that up. I'm with Jarell now," I said, lying, but just so he could understand I wasn't dealing with him anymore. He hurt me, and now, I was over it. He showed he didn't care about me at all.

Mike nodded and clenched his fist like it had taken everything in him to prevent himself from hitting me back.

"Man, that bitch ain't worth it, Mike," one of the other guys said.

"He right, fam. Let her have that dirty little ass wipe," Martell laughed. "Aye, yo stankin ass momma prolly out in the streets bustin' it open for a living to give money to your broke ass, huh? Tell her crackhead ass to come on over so she can suck my dick for some goods. I'll fuck her too and have her call me daddy."

My mouth dropped. "Martell!"

How dare he... That was low. Lowest of the low. Especially knowing Jarell's mother would never. She wasn't even a crackhead.

I glanced over at Jarell, and his fists were literally balls. And his entire body shivered as he bit down on his bottom lip. To the point where blood profusely seeped from his lip and onto his teeth. A very, very intimidating sight.

"Jarell?" I called out.

"Aww, look at that bitch. He think I'm supposed to be scared because he popped a blood vessel. What you gonna do? Huh? Is poor little momma's boy triggered? You mad 'cus I'll fuck your momma?"

Then, he snapped. I didn't even know how he did it without sight, but as Martell cackled at his own joke, Jarell sprinted towards Martell, completely tackled him onto the ground, and wailed on him. At first, I was glad for it, but the more I watched, the more horrified I became.

Jarell was going to murder him.

He had punched Martell maybe three times tops, but the second punch was so hard that Martell's entire face was already bleeding. Literally gushing.

I realized Jarell had strength when he crushed the rest of his old, broken glasses in one squeeze and stress cracked a school door not too long ago, but this was complete and utter rage. His sunglasses tumbled off his face, so his eyes were bare. If I was Martell and looked into Jarell's eyes at this moment, I would have had a heart attack as he threw the worst blows I'd seen on anyone. Ever.

"You ain't doing a mothafuckin' thing to my momma nigga! You thought because I ain't said shit to your ass these last four years that I wasn't gone fuck you up, huh? Now what? Say something, nigga! Say it!"

Poor Martell covered his head to avoid the blows, and the people who were still at school had surrounded the area to watch. Nobody was even egging it on or recording it. Everyone looked scared because Martell couldn't even fight back.

"Jarell! Stop!" I screamed.

Mike and his guys just stood there with wide eyes, not even wanting to get involved. I ran to pull Jarell off since no one else would, but he pushed me to the ground and started throwing body blows because he could no longer get to Martell's face since Martell covered up.

Then, Jarell grabbed his shirt and slammed his back into the concrete. At this point, it looked as if Martell fell unconscious, since he may have hit his head. I just stood there and cried because if this continued, Jarell would have a dead body on his hands.

"Jarell, please! Stop!" I cried.

Before Martell could take his last breath, and before Jarell could do it again, out ran one of the large male teachers and Ms. Jenson that saw the horrific sight, and bear hugged Jarell, picking him up off of Martell. Before he was too far away, Jarell spat at Martell's face with the most disgusting glob that made me gag. Thankfully, he missed.

"Fuck you! You met your match today, you asshole!"

As the teacher dragged Jarell away, he continued writhing, trying to get out of his grip.

"Get off me!"

The teacher moved Jarell away in that same bear hug as Jarell growled and punched many lockers off their hinges nearby when the teacher let Jarell go. *Jesus was he strong.*

Ms. Jenson and others knelt to help Martell off the ground, but he was unresponsive. Blood was everywhere on his face and the concrete. One of his eyes was swollen shut and his lip was huge. The side of his face was red and was going to be bruised later. I shook my head, and Mike went over to help. I wanted to say that's what Martell got, but he was so messed up that I couldn't even have the heart to say it.

Jarell's rage was unmatched. Everything he just did solidified what everyone said about him.

Jarell was a monster.

And now, I believed them.

Chapter Twenty-Eight

THIRTY MINUTES LATER found Jarell and I in the office of the principal as police surrounded the area asking people questions along with an ambulance. Ms. Jenson and I had gotten him to calm down after him punching and breaking several lockers. He had stopped after a while, but Jarell's gritting jaw and clenched fists told us that we were far from getting him to our desired state. Ms. Jenson had called Jarell's mom the moment after she had gotten someone else to help Martell. She was on her way now in a taxi.

I didn't peep a single word to Jarell, who was shaking his knee in the office chair with a blank look on his face and his sunglasses back on. I couldn't take being this intimidated around him after getting to know his softer side. I could deal with off-putting, sarcastic Jarell, even. But not this.

As he sat seething, I looked at his hands and was horrified. They were as big as softballs. Especially his left one. His knuckles were covered in bruises with deep wounds seeping blood. To make matters worse, he didn't seem to have any perception of pain.

The ambulance finally took Martell on a stretcher, who had finally woken up after a half an hour. Then, one medic came into the office and approached Jarell.

"Hey, buddy. Looks like you got into a fight there," he said cheerfully. Jarell's nose flared. "May I see your hands?"

When he saw them, his eyes widened. He looked at Jarell as if Jarell would tear him in two with his bare hands, but that was short lived. He blinked and swallowed to clear his throat, possibly playing off his reaction. He took out some gauze and tape.

"These look really bad, man. You're going to have to go get this checked out at some point. Your left hand looks worse. Could be either broken or severely sprained," he said. Jarell didn't budge or even wince.

"Is it painful?" the medic asked.

Slowly, Jarell shook his head.

"Is it numb? Can you tell me what you're feeling?"

"I don't feel anything," he mumbled.

"Well, that's even more alarming. We don't want you to lose feeling in your hand due to numbness. That sounds more like amputation symptoms."

"It hurts. I just don't care," Jarell said, shrugging.

"Oh." The medic blinked. With no hesitation, he packed up any first aid items he had into the little medic bag and stood to his feet in haste. "Well, I shouldn't be talking much to you. I think you're still coming down from a hell of a lot of adrenaline. Come back to the ER to get this checked out."

The medic left as quickly as possible and left us alone again. We weren't alone too long because Jarell's mom charged in with Kylah – a worried look on her face.

"Jarell, Ms. Jenson called and told me to get here asap because you got into a fight. The police are everywhere. What happened?" She looked at him frantically.

Jarell didn't respond, and Kylah was so happy to see me that she didn't even pay her brother any mind. I was glad to take her off his mother's hands so that she could deal with this problem. I sat Kylah on my lap.

"Are you going to answer me, Jarell or what? You know I don't like coming up to this school. So it better be a damn good explanation as to why I got called up to this mothafucka."

Whoa. My heart started racing. If I thought he was in deep shit at school, he was definitely in deep shit at home. She was a whole different woman.

Before Jarell could even have an opportunity to say anything, the principal, and the police barged into the office.

"Get up!" the police yelled at Jarell. Jarell stood in confusion, and without a single word or even a glance, the police made a beeline for him and grabbed his wrists to cuff him. Jarell winced and clenched his teeth, the first visceral reaction to his injured hands.

"Hey, hey, wait! Do not arrest him. Get off him!" his mother screamed, clawing at the police, but the other officers held her back. "We don't even know what happened!"

"What's going on, Mommy?" Kylah cried in my arms, and immediately, I headed for the door so she wouldn't have to see her brother like this. I made sure I stood at the office window to watch.

"Ma'am, we have enough evidence and probable cause to arrest him, alright? He beat someone out there, and it's definitely going to be a battery charge."

"Are you kidding me? My son is blind! Could you at least show some lenience with someone with a disability?"

"Apparently, him and his blindness didn't show much lenience out there when he sent someone to the hospital," one of the officers said as he continued to shackle Jarell.

"Before you take him," said the principal, "let's at least get his side of the story. I don't know the details of what happened and why, so we are going to figure this out together. I'd like to know your side of the story, Jarell. What exactly happened?"

The police secured Jarell's hands behind him and made him stand to explain.

"He was talking shit, so I beat the fuck out of him. No regrets," Jarell bluntly said with an evil rage that I could just not believe. I had to be dreaming.

"Jarell!" his mom exclaimed and punched him dead in the chest. He didn't even budge. "Do you want to be in jail forever? The hell is wrong with you?"

Then, the principal looked at me. I rolled my eyes and sighed. I didn't want to be snitching on Jarell right in front of him because Martell truly deserved it. I mean, maybe not the severity of it. But he deserved something.

"You were there the entire time, Jade. Correct?" she asked.

"Yes."

"From your point of view, what happened?"

"Well, the short of it was that Martell said some really cruel things about Jarell's mom, and Jarell snapped. I'm not repeating any of what Martell said, so don't ask."

"Ma'am, this is a police report. You need to share every detail so that we get the story straight," said one of the officers.

I rolled my eyes and sighed.

"Fine. Martell told Jarell that he was dirty and broke. Then, he said that Jarell's mom was... you know... these are his words... 'busting it open' to give him money. Then he said that he'd have his mom 'suck his own dick' to prove a point."

Ms. Hendrick's eyes shifted to Jarell. I couldn't read a single thing she was thinking. Was she still upset with him? Did she have any sympathy now that she understood why?

"Alright. Well, here's the deal. Charges may be filed because Martell was sent to the hospital, Ms. Hendricks. We do not know fully what the charges will be, but it is a high possibility the charge will be assault and battery," said the principal.

"Jarell," his mother said softly. "Why did you let that boy get you that angry? You shouldn't be sending folks to the hospital. Are you kidding me? And now, you're going to be booked in the system with thousands of dollars in fines. What the hell were you thinking?"

Jarell stood silently with no sign of emotion.

"I understand your frustration, baby. I really do. But you need to channel it and go to therapy like the school has been asking you to do. Sending folks to the hospital because you're upset is unacceptable. Do you understand me?"

"I'm sorry," he grumbled as she walked around him.

"Look at your hands. Jesus. What did you do?"

"Ma'am, I'm afraid he really hurt this individual. I can't really say the extent, but what I do know is he has lacerations on the back of his head, a black eye and bruised face, and a busted lip," said an officer.

Jarell's mom tilted her head back and her eyes watered as she looked at the ceiling, trying to keep her composure. I wanted to say so badly that Martell had been bullying Jarell for quite some time and deserved some of it, but I didn't know if she had already known this. I didn't want to bust Jarell out if he had opted not to tell her.

"In addition, Ms. Hendricks, Jarell punched and broke several lockers out of anger," the principal said, showing her photos on her phone that she took. Ms. Hendricks' eyes widened in disbelief. "These will also need to be paid for."

"You did this Jarell? This isn't you. This is the old you. This isn't my son that I know now." She shook her head. "How terrible. Don't you know your actions have consequences, Jarell? I tell you this all the damn time. I worry about you, but you've got to start making better decisions. Your actions have consequences for me, too. I don't have money to be paying your legal bills. I don't have money to repair vandalism, either. What the hell is wrong with you? Are you serious right now? So you beat a kid damn near to death, you vandalize a school. You damn near dropped out of school. You won't go to therapy. What do I even do anymore?"

Jarell said nothing.

"Moral of the story here is that Jarell will be suspended for two weeks, if released from jail before then. Martell will be suspended for one week. And if the severity of something like this happens again, Jarell will be expelled."

"Understood. Thank you, Mrs. Kilburn. We're going to figure something out with Jarell's case manager and social worker. This is getting to be too much, and I don't know what to do. This is the last straw, now."

"It isn't entirely his fault, Ms. Hendricks," I interrupted. I couldn't let them keep going on without having the full story. At least more of it. "I think you officers should stay to hear more of the story."

"What do you mean?"

"Martell has been asking for it for a long time. He shouldn't have gotten what Jarell gave him maybe, but he was asking for something. He and his friends have been constantly picking on Jarell. Throwing his books around the hallway. Breaking his glasses. Verbally assaulting him. I told the principal about some recent threats Martell has made, too."

Ms. Hendrick's gaze landed back onto the principal.

"Well, Jade came to me earlier this week notifying me and Ms. Jenson about possible threats that two individuals were making about Jarell. One of the individuals, Martell, had made a threat as well," the principal said with her hands up.

"Well, what were the threats? Why are they threatening him, anyway? Don't you realize that he's blind? How can Jarell even anticipate a threat if he cannot see? Have you even sat down and talked to these individuals?" his mom interrogated.

"I don't know why they threatened him, but I talked with them this morning, ma'am."

"And?"

"And I said if I hear anyone carrying out these threats, then they'd be in trouble. I'm assuming that it could be possible that one of them tried to carry it out, but Jarell..." the principal stopped at the end with a knowing look.

"Alright, see, we didn't have this information before," one of the officers said as he wrote these things down on his notepad.

"Mmm. Well y'all need to own up to your end of the deal. Y'all out here criminalizing and vilifying my son and y'all haven't done shit to stop the other perpetrators. You know my son has been dealing with bullying since Freshman year and it seems like y'all don't give a fuck at this bad ass school. Either way, it still doesn't excuse the fact that Jarell can't control his goddamn anger. Jarell, you're going to therapy. That's final. I'm not accepting no anymore. You don't have a choice in this matter. Alright? Let's go."

With that, Jarell's mom stormed out of the office, snatched her daughter away from me, and rushed out of the building. The police wasn't too far behind as they hauled Jarell to the police car. I quickly followed to catch up with both parties. Many people were outside watching the scene like it was a movie, visibly showing scorn at Jarell.

"Jarell, I'll meet you at the county with your mom, alright?" I said to him before they put him in the car.

He said nothing.

"Ms. Hendricks, wait!" I called out to his mother as soon as Jarell was away. She was walking down the street, dragging a crying Kylah whose poor little legs couldn't keep up with her pacing mother.

I wished I could do something to take her pain away because I knew that she was frustrated with Jarell and frustrated with the school and could do nothing about it. A least with me, she could find some solace.

"Ms. Hendricks!" I screamed and ran to catch up with her. Once I did, I stopped her by standing in front of her, blocking her way to a path forward.

Her usually beautiful face was priceless and red with tears.

"Why would Jarell do something like that, Jade? I'm so fucking pissed with him!" she screamed, and then buried her face in her hands. "He knows I don't have any money to get him out. I don't have any money to pay any fines. I don't have any money if that family presses charges on Jarell. I don't have money for a lawyer. What am I supposed to do? All that money you gave us is to save up for rent."

"Ms. Hendricks, don't worry about that, okay? I'm just as pissed with him, but I will get Jarell out of there, we will get a lawyer, and we can work things out. Okay? Trust me on this. Martell and those boys aren't as innocent as the police and the principal are making them out to be, and I'm sure Jarell's charges will be dropped. Everything will be alright. I just need you to get in my car so we can get him out of there."

Everything I said seemed to register since she physically calmed down. She swooped down to pick up a still weeping Kylah and hugged her close, kissing her forehead that was covered with sandy brown curls.

"It's okay, baby. Mommy is just upset with your brother."

With that, Ms. Hendricks and I walked to my car with Kylah's arms tightly wrapped around her mother's neck. We drove down to the county jail and had to wait hours for Jarell to be booked and for bail to be posted. Then, it took another four hours for Jarell to be bailed out, which caused for all of us to spend the bulk of the night in the county. Jarell wasn't released until midnight. So much for me cheering at the game tonight.

The moment he was released, we all could tell life had been drained out of him, but he didn't say or express much else other than that in words or body language. We all just silently got back into my car as Kylah laid asleep in the backseat.

"Jarell, Jade's going to take you to the hiking paths tonight," Ms. Hendricks spoke out after a while. "I think that's a good opportunity for you to think about your actions. In the meantime, I need to get away and think myself about what I'm going to do with you and how we're going to get through this legal stuff. I'm very disappointed with you, Jarell. You're so much better than this."

Jarell said nothing the entire time. He just stared out of the window with his hood up, closing himself off to his mother and everyone else.

"Jade, are you okay with this?" she asked.

"Yeah," I nodded, although I really didn't know how I felt and couldn't really express it.

Not another word was said in the car as I dropped Jarell's mom off at the house along with Kylah, leaving us alone to process everything that had transpired.

Chapter Twenty-Nine

WE DIDN'T SAY a single word to each other for the entire car ride to the hiking paths in the dark, and the silence didn't make my anger better. In fact, it was the perfect quiet before the storm as contempt brewed in my stomach, waiting to burst at Jarell at any moment. If I was really being honest, Jarell deserved all the fines coming his way. Maybe not a criminal record, but assault was appropriate for his actions. And I wasn't going to pay a single dime of his fines because five hundred dollars out of pocket to bail him out was enough. He had no business nearly killing someone over a dumb ass insult.

When we arrived, Jarell requested to take the harder route as he picked up a thick stick from the ground to guide him. It wouldn't have mattered to me anyway because I wasn't familiar with any of the paths, nor was I even focused on that. I was trying to figure out what the hell I was going to say when I finally spoke.

Within the first ten minutes of hiking, I got tired out fast. I thought I got used to it after the first time, but I didn't. In fact, I stopped to take a break when I was out of breath. He noticed and had paused to wait for me. As I still caught my breath, he found a large stick on the ground to give to me to assist me. It was this gesture that I finally exploded.

"Jarell what the hell was that today?"

He was living up to what everyone had said about him – that he was this ruthless monster and at this point, I couldn't help but to believe everyone. What kind of relationship or friendship was I getting myself into? Would I be subjected to the Jarell that I saw out there? Would he become abusive? There was no way in hell I'd set myself up to be killed after watching what he was capable of. No way in hell.

"Excuse me?"

He paused, throwing a disbelieving look my way coupled with something else I couldn't quite decipher.

"You heard me. What the hell was that? You acted like a maniac! You almost killed him! What is wrong with you?"

"You really gonna sit here and take his side, Jade?"

"Hell yeah, I'm taking his side! You took it way too far, Jarell. Slamming his head on concrete, bruising his entire face... how did you not think that was going too far? You tell me!"

His disbelief morphed into a bewildered look, yet he laughed. It was that same manic look he had on his face while punching Martell.

"You gotta be kidding me. You don't have a clue," he uttered, and turned his head away from me.

"Well I'm not kidding. Are you gonna answer the question? I'm not gonna sit here and act like what you did was okay. I don't care that we've built our relationship. I don't want to be friends with someone who is batshit crazy while they act like it's normal!"

"Then get the hell out of my life, Jade. Nobody asked you to be here but you. You don't know me!"

"After that, I might have to if you're truly anything like what you just showed me out there. I didn't believe anybody when they called you crazy, but this might've confirmed it. You're a piece of shit who can't handle anger and you're a monster."

"What?" Jarell blinked.

"You heard me," I said, holding my breath. "You're a piece of shit for what you did, and you deserve any wrath coming your way."

The forest fell silent, and Jarell looked my way, shaking his head.

"Really? So it's just like that, huh?" This time, he genuinely looked hurt, but I refused to let myself feel bad. He needed to know and understand how I felt about all of this.

"Why did you nearly kill Martell then, Jarell? Explain it to me. Explain it so that I understand because whatever the hell you're saying ain't convincing me. You owe me an explanation."

"I don't owe you anything!"

"You're right. You don't. But if you're going to act like this over some stupid your momma joke that no one cares about, then I want no parts of you. You're really going to beat someone to a pulp over some shit your mom was never gonna do? Why would you even take him seriously?"

"You don't understand," he said, shaking his head.

"What is there to understand? I will never understand nearly killing someone over something silly."

"You don't understand!"

"Make me fucking understand! Who beats someone for saying they'll fuck your mom because it's not like it's ever gonna ha-"

"Because my mom got raped, Jade!" he screamed with a look that made my heart drop. It was a mix of fear, confusion, anger, and a deep despair that slapped the frown off my face instantly. Snatched words I thought I was going to say from my soul.

"My mom..." Jarell faltered, and then turned his head away to hide whatever he was feeling.

Silence. For a while.

"Jarell?"

"I was there, Jade. I let my mom get raped and I did nothing. I hate myself for it every day."

"Jarell I-"

"No!" he bellowed. "I'm going to tell you some shit I shouldn't tell you since absolutely no one knows. Except maybe my teacher does, but I'm desperate, and I don't want you to see me as some psychopath because I value this...friendship or whatever the fuck you wanna call us. Maybe even after I tell you, you might still regret knowing me in the end just like everyone else regrets me. It'll be nothing new. So shut up and listen."

My mouth instantly snapped shut. The only thing I could do was stare at his back in anticipation. I wouldn't dare touch him. Wouldn't dare say a word because now, I wasn't worthy of saying a thing after that revelation. I hated when Jarell proved to be right. I really had no clue.

For a while, you could hear nothing but the wind, the creak of water flowing, and the animals chirping in the distance. Jarell stood by with his back turned, but he hadn't said a word.

"What happened, Jarell?"

The longer he stood silent, the more I felt even more ashamed for asking because it was evident that it had hurt him to think about it. I started, about to just tell him to forget it and apologize for everything I said, but he interrupted me.

"I was twelve."

My heart sank. *Twelve.*

"I was... my mother was in an abusive relationship. With this big, huge dude."

I didn't know if I wanted to hear anymore, but I swallowed my thoughts and listened anyway. This was his story, and I needed to be there for him to hear if he was going to tell.

"Um... he... beat on her every day. And he always had a gun. Usually in the waist band of his jeans and would threaten to kill me if she didn't do what he said. His favorite phrase was 'I will spill his guts.' I was too scared to do anything. We were too scared to leave. My mom feared getting caught. So, I would just go to my room and listen to him beat her every single day and listen to her scream. After a while, I learned to just turn up the music and dance like it was never happening. That was my only escape," he said. His head was leaned back as he gazed upwards towards the sky.

Damn. *I will spill his guts.* Fuck. I remembered. I remembered Martell saying that to him the first time I had ever saw him on D-Block.

"Whenever he didn't get his way, he would come and put his gun to my head, forcing her to do it because she didn't want to lose me. Sometimes he'd shoot in the air to let her know that he was serious. I never tried to fight back because I didn't want to die. I didn't want to leave my mom alone. So as time went on..."

I watched his back keenly in anticipation for him to continue. He opened his mouth and tried to keep going, but only a squeak came out.

"I'm sorry, Jarell," I whispered. I slowly walked towards him and reached out to rub his back, but at the very last second, I didn't touch him. Didn't know how he'd react.

The moment my hand fell to my side, a single tear trickled from my eye, but I quickly wiped it away. I had no right to cry after everything I said to him.

He didn't say anything for a while. He just kept his back to me with his head down, hood up, and shut me completely out. We were that way for about thirty minutes – me watching his back as I leaned against a tree, and Jarell rigidly standing there without a single sign of movement. It was fascinating, but I knew better. This was trauma, and it had a hold of his entire body. I had never seen anything like this before in my life. But I knew if I walked away...

"Over the months, it got worse," he randomly spoke out. In shock, I perked my ears up. I barely wanted to be heard breathing. I was a fly on the wall, just ready to listen.

"When he realized that I'd turn the music up to dance to drown my mom's screams out, he'd get annoyed. Then because of it, I started to become a part of her beatings. Except a lot worse because he wanted to show me what it meant to be a man. It was usually with this thick brown belt, extension cord, a wooden paddle, or sticks. Or glass bottles. And each time he beat me, it was worse than the last. It got to the point where..."

He paused for a long while, and I was bawling as quietly as I could. I couldn't even imagine...

"It went on until I turned thirteen. The beatings stopped hurting after a while because he forced me not to cry or else he'd make it worse, so I just don't register pain the same anymore. And if my mom tried to stop him, he'd pull his gun out. Or he'd just stop beating me to beat her again. It started with just him beating me because of the music, but later, it had become for every little fucking thing. I remember sneezing too loud, and that day was the worst one I had ever gotten. So I stopped dancing with music and danced in silence to avoid another reason to be beat. And at night, I never slept because I did hundreds of push-ups so I could grow strong and murder him."

"Jarell," I wept, but he put his hand up to stop me.

"One day, he had threatened my mom to have his baby. She said no so many times that day, but he kept begging and begging. I was in the room doing push-ups when he told me to come here. I knew him calling me over wasn't good, but for him to not have come in to beat me or put a gun to my face by now, it felt different. I went into the kitchen with him where my mom was cooking, and he had my favorite ice cream on the table. He never bought me treats, and I hadn't had ice cream in so long. Then, he told me I could have it if I asked my mom if she'd have a baby by him. I told him that she already said no, so I really couldn't do anything about it."

Jarell paused again, his entire body tensed as if having a flight or fight response. I held my breath.

"Then, he said he'd shoot me if I said something like that again. My mom said that she didn't believe him anymore. That he was just talking shit because he never did it. I still remember his face after she said that. He looked so surprised. So he pulled out a bottle of bleach from the kitchen cabinet under the sink."

I couldn't help myself. I gasped, clutching onto my shirt, my heart pounding out of my chest. I knew that if I made another sound, another crying sound, that it would be too much for him.

"He poured the bleach into a red plastic cup. He warned her one more time, that he would poison me if she said something like that again. Then she said, 'Fuck you.' All I remember was him splashing the cup of bleach on my face. I fell to the ground screaming, trying to get it out of my eyes. It burned. It burned so bad, Jade."

His swollen fists were balled so tight, I was afraid his nails dug into his palm to make them bleed again.

"Then, he took her and raped her. Right next to me on the kitchen floor. I tried to open my eyes to help her, but my eyes were on fire. She screamed my name out. For me to help her, and I just gave up. You wanna know what happened?"

I didn't say a word. But he knew I was still there.

"She reached out and grabbed one of my hands away from my eyes. And she held my hand through every disgusting thrust he made. To protect me. And I just laid there, balled up, crying as my eyesight burned away."

I was bawling audibly. There was no way that I was keeping that inside.

"When it was all over, he kicked me as hard as he could. Twice. Once in the stomach and once in the groin. My mom called the ambulance, and they rushed me to the hospital after she tried to flush my eyes with cold water in the shower, but it was too late. Doctor said I would have complete and permanent vision loss. On top of that, broken ribs, and testicular damage. I officially can't have kids."

"Jarell...please..."

"The worst part about it? He skipped town, and later she found out she was pregnant with Kylah. Authorities couldn't find him, so they dropped the case."

My God. This was the most second-hand heartbreak that I probably would ever experience.

"So, now you know. I didn't mean to hurt Martell, Jade. I thought of my mom's ex and I just snapped. And now I fucked up and got booked in the system and I know my mom can't pay for this shit and..."

"No. Please stop talking. Come here," I whispered.

"Why? What do you want?"

"Come here. Please."

With reluctance Jarell turned to me, showing his face for the first time since talking about this, and it was priceless. The level of anguish he exuded couldn't even be described. I rushed to hug him. Tight. I felt so shitty for everything I had said prior to this. I didn't know how often he received love, but he deserved it. Literally no one deserved it more. Jarell often appeared stoic, heartless, and hardened... like he didn't feel. Like he was crazy the way everyone made him out to be. Like he wasn't human. I called him Ghost in my own way of perpetuating that, but I would never, ever call him that again. He was somebody. He wasn't dead. He wasn't made from steel or air. He felt.

I experienced first-hand how deeply he felt when my neck seemed wet as I hugged him against me. I was puzzled at first, but when a sniff that wasn't my own split the night, my heart shattered. It was such a quiet release, but so powerful and abundant that it took my breath away. Like his soul was flooding.

"I am so sorry Jarell. I won't leave you to be alone through this."

Jarell's forehead sunk into my shoulder, and his silence completely broke. His cries had become heartbreakingly audible as they joined the chirping crickets of the night. Goodness. I tried to keep it together, but I had never, ever heard a man's pain the way I heard his.

"Promise me you won't go, Jade. Please," he wept.

"Shhh. I'm not going anywhere. I promise."

Chapter Thirty

IN SUNNY SOUTHERN California, it rarely rained. When it did, it poured. On a cool, Saturday, rainy night like this in late March, dance was the only thing to do since mostly everyone stayed in the house when the weather was like this. Sometimes, it seemed like everything shut down; most people didn't come out to play.

So, I went to the studio and danced for a long, long while. I hadn't practiced for some time, especially after being kicked out of my mom's place and all the drama that came with. Over three weeks had passed since I was out of her house, and the apartments I applied for were at last going to get back to me with their responses this week. I couldn't wait so I could get out of Alise's hair. Consequently, this dance was a passionate one. One where I let the thoughts of life fade into oblivion, and I was the only one in the world. I didn't think about my mother. Didn't think about my finances. Didn't think about graduation. Didn't think about these dance gigs. Didn't think about Laurie. Didn't think about Mike and Martell. Didn't think about anyone at all. So soothing and refreshing. Therapeutic.

When I was done, I had nothing left to do. It was close to midnight. I just sat on the cold, wooden floor of the studio and brought my knees up to my chin, enjoying the reticence and peace of existing.

Then, reality hit me again, and I started to think.

During my dance, I didn't even think about Jarell.

I missed him. So, so much.

Ever since our time on the paths, Jarell of course was suspended, but I couldn't even have access to him outside of school. He had been grounded for the duration of his school suspension. His mother told me that he wouldn't and couldn't be with me until he worked out a plan to address his pent-up anger and his pending court dates when I dropped off his schoolwork. No check-ins, no calls, no nothing. So, it had been two long weeks without seeing or hearing from him after his revelation in the forest. It especially felt long because I really didn't have my old crew anymore that I could just go to on D-Block for any social reason.

They all hated me now. I was officially ex-communicated.

Everyone had heard all about what had happened to Martell. He was hospitalized for a day, and then released to serve his one-week school suspension. When he came back to school, all of the evidence was there on Martell's face. One side of his face was a dark, bruised purple. His lip returned to normal, but his eye on that same side was still blackened, and sadly, he wore a neck brace and had cuts on the back of his head that were healing. When everyone saw that sight, it was over.

Martell hated me. Mike definitely hated me. Everyone on D-Block hated my guts. I couldn't even go to Laurie. Why? Because her parents pulled her out of the school temporarily because they found out about her dating Martell. Now, I had to deal with defending Jarell and listening to everyone build this narrative about him about how crazy he was, how much of a monster he was, how much he needed to be locked in a looney bin, or how much they hated him too, simply because of what he had done. No one cared about what Martell had said or done to push him over the edge because no one knew. I wasn't going to tell them out of respect for Jarell's situation, and Mike's friends wouldn't tell to protect Martell's image. So as a result, they only targeted Jarell. And I had to deal with that all by myself with everyone knowing I was right there for it all. Taking his side.

I had no one, and it was one of the worst feelings. It took this to truly now understand how Jarell felt every single day.

There were some days when I wondered if it was worth it. If giving up my popularity for Jarell was even anything I should've been doing. But when I thought of him day after day, night after night, I got my answer. It was clear as day how I truly felt.

And that feeling in and of itself had me leaving the studio and driving over to his place in the pouring rain at midnight, knowing that I wasn't allowed to be there.

I missed his company. I missed his genuine friendship. I missed growing with him. I needed to check on him after pouring out something so traumatic and trusting me with his heart. I promised I wouldn't leave him, and I meant it. But for some reason, even with him revealing something so horrific like his mother's dignity taken away in front of him along with losing his eyesight and fertility through abuse, deep down, I felt there was more to Jarell's life that was just as traumatic and devastating.

It was the way he hugged me that told me so. The way he pleaded with me to not leave his life, the way his tears poured out as if the levies had broken inside had told me so.

So I had to see him. Two weeks felt like an eternity. So was he worth losing everything? Hell yeah, at this point he was. I wasn't taking that thirty-minute drive downtown to Alise's. I just couldn't.

Getting out of my car quickly and into the cold thunderstorm, I ran up to Jarell's house and looked for his window on the side. All of the other windows looked as if the lights were off from the inside, but there was one that was on. The blinds were closed, but there was a hole in one side of them. I jumped up to peek to see what was inside and saw a piece of origami hanging from the ceiling. This is it. I knocked softly, but loud enough to for him to know that it was frantic. The rain was chilling my skin to the bones in this skimpy, dance outfit. Shaking back and forth in place and waiting, Jarell pulled his curtains back in an angered confusion.

"It's me!" I said through his window, hoping he could recognize my voice. "Jade."

The frown on his face eased as he searched for the lock on the window. He found it quicker than I would have thought and opened it.

"What are you doing here? It's midnight and pouring," he said softly, jumping back from the rain.

"You gonna let me in?"

"Yeah," he said, stretching his arm out to help me. In gratitude, I grabbed on to him and catapulted myself into his window. Once I was safely inside, I shut his window and curtains myself.

I was almost soaked, and my wet hair stuck uncomfortably against my neck and shoulders as it kinked up from water contact. With a free hair tie decorating my wrist, I pulled it up into a ponytail and wiped my neck dry with my hand. By the time I finished readjusting myself, Jarell had already sat on the bed, looking my direction in a weird way.

He had always looked handsome every time I saw him, but tonight, there was a beauty to Jarell I had never, ever seen before. I couldn't quite pinpoint why it was different. He still had his hoodie on, but there was nothing on his head to conceal or hide any of his features, but I had seen that on multiple occasions now. Maybe it was because he was at home and it was late, but he looked super vulnerable. All emotions seemed to be fair game and laid bare before me in a myriad within his eyes. It was fascinating. It was like watching his brain; he couldn't see anything, so the only thing that would show were his feelings. And that made him more attractive than ever.

"You look handsome," I blurted out, staring at him like a fool. "How you holding up?"

He shrugged and turned away from me with an indecipherable look. It was silent for a moment after.

"I missed you," I confessed. "Couldn't wait to see you."

He dipped his head and smiled small, fiddling with his hands like he always did when he didn't know what to say. I didn't want him to say anything. I just wanted him to hear it.

"You know?" he started after a while.

"Yeah?" I raised my eyebrow.

"I wish I could see you."

It pained him to say that. The way it tore from his mouth, the way his shoulders sagged. The way the vulnerability in his eyes matched his tone. I had no idea how to respond. I was always so fascinated with Jarell's blindness and the wonders of how he navigated the world, but it never dawned on me just how grateful that I was to even be able to *see*. Nor did it dawn on me on how much he must've yearned for that ability again.

"Jarell..."

"I been thinkin' about this a lot. I could touch your face and dream what you might look like, but it's not the real thing. I just want to experience you."

With a sigh, I sat next to him and placed a comforting hand on his thigh.

"Can I just... can I touch you?" he asked. At first, he looked ashamed to ask. I didn't want him feeling like that.

"Of course you can," I whispered.

I closed my eyes. I grabbed his hands and placed them upon my face as he began to feel every curve and crevice. His thumb brushed down my nose and over my lips in a tickle that made me smile. The rest of his fingers smoothed over cheeks to my eyebrows and gently touched my eyelashes. His hands were surprisingly soft, and he touched me with care, like I was fragile china.

"You're beautiful," he said with confidence. "High cheekbones and long eyelashes. Your lips are full. And you have a dimple in your left cheek. God. I wish I could see you."

I grabbed his hands back into mine, wanting to cry. I knew there was something up when I noticed that Jarell looked defenseless. No matter how far we'd come, he always shielded his emotions around me. I didn't know why, after all of the barriers we had broken, but I guessed that today was the end of it all. He looked tired. Tired of hiding.

"I don't know what to say to make you feel any better," I whispered, laying my head on his shoulder.

"You don't have to," he said. I could feel his body stiffen up, but I ignored it. If he was going to open up, I wanted him to open up forever.

"I wish I could."

I looked down at his hands. They were still bruised and scratched, but they started to look better than before. His left hand was wrapped in a small bandage while his right hand was free.

"Jade?"

"Hmm?"

"I think about this a lot, too."

"What is it?"

"I um –" he paused, and then laughed. "This is putting myself on the spot, but I really care about you. For real. I wish I could be more for you. I'm nothing like you're used to."

"And that's why I like you, Jarell. You're not like anyone else. You're such a mystery. Every time I'm around you, I discover something new about you. New things that fascinate me every day. Honestly?"

"What?"

"You're special."

"Me?"

"Yeah! The way you dance, the way you go through the world using your other senses, the way you appreciate nature, your sense of humor... you're just a really cool and unique person. A kind of person you don't get at our school."

"No one likes me, Jade. No one ever has at our school."

"Because they don't understand you. I didn't either. And now, I do. And getting to know you was the best decision I've ever made."

His shoulders relaxed as he let out a deep breath, gazing towards the ground.

"Hey," I whispered, grabbing his chin softly and turning it towards me.

I began to caress the side of his face with the back of my hand. The scratchiness of his growing beard felt surprisingly good against my skin. With closed eyes, he snuggled into my hand like a big cat. My heart crushed into a million pieces. Even with a supportive mom, there was something different about an intimate touch that doesn't come from moms that he longed and wished for. I could just feel it.

With no hesitation, I pressed my lips against his.

His lips were motionless at first, but he eventually puckered them in the slightest. I sucked on his soft and moist bottom lip and opened my mouth more, hoping he'd let me in. He recoiled a little, a slew of emotions swirling in his eyes. I couldn't even read them all, but I could sense he was holding something rigidly in check inside of him. Something he so badly wanted to unleash. Either way, I stopped with a frown feeling rejected because I didn't understand why I was the only one acting.

"Kiss me back, Jarell."

He swallowed and closed his eyes, cutting me away from what he was feeling. Then, his forehead rested on my cheek.

"Is this really what you want?" he asked.

"What do you mean?"

"You know… this. You know where it's gonna lead."

"Would I be kissing you if I didn't?" I jerked my head back, breaking all physical contact.

"It's not like that. It – it's not what you think. I just – I just wanna make sure. I don't want to force anything. I wanna make sure that – that I'm the one you want giving you this whole experience."

I blinked, and my cheeks burned. *My goodness.* I had no idea he was thinking that this entire time. I paused for a moment to think. Hell, I've never felt surer.

"I want this, Jarell."

"You sure?"

"I'm positive. Now kiss me."

He licked his lips with a smile, and this time, he kissed me. For real. It wasn't those cute little pecks we had experienced before. This was the real deal, and he gave me his all. His whole self, and there was no holding back.

The both of us fell onto his bed as I was on top of him, trying to get him to open his mouth more to let my tongue inside. It had become more and more apparent he had never really kissed much before because I had to constantly give him cues, but Jarell was a feeler. He was going to get the hang of it.

I tugged at the hem of his hoodie to take it off, and immediately, his hand vice gripped my wrist.

"No." He shook his head frantically, separating his lips from mine.

"Ouch, Jarell, let me go!"

He dropped my hand like a hot potato.

"Sorry. Didn't mean to hurt you."

"What's wrong?"

"Don't take it off," he said firmly.

"Jarell, if we're going to do this, you can't have this big, dirty hoodie on. What's the matter?"

"It's just..." he faltered.

"What is it?"

He looked my way with an expression of shame and something else I couldn't interpret.

"Come on. After all the barriers we've broken. You can feel safe with me. Trust me."

Jarell closed his eyes. For what seemed like forever. And I just waited.

Suddenly, without another word, he sat up and slowly pulled his hoodie off.

And then, his t-shirt.

What I saw told me everything. Everything I needed to know to understand why I had never, ever seen him without that hoodie.

Old scars and lacerations from his stepfather's beatings decorated the entire front of his body. Wicked looking scars that even wrapped around to his arms. You'd have thought he was an ex-slave.

"Oh my God..." I whispered.

I turned around to his back and it was worse than the front. The scars were much more pronounced, larger, raised, and scarred over in black, brown, and blue. And then, my eyes landed on a huge, dark, rough scab across the bottom of his back that I almost gagged at.

"Jarell... is that a burn?" I asked, not wanting to touch it.

I hoped it wasn't true. I hoped he wasn't set on fire and severely as burned as this scar looked, but I was disappointed. He confirmed it with a nod. I held my head up, trying desperately to hold the tears away. I had done pretty good so far.

But the tears welled when, through all the staring, I finally noticed the beauty underneath all the ugliness.

Here lay the source of his physical strength I often wondered about.

The deep ripples of his abs and pecs, and the way his arm, shoulder and back muscles flexed to call my name. Jarell was more than strong. His body was a physical specimen. Strapped. Ripped. Cut. Defined.

All hidden beneath brutal scars and a dirty, oversized hoodie. All because of some idiot.

I finally broke and started crying. Why would that man want to bruise such a sweet soul like Jarell's? Destroy such a beautiful canvas?

"Please don't cry," Jarell whispered. "This is why I didn't want to show you."

"I just don't understand why he'd hurt you like this, Jarell," I cried.

With a sigh, he grabbed my hand from his shoulder into his and squeezed it.

"It doesn't matter anymore."

"What the fuck? Yes, it does, Jarell! That man destroyed your entire body. Don't downplay this shit anymore. It does matter. I wish I could fucking kill that bastard. Where is he?"

"No. I'm not giving that man any more of my thoughts, energy, or sorrow. My body is far from destroyed, so don't worry about that. The only thing that matters right now to me is you," he said softly, his forehead meeting mine.

I surrendered, letting us connect in a way that we never had before. Without shame, Jarell pulled me in for a kiss, which led to a heated make out session. He hadn't taken anything off of me yet, but his hands roamed my back and my shoulders, rubbing me lovingly in his hands.

Now that I had his shirt off, I had no idea what to do except for look at him. I had never seen a body so beautiful yet horrid at the same time.

"You alright?" he asked when I hadn't moved or said anything for a little while.

"Yeah. Just taking you in," I said and kissed him again. I didn't want to be the one to pull down his pants and say let's have sex. Making out was the furthest I had ever gotten with someone, and the next steps were like – up in the air. I was super dependent on the other party to take over where I lacked.

As we kissed, Jarell pulled my shirt. I rose up quickly from on top of him and took it off as fast as I could along with my bra. The thing that made undressing easy for me was that he couldn't see. So it made me feel more confident and comfortable, even though it wasn't much of an advantage for Jarell.

"Um…Jade?"

"Yeah?"

"If we're gonna do this, what about condoms?"

I lowered my head. *Fuck.* I forgot all about condoms. But my goodness, I was already half naked. My skin was searing hot in need, especially from his touches. Did we really need to have protection?

"Are you a virgin?" I asked.

"Why?"

"Just answer the question. I promise, it's related to the protection thing."

"Yes."

"So am I. Why don't we just say no to protection. If you're a virgin, I trust that you don't have any diseases."

"What? No. I don't think that's safe, Jade," Jarell said.

"What's not safe?"

"I mean, I know you won't become pregnant because… you know… but… I don't know. You sure?"

"Yes, Jarell. Trust me on this."

He took a deep breath and closed his eyes.

"Alright. Come here," he said, biting his lip, and I gladly obliged, falling into his arms, and let him kiss all over me again. I sensed he felt awkward about touching my breasts that were now bare. I couldn't lie and say I didn't feel awkward to touch him either. I didn't want to feel like I was bad at it. So I just didn't do it.

We kissed for a little while longer, and Jarell found the band of my leggings and slid them off my legs along with my underwear. I laid naked on top of him, feeling something growing upon my stomach.

I swallowed.

I had never felt a real, full-on boner in person before. I've seen them through jeans and pants like I saw Mike's, but I've never felt them. It felt... scary. I didn't see what he looked like down there, but just from the way he felt through the thin materials of his boxers, I already knew that he was going to be a lot to handle.

"How do you like to be touched?" he whispered in my ear and kissed the side of my neck. That made me shiver and knocked me from my thoughts about his erection.

"What do you mean?"

"You know... down there. How do you like to be touched?"

I blinked. When Mike and I were close to doing it, Mike never asked me that. He was just ready to go. So, I didn't think that was something that would even be considered. I mean, I knew how I liked to be touched, most definitely. I was pretty well versed with my own body because I explored and pleasured myself from time to time. But I didn't want him knowing that. What would he think if I knew how I liked to be touched, but I said I was a virgin? He'd probably think I was lying about my virginity if I told him the truth.

"I don't know."

"Alright. I'll just have to learn your body. Just let me know if you feel uncomfortable, okay? I'ma try my best, but you just have to tell me. You okay with that?"

I nodded, amazed at his care for me. I thought sex was more about what guys wanted, but he was really interested in making me feel good too. I loved it and took note to make sure that happened every and any time I had sex.

Jarell told me to switch positions and lay on the bed. His hands moved slowly over my entire body, feeling its dips, shapes, and quirks.

I bit my lip as my brain ran a million miles an hour about what he was thinking. His breathing became more audible, so that was a sign that he was just as aroused as I was.

"You're so soft," he murmured.

His exploration made its way down to my stomach, deeper, and his fingers discovered what was once unknown territory. I moaned softly as he began to rub me. The way he touched me was a little uncomfortable and I tried to get with it, but it was to the point where I had to direct him to my favorite spots.

He listened to everything I said, learning his way around, and that's when I really started getting hot. I was breathing heavy, trying to muffle my moans because we were still in Jarell's mom's place without her knowing I was here.

"Love the way you sound. Can't wait to hear that when I'm inside," Jarell whispered, and I moaned out loud.

Where'd he learn to talk like that? My goodness was it sexy, bereft of inexperience, and so authentic. He meant every word. It was nasty, and I treasured it. It was the one thing that wasn't awkward about our journey to sex tonight. It opened up and showed more new avenues of him that I just loved to continue to reveal.

His hands came up from my folds, and he grabbed my hand.

"Can you touch me, too?" he asked.

"What do you want me to do?" My eyes widened.

"Just wrap your hands around it and move up and down. At least that's what I do."

"You do that?"

"I mean… yeah. Every now and then when I'm bored and need a release," Jarell disclosed. "You down?"

I nodded, shocked that he even opened up so candidly about his experiences. I felt ashamed that I opted not to share mine. It just showed me that Jarell was truly done hiding. This was him. The real him laid out here before me. Raw and uncut.

"You sure? I don't want to make you do something you're not comfortable with."

"Yeah. I'm okay."

My hands went up to him and massaged his abs first before I made my way to his boxers. I took a deep breath, hoping I wouldn't fuck this up, and slipped my hand inside. Jarell bit his lip. I felt a bush of hair first and kept moving south for the gold. The moment a hot, hard, and heavy rod of flesh touched my fingers, my hand slid right back out. Anxiety rushed into my chest fast. I jumped so hard from the feeling that my temple smacked into Jarell's eye.

"Ahh, fuck," he uttered.

He winced, and I yelped out in pain at the same time.

"I'm sorry."

"What did I do? Did I do something wrong?" he asked, covering the blow I made.

"No, no... it's just... listen. Maybe we shouldn't do this."

I lightly pushed him off of me and rose up from his side, looking down at him. The tips of my cheeks were on fire. His boxers were sticking straight up from a serious erection, and that both scared and excited me at the same time. I couldn't really describe the feeling. But I just didn't picture my first time going down like this. We were both nervous. Every move we made was awkward. It was just so unlike me, and I couldn't face him anymore.

I fixed my arms to slide out of his bed and did so. Jarell hadn't said a word. He just laid down and stared blankly at the ceiling, but the look on his face said it all.

There was something that Jarell could never really master, and that was hide the emotion in his eyes. He didn't want me to leave but didn't want to force me to have sex either. His silence in that regard made me love and appreciate him more. But I just didn't think either of us were ready.

"I'm sorry, Jarell," I whispered.

"S'cool," he mumbled, and then turned on his side, cutting me completely off with his back.

"No it's not. You're not cool," I said, picking up my shirt off the floor.

"I have to be."

"This just... this didn't turn out the way I thought it would've."

"What did you expect?" he crassly uttered.

"I ... I don't know. I didn't expect anything like this to happen."

"Did you think we were going to be out the gate fucking like porn stars?" he asked, his back still turned towards me, but damn I wanted to laugh.

"No! I'm not saying that."

I chuckled, and for some reason, that had completely eased my nerves. He didn't even have to try.

"Then, what? You thought I was going to be daddy long dick the expert and blow your mind? Tell me what you expected to happen? I'm a virgin, and so are you! I'm just tryna make sure you're okay, tell you what I think I might like, you tell me what you like so we can please each other. That's all."

I didn't mean to laugh. I promise I didn't because Jarell was serious and obviously angry. But damn. Jarell had an uncanny sense of humor that destroyed me every single time. Because he was so serious about everything, he never realized that the things he'd say were off the charts funny. And that was what made it even better. There was something about his curt tone and the delivery that made it priceless. He was so often times reserved that him saying things like this were pretty unexpected.

"So now you think this is funny?"

Smiling, I dropped my shirt and curled my arm around his body, laying my cheek on his shoulder.

"No, I don't think it's funny."

And just like that, any of what I felt disappeared like it had never existed.

"Then tell me what it is, Jade," he said and turned towards me, holding onto my waist with a gentle hand.

"This is what it is."

My lips met his again. This time, in urgency.

We were at it again. No matter how much I tried to fight it, my body had its needs, and if I would have left out of that window, I would have been aching all night.

"You don't have to touch me if you're not comfortable," he said out of breath, and shifted on top of me again. With his hands, he gently spread my legs apart and rested himself in between. "Let's just make this about you, okay?"

Then, he took his boxers off.

I took a deep breath and one good look. And that was enough to send my heart to my throat. I hadn't seen any male goods in person before, so I didn't know what was considered "packing" or not. But from the word on the streets about what I should expect, Jarell was working with something. It looked beautiful and scary all at once.

I made a point to avoid looking at it for the rest of the night because if I didn't, I was going to be running scared.

Without further ado, he crawled on top of me and adjusted himself between my legs. His weight on top of me was a little uncomfortable, but I forced myself to ignore it. He couldn't help that he couldn't see.

"You okay?" he whispered. "You feel tense."

"Yeah. Yeah." I nodded erratically. His senses always amazed me.

"Alright. I'ma try not to hurt you, okay? Let me know if you want me to stop."

"Okay."

Before his grand entrance, Jarell reached down and rubbed my hot spots to diffuse my nerves. His growing beard scratched my cheek, but I didn't mind. I was happy to feel so close to him as I held him tight.

The tingly feeling in my chest began to slowly subside while consistent, soft moans from me filled the air. A couple of intimate kisses along my jawline made me feel breathy and way more turned on than I would've expected such a simple move would do.

Man, he was good.

Without waiting any longer, Jarell grabbed and guided himself towards me. The warmth of his flesh moved through me with a slick wetness that I didn't expect. This was just all so new. So I just wrapped my arms around his neck for security.

"Ready?" he asked in a raspy voice. "You sure you okay with all of this?"

"Yeah." I nodded.

"Well, I'm nervous. I don't know if I'm okay." He laughed, and just him expressing that made me feel so much better. "I just wanna be good for you."

"You're doing great. Honestly, it's like you've been here before," I admitted.

With a smile and a grateful look, Jarell continued. He slid himself through me again, searching for my entrance. His soft, velvety skin against my flesh felt so good that I was reluctant to even have him inside of me, but I gave him a couple of verbal directions to find it, so he could feel what he's been waiting for all night. I wanted him to feel just as amazing as he made me feel.

"This it?" he whispered, the tip touching the opening.

"Yeah."

"Alright. Here I come."

He pushed softly. I gasped, feeling a heavy, blunt pressure. A pressure trying to break something small open with something much larger.

"Sorry. Did I hurt you?" he asked in panic.

"No, no. It's just… it's just …you're okay. Keep going."

"Are you sure?"

"Yes, Jarell. I promise."

"Alright," he said, taking a deep breath.

I felt the pressure again. A poke. A sort of twist. A poke. Then, he pushed a little harder, sensually splitting open a part of me that will never be intact again. A feeling I would never forget.

He pushed forward again, inching more of himself inside of me. This time, it wasn't a pressure. It was a stinging of blissful fullness that I never, ever wanted to let go of. The fullness of becoming a real woman, the fullness of feeling sexy, the fullness of… him. I wanted more.

And he gave me more. A lot more. He still inched his way through, and my mouth dropped open in pain the further and further he sank inside. He was all the way in when he gave me a soft thrust with the rest of himself, pushing me forward in a way that made a noise come out both of our mouths. He stayed there for a little while with him all the way inside me like this, simply enjoying my walls fully clutching around him. I didn't want him to leave as the pain subsided.

"You good?" he panted, not asking me this time, but just a check in as he pulled himself slowly out of me.

"Wait. Don't leave. Where you going?" I pouted as the fullness disappeared. He was almost completely out of me with his tip barely touching the orifice.

"Nowhere."

I gave him a confused look when he delivered a full and firm thrust from tip to base that sent my brain flying everywhere in a mix between pain and pleasure as the fullness came back in its entirety. Stealing every bit of breath in my lungs.

"I'm right here, Jade," he whispered in my ear.

Those words meant a thousand different things that settled me in comfort. He grunted as he slowly moved back and forth inside of me, irregularly at first in awkward movements, opening me up and breaking me in. After a while, fluid movements, and a steady rhythm began to play against the wall, his bed creating the sound. I tried not to moan, but I couldn't help it. It hurt to get used to his size, but the closeness I felt with him obliterated all of that. He felt amazing. An amazing that I would have never thought I'd ever feel, let alone from him.

"Shh, shh," he said, groaning, trying to get me to stop so that I wouldn't wake his mom and sister.

I had my eyes closed the entire time, but for some reason, I thought to look up at him to take in everything that was happening. Surprisingly, he was looking down at me. His eyes were still a washed shield to really seeing anything, but I could tell I was making him feel as good as he made me feel. He rolled his eyes back and kept his eyes closed for the remainder of the time as he rocked me back and forth.

The connection in the air was so strong... so meaningful. I wouldn't have wanted to experience this moment with anyone else. This was way more than I would have ever imagined my first time having sex would be.

Jarell reached above me and held onto the wall to stop the bed from hitting it, showing his flexed muscles in a way that fascinated me. His body was so chiseled. I had never felt so protected anywhere else in my life. Not only did him reaching up like that look visually pleasing, but it also caused a position shift with him hitting another dimension deeper in me that I didn't think I had.

"Oh my God," I gasped, trying to get used to a new length after barely getting used to the first position.

"Shit. Sorry," he groaned. "You want me to stop?"

I shook my head. The look on his face was priceless, and I'd be damned if I wiped it off by forcing him to stop. His moist lips, his closed eyes... Jesus, I couldn't get enough of watching him. He kept going in this same position, but after a while, he simply gave up trying to stop the bed from hitting the wall. He let go and let it happen with his strong arms holding himself up at my sides. He didn't care what his mom would say because the bed hit wall a little louder, and his soft groans drifted frequently into my ear as he sank into the moment. It was the most erotic, beautiful sound. An intimate gift that only I ever made him produce.

I was loving every minute of this as the pain had fully subsided. He kept driving in between my legs, until I heard him again.

"Damn," he groaned. "I'm so sorry, Jade."

With one strong thrust, Jarell went stiff, then shivered as his eyes squeezed tight for a moment. I didn't know what was happening, but I watched him closely as he lingered above me for a while to catch his breath.

Ahh. Now I understood as a new sensation appeared between my legs. With a sigh, he collapsed on the bed next to me with an exhausted, but satisfied look.

"I'm sorry," he panted.

"For what?"

"I finished way too fast," he said.

"Don't worry about that. You made me happy, Jarell."

"You sure? Did you... I don't know... you know what I mean..."

"No," I said, knowing exactly what he meant, "but I didn't expect to. This was just as great. Trust me, okay?" I said, wrapping my arm around his torso and hugging him close to me.

"Okay," he said, wrapping his arm around by back and bringing me close. "Thank you for trusting me, Jade. I'll never forget this."

"I won't either," I said, yawning, and falling asleep on his strong chest, feeling wanted, loved, and protected.

Chapter Thirty-One

A **STINGING SENSATION** in between my thighs thrusted me awake. Wincing in pain, I sat up with my hair plastered over the side of my face and looked at my surroundings. It was morning, and Jarell's room was a still quietness that made me nervous yet made me feel safe. I turned my body to gaze at the source of deep breathing. Jarell lay next to me, again with his arm draped over his forehead. His mouth was open, and he was snoring softly as drool trickled down the side of his cheek. I smiled. As gross as that might've been to someone else, it was so cute to me on Jarell. He looked so at ease and peaceful. A way I rarely saw him.

Sitting all the way up, the stinging in between my thighs shot back, and I squeezed my eyes shut. Nobody ever tells you about the pain after your first time having sex, apparently. I reached down in between my legs to touch down there because it still felt strange, and my hand came up with.... *blood.*

My heart raced. I didn't think that I'd be bleeding! I expected to see something else entirely. Did I get my period? Did I get it all over his bed? Did he tear me? Was something wrong? He was going to kill me! I was so thankful that he couldn't see although that was such a wrong thought, but I couldn't help it. Him seeing me like this would be so embarrassing.

I slid out of bed hoping I wouldn't wake him, pushing the covers back and looked at his sheets. There was a wet spot that was dried, but thankfully, it wasn't my blood. I at least felt better about that, but I still felt anxiety about what was going on down there.

I reached into my small purse that was on his floor and pulled out a sanitary pad. Now, I had to muster up an insane amount of courage to walk out of his bedroom and to the bathroom without facing his mother or his little sister. I didn't even think about how I was getting out of the house without his mom knowing I was here. Climbing back out of the window in broad daylight wasn't an option. Too many people were outside and driving by.

So, I had to leave out of the front door. There wasn't a better choice. And now? I felt truly mortified. I couldn't face his mother knowing that a teenaged girl like me was sneaking into her home. And what if she heard us last night? Was I loud? Did she hear the sound of lovemaking against the wall? I felt dirty and whorish.

No one tells you these feelings after the first time you have sex, either.

Taking a deep breath, I slipped on my underwear from last night. Then, I pulled on Jarell's oversized hoodie that he wore every day because I didn't want to put that skimpy dance outfit back on. I would've really felt like a hoe then. His hoodie had swallowed him, but it had completely drowned me to the point where it was nearly dragging on the floor. His musk was all over this thing, and though it didn't smell the best, it was him, and that alone was comforting.

Man, there was something about Jarell that completely changed me. I, Jade Williams, didn't care about a musky smell anymore. Growth, I guess. Worrying about the shit that actually mattered.

Wobbling over to his bedroom door, I pulled it open slowly, trying not to make any noise. As soon as it was beyond a crack, the aroma of pancakes drifted lovingly through the air while sizzling pops of what smelled like sausage or bacon mixed in as a second. For a moment, feeling like a slut had dissipated just from the smell of that breakfast. And knowing his mother worked hard as hell to get that breakfast on the stove because I knew Jarell and Kylah sometimes didn't know when their next meal would be.

I tiptoed to the bathroom without a single peep, closing the door just as quietly as I opened his bedroom door. I let out a huge sigh of relief. My heartbeat slowed down, accomplishing what I felt was the biggest feat of my life. I sat on the toilet and put on my pad. A strong need to take a shower ached at my stomach, but then that would require me to ask someone for a towel and soap. I wasn't ready to face anyone yet, so here was this new dilemma.

I exhaled again, opting to stay in the bathroom a little longer to rebuild the courage to go back to his room without getting caught. I took this time to feel in between my legs again. I was still bleeding. I wondered where it came from? I would have to just suck it up for now.

I tried not to worry as I pulled up my panties and washed my hands. I hesitated, but I pulled the bathroom door opened again to head back to his room. No one was around, thankfully. I assumed his mother was too busy cooking. More aware of my surroundings, the sound of Sunday morning cartoons wafted through the breakfast smells, so Kylah was also pretty occupied as well.

When I made it back to Jarell's room, his eyes were opened, looking at something arbitrary. My instinct was to ask him what he was looking at, but then, I remembered. It made me sad all over again just to know that he would never know the difference between what it looked like to be dead, sleep, or alive. At least that's what I thought. Maybe he could see things differently behind his eyes. Now that we were more intimate and closer than ever, I thought I'd ask what he saw. *Just not yet.*

"Good morning, Jarell," I called out to him.

Hearing my voice made him smile. It wasn't a smirk or anything sexual. It was a gift that I rarely received from him. It was a "happy you're here" toothless and shy smile.

"Are you okay?" he asked. "I woke up and you were gone."

"I was just in the bathroom. I'm okay, I think. I'm bleeding."

"Did I hurt you?"

"No... well, yes. But not intentionally."

I walked slowly over and sat on his bed next to him. He sat up, his blankets covering the naked part of his lower body. For some odd reason or another, my eyes kept lingering down at his crotch, wanting to see more, but didn't want to say it. Instead, I just appreciated what was visible to me, which were his abs. They were just as sculpted and beautiful as they were last night. I was already starting to see through all the scars.

"I'm sorry," he mumbled. "I didn't mean to hurt you."

"I know you didn't, Jarell. I honestly don't know if it's my period, or the sex."

"I think you'd know what your period feels like," he said.

"True."

"Maybe it's just... I don't know... the whole pop the cherry thing."

"That could be it." I nodded, realizing that was exactly why I was bleeding. He had broken my hymen. The way they talked about it in sex ed.

"It probably is it." He laughed. "How'd it feel?"

I blushed, feeling my entire body turn red. Is that what the first time having sex does, too? That if you bring it up afterwards, you feel all hot and bothered again?

"It was good. You made me feel amazing."

"I feel the same way. I want to make you feel better, though. I want to make you... you know... get off," he said, winking.

"Hmm. One day."

"Well, let's look forward to that day," he said softly, grabbing onto my hand and caressing it in his.

Sometimes, Jarell's senses were so strong that I felt that he could see. How the hell did he know where my hands were? Every single waking moment, he fascinated me in some way, shape, or form.

"Yeah..." I said, breathlessly.

Without another word, Jarell whipped the blankets off of him and stood up as naked as the day he was born. Watching him, I blinked several times, trying not to get turned on by every inch of his flesh. Even his butt was nice, firm, and sat round on his back. I forced my eyes away so that I wouldn't look at what was inside of me last night. I was too scared to look at it for some odd reason even though thirty seconds ago, I wanted to see. Thankfully, he quickly slid his boxers over himself, and I was able to look at him again without feeling all antsy.

"Where's my hoodie?" he asked.

"Oh, sorry," I said, breaking out of my thoughts. "I have it on."

"Oh... alright." He paused, and then shrugged like it was no big deal. Instead, he put on some sweatpants and a long-sleeved shirt that were lying haphazardly on the floor as he seemed to know exactly where they were and slid them over his boxers.

"Mmm. I smell some pancakes out there," he said, rubbing his belly while his eyes held a hungry tint.

"Yeah, those are pancakes," I said, amazed that he was able to smell them from here because I sure couldn't. I had to open the door for that to register to me.

"Yum. I haven't had pancakes in years. Take my hand. Let's go eat."

"Wait, Jarell. I'm not supposed to be here, remember? What are we going to say to your mom?"

His eyes expanded with realization, and then he swiped a hand down his face.

"Oh yeah. Damn. Well I mean... let's just face the music. Don't run from it," he said with a shrug.

"No! I'm not that brave, Jarell. She's going to know. She probably heard us."

"Well, if she really didn't want you here, she would've kicked you out, especially if she heard it. My mom's a hard ass sleeper anyway. She didn't hear us."

"Jarell, please. Can we just come up with a plan or something?"

"What do you want the plan to be?"

"I mean... I don't know."

"There is no plan other than the truth, Jade."

"You're suggesting we tell her we had sex?"

"No, but if she asks, fuck it. Say yes. Jade, trust me. Yeah, my mom's pissed with me about fighting, but she don't stay mad for long. And we're eighteen. My mom ain't all strict like that," he explained. "She'll probably be happy I got some action if I'm honest."

"Alright. Fine."

Taking his hand, I didn't have a choice now. At least I didn't have to do it alone or while vulnerable and wondering what the hell was going on with my vagina.

I walked slowly with Jarell to the kitchen. There his mother was, humming to an unrecognizable song as she seemed to be finishing up breakfast and his sister glued to Dr. McStuffins on the TV. I opened my mouth to say something, but I couldn't. I still felt disrespectful.

"Morning, Ma," Jarell called out softly.

His mom turned around and faced us. She had a warm smile at first, but then she gave a clear double take at my presence. She looked the both of us up and down with a suspicious glare.

"Jade, when did you get here?"

"Uh... last night?"

"I know I didn't let you in..."

"Yeah I mean, it was really late last night. I was caught on this side of town in the huge rain and thunderstorm, and I didn't feel safe driving home. So I just... hopped through Jarell's window. Didn't want to disturb you."

That was the closest story to the truth I would approve. Flat out telling her I came to the house unannounced just because I missed Jarell with sex being the end result was not going to fly.

She looked at me, and then her eyes landed on Jarell.

"And you let her in? Knowing you're grounded?"

"Yeah, you want me to let her just sit outside in the rain?" he asked full of sarcasm.

"Hmm. Okay. Let that be the last time you sneak in here, okay?" she asked with a serious look. "I'm happy to have you but knock next time. I don't want my house being unsafe. And I guess Jarell has been grounded long enough to get off."

"Okay, Ms. Hendricks. Sorry."

"It's okay, baby. Good morning to the both of you. Are y'all hungry?" she asked.

I nodded, and Jarell audibly expressed the same sentiment.

"Alright. Why don't y'all have a seat? I'll make your plates. It's been a while since my kids had Momma's pancakes! Kylah, come and eat sweetie."

"Relly! Jade!" Kylah yelled out and ran over to us. Well, she ran to Jarell and hugged his legs. Jarell ruffled her hair.

"Sup, baby sis."

"Good morning, Jade!" Kylah said with a smile so bright, that she just lit up my entire world. I had never seen someone so excited to see me as Kylah was.

"Good morning, sweetie."

"Relly, I've never seen you hold a girl's hand before!" Kylah said, and for the first time, I realized that we were still holding hands. My true intention was to simply lead him to the kitchen, but our hands so naturally intertwined that I didn't even feel us connected. In response, Jarell's hand tightened around mine, signaling that he wasn't trying to let go either. A faint smirk lingered on Ms. Hendricks' face at Kylah's statement as she set the table. Wonder what that was about?

"Because you're never around," Jarell responded jokingly.

"No, it's because you've never really had girls over. You really like Jade, don't you, Relly? I like her."

"She's alright," he said with a shrug, and my mouth dropped, turning towards him to nudge him.

His mom simply stared at us and laughed.

"Be nice," I said.

"Mommy, you like Jade too, right?"

"I love Jade for Jarell, honey. I've never seen my son so open," she admitted, and my heart just melted.

"Yay! Relly has a girlfriend!" Kylah said, jumping up and down and twirling around me. I laughed, kneeling to her and touched her little nose.

Soon, everyone's plates were made, and everyone was at the table eating. Like a family. There was laughter, jokes, and just a general sense of feeling at home. I watched them in awe. For a family to have been through so much, yet to still stick together and laugh was something commendable. But it was still incredibly sad to know the real people behind those smiles. A domestic abuse and sexual assault survivor. A child abuse survivor. A little, beautiful girl created from such monstrous acts and didn't even know. It put my life in perspective, and I suddenly felt so ashamed for how I was raised.

"So, Jade, you mentioned that you dance right?" his mom suddenly asked. "I've been telling Jarell that you look oddly familiar."

"Yeah, I run a studio downtown, and have worked with people like Usher, Missy, and some other big names."

"That's why! I'm sure I've seen you in some music videos. That's awesome! Jarell, why didn't you tell me that she was also in music videos?"

"Because that's not all of who she is." He shrugged.

"It still would have been cool to know! So of all the people you could be with, you choose my son?"

"What you tryna say, Ma?" Jarell asked, holding his chest. He was so dramatic.

"Boy, shut up," she said.

"I chose your son because he is special."

"Yeah, he is special. My big baby," she said, pulling him in for a hug and a kiss on his forehead. Jarell easily accepted it with no fight.

"You need to push him to dance more. He's way too talented not to."

"Trust me, Ms. Hendricks. I've tried," I said, giving Jarell a side glance, and he simply smiled.

"See he treats you just like he treats me. He will snap if I even mention performing at all."

"Sounds about right."

"Why y'all talking about me like I'm not sitting here?" Jarell asked with doughy eyes.

"Because we can!" his mother said. "But I have to get serious for a second here, Jade. Jarell will be seeing his therapist twice a week on Tuesdays and Thursdays. After school. That's what we've decided during his grounding. So will you support him in that? They're going to pick him up at the school."

Jarell rolled his eyes at her talk, and I nodded.

"Of course I will, Ms. Hendricks."

"Good. Now speaking of dance, he loves it and I don't want to take that away from him. It's actually more important for him to dance now that he's going to therapy."

"You know I'll dance with him," I said with a smile, nudging Jarell. "He knows I can out dance him any day."

"What? Never!" Jarell said out loud, and we all laughed.

Jarell, me, and his family continued to joke around at the breakfast table with no mention about the sex or me sneaking into the house until it was apparent that everyone was stuffed, and it was time to get ready for the day. Well, it was Sunday, and usually Sundays were lounge around days, but I still needed to get into the shower.

Jarell's mom had given me all the necessary materials that I needed to shower and feel refreshed. Thankfully, I was no longer bleeding and was just simply sore, which made me feel a whole lot better than this morning. Jarell had done the same after me while I went outside and grabbed some spare clothes in my trunk which were more leggings and a tank top. It wasn't the most appealing outfit ever, but it wasn't like Jarell could see it anyway. Besides, he wouldn't have really cared.

Along with my spare clothes, I grabbed my backpack with my school stuff. I had to help Jarell study for his biology test since his suspension was over. He had to make up what he missed. When I suggested that we study, he seemed closed off to the idea, but of course, I had to remind him about the end goal. That was the only reason why he obliged.

So, the plan was to spend the afternoon hours studying, especially while his sister napped, and the evening hours making origami the way I promised that we would do. It was his only incentive besides the whole graduating thing.

Jarell sat on the floor and opened his textbook to the chapter he was testing on, and it actually was asexual and sexual reproduction. At first, I thought he was messing around with me in the library, but he was serious. Maybe I was the one who had my mind in the gutter the entire time.

"I've always found this whole reproduction thing interesting," Jarell said as he read his chapter aloud, his hands feeling all over the pages. Watching someone actively read in Braille was fascinating. He was extremely fluent because the way he recited some of the passages were flawless.

"Why's it so interesting?"

"Just the way it happens, you know? Like, how the sperm can just swim and look for an egg. But the sperm has to be there at a certain time and all of that. It's crazy."

"Now that you put it that way, it is. It's like, we're literally one in a million," I said.

"Right. Because if we weren't, the world would have been overpopulated a long time ago."

"That's true. Now see, Jarell, I thought you told me that experience was the best teacher? You seem to know a lot and you're telling me right now instead of showing me."

"I mean. Didn't I show you last night?" he asked, licking his lips.

"But you ain't say anything about how your experience relates to reproduction."

"What I showed you was the process."

"You gotta tell me the process before I leave from here. That's how I'll know you're ready for the test."

"Who says I want you to leave?" Jarell asked in a low voice, scooting over towards me.

"Jarell, no flirting. We have to study."

"Who said I was flirting?"

"Because you're coming closer to me," I giggled, blushing like an elementary school girl.

"So?"

"So, no."

"No what? I didn't do anything."

"Yeah, you are."

"I just asked who said I wanted you to leave? What if I don't want you to leave?"

"You don't have a choice in that, Jarell."

"Can I get a kiss before you leave?" he asked, laying his head on my shoulder and wrapping his arms around me. Man. I just loved this side of Jarell. He was such a teddy bear and super affectionate. I could live with this any day!

"Of course you can."

"Can I get a kiss now? Please?" he asked.

Looking down at him, although his eyes saw nothing, they were so cute and puppy dog like. I would have never thought that I'd say anything like that about his eyes. I didn't know. Maybe I was starting to get over the aesthetic of them and really started to understand the emotions that were so vividly displayed in them. I chuckled and rubbed his face with the back of my hand.

"If you weren't so cute, I'd say no."

"Come here," he whispered.

And just like that, our lips softly touched, coming together in a sort of calm, but steamy passion. I felt myself fall. Our lips wouldn't separate no matter how much I wanted to try and stay on the task at hand. Eventually, I gave up and let it go, forgetting all about studying. I was so focused on him that my body started humming again in that familiar arousal that I felt last night. My mind on the other hand was screaming no because I was still raw down there. Or at least felt that way.

My body was much stronger than my mind because I began to softly moan at Jarell's gentle touches up my thigh.

"How do you feel?" he whispered in my ear, pulling me on top of him.

"I feel... I feel... I don't know. I just want you."

The moment those words left my mouth, my heart fluttered. He knew that sounded different than just sex. He paused, pulled back, and gave me a weird look. It wasn't repulsive or anything. Actually, it was that same vulnerable look from last night, but intensified.

"You want me? You sure that's not the lust talking?" he asked.

"No, Jarell. I really want you."

Jarell continued to look my way for a second. Then, he closed his eyes and brought me closer to him, our foreheads touching intimately. I closed my eyes and just let us connect. This meant the world to him. I could feel it. Never felt an energy so tangible. We stayed that way for a while, our hands caressing each other's bodies in a way that showed we cared for one another. More than just lust.

"I want you too," Jarell confessed, and then kissed me again. This time, it was short.

"Well then I'm yours," I whispered. "I promise. I'm yours."

Chapter Thirty-Two

It was Jarell's first day back to school, and I needed to be there. For sure. Graduation was in a little over a month, and we needed to be focused. No more skipping. I had no idea how everyone would react with him being back, but the last two weeks weren't pretty when it came to the things that they were saying about him. To be honest, it had me kind of scared, hoping he'd be able to handle it. But I would be there by his side no matter what. Jarell didn't deserve the kind of talk that was going around about him because none of it was his fault. I wished that I could just express that without revealing any of his business. I hadn't found a way to do that yet.

I got dressed and gave Alise a farewell before heading to Jarell's spot. His cute ass was already on the porch with his hood up, sunglasses on, his usual old jeans, and his backpack hauled over his shoulder. He simply sat, meddling with a piece of origami in his lap with a pensive look. I smiled, remembering the weekend's escapades. I couldn't believe he was my new boyfriend. I deserved none of him.

"Jarell!" I called out of the window finally after I had had enough staring at him.

He raised his eyebrows and stood up, hiding whatever origami piece he was working on into his pocket. Then he walked slowly to my car, hopping into the passenger seat. The moment he was settled in, he gave me a warm smile and leaned in for a kiss on my cheek.

"Morning, beautiful," he said softly. "Well, I know you look beautiful."

My heart melted. If this was how my man was going to greet me every day, I would cherish it forever.

"Hey, Jarell."

"How you feeling?" he asked and put his hand out to take mine. I put my hand into his as he caressed me softly. "Still sore down there?"

"A little. And I'm kinda tired from the weekend, but other than that, I feel great," I said, pulling off from the curb.

"Man, you had me thinkin' 'bout that shit all last night. Is there anything I can do to make you feel less tired?"

"Not really. I'll catch up on sleep later. How are *you* feeling?" I said with a wink he couldn't see, but he heard that intonation because he smirked and licked those sexy ass lips.

"You know how I feel after all of that."

I laughed. "I just wanted to hear you say it again."

"Nahh," he said with a chuckle. I loved making him blush. Jarell was never going to brag or talk candidly about sex. Especially since he was private and cared way too much about how I felt through it all. We'd have to date a little longer.

Jarell rolled down the window to feel the air with his hands. It was a little too chilly this morning for me to bear, but I didn't say anything because I knew how much he liked to interact with nature. Plus, for him to be stuck in his house for two weeks on punishment, I was glad to give him some air. His small house was stuffy.

"So... are you ready for your test today?" I asked with a deep breath, not really knowing how I was going break down the whole school climate thing with him.

"Yeah. I'm probably going to ace it, thanks to you," he said with a tinge of wickedness in his voice that made my skin heat up a bit.

"Jarell, you didn't even let me help you study." I chuckled, squinting at him.

"But you let me show you a few things that's very much related," he said. "If I could have kids, I'd have probably popped a kid or two up in there already."

"God, you're so damn nasty." I blushed. "I would've never, ever thought. You're like nowhere near as innocent."

"What eighteen-year-old man is? And you're my girl. I get to talk like that."

My heart just melted. I smiled, drawing my bottom lip between my teeth, trying not to squeal.

"You're right. I guess no one."

Jarell and I engaged in our flirty and usual banter until we pulled into the parking lot. I took my seat belt off, then looked at Jarell. Man. He was genuinely in a happy mood, and it was all about to be destroyed the moment he stepped foot in those school doors. I had to say something, even if I had to be the one to suck the happiness out of him. I just needed him to understand what he was about to be facing today, and for I don't know how long.

"Jarell?"

"Yeah?"

"Before we get out, I have to tell you something."

"What's wrong? Everything okay?" His smile disappeared.

I shook my head.

"No. Everything isn't okay."

The relaxed look on his face was replaced by a small frown that made me upset. *God, I didn't want to do this.*

"What is it?" He looked my direction, and took his sunglasses off, letting me connect with everything that he was feeling right now. A sense of foreboding wracked his entire body. I sighed.

"I just want you to know that people have been talking," I began.

"Okay?"

"These past two weeks, people have been saying some really negative things about you because of the whole fight with Martell. I've spent the last couple of weeks defending you but... it's gotten really out of hand."

"Oh, well that isn't anything new to me, Jade."

I closed my eyes. He didn't get it.

"Jarell, this is... this is some next level shit that I don't think you've experienced. People are saying some real, real messed up things."

"What are they saying?"

"I'm not repeating it."

"Jade, it ain't anything that I haven't already endured in my life, I'm sure."

"I just don't want to see you hurt, Jarell."

"Jade," he whispered and put his hand out towards me again. I placed my hand into his and he kissed it. "It's going to be fine."

"I hope so. But no matter what, I got you. Okay? I'm not going to let anything happen to you. We ride or die today, alright? Just be ready."

He smiled.

"I like that. I'm ready."

He kissed my hand once more, and we got out of the car. Together, arm in arm, we walked to Crenshaw's school doors and through them. The scene was already buzzing. People chaotically walking around to get with their friends before school started, going to the bathroom, seeing teachers, and the whole nine. Jarell was a bit tense and so was I, but so far so good. No one really noticed us yet.

Until we got deeper into the school.

We passed the Freshman wing, but when we started passing the Junior wing to get to the Senior wing, the stares started to come. Then stares turned into comments.

"Snake ass bitch."

"She's so fake. Got the nerve to defend him after what he did."

"She ditched Mike for his weird ass. Stupid."

"Yeah, she got dropped by D-Block because she betrayed Mike and Martell. How could she walk around with him after what he did?"

"She's an idiot."

So many comments. I closed my eyes and took a deep breath but pressed forward with my arms locked with Jarell's. Jarell shook his head and whispered to me.

"This is crazy. The energy is so hostile."

"I told you. You haven't heard nothing, yet."

"Don't say anything back to them," he warned.

"I'm not."

Jarell and I kept walking with our arms locked together until we reached the Senior wing. I avoided D-Block at all costs, taking a whole different route. But still, the Senior wing was the Senior wing. If they weren't in our congregation spot, they were elsewhere. My heart was now pounding as we turned the corner to the hallway where Jarell's locker was. The corridor was a long stretch to his locker, which gave people plenty of time to stir up some shit.

"Look at that killer. We should take his ass out before he takes us out."

"Look at him. Who the hell wears sunglasses in school? Fucking psycho."

"He needs to be locked in a cage. Crazy ass nigga. He's a whole animal!"

"Him beating on me would never happen. I'd have stabbed his ass. He better off dead anyway."

"Crack head babies make crack head behavior."

"No way he should've beat Martell like that."

"He's fucking unstable. Why isn't he in jail?"

Jarell really started to tense up. I didn't think he'd ever heard them in a string of insults back-to-back the way that he was getting them right now. I just took a long breath and kept walking, holding him tight.

Then, the comments turned into harassment the further we got down the hall. Out of nowhere, one of the girls in the hallway threw several notebooks at Jarell, aiming for his head, but missed.

"Crazy asshole!" she shouted at him.

Another spat at him as he walked by.

"Go kill yourself, punk."

I picked up the walking pace with Jarell because he started to look physically shaken up. I felt so helpless. I wanted to beat the shit out of that girl who threw those notebooks and the girl who spit at him. But at the same time, I didn't want to exacerbate the situation by stopping to fight because then, it would have left him alone to possibly get jumped.

"Let's hurry," I said.

When we made it to his locker, Ms. Jenson was standing there with his locker opened. She looked just as worried as I did.

"Ms. Jenson –" I started to vent about everything going on, but she put her hand up to stop me.

"Yes, I know. Listen. I have already communicated with the principal, and the security guards will be down here in the next few minutes to make sure that Jarell doesn't get hurt. She had no idea the reaction to him coming back would be this intense."

"I guess that's what happens when you're popular like Martell and something happens to you," I said, shaking my head. "But that principal isn't doing enough. She knows he's blind. She needs to do more to protect him. She knows Martell needs to be held accountable."

"Yeah, I know. But it's not going to happen because she fears for her own safety."

I shook my head. This school was so fucked up. The sad part about it? I played a huge role in making it this way.

"Jarell," I called out to him to check in to see if he was okay.

He silently grabbed the things he needed out of his locker without answering and then slammed it shut, walking away from us. *Ooooh.* Not good when the anger inside of Jarell was starting to brew like that. I didn't want him to snap and get into any more trouble. It was his first day back, after all.

"I'll get him. Please go let the social worker know," I said to Ms. Jenson, and ran after him. "Jarell stop!"

As he paced towards his class and before I could reach him, someone purposely pushed him from the side, causing Jarell to bang his shoulder pretty hard against the lockers, and his sunglasses tumbled off his face. Shit. Another bruise on Jarell's body was going to develop later after that. In fact, Jarell got pushed so hard that his arm might've been bleeding underneath his hoodie.

"Punk ass nigga," said the guy who pushed him. A guy named Marcus. "What you wanna do boy? I ain't Martell, but that's my cousin, boy. I'll fuck you up."

Everyone, and I meant, *everyone*, feared Marcus. Marcus was also on D-Block, but he rarely came to school because he was always in trouble with the law. Marcus was at least six foot five with a hefty, sturdy stature and big hands. He was way bigger than Jarell. One punch from him would probably have sent Jarell crumbling like a ragdoll, even though Jarell was strong himself.

It seemed like the world froze as passersby stopped to watch what they hoped would be the end of Jarell.

Much to my dismay, as I picked up his sunglasses, Jarell dropped his backpack and rolled up his hoodie sleeves. *Oh no. Oh no, no, no.* I wasn't going to let him fight again and get expelled because of someone else's bullshit. But not only that, Jarell definitely was losing this battle. Might even be killed.

But I also had to remember that his mom's ex, as he described, was big like this. It might have been something Jarell was preparing his whole life for as he did all those pushups at night to grow strong – to fight back and possibly kill as well. Either way, it wasn't good for either of them.

"Would you fuckin' leave him alone!" I screamed at Marcus, stepping in front of Jarell. I knew Marcus wouldn't hurt me. We were cool in the past. "I'm so tired of y'all treating him like this!"

"What you wanna do? You rollin' up your sleeves like you 'bout it. You really wanna send niggas to the hospital for no reason... I'll show your retarded ass how it feels!" Marcus ignored me, giving Jarell a look that held so much disgust and hate that you'd think Jarell was from another planet.

"You're not touching him!" I screamed.

"Shut up bitch. Martell might've listened, but I ain't Martell!

Look at him. Looks like someone gutted his eyes out. He's a demon from hell with no soul and you standing up for him. Somebody needs to kill him! Fuck it, I will!"

"No you won't! You don't even know him!" I said, beginning to cry as I watched a circle form around us. I just didn't want Jarell to get hurt.

"Get your bird ass out of this. Let's go, nigga. Let's see if you really bad."

"Okay," Jarell said. Way too calm. "I ain't scared and I'm not letting you talk to my girl like that. Hit me. I dare you."

"Shut up, Jarell!" I screamed, and slapped the dog shit out of him across the face.

Fuck.

I shouldn't have done that, but I was just so scared for him. Forget him standing up for me. I was trying to protect him as best as I could. Who knew what Martell's cousin was capable of? Last time, Jarell was lucky because Martell didn't expect to get rushed, but a one-on-one fight squaring up? Jarell was clearly at a disadvantage due to his eyesight. I didn't want to underestimate him, but hell, I was being realistic.

Either way, it was like I didn't slap him at all. He didn't even flinch.

"Don't hit me like that again, Jade. Move out of the way," he said, in a nonthreatening way. No bass in his voice. Nothing. He just turned his head back towards Marcus and stared into space, waiting to be punched by him.

My skin began to pebble. He really just acted like I didn't almost knock his head off. Even my own hand still stung after slapping him. His lack of pain perception really frightened me. And he damn near had that same look he had before he almost murdered Martell.

I just knew he was doomed. I was desperate, and now didn't know what to do. I started bawling as I stood in front of Jarell face to face.

"Please, don't do this. Please. You're better than this. I didn't mean to slap you, but I'm scared. Please, Jarell."

"Move out of the way. Let him do it. He talking all that shit like a nigga scared. You know what I been through, Jade. I been quiet for too long." His face was devoid of any expression, any emotion that usually lived in his eyes, and that wasn't a good sign at all.

"I'm begging you Jarell. Please!"

The growing crowd that had formed around us had grown larger and larger, and everyone was egging Marcus on.

"Kill his ass, bro!"

"Fuck him up!"

"Paralyze that bitch!"

"Take his ass out, man."

It was the scariest, most horrifying thing that I had ever experienced. I couldn't imagine how Jarell was feeling, hearing everyone wanting him to be dead.

"Are you listening to me, Jarell? Please..."

"Get your skinny, begging ass out the way. He said he wanna fight, so let us fight. I'ma fuck this nigga up so bad..."

"I'm not fucking talking to you!" I whirled around and screamed at the guy.

"Suck my dick."

Without further ado, Marcus pushed me away and to the floor, breaking the barrier between him and Jarell.

"Jarell, watch out!"

Marcus cocked his fist back and threw a haymaker that would've easily slept him. I was so glad I warned him because Jarell ended up ducking and the punch completely missed as Marcus' body ran into him. Much to my surprise and horror, when Jarell ducked and felt his body run into him, he picked Marcus up by his legs as high as he could and slammed him to the ground so hard that I just knew Marcus broke a bone somewhere. It was confirmed the way Marcus yelled out in pain when he tried to break his own fall.

It was over.

There was no way Marcus was defending himself nor winning this fight anymore. The first punch he threw at Jarell was his only chance, but that ship had sailed the moment he missed. Once again, Jarell never ceased to surprise me. His power really was unmatched. Almost hulk like. And it was being released in the wrong ways. I knew all of that strength in him was meant for his abuser, but goodness...

"Jarell, no!" I screamed. "Don't you dare!"

He didn't listen. This time, it was worse than what he had given Martell.

Much worse.

Jarell took one hand and choked him to the ground with his fingers enclosed viciously around Marcus' neck and his other hand peeled back, ready to end Marcus' life with one blow.

To seal the brutal deal, there was absolutely no way for Marcus to escape this lock hold or to tumble a smaller Jarell off.

At all. Not even a little bit.

One of Jarell's knees sunk deep into Marcus's chest while his other leg gave him balance, along with helping his ability to locate Marcus' different body parts without sight. Either away, the move completely eliminated any source of air or ability to get up, quickly expediting Marcus' chance of death.

It was definitely an advanced military or martial arts type of move, and I had no idea where Jarell learned it from. Nonetheless, it was just ruthless. I wasn't prepared to watch either someone suffocate or get killed by a brutal punch right in front of me.

"Go 'head and tell me what you were saying," Jarell threatened as tears of straight horror streamed from Marcus' eyes. "You alright? You had a whole lot to say before. Your little friends hyped you up. They told you to kill me, and you thought it was gonna happen, huh? Actually? How about I kill *you* instead..."

I screamed again, scrambling up off the floor as the worst possible scenario flashed before my eyes. "Jarell, don't! Let him go! It's not that serious!"

Jarell didn't listen. He actually pulled a pocketknife from his back pocket and put it to his forehead. *Now?* Marcus was convulsing, frothing at the mouth, and wheezed for air, clawing at Jarell's hand and looking like he had seen his worst nightmares come to fruition. If Jarell strangled him like that for thirty seconds longer, Marcus was dead.

The entire hallway went completely silent, watching Jarell in terror. The few people who saw the fight between Jarell and Martell had looked this way, but it was entirely different when there was five times the amount of people and they had a similar look.

"Get off of him, Jarell," I squeaked, pulling Jarell away from Marcus and snatching the knife away. Marcus immediately started coughing.

"Yeah. You lucky. I could've killed you already if I really wanted to. So don't fuck with me for the rest of the school year. That goes for all you weak ass niggas who think you run the school by bullying everybody. I ain't said nothing for four years because I'm trying to contain my anger, and now I'm done. So come collect this nigga off the floor that y'all hyped up. You scared of him, but this nigga weak as fuck to me. He can't even get up," Jarell demanded and kicked Marcus one last time, coincidentally as he tried to get up, which knocked him back down.

Wow.

This was a Jarell I just... I couldn't even *imagine* existed. Cold-blooded. Heartless. But no matter how I felt though? It was checkmate. He put every last one of them in their place. That quick.

Marcus was hyperventilating to get that much needed air and held on to his neck that I knew for sure was going to be bruised later. Jarell was right. He couldn't even sit up. Meanwhile, Jarell kept his back turned and his eyes closed, clenching his fists, trying to regulate himself by taking deep audible breaths. I gave Jarell his glasses back, stood in front of him and slowly faced the silent, stunned crowd.

"Let this be a lesson learned to everybody," I said, voice shaking.

Mike's face had appeared with a stoic look, Erica looked like she was shitting bricks, Laurie stood with wide eyes, and Martell was there, still in his neck brace, picking up his cousin off of the floor who still laid there and cried.

"Jarell is human. You don't know what he has been through. You don't know his situation. You don't know him at all. So stop pushing him over the limit because it's pretty fucking clear that he'll kill you."

"Hey! What's going on here!"

The resource police officers came and rushed the scene with their batons in hand, ready to escalate the entire situation. Everyone scattered like roaches when they arrived, so no one was able to even respond to any of my comments. Jarell still stood standing, facing the lockers with his fists enclosed.

"Young lady!" the police shouted towards me. "What's going on?"

"Nothing officer, damn! Everyone is fine."

They looked at me, and then looked at Jarell who was still tensed, shaking, and fists in tight balls. And if the day couldn't get any worse, it just did.

The police slammed Jarell into the lockers chest first and brought his hands behind his back.

"What are y'all doing!" I screamed. "He's blind. Stop it! Get off him!"

"What happened here?" they ignored me and asked Jarell.

"Nothing!" he roared. "Nothing."

My goodness. Every emotion in Jarell's eyes were so raw at this point. He was scared, he was hurt, angry, frustrated, sad… everything. As the police had him pinned against the locker and patted him down, his Adam's apple was bobbing at work, and I could tell that he was trying so hard to keep it together. Thank God I took his knife. Otherwise he'd be back in jail.

Eventually, when they found nothing, they walked away without apology. Jarell released himself from the locker and closed his eyes, trying to regain control of everything inside of him. I hugged him tightly from behind, feeling every tensed muscle in his body, hoping my touch would calm him down, whispering that we just needed to get through the rest of the day if we could.

Chapter Thirty-Three

THIS DAY WAS the longest and arguably the worst day of my life. It couldn't have been any worse than Jarell's day, though. No matter what, I had to stick by him because it didn't matter that he had almost murdered someone else or that he had gotten roughed up by the police. We continued to get cruel comments and stares, mostly from people who didn't see what happened this morning. It was so bad, I couldn't even enjoy being with Laurie or anyone else because I found myself with him, making sure that no one else tried to harm him.

As a result, the Jarell I had gotten to know had completely disappeared. It was like he never existed. He was mute, withdrawn, and emotionless for the entire day, speaking only when he absolutely had to. He had completely reverted back to the old him. I felt so helpless; I was trying to do everything I could to be there for him. The principal seemed to not give a shit except to get the police to criminalize him, his social worker was out of the building for the day, Ms. Jenson was too soft, and it was literally as if the school could do nothing for him. Everything had just become out of control.

It was now seventh period Gym, and I was so glad that this was the last real class of the day before having study hall with Jarell in which we weren't going to study. We needed to debrief the day for sure.

Swimming class was literally the knock off Sports Illustrated Swimsuit modeling contest. Girls tried their best to make sure that their swim gear was on point, titties out and up, and all. It wasn't even about learning how to swim. It was about which girl could get the most compliments about their body from the guys who would get these disgusting ass boners in their trunks after checking out the girls in class. Honestly, it was a hot mess, but I was just there so I wouldn't get fined. Or an F, I should say.

Laurie was in this class, and I was glad so that I could at least still spend some time with her and get her thoughts about what happened earlier. Like she'd even care. She was always looking for guys to give her attention whether she was with Martell or not, even though she could have most definitely gotten it without doing the most. She was pretty anyway, but she got attention in the wrong ways.

I was sitting on the ledge of the pool of the shallow end, waiting on Laurie to come out in her skimpy little swimsuit when many of the boys started to come out of the locker room.

Jarell was the last to come out. He stuck out like a sore thumb too as Ms. Jenson met up with him. His swim trunks were long and past his knees, and he had his hoodie on with his hood up. No matter what, Jarell was never going to give up that goddamned hoodie, even if it was for swimming. I knew why, but still.

I observed him for a while as they walked the pool deck. His shoulders were sunken, his hood was tightened, and his glasses were off, but he looked towards the ground so that no one could truly see his face. At this moment, he truly looked like the grim reaper, and I wanted to cry for him. But we were almost at the end of this day. And we were going to have to figure out how we were surviving the rest of the school year after this.

I just stared at him with sad eyes when he and Ms. Jenson were interrupted by a student walking to the other pool for the special education students, which was one-hundred percent shallow. Two-point-five feet deep. I listened in closely.

"Ms. Jenson. Do you know where I can put my backpack and belongings while I'm swimming? I don't have a lock and people steal too much. So I just want to keep my stuff safe."

"Sure, Miranda. Let me show you some of the cubbies that are around here that you can stick it in."

As Ms. Jenson helped her, Jarell squatted down to feel the temperature of the water in the twelve feet deep end of the pool that was closest to them as he waited. Ms. Jenson proceeded to answer the girl's question, pointing in several directions.

As Jarell's hand grazed the water, suddenly, some random guy in the class, who wasn't that popular himself and even was bullied occasionally by us since he was a Sophomore, kicked Jarell as hard as he could in the back. Jarell went flying into the deep end of the pool in a huge splash face first.

"Oh my God!" I screamed out. "You asshole!"

Everyone around laughed hysterically, but I was petrified and so was Ms. Jenson.

"Oh my God. Oh my God, help! Somebody help!" Ms. Jenson screamed in bloody murder.

I was completely frozen. My entire heart was caught in my throat as I stared at the water for a good fifteen seconds, and there was no sign of him coming up. Just bubbles where he had fallen. I had no idea how to swim or how to get him out, but the flight or fight mode in me kicked into third degree. All I felt myself doing was leaving the shallow end and sprinting to the deep end, screaming for a life guard to help.

Class hadn't started yet. There was no lifeguard in sight.

Shit. I couldn't just stand here. So I went for it.

Didn't even think twice about it. I punched the emergency glass with my bare hand, grabbed the emergency rope from the wall, pushed my goggles on and dove into the water as if I had done this a million times. The coolness of the pool chilled my entire body as the water abruptly splashed over me, but what I saw in that water chilled my entire soul.

Jarell was sinking in his hoodie as he literally struggled. Fighting the water, and for his life. To come up for air. He had to be scared. Had to. He couldn't see. I didn't know what to do. I just started kicking and moving my arms the way I would imagine swimming under water. I was so scared that I was literally out of breath myself, but I couldn't let the both of us die.

When I reached him, I tossed the rope to his nearest hand, hoping and praying that he could feel it and grab on. And luckily, he did. He grabbed onto it like it was a lifeline, which it was. *Now what, Jade? You got him, so what do you do?* I started to panic.

Come on, Jade. Push the water down if you want to go up. Push down, go up. You can do it. You're strong. You're a dancer. You're an athlete. Pull him up.

I let my inner self talk me through. I pushed down, pulled up and before I knew it, I was surfacing above the water in a panic attack and coughing fit. But I had another problem. I didn't know how to tread water, so I went back under with him. And just like that, I was drowning. The both of us were. I tried my hardest to keep him a float.

I could hear his panting, hyperventilating, and coughing. Suddenly, he was grabbing a hold of my shoulders, climbing on top of me in fear, pushing me down so I couldn't surface.

Now, I was breathing in water.

It hurt like hell, and I wanted to scream in pain. I didn't want to cough because more water would just seep into my lungs. But it was the only thing I could do instead of screaming. So, I coughed enough water into my lungs that the result was excruciating pain that had me wanting to pass out. I couldn't muster up the strength in my now weak arms to push him off of me, so I just struggled and tried to hold my breath, praying inside for someone to come and save us with the few seconds of my life that I had left.

The last seconds felt like forever and a day until I felt the release of Jarell's weight off of my shoulders and myself being pulled away from the weight of the water and onto the ground. The only thing I felt were my knees on the deck and my back in a searing pain as I tried to breathe normally. All I could hear were my rough, wet coughs, yelling and chaos from classmates, Ms. Jenson cussing someone out, and heaving from Jarell. I hadn't yet opened my eyes because my chest hurt so bad that I was clutching on to it. But when I did, I looked up to see Ms. Jenson crying. Jarell was next to me throwing up water.

And that was the last thing I saw before everything went black.

Chapter Thirty-Four

THE SMELL OF sickness in the air, the feeling of foreign objects in my body, pressure on my face, and the beeping noises woke me up out of a deep, deep sleep. My eyes blinked open several times to take in my environment, and I shot up in bed in a panic. Tubes were in my arms, a mask over my face, and I was completely naked underneath a gown.

"Don't. It's okay," I heard an unfamiliar lady voice.

Someone was standing over me, and it looked to be a nurse. That didn't stop me from panicking inside, but physically, I was so scared that I listened to her. I'd listen to anything she would say. She adjusted the bed and helped me sit up. That gave me full visual access. Darting my eyes around, a small room with random picture decorations encompassed me. A TV sat on the high wall. And last, sitting across from me was Jarell wrapped in a blanket like he was freezing and Jarell's mother, hugging him close to her.

I frowned in confusion. *What happened?*

As if Ms. Hendricks could feel my gaze, her head turned towards me, and she got up from Jarell instantly and walked over my way.

"Oh sweetie. I'm so glad you're awake," she whispered, and then rubbed one of my hands in a motherly way.

"What's going on? Why am I in the hospital?"

"You almost drowned saving my son because of some piece of shit at school. I swear to God, it's taking everything in me not to go and shoot that damn school up. The kid got arrested. I'm pressing charges."

I blinked. *Drowned?*

I gave Jarell a bewildered look, and he was looking towards the ground with the most defeated look I had ever seen from anyone. He was wrapped tightly in his blanket, his eyes were bare, and no hood over his head. I hated calling him Ghost now, but it really did seem like he was lifeless. He didn't even react to me being awake. I watched him, feeling my own sadness, wanting to say something to him, but not really knowing what because I truly didn't know what happened. He clearly wasn't in a place to explain it either if I had asked.

"He isn't responsive right now," his mother whispered to me when she realized that I was staring. "He might be in shock."

"What happened?"

"I don't know any real details. But he had just got released from the hospital himself. He wasn't out like you were. But that's because you saved him," she said, rubbing my arm now in gratitude. "I don't know what my son would do without you, Jade."

Her eyes began to water.

"Ms. Hendricks..."

Speechless was the best way to describe this feeling. I was just so confused.

"Someone pushed him into the pool, and he almost died. But you saved him. I know you don't remember because you blacked out, maybe had a concussion, but you did. You saved my son."

I blinked. Someone did what? Why would they do that to him? Well... if I saved him, I would do it again. I would do it a million times over. Jarell had enough of being alone in this world.

"I'm not going to let anything happen to him, Ms. Hendricks. I made a promise."

She nodded, her tears falling. My heart broke. My goodness. This family had gone through so much suffering and pain... It was my turn to rub her hand. She needed to know how much she was loved and appreciated, too. I didn't know what the hell was going on, what I had done and why, or what happened for Jarell to end up in the pool, but I just needed to be there. Be there for this family.

For a little while, we all just sat in silence and watched the hospital TV as the nurse periodically came in to check my vitals. She said that I wouldn't be released until tomorrow morning or the day after to check in on my breathing and my lungs in case I developed pneumonia. Not once did Jarell ever look up or even budge. He stared with his sightless eyes at the same spot on the floor for minutes that turned into over an hour. His mother just embraced him like she didn't care. Poor Jarell.

A few minutes passed by, and the hospital door burst open. It was my mother, rushing into the room and hovering over me. Her hair was pulled back in a tight bun per usual, and she had on a business suit.

"Jade, baby. Are you alright?" She swarmed, touched me, and felt my forehead. It was super overwhelming.

"What happened? How's your breathing? What do you need from me? Oh my God, you scared me so much. You scared me; I thought my baby was gone."

I didn't know what to do or say, but to be honest, I was so glad she was here. There was something about a mother's presence during times like this that was so needed, no matter what our relationship was. I was relieved to know she hadn't completely forgotten about me. That she did love me.

"I'm so glad you're awake and okay. My god, when the school called to tell me that you nearly drowned, I tried to get here as soon as I could."

She rubbed my forehead with her thumb and caressed the rest of her fingers through my hair that was usually straight but was kinked over into thick curls now.

"I'm okay, Mom. I think. I don't know what happened, but I'm so glad you're here. Thank you for coming."

With a small smile, one of the most loving smiles I received from her, she backed up and then turned her head to look at the other guests in the room. I hadn't even realized Ms. Hendricks had stood up and waited for my mom to stop swarming over me.

"Hi, I'm Rachel," Jarell's mom warmly greeted my mom and stuck her hand out for a shake. She looked at my mother with so much admiration, so much respect. "It's so nice to finally meet you. You're stunning. I see where Jade gets her beauty."

Much to my disappointment, she simply looked at her hand, and then back at her face, backing away with her lip turned up. Jarell's mom began to understand that was an insult, and she frowned, slowly putting her hand down. Jarell still didn't move a muscle. I closed my eyes and prayed for my mom to just be mature for once. For once, to not make it about her or her antics. I was sick, goddamn it. Could she just focus on me?

"What happened?" my mother coldly asked.

Ms. Hendricks blinked in response, taken aback by my mother's aggression.

"Hello? Oh, so he's blind, and you're deaf? Go figure. Are you going to answer me, or what? Is the reason my daughter is in this hospital bed because of that bum?"

Ms. Hendricks physically jerked her head back in offense.

"Excuse me? What did you just say about my son?"

"Let me repeat it for you, since you're both slow and deaf. I said, is she here because of that bum? If you're here invading my daughter's space before I can even get to her, I'm assuming that it's the reason. And yeah, I said it. Ever since she has been messing around with *it*, her life has gone to shit. I told her to stay away from *it*."

Ms. Hendricks closed her eyes and crossed her arms, taking a deep, deep breath. It looked as if she was literally counting to ten in her head.

"Listen, lady. I don't know who you think you're talking to, but I won't allow you to talk about my son like that and dehumanize him. Say whatever you want about me, but my child is different. You ought to watch yourself before something happens in this hospital. I'm trying to be civil."

"Momma, are you serious? If you're going to act like this, just go. You always do this. This is the worst possible time right now. Please," I said, trying to diffuse what was already a quickly heating situation.

"What you gonna do? Girl you're like three feet tall. You can't afford to get into a fight," Janet laughed, and stepped into Ms. Hendricks' face, baiting her. My stomach began to churn, and my breathing started to quicken. I couldn't even breath properly to begin with since I've been in the hospital, so I started coughing, waving my hand to get them to stop.

Ms. Hendricks' anger was rising in her eyes, and she tried to step back, but Janet moved in closer.

"Mom! Stop!" I managed to scream.

"Jade is my daughter. Mine! Not yours. She's going to do what I say. She won't be around that ugly thing."

"Stop! You need to leave," I said, buzzing my nurse and telling her that I had an unwanted guest and that they also needed to bring security.

"Listen, bitch. Say what you want because you're clearly trying to get a rise out of me. I ain't gonna fight you in this hospital. But it looks like you're the bum who can't fathom their child loving who they want to love," Jarell's mom said.

"You call that love? Ha! She doesn't love that thing. She's in this phase. The phase all of us dumb asses were in when we were young. She'll wake up soon, hopefully if this hasn't already been a wakeup call."

Ms. Hendricks looked Janet up and down and scoffed, shaking her head.

"You're immature and pathetic trash. Your daughter is so much better than you."

"Hmm. You're right. She will be better than me. Because I taught her not to be with filthy cockroaches. Dirty ass peasant," she growled and picked up a Styrofoam cup filled with water.

Without hesitation, she threw an ice-cold cup of water at Jarell's face and threw the cup at his face, too. Jarell flinched and covered to avoid any further items that she might've tossed. If I wasn't bound to the IVs, I would have gotten up, but without further ado, Ms. Hendricks threw a mighty punch that would have squarely connected in her face had security not swooped in and picked her up with ease. She started shouting at Janet as security held her back in the room. Just as quickly, another security guard pulled Janet out of the room as she laughed and started throwing things at Jarell that she could find on her body or in her purse like a small bottle of lotion, jewelry, and deodorant that missed, but the ones that did connect with Jarell's face were her shoes.

I covered half of my face with my hand. I couldn't believe what I was watching. She embarrassed me again. Not only in the hospital, but utterly disrespected Jarell and his mother like they weren't even human. How in the hell were they going to perceive me now?

Jesus. I didn't know what to say. How could I even apologize for this moment? There was no apologizing for that. The remorse inside of me ran as deep as the ocean.

"This ain't over, bitch!" I heard my mom scream from the outside as she was escorted out.

The security guard must've said something good in her ear because Ms. Hendricks relaxed in a huff, ignored Janet's comment, and adjusted herself. The security guard watched her for a little while to make sure that she was really okay, and then he took off to report what happened. She knelt down to Jarell, making sure he was okay, telling him not to listen to her, telling him that she'll handle her as the nurse checked to see if I was okay. She had taken my vitals, and my blood pressure had gone up a bit, but it was still in the safe zone. Jarell was just sitting there with his head lowered even more, shaking his head as he was still wrapped in his now moist blanket. His mother continued to soothe him and tell him not to believe any of what Janet had said. None of it mattered.

Jarell started crying.

It was the first sign of life or emotion from him since he'd been in this room. It was one of those infamous quiet releases from him, and that was what made it so painful to watch. But it wasn't the kind of cry I saw in the forest. That was cathartic. This was different. Way different. This was pure angst, sadness, and devastation. His eyes were bloodshot, veins popped from his neck and face, and his skin turned red.

"Why does everyone hate me so much?" Jarell wept. "What am I doing so wrong, Ma? I only respond to what people do to me. What did I do so wrong?"

"Oh, Jarell," his mom said, dropping to her knees and she wept with him.

"I don't know how much more I can take," Jarell whispered. "I can't keep taking it and taking it and taking it and taking it over and over and over and over. I don't want to live anymore."

"Don't talk like –" his mother said, but he interrupted.

"I can't do this anymore, Ma. I can't keep getting treated like this."

"We're going to get you to your therapist on Thursday. Alright? Please. I'll do whatever. I'll pull you out of that school. Just please..."

"I can't take another day. I don't want to take another day."

"Jarell, no. No. You're all I have. You're all I have. I swear it."

Now, Ms. Hendricks was on her knees begging, clutching at him.

"You're my everything. I wouldn't know what to do if something happened to you. My son," she said, pulling him tight into her chest as she cried hysterically. "I don't care what you do, but don't talk like this. I don't want to lose you. I can't take anything else horrible happening in my life. Please. I love you. I love you so much, Jarell. Promise me. Promise me right now you won't dare take your life."

Jarell looked her way for a little while, but he looked away and shook his head.

"I can't promise you that," he whispered, but damn was it full of conviction. It sounded so final.

"Jarell... please..." his mother begged.

"Jarell, don't say that," I called out to him, but I couldn't even blame him for how he felt. I still only knew a piece of the pie that was his life. "Don't say that. That would crush me."

"No! Fuck that, Jade. I hear why *you're* saying that, but I've spent my whole life getting physically abused and forgiving. Getting mistreated and forgiving. Suffering and forgiving. Getting sexually abused and forgiving. I'm trying to be in a happier mental state. Trying my best to make others happy. I need to know what I did so wrong," he cried.

"Wait, what? Sexually abused?" His mother gasped. "Jarell..."

"Yes!" he bellowed, now completely distraught, his entire face covered with tears. "By that asshole you brought home. Every time that stupid fuck beat on me after beating you, he'd come into my room at night to apologize, putting his hand in my pants, touching on me and shit. Promising me he'll never beat me again. Promising me he won't hurt you again. And I let him because I believed that if I just let him fucking do it, he wouldn't beat me no more."

My head hit the pillow and I stared at the ceiling, bawling my eyes out. I literally, literally, couldn't even imagine... how could someone endure so much pain...

"Jarell baby why didn't you tell me?" his mother cried.

"What was that gonna do, Ma? Huh? So you can bring it up to him just for him to beat you? I didn't want to watch you get beat for another reason. It's the shit I'm talking about. I'm always sacrificing something in order to make others happy. So I don't understand why I'm the one out here getting shit thrown at me, getting grounded, getting arrested, people attempting to murder me, getting beat, molested, starving because Kylah needs food more than I do because I know what it feels like to go weeks without a meal and she doesn't, getting bullied at school by everyone, and all of this without a single thing in return! I don't deserve none of this shit!"

The room was dead silent. The only thing you could hear were Jarell's cries as he fell deeper into his misery.

Ms. Hendricks brought his forehead up for a kiss, and they cried together. Forehead to forehead. Tear to tear. Releasing everything they've been through together as she caressed his head in a motherly way. I wasn't even there to them. I just watched like a fly on the wall bawling to myself feeling a permanent agony I didn't think I could ever shake in my soul.

I hadn't known Jarell long, but what I did know was that he had an uncanny capability to be strong. Physically, emotionally, and mentally. And now? He was crumbling before my very eyes.

And that was devastating to watch, especially since I've known him to be tremendously composed.

"It's all coming out, now," his mother said. "So much that you've kept bottled. Let it out, Jarell. Anything else you want to pour out to me? What do you need from me, baby?"

"I don't need shit from you, Ma. Except for the words 'I'm sorry, Jarell.' That's all I want to hear from you. At the end of the day, the only person I can say truly has given a flying fuck about me is Jade. And I kept pushing and pushing her away because I thought she was like everyone else. But now I have to deal with her mom. I can't catch a break!"

"I care about and love you, too Jarell. You know that."

"Oh, do you? Really? Because you haven't apologized a single fucking time for all the shit you put me through because of your bad decisions. And not once did I ever complain. And even now, I still stick by you because you're doing the best you can as a mom, and I can't blame you for what you've faced either. But own your part of it, Ma. Own it! Apologize to me! It's all I want!"

She huffed and dipped her head. It was silent for a long, long time.

"I'm sorry, Jarell," she confessed.

"Thank you."

Then, without a single word, he got up from his chair and proceeded to head towards my room door. *God.* If he walked out of this room, I just knew I'd never see him again.

"Jarell..." I called out, my voice shaking.

"Where are you going?" his mother asked. "Don't go anywhere. You're not going anywhere, Jarell."

He said nothing. Just proceeded to the door.

"Jarell? Please stop. Please," she begged, standing in front of him.

He ran into her from lack of vision, but he simply pushed her out of the way with his strong arm.

"Jarell, you're not leaving. You're not. I won't let you."

Ms. Hendricks kept moving and standing in front of him every time he shoved her away. The closer he got to the door, the more hysterical she became.

She grabbed onto his clothes and kept tugging them, hanging onto his life. Jarell kept pulling his clothes out of her hand until she grabbed it one good time, digging her heels in and yanked it, tearing his hoodie apart that provided him with so much security in his life.

"Jarell, would you stop!? I'm not letting you go! Please!"

That didn't stop him from trying to leave and her from trying to stop him. She grabbed on to his now white t-shirt as he kept trying to push her away, but she ended up tearing that too. Jarell pulled away from her to the point where she fell to her knees when she tore the rest of his shirt and had nothing left to grab on to. It wasn't like she could pull his scars away. The way I wished she could.

I called out to stop him several times, but he wouldn't listen. It wasn't like I could get up from my IVs, so all I could truly do was weep. He kept telling his mother that she'd needed to be okay without him and my hand was on the red buzzer to call my nurse in.

I knew he'd hate me for this, but there was nothing else I could do.

"Everything okay, in here?" the nurse came in with concern.

"Hurry up and get someone! My boyfriend who just walked out of the room needs to be on suicide watch!"

Chapter Thirty-Five

AFTER TWO HAUNTING days, I was physically free. But knowing that the person I cared about so much wasn't free because he was admitted to the mental health wing of this very hospital made it feel like I was in psychological bondage. I felt even more bounded after finding out the truth about what happened at school to cause me to be in the hospital, since I couldn't remember due to my concussion. People truly were cruel, and I didn't know if I wanted to even go back to that school tomorrow. I knew that I wanted to graduate and all, but just not at Crenshaw. I didn't want to be around people who wanted my boyfriend dead, and he had done absolutely nothing wrong.

I even thought about how I was showered with love from people who eventually came to visit me. Laurie, Corey, Alise, the studio crew, and so many others came to tell me how much of a hero I was and had given me get well and thank you cards. It honestly felt great. I couldn't even imagine being in this place a year ago. The old me would have let Jarell die and not give a care in the world. Things were just so much different. But I just knew Jarell wasn't getting the same kind of love that I had received from everyone, and that was heartbreaking.

That was what haunted me.

Everyone's hatred towards him. My mother blatantly throwing things at him like he was trash. Replaying his words and giving up on life had me up all night for the past couple of days.

I couldn't lie. Jarell deserved to feel that way.

I signed my medical release forms and asked the medical staff where the mental health/crisis wing of the huge building was. They had told me, and I found myself walking slowly down the corridor of the mental health extension. I've always heard stories about how these facilities were full of people with schizophrenia and bipolar disorder running around screaming with their unstable mental disabilities and a stressful environment for the workers.

I found none of that to be true. At least in my experience at the moment.

The facility was quiet, and the rooms were extremely domestic and comfortable. As I was walking by some rooms, family members were in there and spending time with their loved one as if they were in their own homes. Other rooms were closed. I heard a scream as I walked through the halls, but it wasn't to the point where it matched my prior assumptions of what this place would be.

I reached the middle circular receptionist desk at the end of the hall. Only one red-headed lady was at the desk with this weird eighties looking hairstyle.

"I'm looking for the room number for Jarell Hendricks," I said. Now that I was closer, she appeared to be doing nothing at all and looked as if she'd rather be any place but here. This made me rethink my assumptions about a place like this.

"Thirteen-oh-three."

Curt, short, and sweet. I didn't take offense. I could tell that she wasn't going to be helpful the moment I looked at her, so I just found the arrows on the walls to figure out where to go myself. I followed the signs, and Jarell's room was the second door from the corner hallway. With a deep breath, I paused before appearing in his doorway, hoping that everything was okay. I had no idea what to expect. No idea what he would say to me after Janet had, without question, destroyed any dignity Jarell had left inside of him.

Would he blame me for what my mother had done? Would he not want to talk to me or have anything to do with me anymore because of that?

No idea what he would say. Would he continue talking about his ideas of ending it all? Would his mother tell me to leave? Was he going to shut me out the way he used to before I worked so hard to break those barriers down?

I was so nervous.

I knew that Jarell wasn't that kind of person, but I also didn't think he'd want to end his life either, whether I felt it was warranted or not. To be honest, if I had even experienced a quarter of what Jarell had experienced in his life, let alone from Monday, I would've hung myself long ago. I was surprised that these feelings he had didn't appear sooner.

Swallowing, I closed my eyes and walked up to his door in a tip toe. His room was relaxing and cozy. A twin sized bed was in the middle of the room against the wall with what looked to be some pretty comfy blankets. There was a huge window that Jarell sat at and looked out of in a large cushioned chair like he does at home. He was dressed in plain white t-shirt and oversized sweatpants, but no hoodie. I knew that he was just dying inside not to have his hoodie after his mother tore it apart. I made a mental note to make sure I bought him a new one later.

To my surprise, his little sister Kylah was on the carpeted floor with two naked Barbies in hand and her sandy brown curls falling all over her face, but she didn't seem to have a care in the world. She was having the time of her life playing a scene of the two Barbies going to the grocery store to get some food for a birthday party they were going to throw when they got back from the store. My heart warmed. I didn't know where she was for the past couple of days, but she was the light in everyone's life, and I was sure Jarell appreciated having her here. There was no doubt about the fact that she had probably showered her brother with so much love when she saw him that would lift his delicate spirit.

I smiled at her cute little face and her rosy cheeks. It was like she sensed someone was there, and she looked up with her bright, gray eyes.

"Jade!" she screamed and ran over to me with her arms wide opened, ready to receive a hug.

I laughed and knelt to her level to give her the hug she wanted.

"Hey, honey bun," I said and tapped her nose.

"I'm playing Barbies. Relly won't play with me. Will you?" she asked with sad eyes.

"Well," I said, and then looked over at Jarell. I expected him to still be looking out of the window as if I had never showed up, but his head was turned in our direction. That was a good sign. "Let's see what's up with your brother, and then we can play. Okay?"

"Okay," she said, and I stood up from her. Without further ado, she hugged onto one of my legs in a giggle. I tried to walk while she hung on, but it was difficult. I did it anyway to play around with her as I wobbled over to Jarell. At the table near him, there looked to be some new origami pieces that I also made a mental note to ask him more about later. Talking about his pieces always made him happy.

"Hey, Jarell," I said softly.

He returned my greeting with a small tilt of his lips upward, but I wouldn't quite call it a smile. His eyes told the story. He still looked like he would rather just end it all, but another part was happy to see me. I sighed and opted not to say anything else until he was ready. I simply caressed the side of his face like I always did when I wanted to show how much I cared about him.

It never failed.

He burrowed into it with closed eyes and kissed it lightly when he brought it up to his lips.

"How are you feeling?" I asked as Kylah still unapologetically hung tight to my leg.

He said nothing. He just dipped his head and reached out to my waist. I took a step closer to him and let him wrap his arm around me and pull me closer. His head rested upon my stomach, and he held me again, like it was the last hug he'd give on earth. I rubbed his back, paying Kylah no mind. With a slight dip of my knees, I hunkered down to kiss him on the lips.

"Oooh!" Kylah squealed and jumped up and down in giggles.

I chuckled and ruffled her wild hair the way Jarell always does. She cheesed and ran away from the both of us.

"Everything okay, Jarell?" I asked, comfortable to really speak with him now that his sister had gone away.

Jarell looked back towards the big window and shrugged. I could tell he wasn't quite ready to talk about it or show much of what he felt. I respected it. I was just glad that he showed signs of life and affection.

"Jarell…" I called out to him.

No response.

"Jarell, I had to do it," I said. "I couldn't let you walk out that door and hurt yourself."

No response again. For a long time. Just breathing and a sightless gaze out at the skyline.

"No matter what, Jarell. I'm still yours. And trust me. You're still mine."

Silence, for a long time as I finally sat down at the small table and its wooden chair.

"Why did you save me?" he suddenly asked. "Why did you even do that?"

"What do you mean?"

"Why didn't you just let me drown?" he said in a low and thick voice that worried me, but I heard how much he wanted an answer. That same inescapable, emotional hurt began to knock at my stomach's door that I couldn't seem to shake at the hospital. I swallowed.

"It's because I love you, Jarell. I've grown to care so much about you. I wasn't going to let you die. I wasn't going to let anything happen to you. You need someone to stick up for you."

He blinked, but that was really the only sign he had given me that he was alive. A few minutes passed with him sitting and saying nothing. Processing.

"I – I don't know if I have anything left inside me to love you back the way that you deserve to be loved," he whispered. "I want to love you so bad, but …"

My heart shattered. I closed my eyes. It didn't matter that he didn't love me back, or at least verbally express it. It was the fact that Jarell had felt so empty inside. That there was nothing left in this world for him to even love. *Man.* That's another level of broken that I didn't know if I could bear. How was he supposed to be my boyfriend? Was I ready to take on the baggage of someone like Jarell? What if my mother was right? What if he sucked the energy out of me and pulled me down the emotional toilet with him?

"It doesn't matter. I just want you to know how much I love you. That's all that matters to me, Jarell. And I'm happy you're here. Happy you're alive. It would honestly hurt me so much if you were gone. I really appreciate you, and I care about you."

The minute I gave my mini confession as I wouldn't allow my mind to plant any seeds of doubt with someone as vulnerable and broken as Jarell, Ms. Hendricks walked into the room with some bags of McDonald's in her hand. She looked disheveled with a wild ponytail sticking out everywhere. I immediately ran to her to take some of the things out of her hands. Exhausted and defeated were additional things I picked up on as she walked inside. Huge, dark bags were under her eyes, and they were bloodshot. It was clear that she hadn't slept and had been crying for the past couple of days.

"Let me get those," I said, taking the load away.

She shot me a grateful look and didn't hesitate to accept my offer. I set the bags and drinks down on another table in the room. Before I could even set it down, Kylah sprinted towards the food full speed, but she was stopped mid-stride by Ms. Hendricks grabbing tightly onto her and yanking her back so hard that I thought she might snap her arm off. Kylah yelped out in pain.

"What I tell you about rushing to food, huh? Because the last couple of times you did that, you spilled it everywhere, and I don't have no funds to be buying this shit all over again. Do you understand me? Be patient, and let Jade set up your table. Go sit your ass down," she growled at her, and Kylah gave her a sad glare, backing down in intimidation.

That's how you knew Jarell's mom was at her limit.

"How do you want me to set up the table, Ms. Hendricks?"

"Thank you, honey." She sighed. "It doesn't matter. Set it up how you want. If I would've known you were coming, I'd have brought you something. And call me Rachel. Please."

"No worries. I was just released from the hospital myself and wanted to check in."

"Okay. Well, thank you again. Come out in the hall? Let's talk there. Kylah, don't you dare touch that food, you hear me?"

With her little body balled up into a corner with her knees up, she gave her mother a long, dirty glare. It was quite scary for a five-year-old to look at their mother like that and I just knew that she looked like the demon that was her father.

"Girl fix your face! Looking at me like you crazy, I'm not playing with you."

She didn't listen and ended up frowning deeper, but Ms. Hendricks ignored it. We both stepped just a hair out in the hall.

"I'm glad you're released. How are you feeling?" she asked and ran her fingers through her hair to fix it.

"I'm well. I got a lot of visitors the next day after you and Jarell left, and I found out about what really happened at school."

She rolled her eyes.

"And I just want to say that I am so sorry about my mother. I honestly left her place some time ago because she is just…"

"It's not your fault, Jade. She is who she is and will be."

"I know, but I just feel responsible."

"You shouldn't. I'm just so tired of everyone treating my baby like he isn't human. He was right. He ain't never did anything to anyone. Ever. I swear it, Jade. He was the sweetest kid. Never, ever gave me trouble. Always been respectful, loving and so helpful. Even as a baby. He rarely cried and he always, always smiled. And he loved. He loved hard. I ruined everything by putting him into my bullshit. He was the best child a mother could ask for... it's all my fault."

The tears started welling in her eyes, and she covered her mouth with her hands, looking over at Jarell. Before I knew it, she started bawling.

"I ruined my son's life, Jade. The moment that... monster I was dealing with took his vision away from him, it was the day my son died. He was never happy anymore. He lost all of his friends. Everyone treated him horribly, no matter how nice he was. Like he was a disease. He began to withdraw from me, and the world. And now my baby wants to take his life. You're the only one that can get him to be his old self again. I don't know what to do. I seriously don't know."

I pulled her in for a hug as she cried on my shoulder. I cried with her, feeling that unshakeable pain intensify. I couldn't imagine watching your son morph into something you didn't know, but I didn't want her to blame herself completely, either.

"Listen. Why don't Jarell and I go out for a dance? I'll leave you and Kylah to eat, but I think that Jarell should take a break from this space because all he's gonna do is think. He doesn't need to be in a place where he is forming these self-harming ideas."

She wiped her tears away and nodded.

"As long as my son is happy. I don't care."

"Alright. I'll set this table up, and then I'll ask him."

"Okay. If he says yes, we have to let his doctors know. He's on medication, so he's sedated and drowsy. And if he leaves the building, he needs to have a tracking device on his ankle or wrist that I can monitor because he's still under suicide watch."

"Will do."

Chapter Thirty-Six

OUR FAVORITE ABANDONED park. It was a warm spring night, so it was perfect for a passionate dance. But the thing was, we didn't even dance. Jarell wasn't up to it and it was heartbreaking to watch him walk around and try to feel a beat come over him, but nothing actually came. He was lethargic and completely out of his element. Nowhere near himself, since he was on medication.

So we just sat in the middle of the lot like we always did to talk after we danced. I leaned my head on his shoulder and wrapped my arms around his waist. Thankfully, he caressed me in this position, letting me know that he truly was thinking about me.

"Jarell?" I called out to him.

"Hmm?"

"I'm so sorry about… you know… about you being molested. I didn't know, and it was honestly heartbreaking to hear."

"Yeah. It don't matter."

"It does, Jarell. It does matter. You've been through way too much."

"Yeah. Many people get molested every day. I'm not ashamed about it because I know it wasn't my fault. I've come to terms with it the way I've come to terms with everything else. I didn't let that shit confuse me or make me question my sexuality or nothing. It's just a memory I try to put in the past."

"You're incredibly strong, Jarell. I need you to know that."

"I wouldn't have survived if I wasn't." He shrugged. *Damn. That was true.*

"Yeah." I sighed and pulled him close to me.

We were silent for a while until I thought of something else.

"Can I play the question game with you?" I asked.

He smiled for the first time in a long, long time.

"Why you always wanna interview me?"

"Because you're my man now. And I wanna know everything about you."

"Fine. Go for it."

"Yay! So... what does one of your poems say?"

"You're still stuck on those poems, huh?"

"Yes! At least tell me one."

He tilted his head back, rolling his eyes in exasperation. I laughed and hugged him tighter.

"You know you want to share. Please? Pretty pleaaaseee?"

"Alright. Damn. Stop begging. Here's one. When I tell you it, you gotta guess what I'm talking about."

"Ooh, this'll be fun!"

"Okay here goes:

Limbs move,

with the wind.

Glide thru

space; creating

trebles and clefs.

I'm floating

in a world

not like

my own, when

I spend time

with you."

"What does it mean?" Jarell asked.

Hmm. I had no idea. *When I spend time with you…* he didn't really spend much time with anyone before I met him. At least that's what I thought.

"Are you talking about your mom? An old girlfriend?"

"Nope. I'm talking about dance."

"Ohhhh! Damn, that's so obvious now!" I exclaimed. How the hell didn't I guess that? Trebles and clefs were about music. "Can you share another one?"

"The other ones are too deep. I don't want to think about them right now."

"Touche,'" I said. I didn't want to push too much. He was already in an incredibly vulnerable state, so I didn't want him thinking about anything that would set off any thoughts of self-harm.

"Okay, here's another question. What do you see?"

"What? What do you mean? I'm blind Jade, I don't see shit." He chuckled.

"No. I mean, what do you *see*? Do you see complete darkness? What is it like to have vision before, and then lose it all?"

I knew it was a random question, but I just wanted him to take his mind off of being in the mental health facility and everything else that was going on. I really wanted him to focus on how unique he was. How special he was. Plus, I always wanted to know.

A ghost of a smile lingered at his lips, and I smiled fully at it. Even if it was just a little bit, I was happy to see something other than a blank face.

"It's funny that you ask that because I never really knew how to explain it to myself," he replied, yawning. That medication was really getting to him.

"Tell me."

"Sometimes I see nothing at all. Like... it's not even black. It's just nothing. I can't explain it. It's the kind of nothing that you saw when you weren't born yet."

"I don't know what that is because I don't remember what not existing looked like."

"Exactly! That's what being blind is like. But when I touch things and my brain knows what I'm touching, an entire visual pops into my head. Like I can completely see all over again, depending on what it is. But when I stop touching it, or after a while, the visual fades into nothingness again. It's kind of cool sometimes," Jarell said. "That's why I can fight so well. I spent so much of my childhood fighting a lot, so I have those images in my head. That's why I don't get beat up. My brain uses it's prior knowledge and images of what it saw before I went blind."

"That's actually awesome, Jarell."

"Yeah. So like, when I touch flowers and trees, a visual comes into my head of what that might look like. So then, I recreate it with origami."

"What about people?"

"I make people, too."

"No, I mean... do you have a visual in your head of what someone looks like when you touch them?"

"Yeah, but not very often. Because I don't get the chance to touch people. I can try to imagine it based on someone's voice, but that's as far as it goes. I have to touch them. Especially if it's someone I met after I went blind. I can still picture my mom, and other people I used to know."

"What about me?"

He froze and gave me a toothless grin. I was mesmerized.

"I met you after I went blind, so I have to work harder to know what you look like. Besides, I told you how you looked when I touched your face."

"Can you visualize me?"

"Kind of. Here... I have something for you that I've been working on for a while. I hope you like it. I guess it's a gift to you. I'm sorry that it couldn't be more, but this is the best I got. It's a representation of what I think you look like."

"For me?"

Jarell nodded. He reached into his pants pocket and pulled out a small piece of origami. Then, he grabbed my hand softly and placed the piece in it. My mouth dropped. It looked like an origami piece of me.

My eyes watered.

Where it was so simple, it was so intricate. It was a brown woman of my complexion with a slight hourglass shape and straight, black hair that was shoulder length. The bone structure of the origami woman's face was so similar to mine that it was scary. The actual face of the piece was blank, but everything else was so spot on. The white t-shirt, the blue pants... it was everything to me. My chest fluttered the more and more that I looked at it. I'd cherish this forever and ever. This was the best gift I had ever received.

"Jarell! This is beautiful!" I cried.

"You think so?"

"Yes! I love this!"

I wrapped my arms around his neck with a hug, and I was sure I was choking him, but he needed to understand how much this meant to me. This gift was completely him. Straight from the pieces of heart he still had left intact.

"What's that sound?" Jarell suddenly asked into my ear as I embraced him.

"What do you mean? I don't hear anything."

I looked up at him, and then behind him. My eyes had to have gotten as wide as saucers because a big, black SUV drove up behind him full speed into the parking lot.

"Oh my God. Oh my God, Jarell! Get up!" I screamed and pushed him to rise.

The SUV was closing in on us and stopped just before running Jarell completely over and killing him. I tried to grab Jarell's hand to run the opposite direction as I was in fight or flight mode, but another black SUV drove up behind me and surrounded us. We were trapped.

"Get the fuck on the ground!" yelled out a guy in a black mask that exited the truck with what looked to be a shot gun. He pointed it directly at me, and I screamed, falling to my knees with my hands in the air.

"Get down! Don't move or I'll blast your ass!"

Two more guys came out of the other truck with what looked like Uzis and pointed them at Jarell. Jarell paused and one of the guys pushed him down.

"Stop! What do you want from us!?" I screamed, ducking my head. "Please don't shoot!"

"Shut up," one of the guys said, and then without warning, gripped my hair in a tight, tight fist. Felt like my scalp was scorching from the impact.

"Ahh!" I screamed, grabbing onto his hand in reflex for him to let it go.

"Shut up dumb ass girl!"

Without hesitation, he grabbed my hands from the top of my head and forced them behind my back, tying them with brutal tightness with some sort of rope. Then, he threw me into the trunk of the SUV.

"Jarell!" I screamed out. "Please don't hurt him! Please!"

I kept crying out not to do anything to him, but the two guys in the masks circled around Jarell with their guns pointed at him.

"If you try to run, I swear I'm going to blow your head off!"

Jarell said nothing. Just stood there with his hands in the air. Then, the two guys also tied his hands to his back and threw him in the same trunk that I was in and slammed the door shut.

What... the ...entire... fuck just happened!?

It felt like I was having a heart attack. My heart was skipping over beats, and tears were flowing relentlessly down my face. *Seriously. What in the whole entire fuck just happened? Did we really just get kidnapped?*

"Jarell," I whispered to him, who looked just as scared as I did.

"Who the fuck?" Jarell whispered, too.

"I don't know. They all have on masks."

"Shit," Jarell hissed and dipped his head low.

"What's wrong? Do you have any idea who it is?" I asked in a panic. "Marcus? Martell? Mike? Anyone?"

He shook his head with his eyes closed. I sighed and continued to cry. I just hoped that they wouldn't kill the both of us, whoever they were. It had to be someone from school. No question. Or at least someone associated with the school was up to this.

"Was it worth it?" Jarell suddenly asked me with his head still hung low.

"What?"

"All of this shit that I'm putting you through because you're with me. Was it worth it?"

I blinked several times, opening my mouth to respond, but nothing but a squeak came out.

This time, I really had to think.

I had lost my mother. Lost my friends. Lost my popularity. I was hurt, nearly died... and now, I was being kidnapped and strong armed. I had lost so much, been through so much in such little time at the expense of my mental. The expense of my future.

I couldn't answer that. I couldn't. Maybe my mother was right. Maybe right now, I was giving so much of myself to Jarell that it was costing me my entire life and wellbeing. *And was that worth it?*

I sighed and looked at Jarell. His head was dropped, anticipating my response, bracing for the worst. I looked down at the floor of the trunk, and there lied his origami piece of me. The tears continued to fall as I stared at it, knowing it was now my most prized possession.

I opened my mouth again to give him my real, sincere answer.

"Shut the fuck up!" one of the men in the masks yelled out and cocked his shot gun at the both of us.

I snapped my mouth shut.

"If I hear one word out of either of you, or you try to look out of this window to see where we're going, I will blast you to nothing. You hear me!?" he yelled.

I swallowed every word that I was about to say as the truck screeched off fast and to some unknown place. Words that Jarell was going to know and understand forever.

That hell yeah, he was worth it. He was worth everything.

At this point, I was here. I wasn't going anywhere. I was his ride or die forever into this unknown place that we were now going. And if I had to die? I'd die with him.

Born and raised in Wisconsin, author and educator Janeé Thompson pens novels that capture the experiences of Black teens and Black new adults in ways that are raw, relatable, accessible, and unapologetic. These novels transcend the notion that leisure reading for Black people must be about navigating racial stereotypes, racial trauma, and overcoming pain caused by anti-black violence such as police brutality or slavery. The experiences of Black teens and new adults are multifaceted and dynamic. We deserve to read more of these diverse experiences absent of white supremacy, and Janeé is intentional about making these stories known.